THE PRIVACY ACT

Linda Jayne

For Billie,

I hope you enjoy The Privacy Act.

Happy Holidays and best wishes

from your friend,

Linda Jayne

Published by Createspace.

Cover design by Bespoke Book Covers, UK.

ISBN-13: 978-1511915120

ISBN-10: 1511915129

Author's Notes:

While the characters and events in The Privacy Act are fictitious, most locations are real and accurate. Layout and functionality of some buildings, including Homeland Security's Nebraska Avenue complex in Washington D.C., the Butler County, Ohio, morgue, and the Hamilton, Ohio, police station, have been changed to better accommodate the scenes in the story.

Special thanks to Susan Burgess, Diane Jacks and Sandy Jacks for their feedback and support.

PRELUDE

She was now certain that she was being followed. It was a terrifying revelation and she tried to quell the panic that was rising in her by focusing her mind on what she needed to do. I need a weapon! she screamed to herself, but all she had was the car key in her hand, which she readied by sticking the shaft out of her fist.

Her car was still three blocks away. There was no moon. The night was dark. She no longer had her cell phone. They made sure of that. She was in a residential neighborhood and wanted to go to a door and ask for help. But she knew no one could help her. If those after her wanted her dead, she would be dead and so would anyone who tried to help her. Her only hope was that they wanted her followed, not killed. Or, if she were attacked, that she could strike a well-placed blow of the key into the eye or ear and subsequently into the brain of the attacker. Slim chance.

She thought of Danny and how she wished she had told him she loved him. She thought now she would probably never see him again. She wished her father knew where she was, for if she died tonight, chances are no one would ever find her body or know what happened to her.

Focus! Two more blocks. She knew she could probably outrun her stalker if only she knew where to run. It was 3 a.m., pitch black, and she had never been in this neighborhood in her life. So running would be futile. If the person following her was unarmed, she would have a fighting chance. She was strong and agile.

Would they at least have the decency to tell her father she was dead? He knew these people; hell, he trained these people. But no, they probably wouldn't tell him and he would agonize the rest of his life, wondering what happened to her. So would Danny. Maybe not the rest of his life, since he was only 33 and would hopefully find someone else to love, but it would hurt him deeply not knowing where she was or why she had left without saying goodbye.

I should have gone on vacation with Danny. I should have kept my nose out of this. I have only made things worse, not only for me, but for others. What was I thinking? I was trying to help someone, that's what I was thinking. I was trying to help a lot of someones, that's what I was thinking. I'm trying to do the right thing, and it's probably going to be the last thing I ever do.

One block to my car. Then she was struck with another thought and stopped running. What if they have tampered with my car? Is that how they plan to kill me? But I have to use my car to get out of here. I can't keep walking aimlessly. I don't know this area at all. I have to risk using my car. And if I die in the car, at least Danny and dad will know what happened to me. She continued her brisk walking and could now see her car up the street.

An occasional streetlight cast a circular glow around its base, and fortunately her car was underneath one such light. Unfortunately, so was the man who was after her.

Four Days Earlier
THURSDAY

"Nice work on finding that terrorist cell, Jeremy."

Jeremy turned on his swivel stool to see four identical faces of an Al Qaeda leader looking at him. After only momentary startlement, Jeremy grinned at the paper masks covering the faces of four of his co-workers. The news had hit the major television networks all over the world last night. *Terrorist Attacks on Disney World, Sea World and other Orlando Area Theme Parks Thwarted by Homeland Security.* The largest terrorist cell found in the United States to date, near Miami, Florida, was eliminated the day before by special forces squadrons. Most of the identified terrorists were arrested; the Al Qaeda cell leader and several other cell members were killed during the operation.

Jeremy played a major role in finding the exact location of the cell members and in positively identifying each individual and his or her terrorist ties. His satisfaction at the news of the successful operation was evident – he was grinning from ear to ear. His co-workers had huddled as soon as they arrived at work that morning and decided to surprise him with some congratulatory donuts and a bit of humor in the wearing of the masks, which they printed from the on-line news story that morning. The masks were complete with pencil holes punched into them to denote bullet holes. The cell leader had been shot in the head and face several times.

"It would be nice if you guys would get off your asses and help so I didn't have to do all the work around here." Jeremy tried not to grin as he accepted the box of donuts and began chomping on a glazed with chocolate icing.

A tip received by the Department of Homeland Security less than two weeks earlier alerted them to the possible attacks in Orlando. A private citizen made the phone call and backed up his suspicion with a document found in his company's copy machine. "I was starting to make a copy but the copier was jammed. I had to open the machine and pull out the piece of paper caught inside. It had already been copied onto for the most part," the caller had told the DHS agent. "I started to throw the paper away, but then noticed little pictures that looked like explosions on a map." The caller knew the name of the person that had just been in the copy room, a new employee of only two months. That information, followed up by an in-person meeting with the informant that same evening, was enough to convince DHS that the threat might be real and imminent.

The DHS Secretary, head of the country's third largest government agency, personally assigned the agency's most talented surveillance expert, 24-year old Jeremy James, to follow and watch the new employee that had allegedly copied the map that planned for the simultaneous bombing of six theme parks. Jeremy immediately placed a surveillance satellite over the employee parking lot where the 1992 Chevy driven by the suspected terrorist was parked. He hacked into the suspect's work computer and checked his e-mail, C drive and internet sites for anything suspicious although he didn't expect to find anything. No moderately intelligent terrorist would risk exposure by leaving evidence on a computer, especially a work computer. But then again, this terrorist had left a map with "bombs" on it inside a copy machine.

Jeremy got lucky. One deleted e-mail sent two days before stated "I've never been to Disney World and I'm ready to go! See you in two weeks!" Jeremy informed the Secretary that they might have up to twelve days before the bombings were scheduled to happen. He followed the suspect after work that evening with his giant video camera in the sky, which produced very beneficial results as well. The suspect nonchalantly handed off a piece of paper to a woman who passed him on the street. Jeremy quickly maneuvered another satellite to follow the woman.

The first suspect stopped outside a bar and met with two other men. Both received a piece of paper.

Jeremy's job as Surveillance Technician was to utilize satellite and other surveillance technology to find the terrorists' exact locations. He could position the satellites above his targets and could see them from as close as a few feet away. With these satellites, however, he could not get close enough to read the papers, or position them to see the faces of the suspects. He could not follow the suspects inside a building. And there was no sound – he could not hear anything they said. So while his $500 million, 14-ton toys were very helpful, they were also very limited in what they could do. He would need better technology if he was going to find out exactly what was going on.   But first, he needed to find out enough information to verify there was a plot.

Even though their faces were not in view, Jeremy took photos of the men before they went inside the bar. He left the satellite positioned high enough to watch all exits, then focused his attention on another monitor where he was tracking the movements of the female suspect. She was walking in a residential area of apartment buildings.

He snapped several photos of the woman but, as with the men, nothing that his facial recognition software would be able to use.   However, it was helpful to him to enlarge the photos for detail purposes on clothing, tattoos and hair.

The woman turned onto Palm Avenue, and soon stopped at the entrance of a two-story building. She appeared to be rummaging through her purse, perhaps retrieving her key to the door, when the door was opened by someone inside the building. It was at this point that Jeremy took his soon-to-be famous photo of the Al Qaeda cell leader, the one printed and held up to the faces of his four co-workers.   The man who opened the door made the mistake of stepping outside to let the woman in and glancing up at the sky as he did so.

"Smile!" chuckled Jeremy as he snapped a picture of the upturned face - a face he didn't know at that time was of the terrorist who most probably would have killed tens of thousands of innocent people and destroyed the city of Orlando had he not been stopped the day before. Seeing that face as a mask on his co-workers now, he laughed exuberantly. While he would never be a hero among the American people, as they would never know who, behind the scenes, was just doing the job he was hired to do, Jeremy still relished the praise and recognition of the other techies in his division who knew who really stopped the terrorist attack. Well, he and the guy who called in the tip. And the special forces squadrons of course.

Jeremy lived for these huge successes.   His biggest surveillance win was shortly after he had started with the agency - finding and watching the world's number one terrorist at his compound. He had spent weeks keeping constant vigil on the Al Qaeda leader before the terrorist was finally killed. Even when he wasn't working, and another surveillance technician was assigned to keep watch, Jeremy monitored him from his personal laptop with software programmed to audibly let him know if the man left his compound, which he never did. He remembered the Monday morning after the announcement of the terrorist's death and the palpable excitement at the Homeland Security office that morning.

"Finally!" Jeremy had exclaimed. While the wheels of counter-terrorism had been moving, they didn't move quickly enough for Jeremy. "It took them weeks to kill him!" he complained good-naturedly. "I guess they had to rebuild the frickin' Blackhawk first. I'd have been there by 6 a.m. that first morning to take him out."

"That's because you don't believe in following the rules," chided the one female co-worker in their techie group, "like informing the President, and carefully planning the attack to make certain it's successful, and thinking through the ramifications of your actions, etcetera, etcetera."

"That's our problem – way too much etcetera, etcetera in government," Jeremy spewed.

Jeremy was a card-carrying conspiracy theorist. He believed the government was part of the New World Order and that they were watching our every move through the many surveillance cameras now positioned everywhere. And he should know since it was his job to do this very thing. He had been on the FBI's watchlist since he was fourteen years old because he was always looking up information on the internet using search words which popped up on the FBI's list of spook words. Five years later, he was recruited by the Department of Homeland Security when they caught him hacking into their confidential files. He was arrested, interrogated, then hired for his excellent hacking skills. While at first Jeremy was opposed to working for one of the government agencies that he felt was taking away many of his freedoms, he decided that perhaps it was better to work for them. *Keep your friends close, and your enemies closer.* The Secretary of Homeland Security felt the same way, he knew.

The Orlando plot had taken less time to quell, primarily because they had less time in which to stop it. After taking the photo of the cell leader outside his apartment the week before, Jeremy had immediately run the face through the agency's facial recognition software program and got a hit. The Syrian-born man had been questioned, not once but twice, in the past year regarding his possible terrorist ties. He had been released both times, but surely, Jeremy thought, someone in the CIA was watching this guy, right? Perhaps that is when and why the terrorists began passing notes instead of communicating in other ways.

Jeremy had immediately notified the DHS Secretary of his findings and requested one of the newer satellites that could see through walls, listen in to whispered conversations, and take photos so close you could count the person's nose hairs. He also forewarned her that there might be a need to plant 360 degree ISIS (Imaging System for Immersive Surveillance) cameras in numerous locations once he identified key home and work locations of the terrorists. She requisitioned the equipment immediately.

With this information, the DHS Secretary immediately alerted the CIA and they put their computer surveillance technicians to work. They combed the internet for any chatter regarding the various theme parks in Orlando. There was none of a sinister nature, which verified the belief of the CIA, DHS, FBI and NSA that the terrorists were returning to old-fashioned, non-electronic methods of communication when possible. This particular cell, as was soon discovered, was close-knit, both physically (they all lived and worked within a ten-block radius of one another) and in the single-mindedness of their purpose, which was to kill as many Americans as possible.

Utilizing his new toy, a $2 billion satellite affectionately known as Samuel, Jeremy's surveillance work was a piece of cake. One suspect led to another, and then another, and he methodically, efficiently and accurately documented the involvement of 34 individuals, most, but not all, of Middle Eastern descent, as part of the plot.

The day after he received the use of Samuel, he witnessed a meeting of five individuals in a park under the cover of two large trees. He was able to record every word of their conversation as well as read and photograph the information on the paper laid out on the picnic table where they sat. The plan was well thought-out, with enough individuals involved to have a Plan B and a Plan C for every theme park should any Plan A not materialize. The attacks were scheduled for Memorial Day, ten days from the date Jeremy was watching the group.

Over the next six days, eighteen to twenty hours a day, Jeremy followed each one of the core groups of the terrorist cell. It was a tough assignment, following so many, but Jeremy thrived at this type of work and by the end of six days had videotaped, audiotaped and documented the role of each of every one of the 34 individuals involved, along with their daily routines and where they lived, worked and met.

The rest was up to the FBI and military operatives, who also performed their work with extraordinary precision and exemplary results. Within two days the operation was coordinated and carried out, resulting in the capture or killing of 34 terrorists the day before.

Jeremy felt great about the outcome of this assignment. While he ordinarily did not condone the United States sending assassins to murder people, there were always exceptions, and this was one of them. As for his part in the outcome, he did this job the same way he did all of his surveillance jobs, with absolute determination to find and follow the target. He surprised even himself that he had turned out to be a very dedicated and conscientious employee.

"Well, enjoy your moment, bro," one of the techs slapped a photo mask on Jeremy's back. "You did gooooood." With a few pats on the back, the impromptu celebration was over and the five of them went back to work.

As it had been the day after the killing of the world's number one terrorist, Jeremy basked in the glory of his success for the first hour or so of his work day. Although less dramatic, he always had assignments of people to surveil and today was no exception. He needed to get to work.

One on-going assignment that he had been tasked with for the entire four years he had been at the department was to monitor three people, only for short periods of time each day. He had not been able to do this assignment, or any assignments for that matter, for the past ten days since all available resources and time had been focused on the terrorists in Florida. Yesterday, however, he had been able to move one satellite to briefly check on each of the three subjects.

Prior to the past two weeks, Jeremy had never had the use of satellites Samuel or Delilah, the agency's two newest, most expensive, most versatile and privacy-invading spy satellites. And he would not have the use of them again until the next critical surveillance project. The on-going monitoring of the three people assigned to him was not of a nature that required being able to hear, or see inside buildings, so he used the older, less expensive models.

Jeremy cued up two of his eight computer monitors which would soon display live video of the workplaces of two of his three target subjects. At this time of morning, all three should be at work and he would not have much to look at until they either left for lunch or for home at the end of the workday. He would make certain their cars were in the lots as he usually did. He repositioned two of his satellites over the workplaces and parking lots. Since two of the subjects lived and worked within 25 miles of one another, he could use one satellite to observe the two. The cars were in the parking lots of these two subjects.

Of the three persons he had been watching now for four years, which was, without a doubt, the most boring thing he had ever done in his life, one was a woman. She appeared to lead a normal life – husband, child, job, house in the suburbs, SUV. Boring! What possible threat to national security could she pose. Like the two men he also watched, who also led extremely normal lives, he would spot check on them a few times throughout the day – before work, lunchtime, after work – if he had time. If he was extremely busy with other assignments, he would check on them only once a day, or not at all if his surveillance equipment was in use. His assignment was to make sure they were alive and well and that nothing unusual was happening in their lives. That was all he was supposed to do.

For security purposes, and for his own good as he was told by his boss, John Dorgan, who gave him the assignment, he was never told who these subjects were or why he was supposed to watch them. The day before, in his brief check on these subjects, he did not see one of the men at all. That was not unusual. The man could be on vacation or a business trip, or sick in bed or just not at his usual place at his usual time. He had certainly learned the routines of the three people over the years and knew exactly when and where to look for them, but it was not at all unusual for Jeremy not to see a person for several days until he found out his or her location. So today he would focus on man number two. He now had time to look thoroughly in all the usual places. And if he couldn't find him that way, he would look in unusual places as well. For not only did Jeremy know the names and everything about each of these subjects, he hacked into their computers if necessary to access their e-mail, calendars, Facebook accounts and any other information he needed to find out where they were. He prided himself in his work and would do whatever it took to do his job well. And while it might be best for both him and his employer if he did not know who his targeted surveillance subjects were, that scenario just didn't work for Jeremy. He needed and wanted to know everything about them, including why their government was watching them. In this case, he still hadn't figured out the answer to that question. All three of these people seemed like ordinary American citizens - almost too ordinary.

So this morning he was going to find Michael Ray Michtenbaum, who wasn't at work yesterday. He perused the parking lot of Daise, Shultz and Michtenbaum, the law firm in Middletown, Ohio, where Michtenbaum was a partner. His car, a newer Lexus, wasn't in its usual parking spot. He wasn't at home, although two unknown cars were in Michtenbaum's driveway. He snapped photos of the cars and license plates. "Mikey, Mikey, where are you?" Jeremy whispered as he began typing rapidly on his keyboard, accessing Michtenbaum's Outlook account. At the same time, an e-mail came through from the DHS Secretary – "Please come see me a.s.a.p."

As soon as possible was twenty minutes later, after Jeremy had determined from Michtenbaum's calendar that he wasn't on vacation or a business trip. In fact, Michtenbaum was supposed to be meeting with a client at his office at this very moment. He had received over a hundred new e-mails in the past 36 hours, yet hadn't sent a single one since Tuesday afternoon at 5:53.

Jeremy was starting to think the guy might be dead.

When Bernie Kossack was first promoted into the Cybersecurity and Communications Division of Homeland Security, he was estatic. Cybersecurity. Homeland Security. They sounded so much more exciting than Federal Computer Incident Response Center (GSA) where he had worked his entire adult life until 2002, when the Department of Homeland Security was formed in response to the September 11 attacks from 22 smaller government agencies, including Bernie's GSA. Finally, after years of menial tasks of filing boring documents, where his only satisfaction had come from being able to tell people that he worked for an important government agency, he now felt sure he would be able to make a more worthwhile contribution to his country, and that women might now want to talk to him.

Upon receiving the notice of his promotion (he still told everyone that it was a promotion even though he was not given an increase in pay, nor a change in job title, nor an office), he had an uncontrollable urge in the ensuing week to watch every one of his collection of James Bond movies.

In his efficiency apartment on the fourth floor of a somewhat run-down building not far from the Nebraska Avenue complex where he worked in Washington, D.C., Bernie would sometimes act out his favorite scenes from the Bond movies, or create scenes of his own. Standing behind his worn green sofa, intently watching the action taking place on the 17" television screen across the small room, he waited for Pussy Galore to *just try* and snuff out Sean Connery. "Shorry, my dear" (using his best Sean accent) "I hate to terminate shuch beauty, but you give me no other choish," and a full three or four seconds before Sean has figured out what is going on, Bernie whips the pretend revolver out of his sleeve, puts a neat bullet hole in the precise center of Pussy's beautiful forehead, and dives onto the couch to avoid the barrage of bullets that follow this daring act, too daring for even the real James Bond. Bernie's five-foot, five-inch, overweight frame would then stretch out fully on the couch and he would revel in the delight of his fantasies as he continued to watch his hero on the screen.

For Bernie, Sean would always be the real Bond. Even though he had every Bond movie ever made in his collection, George Lazenby and Roger Moore and Timothy Dalton could never truly be James Bond. Now Pierce Brosnan was a different story. Bernie really liked Pierce as Bond, almost as much as he liked Sean. Yep, Pierce was definitely worthy of being Bond. But why had the stupid movie people replaced him with Daniel Craig? What were they thinking? He had refused for several years to even watch the newest Bond movies, but eventually his curiosity got the best of him and he watched Casino Royale and discovered Daniel did a pretty good job as well. He now had all his movies that were on DVD.

On the first day of his new job in Cybersecurity and Communications, Bernie wore his only suit, a light blue polyester with a double-breasted jacket with gold buttons and slightly flared pant legs. He had had the suit for years, but he thought it still looked great. He wore a light blue shirt with a white tie and white shoes. Although his belly pounched noticeably, it appeared less protruding in this attire than in his usual T-shirt and cotton work pants.

Bernie's disappointment was quite evident for several minutes after his new boss began explaining his new duties as Cyber Security Information Specialist, aka, file clerk. Mr. McElroy did not at first notice the look of pain on Bernie's face and continued to rattle on about this system of filing, and that method of retrieving data. When Bernie did not respond and Mr. McElroy finally *looked* at him, the hurt was unmistakable. Not usually one to further kindle such weak emotions, Mr. McElroy did feel a twinge of sympathy for the pathetic little man and therefore decided to attempt to boost his morale a bit.

"Bernie, you realize the extreme importance of this job. You will be handling highly confidential information on a daily basis and will be asked by the Secretary and Deputy Secretary themselves for information. We selected you because of your great work ethic, your organizational skills as well as your ability to maintain confidentiality."

It worked, to some degree at least. Bernie felt better. And when Heather Barnes, Executive Assistant to the Secretary of Homeland Security, and the Bond girl of his fantasies, walked past them and smiled, Bernie was energized and ready to scan or shred every document in the place.

That was more than a decade ago. Since then, his new job had been pretty much like the old one – scanning, classifying, retrieving, delivering, shredding and babysitting boring documents. He rarely read any of the documents he handled. He wasn't much of a reader, but occasionally would skim the first few sentences of the documents he handled. There was one interesting memo about an affair that a high level official was having with an intern, and the consequences that were becoming apparent as a result of that affair. Bernie actually read the whole first page of that document, but that was the juiciest file he'd come across so far. Big fat deal. Nothing about the government's concealment of UFOs, or assassination plots on third world countries' leaders, or anything good. Certainly nothing he could use to fascinate women with by saying that he dealt with such classified material that he was forbidden to have more than one drink for fear he might accidentally reveal some information critical to national security.

Still, Bernie liked his job and it suited him quite well. He was efficient, organized and loyal. He didn't question the why of any request that was given him, only the due date and time. He was smart enough to pick up the basics of the new technology that seemed to come at an ever increasing speed, but not so smart as to understand how that technology worked or even to care. He remembered when all files were paper and he would label his manila folders carefully on the tabs and file them meticulously in their proper order. He prided himself on being able to find any file in an archive room of hundreds of thousands of files in under a minute if it was a file he had placed there himself. In the 70's, shortly after high school and only a year after he started at GSA, he was tasked with copying paper files onto microfiche. For years, he would file and retrieve small microfiche film when his superiors requested certain documents. Then came the floppy disk, and he classified, labeled and filed these in protective sleeves and then in protective plastic boxes.

Now all the computer system files and backup were handled by the IT department. Bernie worried about that sometimes. He had met a couple of those guys. While they were computer geniuses, they knew didly-squat about organization and filing. But he supposed the computer somehow did all of that. Bernie's primary job now was to scan paper documents that came into the agency from outside sources. While he kept expecting his job to become obsolete with everyone's talk of going paperless, that hadn't happened. There was still plenty of paper arriving on a daily basis. It appeared there would be enough paper to last until he retired.

The excitement in Bernie's life was in his fantasies and he was usually okay with that. Not many people actually felt the heights of adventure and excitement that Bernie felt when he immersed himself into a movie and truly became James Bond. He didn't just pretend, he *became* the man. He actually felt the passion, the tension, the excitement of skiing down a steep slope pursued by villains. Even though his true Bond hero Sean Connery never skied as Bond, Bernie still pretended it was Sean, not one of the other Bonds. When Bernie fantasized, his body language and even his voice changed as he placed himself totally in the role he was playing.

At times, though, Bernie felt very lonely. He was 57 years old and had never had a girlfriend for any length of time. He dated a co-worker at GSA for a couple of years but that ended when she quit her job and moved from D.C.

For the past five or six years, he ate dinner every week night after work at a café near his apartment, partly because he wasn't much of a cook, and partly because he wanted to meet a woman. His fantasies sustained him, but he still fantasized about having a real girlfriend.

He always wore his Homeland Security keyfob badge displayed around his neck as a conversation starter when he went to the café. When in his James Bond persona, he wasn't shy at all and would start up a conversation with a woman who was by herself at the counter where he sat. But the interactions always ended the same. They would often start out okay. "Pardon me mish, do you mind if I sit here by you?" "Not at all, please sit." "I jusht came from work (and he would conspicuously hold the plastic badge around his neck so that it was visible to the woman) and always shtop here for dinner. The food is exshellent." Sometimes the woman would notice the badge and ask what he did at DHS, and sometimes she would notice but still didn't want to talk to him. In either case, he occasionally had a nice conversation that never led anywhere else, or the woman completely ignored him or asked him to leave her alone.

Since none of the women ever came back and sat at the counter a second time, a fact Bernie had clearly noticed but was glad the café owner had not, he decided to change his tactic slightly and began talking to the pretty waitress who had just started working the counter. She always spoke to him and would carry on a conversation with him when she wasn't too busy. He soon got into the habit of hanging out at the counter even after he had finished his meal so that he could talk with her. One day the café owner, who was also the cook, scowled at him several times and when Bernie finally got up to leave the man caught up with him outside and said, "Listen mister. You're takin' up too much of my counter time. Dinner's a busy time and you're stayin' way after you're done eatin'. And you're talkin' to my waitress too much. She's busy."

Bernie was taken aback by this encounter and didn't know what to say. He'd never been scolded by a business owner for doing business there. "Are you telling me to stop eating at your place?" he finally asked meekly.

"No, I'm not sayin' that. I'm just sayin' stop stayin' so long and stop talkin' to Mindy so much." He paused. "Forty-five minutes. You can stay forty-five minutes." Then he disappeared into the café.

That encounter had happened over a year ago and Bernie had never exceeded his forty-five minute dinner allotment even once.

This particular morning, something different happened at work. His boss, Mr. McElroy, summoned Bernie into his office, where a well-dressed visitor sat. "Bernie, I'd like to introduce you to Dr. Randall Thyssen, Director of National Clandestine Service at the CIA. Dr. Thyssen, this is Bernie Kossack, our document security specialist. I'm sure he can find whatever files you need."

When Bernie was nervous, he tended to sweat, and his palms were quite clammy at the moment. He wiped his hand along his pant leg in anticipation of shaking Dr. Thyssen's hand, but the Director never offered to shake hands.

"I have an urgent assignment for you," started Thyssen. "Here is the name of the project I am looking for. There are most likely several old files associated with this project name in your archives." He handed a slip of paper to Bernie. "I've also written down the name of a doctor who was involved in this project as perhaps some files are categorized under his name. Your boss and I have been searching computer files this morning and can find nothing with this project name or the doctor's name. I am therefore assuming any files were never converted to electronic form but are still in paper format or perhaps on microfiche. Keep in mind that these files may be very old – fifty years perhaps. I need for you to search the archives and find any files about this project. Okay?"

Bernie could see that the visitor was watching him carefully, uncertain whether to trust him with his important assignment.

"Yes sir," said Bernie with as much authority and importance as he could muster.

Jeremy's supervisor, John Dorgan, had been a field agent with the CIA for seventeen years, then a department director at the CIA before taking the high level Director of Intelligence and Analysis position at Homeland Security. He knew the workings of both agencies very well, and knew that when it came to sharing a project, they usually didn't. So he was surprised when Mr. McElroy, a department supervisor from Cybersecurity and Communications, brought a CIA Director, Randall Thyssen, into his office, indicating they had been working together that morning on a project and needed his help.

After McElroy made the introductions, Thyssen grabbed McElroy's hand and with a warm smile said, "I'll be back for that file shortly - thank you very much for your help," indicating that McElroy could now leave. Dorgan could tell that McElroy was embarrassed by his unexpected dismissal from the meeting.

The two remaining men seated themselves in Dorgan's office and eyed one another for a moment. Dorgan had spent over twenty years in the CIA and although he'd been gone for several years, he'd stayed in touch enough to know the key players. Dr. Randall Thyssen was a relatively new key player, only with the agency five years, and in his current position less than two years. Although he had never met Thyssen before today, Dorgan knew the man was intelligent and ambitious - definite requirements to be the youngest person in such a high position at the CIA. Dorgan had been ten years older before he had achieved the same level on the org chart.

Dorgan could understand why, at least on the surface, Thyssen had achieved his success at the agency thus far. He was an extremely attractive man and every detail of his appearance was immaculate. Dorgan guessed Thyssen to be in his early thirties, but every movement, every look, every word was far more experienced, more confident and more calculated than any thirty-some-year-olds Dorgan had ever known.

"Coffee?"' Dorgan offered as he held up his own cup and filled it from a pot located on a credenza behind his desk.

"No, thank you." Thyssen was leaning back comfortably in the large leather chair in front of Dorgan's desk. "I'll get right to the point." He tossed a file folder onto Dorgan's desk. Dorgan caught it before it slid off the desk and into his lap. "You're familiar with this old project, I believe."

Dorgan opened the unmarked file. All that was contained within was a photo of a man whom Dorgan had seen many times. He checked the file to see if there were any other documents inside, but there were none.

"Yes. So?" Dorgan had spent only one minute with Thyssen and already did not like him.

"I came by to let you know that this man is dead." Thyssen's eyes were directly on Dorgan's and the slight smile that now passed Thyssen's lips told Dorgan that his own eyes and face had betrayed him. He had not known. He, who was in charge of this project and of the man in the photo. He, who should be the one and perhaps only person in the entire world to first know of this man's death, did not know. A young, arrogant newcomer made a special trip to his office to let him know that he was past his prime.

"When and how did it happen?" Dorgan asked grimly.

Thyssen handed him an article from an on-line news source dated four hours earlier. Dorgan read that Michael Ray Michtenbaum had been found dead in his home around 8:30 the night before. There was no apparent cause of death although the coroner stated he had been dead for approximately twenty-four hours. An autopsy would be performed.

Thyssen continued. "The Director has asked that you handle this situation." The last three words were spoken a bit more slowly and succinctly. "And if by some chance his death turns out to have been murder, you should be able to tell who did it, and maybe even why."

"Murder?" Dorgan looked suspiciously at Thyssen. What did this man know that he wasn't telling? "Why would anyone suspect murder?"

"No one does. I'm simply stating that you will have the evidence showing how the man died. Of course, as the news article stated, there will be an autopsy."

So Thyssen knows about this project, Dorgan concluded. He also knows the autopsy must be stopped or managed as it may reveal damaging information, which is why he is here ensuring that I know about Michtenbaum's death. Time is of the essence.

"How did you know about this?" Dorgan needed to know who else had been watching Michtenbaum. No one at the CIA had any reason to have this project on his radar.

"Apparently your three test subjects are still monitored by someone at the agency." Thyssen abruptly stood and left.

Dorgan knew he didn't have time to ponder the political ramifications of what had just transpired, or the consequences to himself personally; yet he allowed himself a couple of minutes to be angry, frustrated and confused. Why was the CIA still monitoring these test subjects…HIS project?

Dorgan couldn't believe one of the test subjects, Michael Ray Michtenbaum, was dead. How? He needed to find that out right away. He, and perhaps four other living people, all current or former CIA, had access to the video file he was about to watch. However, no one else besides himself was charged with this task as the project had been officially aborted several years ago. He, and he alone, or at least he thought so until now, regularly accessed the video footage that recorded the lives of the three test subjects that had been under surveillance by the US government since the day they were born. Yes, it was true that he had one of his Homeland Security employees, Jeremy James, keep tabs on the three subjects via satellite for a few minutes each day just to make sure they were still alive, but Jeremy knew nothing about the information that he himself was about to access. And so much for that safeguard – one of the subjects died without himself or Jeremy knowing it.

Unless he acted quickly and efficiently, this project was going to come to the attention of a lot of people who shouldn't know about it. Already, there were people involved who shouldn't know about it – McElroy for one. Thyssen for another, although Dorgan felt certain he was just a high-level messenger boy from the CIA Director himself. If necessary, Dorgan would do any damage control required to protect the secrecy of the project and the people behind it.

In addition to his agency-issued cell phone, Dorgan always had a throw-away, untraceable cell phone, which he changed out frequently. He dialed the number of an agent whom he'd recently used in another assignment and set up a meeting for five that afternoon. He then called and made travel and hotel arrangements.

Site access required special software on his laptop as well as a 25-digit password, which he entered from memory. He entered the date of Michtenbaum's death and entered a time that he approximated to be one hour before his death. Dorgan then started to watch the video of Michael Ray Michtenbaum's last hour of life.

Bernie was so relieved, and a little surprised, that Dr. Thyssen had not asked to go with him to the archives room. If the information he wanted was so important, and if he needed it urgently, it seems he would have insisted on coming along. Mr. McElroy trusted Bernie, but Dr. Thyssen didn't know him at all. Thank goodness he didn't ask to come, thought Bernie. I would have been a nervous wreck.

Paper files or microfiche! The good old days! If these files existed, Bernie knew he could find them. He entered the security code at the door to the archive area – his domain. He had already memorized the names on the slip of paper in his pocket and he started in the paper files section to see what he could find. He was immediately rewarded. A brown accordion folder was marked with the project name. Bernie checked to see if there was a second folder, but there was only the one. He then checked the paper files for the doctor's name, but there was no file under that name. Bernie checked the microfiche files as well, but could find nothing more than the brown folder that contained a two-inch thick binder.

Bernie had a standing directive from his boss to scan and electronically file any paper or microfiche document that had not previously been scanned, so he immediately went to the scanner in the archives room and removed the binder from the folder.

Rarely would Bernie even consider looking at a file that wasn't meant for his eyes, but he found that he was extremely curious about this particular case that involved both the CIA and

Homeland Security. Not once in his entire life had he deliberately broken a rule or disobeyed a directive. Not many people could say that. Maybe no one besides Bernie could say that. Still, the thought crept into his mind. I could just peek at it. Anybody else would do that and not think a thing about it.

"No, you can't!" he said out loud, and reflexively glanced around to see if anyone might have heard him. No one else was in this room that was seldom frequented, and usually only by himself.

Bernie removed sections of the binder at a time and ran them through the scanner, which made quick work of the process. The entire binder of papers was scanned in only a couple of minutes.

Soon Bernie was in the hallway walking back towards his work area and his boss's office. It didn't matter to Bernie that there were security cameras everywhere in the building that could watch an employee's every move. His own sense of right and wrong guided him and he wouldn't do anything in the absence of a camera that he wouldn't do in front of one.

Still, the thought nagged at him and he stared at the spine of the binder inside the brown accordion folder. Just thinking about looking inside the binder made him feel guilty and Bernie didn't wear guilt well at all. When he looked up and saw someone coming down the hall towards him, he became extremely flustered, as if this person could read his traitorous thoughts. He dropped the folder and as it hit the hard surface, the binder popped open and spilled most of its secret contents all over the hallway floor.

"Oh, my gosh!" Bernie screamed, and he fell to the floor, attempting to sweep the loose papers into his arms.

"Hey man, it's okay" said the young man who had been walking towards Bernie. "Take it easy. I'll help you."

"No!" Bernie screamed again. "Go away! You can't see this!" Bernie was so upset and irrational that the young man backed off. "Okay, fine, I'm leaving. Just calm down, man."

"Calm down," Bernie muttered as he sat on the floor, still sweeping papers towards him. "How can I calm down? The papers are out of order now. I don't know how they go." He began to sob out of frustration. He had failed to bring the file intact to his boss as instructed. This had never happened to him before.

He took a deep breath to try and calm himself and looked at

his watch. He had only been gone from his boss and Dr. Thyssen for twenty-two minutes. He doubted if they expected him back this soon and that thought made him feel better. *I can put the papers back into the binder and still get the file to them in less than thirty minutes,* he thought. *They've never seen the binder so they won't know if the papers are in order or not.* He was beginning to think it would be okay after all.

He straightened and piled the spilled papers and began placing them in small handfuls back into the binder. As he did so, he saw the top page of a section of papers he was holding. It was a photo of a newborn baby whose right eyeball was missing. Bernie almost vomited. He then put the rest of the pages into the binder one at a time, and still delivered the folder to Mr. McElroy and Dr. Thyssen thirty-four minutes after he had left them.

"Jeremy, so good to see you." The Secretary of Homeland Security, Rhonda Watterson, motioned for Jeremy to sit at the conference table in front of her desk. She moved there as well.

"First of all, congratulations on a spectacular job. We're all heroes thanks to you."

Jeremy liked Rhonda Watterson. She was the reason he stayed at DHS. He didn't care much for his direct supervisor, John Dorgan, to whom he privately referred as Dragon. Without these occasional one-on-one meetings with, and special assignments from, the Secretary herself, Jeremy would have accepted one of the several offers he had received over the past three years from the NSA.

"Just name where you want to go on your next vacation, and it will be paid in full."

"Thanks." Jeremy grinned. From the folder she held in her hand, he knew that vacation wasn't coming right away. She had another assignment for him.

"I have a rather delicate assignment for you." She paused. "I'm not comfortable assigning this to you for reasons you'll soon understand, but you are my key choice and you have the skill set that exceeds the person you will be watching."

Jeremy's interest was piqued as the Secretary continued. "One of our own here at DHS has been accused of having possible terrorist ties, and of working on his own, sometimes using departmental resources, to accomplish certain tasks. One of these tasks may even include murdering American citizens."

Her face was grim as Jeremy watched her talk. "I personally find it hard to believe that this man is guilty of these charges – I know him pretty well – but we, of course, must investigate and find out for certain."

The Secretary opened the file for Jeremy to see, revealing a photo of Jeremy's boss, John Dorgan – Dragon – with another man that Jeremy recognized, a former CIA agent, now independent contractor, still hired on occasion by the CIA to carry out assignments outside the United States.

"Now you see why I am reluctant to give this assignment to you. If you don't want to do it, I will certainly understand and will find someone else."

Jeremy was surprised that he was being asked to monitor his own boss and deep down he rather relished the idea. "I'm okay with it," he said to the Secretary.

When Jeremy returned to his department, Dorgan looked up from his desk, which was situated behind a large glass window overlooking Jeremy's work station. He came out of his office. "My wife and I are taking a long weekend, so I'm leaving at lunchtime and will be gone until Tuesday." He waited for Jeremy to acknowledge.

"Ok," replied Jeremy. "By the way, I haven't seen one of our three subjects in the past two days." Jeremy knew the subject's name but didn't use it. "Probably not a big deal, but I have a strange feeling about it. I'll look for him today and I'm sure I'll find him."

"Don't bother," Dorgan said abruptly. "He's dead."

"Dead! What happened!" Jeremy blurted out, but Dorgan had already gone back into his office and shut the door. "Of course you won't tell me," Jeremy muttered. He knew better than to ask Dragon any questions about Michtenbaum's death, or any questions about the other two people being monitored every day. Dragon wouldn't tell him. While John Dorgan was intelligent and technically very adept, understanding most of the technology utilized by his staff every day, he was not respected by his staff. He was prone to bouts of fiery anger, which could erupt in front of his staff, thus his nickname, "fire-breathing" Dragon. He was inconsistent in his reactions to, and treatment of, employees. Jeremy was liking his new assignment more and more.

For now, though, Jeremy would work on his several other surveillance projects. If Dragon chose to watch his star employee work that morning, he would see him monitoring the whereabouts of a senator from Maryland who was receiving daily death threats, and keeping surveillance on several Presidential candidates.

Jeremy realized he had eaten only one of the donuts brought to him that morning, and he reached for another after his stomach started to growl. "Coffee would go great with this," he said as he headed to the break room.

At 10:00 a.m. every day, Bernie took his morning fifteen minute break. He took the stairs up one level to a break room equipped with various snack and drink machines and several tables with chairs. There was an identical break room on his floor as well, but Bernie preferred the one upstairs as there was always the chance that he might see Heather Barnes. Her office was only two doors away from the break room and sometimes he would see her in the hallway or she would come into the break room and get a bottle of water or cup of hot tea from a vending machine.

While he was disappointed that Heather wasn't in the hall or break room, his disappointment was short lived as he saw another attractive young woman in a short red leather skirt and low cut white blouse. He became James Bond and the young woman became Heather and they were on a yacht in the middle of the Mediterranean. He was calling for drinks as he rubbed suntan lotion all over her neck and shoulders. He was smiling and mumbling to himself as he sat leaning back in the small break room chair with his feet propped on another chair - sunning himself in an Adirondack chair on the deck of the yacht - swirling his chocolate milk – his martini had to be shaken, not stirred – staring and smiling across the table at the beautiful Heather – the girl in the red skirt who saw him staring and got out of there as quickly as she could.

Shortly after he returned to his work area, Bernie began scanning vendor invoices into the system. Mr. McElroy walked in.

"Did Dr. Thyssen give that folder back to you to refile?" he asked.

"No," Bernie answered. "I was going to ask if he gave it back to you."

"You did scan it, right?"

"Of course."

"He probably gave it to John Dorgan," McElroy mumbled, although Bernie thought his boss didn't sound convinced of that. "Could you check with Dorgan and get it back. You can make him a copy on USB. Go ahead and do that right away and let me know," McElroy instructed.

While Bernie was not computer savvy, he knew how to do the tasks needed for his job. The tasks of scanning files and moving them into their proper and secure location was his key job, while copying or moving files to a flash or USB drive for a particular employee was also done quite often. Each portable drive was coded and documented as to what was on it when issued, the name of the person to whom it was issued, and the date and time. Each drive also was embedded with a tracking device. Except in rare cases, it was forbidden for employees to take a flash drive, CD, DVD or other file from the building and all computer files on laptops had to be saved to the agency drives, not the hard drive. Storing confidential documents on a laptop hard drive was a firing offense.

Bernie had half an hour before his lunch break, plenty of time to copy the file onto the USB drive. He recorded the required information on his log. He would deliver the file to the Director of Intelligence and Analysis while on his way to the break room for his lunch break. Just the thought of possibly seeing Heather at lunchtime made his heart beat faster.

But for now, Bernie's mind wandered to the photos and pages from the file that had spilled onto the floor. He had seen a great deal as he placed the pages back into the binder, mostly photos but a few large captions of type as well. This file sparked his curiosity. It wasn't any of his business, he knew, but he was actually considering opening the file and reading it. The thought of reading, and of violating one of his top personal rules, made his head hurt. He sometimes wished he was like many other people who would have no qualms about opening and reading a confidential file if it was part of their job to handle the information.

What would James Bond do, he wondered, and then he knew. A short time later a glance at the clock made him jump up. It was five minutes past the start of his lunchtime. Lunch bag and flash drive in hand, he rushed off down the hall, his mind intent on discovering why three newborn babies had their eyes and ears operated on and why the United States government was interested in that.

~~~

Heather Barnes reported directly to the Secretary of Homeland Security. Many people do not have the pleasure of loving their job, but Heather did – she was one of the lucky ones. Although her position as Executive Assistant to the Secretary was not a management position, Heather, and the Secretary, knew her real worth to the organization. Her analytical mind, technological skillset and connections within the government enabled the Secretary, without reserve, to delegate highly confidential and important assignments to Heather to manage.

Few people other than Heather and the Director knew the true extent of her job. While she didn't have the title, or the recognition, she did have the security clearance.

Heather had been with Homeland Security for five years. She was hired out of grad school by the Under Secretary of Science and Technology, a friend of her dad's, where her primary duties were research and analysis. When Rhonda Watterson was appointed Secretary three years later, she persuaded Heather to work directly for her. Heather knew Secretaries, like Presidents, come and go - Rhonda was already the sixth in Homeland Security's brief existence - and that she may not have that job once Rhonda left or was replaced. Such is the life of politics.

Heather graduated magna cum laude from Johns Hopkins University and earned her Masters in Science and Technology Studies from Cornell University. Even if the position at DHS had not been waiting for her, she would have returned to Washington, D.C., the only city in which she wanted to work.

Only then did she seem to find time, or more accurately, the desire, for a love life. She met Danny four years earlier on a Caribbean cruise that her father had given her for her birthday.

Danny lived only three miles from her, and yet they met a thousand miles from home.

Beautiful wasn't quite the right word to describe Heather. Stunning was a more accurate word. One couldn't help but notice her when she walked into a room. She stood 5'10" in bare feet, with an athletic but sensual body that glided elegantly when she walked.

It was almost noon and Heather left her office to heat her Lean Cuisine in the break room microwave.

As he walked to the break room, Bernie was excited about the fact that he had just read portions of an extremely classified document. He felt so important. "This is how James Bond feels all the time," he surmised, "being privy to so many top secrets." He wondered if his newfound sense of importance showed on his face as he entered the break room. Heather was there, standing at the microwave, looking beautiful as usual, but not so beautiful as to be intimidating. "Hello, Heather," said Bernie without a trace of shyness.

A hint of surprise showed on her face. "Hello Bernie. What's new with you?"

Bernie behaved as if the two of them spoke every day instead of four or five times a year. "Well, this week's adventure is about three men and three babies. Whose eyes were operated on," he added. His own eyes twinkled. It felt good talking to her in this way. And he really thought his movie analogy sounded, well, intelligent. He sounded so informed, so secretive. She was sure to be impressed.

"That's nice," she said. "Have a good rest of your day."

What! he thought. She didn't get it! She didn't know that he knew something of great importance to the agency, to the country, probably even to the world! She wasn't even impressed! His great mood was deflated, and he sat at his usual table and ate his bologna sandwich and cookies that he brought from home, drank the chocolate milk that he bought from the vending machine, and mumbled to himself, "I should have said this week's adventure is about three babies who had microchips implanted in their eyes and ears by our government." Maybe then she would have stayed and eaten her lunch with him.

Another employee entered the break room at the same time Heather Barnes was leaving. Bernie could tell the man who had just entered was thinking lewd thoughts about Heather as he lingered in the doorway with his neck craned out into the hallway, watching her walk away. He then recognized the man as one of the techs who worked for Mr. Dorgan, the one who sat closest to Mr. Dorgan's office.

Bernie had the memory stick with the highly confidential file for Mr. Dorgan in his pant pocket, which made him a bit uneasy. He would have delivered it to him on his way to the break room, but Dorgan was having a standing meeting with his staff, which Bernie could see through the glass doors and did not want to interrupt. So now he planned to stop back by and give it to him after lunch.

"Do you know if Mr. Dorgan will be in his office in half an hour?" Bernie said, looking in the general direction of Mr. Dorgan's employee, his confidence no longer evident.

The man getting coffee looked around the room and, realizing the question was directed at him, replied, "Actually, he's leaving in a few minutes. He won't be back in the office until after the holiday."

"Oh no!" Bernie screeched and, flustered, began eating his bologna sandwich furiously.

"Can I tell him something for you?" offered the tech. "I'm heading back right now."

"No...no. I have to give him this before he leaves!" Bernie stood up and pulled the memory stick from his pocket, waving it in the air. He began scampering about, gathering the remains of his unfinished lunch and putting them into his lunch bag, wiping the crumbs off the table and throwing his garbage in the nearest can. He scurried out the door, hurrying to deliver his critical package before it was too late.

As Bernie entered the door to the Intelligence and Analysis division, he was relieved to see Mr. Dorgan still in his office. He meekly tapped on the door frame of the open door. "Yes?" Dorgan just stared at him. Bernie got that a lot. "I have a file for you from Mr. McElroy and Dr. Thyssen." He held out the memory stick but didn't move into Dorgan's office.

"Oh... yes...thank you." He reached out his hand and Bernie

walked in and placed the memory stick in Dorgan's hand.

"And Mr. McElroy wants to know if you have the paper file that Mr., I mean Dr. Thyssen gave you."

"No." Dorgan then looked at Bernie. "Anything else?"

As Bernie left the office, he passed the tech who had just returned from the break room. His name plate said Jeremy James. Oh, so this guy is the infamous Jeremy James, thought Bernie. He glanced back at Mr. Dorgan and saw him toss the memory stick into a drawer.

As Heather walked back to her office, it suddenly occurred to her what Bernie had said. "…three babies, whose eyes were operated on." She dismissed it for a while as she worked on a research project for several hours which required her full attention, but it nagged at her later in the afternoon for she recalled something about an old case involving three infants. But where and when she had heard of it, she couldn't remember.

"Oh wait!" she exclaimed to herself. She had been trying to remember having seen or heard about a case at the agency involving three babies, but that's not where she had read about it. It was a file she had come across in her father's study at home many years ago. She was only a young teenager at the time, fourteen years old. She wasn't permitted in her father's study, but she desperately needed printer paper for a school homework project and that was the only place she knew to get some.

Under the printer paper was a manila folder with Top Secret stamped on the front of it, so she opened it. Photos of a doctor performing surgery on three newborn infants – there were three separate photos so she assumed there were three different babies – was all she had time to see before she heard her father enter the room.

He was angry when he saw her in his office, but when he saw what she was looking at, he became incensed. His face grew red and his eyes bore into her with dark rage. That was the only time she had ever seen her father act that way towards her, or anyone for that matter, and the only time in her life she was frightened of him. She would never forget it.

"Close it!" he shouted, so loudly she was sure the neighbors heard. "Now!"

She did. "I was just getting some..."

He didn't let her finish. "Shut up!" Never had he used those words with her before. Never had he been so angry and so out of control. "Do you not understand what I mean when I say stay out of this room! Is that not clear to you!"

Heather had run out of the room crying and as she recalled that memory, it still hurt her to this day...to know that she had disappointed him so badly, and to know that he was capable of such rage. He had apologized profusely to her the next day for his reaction to her misbehavior, and she had apologized for going into his office, but the hurt and disappointment experienced that day never completely faded away.

That was fifteen years ago. Heather had never asked her dad about that file. She really hadn't given it any thought as far as the contents were concerned, only that she knew she was not supposed to look at it. Now she thought she'd ask her dad about it. They were, after all, colleagues of a sort now. While they almost never talked about work, they discussed politics, science, world events, books and many other topics on an equal level.

She was leaving tomorrow afternoon with Danny on a tropical, romantic vacation to Fiji that she knew Danny hoped would move their relationship towards marriage and kids. She did want marriage and kids, at least she supposed she did, and probably with Danny, but not yet. She didn't feel anywhere near ready for that commitment even though she was almost thirty years old. How much longer would it take for her to be ready? Perhaps I'm one of those women who are never meant to marry or be a mother, she thought. She was too intent on her career, and loved being by herself much of the time that she wasn't at work. She definitely cared for Danny, and loved the way their relationship was at the present – two or three nights a week together with good sex and good conversation.

Both she and Danny were into keeping their bodies in shape, and they worked out together two or three times a week as well. They biked, jogged, worked out at the gym, hiked and even went mountain-climbing and cross-country skiing. They were both excellent swimmers and intended to snorkel and scuba dive during their trip to Fiji.

She should be more excited about the trip, she knew, and she would have been if it could be completed on her terms. She didn't like having to worry about Danny's feelings and intentions. Oh well, she shrugged, I'm overthinking this whole vacation. It will be fun I'm sure, she told herself. She then forgot about the trip, Danny and the babies file and got back to work.

Once Dragon was gone, Jeremy got to work on his new assignment – following his boss and finding out what he was up to. His instructions from the Secretary of Homeland Security included total access to Dragon's computer files, phone taps, use of agency satellites, and he could requisition other resources if necessary, but only through the Secretary herself or her assistant, Heather. An added bonus, he thought.

"Let's see where you and the Mrs. are going this afternoon," Jeremy's fingers were flying on the keyboard as he accessed yet another Outlook account that wasn't his own. Dragon's calendar revealed nothing as to where he was headed or where he would be for the next several days. He checked e-mails as well but Dragon kept them cleared out so there was no useful information there either. Guess I'll have to tap into IT's e-mail storage software, he thought, but decided to position a satellite to view Dragon's home before he did anything else. Dragon would certainly go home to get his luggage and wife before leaving. Now another of his eight computer monitors was active with an overhead view of Dragon's house along with a few neighboring houses and a short stretch of street. It should take Dragon another half hour to get home.

While he waited for Dragon to arrive home so that he could follow him, he accessed Homeland Security's e-mail software program that duplicated and maintained every incoming and outgoing e-mail. He pulled up his boss's account and skimmed through the past two months' e-mail subject lines, looking for travel arrangements, an e-mail to or from his wife, or any other indication that he was going on a short vacation. Nothing. Of course, they could be driving, or perhaps his wife made all the arrangements, or perhaps Dragon was lying to him. He selected door number three.

Forty-five minutes passed and Dragon's car still hadn't arrived home. Jeremy telescoped the satellite in for a closer look at the house to see if Mrs. Dorgan was home. The garage doors were closed so he couldn't tell if her car was in the garage. The door and drapes from the front view of the house were all closed and there was no evidence of anyone being home. He zoomed out again for a broader view.

There was movement in the parking lot on one of his other screens and he watched as his female surveillance subject, Mary Beth Singer, got into her car and drove away from her place of work, most likely going to lunch.

The monitor that displayed Michael Michtenbaum's home was still on, and he continued to look at it frequently, watching the numerous people, including police, who came and went from the house.

Since Jeremy didn't know where Dragon had gone, he decided to look again into his boss's computer for answers. He checked the most recent internet sites visited. Dragon always deleted them, but that didn't mean they were gone. It took Jeremy less than a minute to find the site that Dragon had gone into that morning and stayed in for seventy-five minutes. He pulled up the site, the name of which held no meaning at all for him, and was prompted to enter his – Dragon's – user name and password. This was going to be a bit trickier, Jeremy knew. He knew Dragon was too smart to use his pets' names, or his birthdate or any password that could fairly easily be determined. He was the type to select a long, random and complicated password of a combination of letters, numbers and symbols, using different passwords for different site entries, and changing them often. That's what I'd do, thought Jeremy. This system would mean that he would have to write them down somewhere accessible. Jeremy kept his in his wallet, so he could access from anywhere, but the passwords were encrypted on his various credit, debit, store, insurance and other cards held in his wallet. His system for creating and changing passwords was simplistic to him but nearly impossible for anyone else to figure out. Dragon probably had his written down somewhere, as most people did, but Jeremy didn't have the time or the inclination to go looking for them.

"Going to Plan B," he stated as he typed in code to bring up a program he had written himself that tracked every keystroke on a particular electronic device. The program only worked from point of activation forward on a specific computer or phone. Anticipating he would need it, Jeremy had already activated this program on Dorgan's laptop at 9:30 a.m., shortly after learning of the confidential assignment from the Secretary. He could now see every keystroke entered on Dragon's laptop over the past four hours and indefinitely into the future until such time as he deactivated the program.

It took Jeremy only minutes to find the keystrokes that were equivalent to the username and password entered earlier that morning by John Dorgan to access an unheard-of program. The user name was Michtenbaum. "Interesting," smiled Jeremy. He typed in the next twenty-five keystrokes, which had been typed by Dragon earlier that morning and which Jeremy therefore interpreted as being the password. There had not been another keystroke after these twenty-five for over a minute.

Jeremy found himself looking at a black square approximately nine inches wide and seven inches deep on the left side of his 19" flat screen, which he assumed was meant for a video feed. There were numerous data fields on the right of the screen to type in date, time and speed of video for recorded data, or the selection of live video coverage. He clicked the live coverage icon although it was already highlighted and should be showing live coverage. The 9x7" box remained black.

Well, he's dead, thought Jeremy. Perhaps that's why the screen is black? It no longer has a subject to video? That would make sense I suppose.

He turned up the sound on his computer as he thought he heard some noise. Yes, there were voices, although they sounded remote. He turned up the sound even further, but still could not understand what the voices were saying. One was definitely female and one male. He clicked the live video button again but still the black screen persisted.

He decided to go back fifteen minutes, so typed in 2:10 p.m. The current date was already displayed. This time the results were different. The video block was still dark, but not black. It was as though there was a light shining behind a black screen. The voices were still there, but loud now.

"Mr. Liming, you're not family of Mr. Michtenbaum, so I won't be able to discuss the results of his autopsy with you. If you're law enforcement, as you say, you can talk with our local police. I'll be sharing the results with them."

"I understand, Ms. Curry. Are you able to tell me when the autopsy will be performed?"

"I was ready to start it when you arrived."

"Well, thank you for talking with me. I'll leave you to your work now."

"I'll walk you out."

Jeremy heard footsteps as they walked and then a door opening and closing. After that, all was quiet. He continued to listen and for several minutes there was no sound at all. Then he heard the sound of a door opening again. In the distance he could hear the male and female voices he had heard earlier, talking but not loud or clear enough for him to hear what was being said. So the door must still be open, Jeremy concluded. Did someone walk into the room again? He strained to hear any close sounds or movement, but he heard nothing. A couple of times he thought he heard a slight shuffle, but he wasn't sure.

He switched back to live coverage. Now he could clearly hear the sounds of a person in the room. There was clinking metal, running water, snapping elastic and other sounds Jeremy was trying to identify. He assumed he was listening to the medical examiner, a Ms. Curry apparently, preparing to do an autopsy on Michael Michtenbaum at the county's morgue.

Jeremy jumped when he heard a voice that sounded like it was right next to him. "Deceased is Michael Ray Michtenbaum, male, age 50, weighing 168 pounds." The coroner was recording her notes.

When he heard the high pitched whirl of a power saw and then the lower grinding jolts it made when it hit bone, Jeremy decided it was time to review other data. He was not able to tell exactly what Dragon had watched and listened to for the seventy-five minutes he was on this site, but Jeremy had a pretty good idea. They knew about when Michtenbaum had died, so Jeremy entered

Tuesday's date and a time of 6:00 p.m. as a starting point to review recorded information about Michael Michtenbaum.

This time the 9x7 inch box showed a perfectly clear recorded video of the inside of a house, a kitchen. Whoever is taking the video reaches out and opens the refrigerator door. Jeremy could see a hand and part of an arm taking out a bottle of beer and opening it with another hand. Now how is this person holding the video camera and using both hands to open the beer, Jeremy wondered.

The camera then moves into the living room, where it lowers slightly as the person apparently sits down, facing a large window. Jeremy sees the bottle of beer come up towards the camera, and he could see the end of the bottle raised into the air. "What the heck is this?" said Jeremy aloud.

The scene was confusing to Jeremy. Who is holding the video camera? he thought. Is someone waiting for Michtenbaum to get home – the killer perhaps - and recording the moment? This doesn't make sense.

Jeremy fast forwarded while there was nothing to see but the window and surrounding room, and the beer apparently being drunk by whomever was holding the camera. When Jeremy saw a figure move rapidly in front of the window, he stopped the video, rewound it one minute, and turned it back on at regular speed. A figure of a white male walks in front of the window, but it isn't Michael Michtenbaum. Jeremy has seen Michtenbaum from his satellite video many times and this isn't him. The video camera now moves higher as the person holding it stands up and moves into the foyer towards the front door.

Jeremy hears the doorbell ring and sees a hand and part of an arm reach out to open the door.

"Yes?" says a voice. Could the voice be that of Michael Michtenbaum, thought Jeremy. Is he the one holding the camera? "What! Stop!" the voice cried. The attack on the man with the camera is over in less than twenty seconds. Jeremy can see the man at the door – the killer as he now suspects - who has something in his fist. Jeremy stops the video, rewinds and plays it again in slow motion. It is a syringe, which the man raises and jabs towards the other person, most likely stabbing it in his jugular, thinks Jeremy. Michael Michtenbaum's jugular. The killer is very close to the camera now, apparently holding onto Michael Michtenbaum until he stops struggling, then lowers him down in a chair in the entryway, directly across from a mirror and a table. His eyes are still open but he has stopped breathing. He is dead.

Jeremy tried to figure out what he was seeing, and how he was seeing it. He could see Michael Michtenbaum, dead, sitting on a chair staring wide-eyed at the mirror across from him. Then it hit him. The guy isn't *holding* a video camera – the guy IS a video camera. It must be through his eyes. His eyes are open and staring, even in death, and as long as his eyes are open, he can continue to record what is in front of him. How is this possible? But he's also recording audio? How? What is going on here? What the hell is going on?

Well, I've identified the murderer, thought Jeremy. But I still haven't found Dragon, and that's what I'm supposed to be doing right now.

Still, Jeremy spent the next hour reviewing the same, and additional, recently taped video from the point of view of Michael Michtenbaum's right eye. It was fascinating.

Jeremy still had Dragon's Outlook up on one of his many monitors, and a ping indicated a new e-mail had arrived. Jeremy glanced at it, then gave it his full attention when he read, "Met with curry. Oh topsy on for this afternoon." Jeremy quickly realized someone had left a voice-mail message on Dragon's cell phone and it converted into an e-mail, although inaccurately. "Dragon I'm so surprised at your stupidity!" whispered Jeremy. "You know better than to communicate via e-mail or any method that leaves a permanent record, you moron!"

So Dragon had sent someone to Hamilton, Ohio, the city where Michael Michtenbaum was murdered, to meet with the medical examiner. But where is Dragon?

At that moment, Jeremy's keystroke logging software began recording keystrokes. Dragon was on his laptop.

At 6 p.m., as Heather got into her grey Toyota Camry, she again began to think of the comment about the three babies made by Bernie, the strange little man from the archives area, and about the file she accidentally came across so long ago in her father's study. Could they actually be the same case, or related in some way?

Since she wasn't meeting Danny she decided to visit her father and ask him about the old file folder that had enraged him so. To drive to Fairfax, Virginia, to the house where she grew up would take about forty-five minutes and she dialed her dad's cell phone number to let him know she was coming. Perhaps they could have dinner together, something they hadn't done in several months. She could pick up Chinese from her favorite restaurant.

Heather's father, Jacob Barnes, worked for the CIA in the Intelligence Division. He had told Heather when she was a child that he worked for the government and left it at that. She didn't question him about the specifics of his job until she was in college and the two began communicating on an adult level. By this time, Jacob no longer did field work, at least not often. He assigned and supervised other field agents. So he decided to tell her the truth, or at least a small portion of the truth, about his current position. He never told her about the type of field assignments his agents engaged in, nor about the ones he himself had done for so many years.

There was no answer on her dad's cell, so she left him a message that she was stopping by and hoped to catch him and have dinner. She was still forty minutes away and could he please call her. Twenty minutes later the distinctive ring of Stevie Wonder's "I Just Called to Say I Love You" announced that her dad was returning her call. "Hi, dad," she answered cheerily.

"Hey, sweetie," Jacob Barnes replied. "I got your message, but I'm in New York City until Saturday so won't be able to have dinner with you tonight. How about Saturday night?"

"Danny and I are leaving for Figi tomorrow afternoon for a week, so we'll get together when I get back. It's just been a while since I've seen you and I was hoping to talk to you about something."

"Oh that's right. I forgot about your trip. Is anything wrong, honey?"

"Oh no. Not at all. Everything's good. The talk can wait until I get back from vacation."

"Is it something we can discuss on the phone? I have a little time now."

"No, it's not important at all. It can wait. So is everything okay with you?"

"Everything is more than okay with me." Heather could hear the smile in his voice. "I've met someone, honey." He waited for her reaction.

"Really dad! That's wonderful! When do I get to meet her?" she laughed.

"Soon, I hope. We've only been seeing each other a few weeks and I wanted to make sure we were going to continue seeing each other before I introduced the two of you. She knows about you of course."

"What's her name?"

"Susan Combs. She's a doctor and a very lovely lady. She's the first woman I've even really noticed since your mother died."

Heather's mother died from a hemorrhage shortly after giving birth to her.

"I'm so happy for you dad! And it's about time!"

"Yes, it is definitely about time," he said softly.

"Well, you two have fun and I'll see you when I get back. I can't wait to see you and to meet Susan."

"Thanks, honey. You and Danny have fun as well."

Heather had passed the exit to her townhouse, which was on the way to her dad's house, and decided to get the Chinese takeout from the place another two miles down the road. She had finished her laundry and most of her packing and was now looking forward to a quiet leisurely evening at home, eating sweet and sour pork and watching the latest on the terrorists' foiled plot and subsequent findings. The news wouldn't reveal much, she knew. She had other ways of finding out more information if she wanted to know.

Her mind wandered back to the file and the case she had wanted to discuss with her father. She drove on past the exit for the Chinese restaurant, having changed her mind once again, deciding to go to her dad's house after all.

Heather still had a key to her childhood home and she let herself in, disarming the security alarm. She knew her father's office would be locked – it always was; but that's not where she intended to look for the old file. She stopped in the kitchen and found a somewhat-fresh pasta salad in her dad's refrigerator as well as a nice bottle of red wine on the counter. Hopefully he won't mind, she thought as she grabbed the bottle and a wine glass. She headed down the basement steps.

When Jacob Barnes had the stately two-story colonial built for his lovely new wife, he had three "safe" rooms built in the home, one off of the master bedroom upstairs, one as his office on the first floor, positioned directly below the upstairs room, and one in the basement, which was so reinforced it could withstand a nuclear blast. Jacob wanted to keep his new wife and any future children safe from attack or other catastrophe. Particularly in his line of work, which his wife never knew about even at her death six years later, Jacob was aware of the many horrible things that can, and do, happen to people in their homes. Once, in 1976, when he was single and living on the second floor of an apartment complex, a group of Irish revolutionaries, friends of other IRA members he had recently killed in a raid in Belfast, invaded his apartment and shot 200 rounds from their ArmaLite AR-18s into his bed. It was only by the grace of God, or perhaps undercooked pork, that he happened to be sitting on the toilet with the runs when it happened. Thankful at that moment that he slept in the nude and therefore didn't have pajama bottoms to pull up and thus waste the precious two seconds he had left to get the hell out of there, he dove from the toilet through the glass window a couple of feet away. Rolling down a partial roof and falling the remaining twelve feet to the ground, he jumped up and sprinted off before the invaders were able to see which way he went.

Heather didn't know this story, nor did her mother. They only knew Jacob Barnes loved and wanted to protect his family in case of a home invasion. The steel and concrete reinforced walls went down through all three floors of the house and another ten feet below the basement floor.

Can you say paranoid, dad? Heather thought lovingly as she punched in the code to the basement safe room that he had taught her how to use at age four. Talk about overkill, these three safe rooms, and particularly the basement room, had to add a few hundred thousand dollar cost to the overall cost of building the home. But Heather knew there was another reason her father had built the rooms. She knew his job entailed a lot more danger than he had ever told her about. Fortunately, they had never had to use the rooms, other than going to the basement a few times when tornados or storms threatened.

Therefore, Jacob had taken to storing paper files in the basement safe room. Heather only happened upon this knowledge one day about four years ago when she was helping her dad clean out his basement and he opened the safe room to put a box in it. She glanced in and saw that one wall was lined with banker boxes.

Heather had no idea whether the file she was looking for would be in one of the boxes in this room but she intended to find out. She set her pasta salad, wine glass and wine bottle on a small table by a couch on the wall opposite the files. None of the boxes was marked as to the contents. "Not going to make it easy for me dad, are you," she said out loud. She poured a glass of wine, took a large bite of her pasta salad and pulled the top box off the first column of stacked boxes and set it on the couch.

"I don't even know what I'm looking for!" she continued talking aloud to herself. She remembered the Top Secret stamp on the front of the manila folder but she didn't recall any other writing or name on the outside of the folder. The file wasn't very thick as she recalled – perhaps a half inch at most. Her father could certainly have added more information to the file after that disastrous day many years ago. She decided to narrow her search by looking only for manila folders one-half to one inch thick so she could search from the top of the box without having to remove each folder.

Most folders were brown accordion style and were 3-6" thick. No file folders met her criteria in that box or in any of the next three boxes stacked in that first column. Only six more columns – twenty-four more banker boxes – to go.

She couldn't believe her dad kept this many paper files. Surely this information was in his or some other computer. Well, maybe not. Sometimes, low tech paper is the safest way to go.

There were two folders that were approximately an inch thick in her search of the next eight boxes, but when she lifted each from the box, neither folder was stamped Top Secret, so she replaced the files without opening them and returned each box to its proper location.

Heather went upstairs to the kitchen to search for something else to eat. She fixed a turkey and tomato sandwich on multi-grain bread. Not her favorite Chinese and CNN as she had planned, but she was rather enjoying herself.

It was 8:30 when she saw a file that looked like the one she had seen fifteen years ago. She opened the folder to see if it held the same photos of infants in an operating room. It did. She had found it.

"All right!" she exclaimed excitedly. She set the box on the floor so she could stretch out on the couch and thoroughly review the folder contents.

She began by scanning through the pages. "…test subjects chosen due to timing and location of Dr. William Banks…three infants, two male, one female, born on October 27…each surgery taking approximately seven hours…Dr. Banks assisted by surgical nurses Mrs. Amy Parker and Miss Janice Birmingham. Both terminated following the three surgeries. Hospital night nurse in nursery also terminated."

Heather dropped the glass of red wine which hit the couch then bounced to the hard floor, where it shattered. Red wine now puddled on the couch and the floor. She jumped up more from the shock of what she had just read than from the wine spilled on her slacks. Did the CIA murder these three people? Was her father involved in these murders?

She was now almost afraid to touch the file, afraid to know what other horrors it held. She was glad of the excuse to go and get a broom, rags and cleaner to clean up the wine and broken glass.

Heather's mind was trying to make sense of what she had read so far. Three babies born at Mercy Hospital in Hamilton, Ohio, had been operated on almost immediately following their births by a Dr. William Banks. She had not yet read exactly what the operations entailed or why the operations were done, but apparently, with the exception of Dr. Banks, the other hospital personnel involved in the surgeries, as well as the nursery nurse on duty, had been murdered in order to keep them from talking about the surgeries. Her father had the file so was obviously involved in some way.

The couch was brown leather and the wine did not stain it. She poured bleach onto the concrete to rid it of any pinkish residue, but now the room smelled of bleach. She doubted if her dad came in this room very often so he might not notice. She swept up the glass and moved the couch to remove remnants of wine and glass under it.

Heather realized she was now worried that her father might find out she'd been in this room looking through his files.

Heather started reading through the file page by page. The surgery photos were gruesome and hard for Heather to look at. Heather gasped and turned her head away from the sight of a newborn baby with an empty eye socket. Close-ups taken during the surgeries showed Dr. Banks removing an eyeball from each infant and making a small incision on the back side of the eyeball. A small circular chip about the size of a droplet of water on a flat surface was inserted into the eyeball before it was carefully sewn closed and reattached within the eye socket. Each baby also had a similar chip placed near one of his or her ear drums. A medical report written by Dr. Banks was included in the file stating the surgery procedure in medical terms, but the pictures told the story much more clearly and in a language easy to understand.

Heather read a four page biography about the man who created both of these devices - a small video camera that could work within a human eye and record everything that eye saw and a tiny audio recording device that recorded everything that ear heard. The devices were made of metal, similar to the metal used in some knee and hip replacements, and were designed to last seventy-five years or more.

Heather read every word and studied every photo in the file. She memorized the names of the infants and their parents, the hospital and city where the surgeries were performed, the now dead nurses and the doctor.

The file contained no explanation as to why the CIA was involved in this experiment or what exactly the experiment was designed to do. It also did not mention who from the CIA was involved. Heather already knew her father had to be involved since he was in possession of the file. What was his involvement? Did he order the experiment or perhaps supervise the field agents? Or was he one of the field agents who'd committed the murders? No, of course not, she thought. This was fifty years ago. Her father would have been a child.

It was 11 p.m. before Heather carefully returned the file to its proper box and restacked the boxes along the wall. Would her father be able to tell she had been in here? It didn't matter, she thought. I'm going to tell him when I return from vacation. More than ever, I want to talk to him about this case.

Before she left, she wrote her dad a note saying she'd stopped by after all to get a red suitcase that was still in her old room. She mentioned she had drunk most of a bottle of his wine and had broken a glass. She said she was looking forward to meeting Susan and seeing them upon her return. She hurried to her old room and retrieved the suitcase before leaving for her home at 11:15 p.m.

The Man was one of six in the room. They were a powerful group, and not in complete accord when it came to decisions regarding The Freedom Project. Some were no longer in favor of expanding current and initiating new projects, partly because of the unbridled cost to taxpayers, which now averaged over twenty billion dollars per year and was hidden among the expenditures of numerous government agencies, but also because the Project itself was becoming too powerful for even those in power to control.

Not only was The Freedom Project in contempt of almost every principle and requirement of the original and amended Privacy Act, it egregiously violated the Fourth Amendment of the Constitution. Utilization of the current Freedom Project gave the group the capability to spy on nearly twenty-five percent of U.S. citizens and they now planned to triple that percentage.

Yet, as is usually the case with those who have been in politics for any length of time, personal agendas and rewards outweighed any righteous indignation they may have felt or voiced in the meeting.

The Man, therefore, was unmoved by their hypocritical naysaying and by any reference to the breaking of laws. He was full of power which had corrupted him absolutely. He was an expert at setting events in motion that would lead to the outcome he desired, and with the murder of Michael Michtenbaum, he had set these events in motion. The person he put in charge of the permanent end of the initial Freedom Project, FP-I, was taking his job seriously.

Yet, as was most often the case, these events could lead to unpredictable events as well – of course they would – no one could predict every eventuality – the butterfly effect you know. As long as the ultimate outcome was desirable, he was okay with whatever path the process took. And if the outcome was not desirable, he was also an expert at wagging the dog.

FRIDAY

Jeremy arrived at 6 a.m. and immediately continued his search for his boss, John Dorgan. He had stayed until 7 the night before, watching Dragon on his computer, trying to learn where he was, but nothing Dragon entered on his laptop revealed his whereabouts.

Jeremy would have stayed all night at work – this was an assignment he relished and didn't wish to leave long enough to take a bathroom break – but he had other plans for the evening and didn't want to back out of them at the last moment.

He was a video gamer and belonged to three game leagues that competed regularly on-line. Last night's game competition was Call of Duty. It lasted until 1 a.m. so Jeremy got little sleep before he showered and returned to work. Jeremy and his team were now in the semi-finals and would compete again Saturday night.

Before he left yesterday, Jeremy accessed a secure agency site listing any and all GPS tracking devices assigned to Dragon. There were four, including the standard ones of car, laptop and phone, and a USB drive issued at 11:15 a.m. that morning. Ahh, thought Jeremy. That one was the memory stick given to Dragon by the archive file clerk at lunchtime – the memory stick that he, and he was sure the file clerk, saw Dragon throw into his desk drawer. So it wouldn't do any good to track the whereabouts of that device.

So far, none of the tracking devices seemed to be with Dragon, as the car, laptop and phone were all stationery at Dulles Airport, just as they were yesterday. Jeremy wondered whether Dragon removed or disabled the GPS devices, then took his now-untraceable car, laptop and phone with him; or whether the car, laptop and phone were all sitting in the parking garage at Dulles, which would mean Dragon was with them since he was using his laptop. Normally, Jeremy could find any computer by its IP address but Dragon was adept at spoofing the address by using a proxy server, so he couldn't locate it that way either.

If he had the use of one of the newer satellites - Samuel or Delilah – he would be able to see through the concrete parking garage and find Dragon's car if it was, indeed, there.

Jeremy had positioned one of his older satellites over the city of Hamilton, Ohio, just in case Dragon had gone there as well as sending another agent. He had specifically targeted Michtenbaum's home, Michtenbaum's parent's home and the morgue.

Despite all his efforts of yesterday, he still had not found Dragon. He intended to change that outcome today.

Since it was still quite early, only 6:30 a.m., and no one else was in the office yet, Jeremy decided to break into Dragon's office to get to the memory stick in his desk. He had thought of doing it yesterday but was never alone, even at 7 p.m. when he finally left. Maybe the memory stick would hold some clues as to Dragon's whereabouts. Picking locks was another of Jeremy's many talents that if used for evil could land him in prison. Even when used for good, most of his talents could land him in prison if not sanctioned by the Secretary of Homeland Security. Thank goodness he was allowed to be bad for the good of his country.

Jeremy fired up his seventh laptop, the first six of which had dutifully continued to record or analyze data throughout the night. He glanced at all of them, a practice he did unconsciously, always surveilling the running applications. He poured his second cup of coffee from the large thermos he brought from home and grabbed a donut from the box of a half dozen he had picked up on his way in this morning, and began reading the 150+ page document stored on the memory stick.

Dorgan awoke at 5:30 a.m. as he did every morning, without the aid of an alarm clock. Even when in a different time zone, which was not the case today but often was, his internal clock rarely needed reset. He kept his body fit by running five miles every morning, so he stepped out of the hotel lobby door into the slightly chilly May morning air of Hamilton, Ohio. Dorgan ran two and a half miles down the bike path along the river.

He used this time to think about the events of yesterday and what needed to happen today. Dorgan knew who Michtenbaum's killer was, or at least he knew what he looked like. One of today's jobs was to find out the man's identity. He had run the man's image through his facial recognition software but nothing came up. Chances are, he was a disgruntled client or unhappy acquaintance of

Michtenbaum's. So today he would visit the elder Michtenbaums - Michael's parents - as well as Michtenbaum's law firm and friends if need be, to find out who killed Michael Ray Michtenbaum.

Another job for today was to find a way to remove the implants from Michael as discreetly as possible.

Dorgan's job was to protect the interests of the United States government and those involved in this project, as well as his own interests, and the only way to do that was to retrieve the implants. He was extremely nervous that too many people had already become aware of this experiment now that Michael's death had brought some information to the attention of others. Jeremy, for one, had been surveilling Michael. He might become suspicious as to why he's been watching him for years and do some more digging. Thyssen at the CIA made him nervous, and now both McElroy and even his lowly clerk who brought him the memory stick were aware of the file document. What if they've read the file? It's very possible. Actually, it's quite likely, thought Dorgan. Yes, if, and probably when, this whole mess comes to light, they're going to dig up Michtenbaum's body and look for the implants. I have to make sure they're not there for them to find. They can't find any of these original implants since the old technology makes them so easy to detect and retrieve. Today's technology allows such devices to be implanted without a trace.

One of the reasons Dorgan had hired former CIA agent Johnson was due to his many talents. Johnson would be able to remove the implants, stitch behind the ear and reinsert the eyeball into its socket in less than ten minutes, leaving the body in almost the same condition as he found it.

Dorgan was lost in thought as he pounded the pavement on the running path along the Great Miami River. He had to make sure this old experiment ended as cleanly as possible with all traces of it eliminated. Most importantly, even if this experiment was brought to light, he had to make sure that it could in no way be linked to any subsequent experiments and projects in which the government was now involved. The personal privacy issues are way too compromised, and therefore the stakes are way too high, he thought.

Dorgan was perfect for the job. He knew the politics of getting what he wanted and more importantly he never stopped –

never – until he got it. He was highly intelligent, sly and ruthless when needed. He believed in the concept of sacrificing the few to save the many, even though his definition of save was probably very different from most everyone else's.

As he turned and began the two and a half mile run back to his hotel, Dorgan was encouraged by the thought that he could at the very least contain the catastrophe to the Freedom Project which involved only three subjects – Michael Ray Michtenbaum, Mary Beth Brown - now Mary Beth Singer - and Jonathan Moore. Worst case scenario, this experiment of fifty years ago would be revealed but could be explained away as the maniacal lunacy of a few fanatics, all of whom have since died, and the knowledge of which their current counterparts were not aware.

Best case scenario, which is always the one Dorgan chose to implement, was that the project never come to light of the American people at all. Whatever the cost, whomever had to be silenced, keeping this project quiet was Dorgan's number one priority.

The "Baby Case," as Heather now referred to it, occupied her mind much of the night and she got little sleep. She decided to try and run into Bernie during his morning break, which she believed he took faithfully at 10 a.m. every day, and ask him a few questions about what he said the day before.

She had a million things to do at work before she left for vacation but her mind kept returning to the "Baby Case." Did the parents of these babies know that their newborns were having implants placed in their heads? She doubted it. She knew she shouldn't take the time to go on a break with the express purpose of talking to Bernie, but she had to find out what had happened to make him mention it, if truly it was the same case. She felt for certain it was. But what could he possibly know – he was only an archive file clerk. Well, she would find out soon enough, and tried to concentrate on her work.

At 10 a.m. sharp, she walked to the break room. Bernie was already at his usual table when she walked in. He was talking low to himself but looked up when he heard the door and left his mouth open as if in mid- sentence, staring at her as she walked across the small room directly towards him. Bernie looked behind him once to see if perhaps there was someone else she was looking at and walking towards, but the wall was empty.

"May I sit here with you, Bernie?" Heather asked as sweetly has her impatient, serious mood would allow. Mouth still agape, eyes wide, Bernie nodded and managed to utter "uh huh."

"Bernie, I was intrigued yesterday by your mention of a case involving three babies, remember?"

"Uh, huh," he closed his mouth finally.

"I'm somewhat familiar with that case as well. Did something happen that caused renewed interest?"

His eyes and face were smiling at her and his lips were moving a little as if he were talking to himself, but he said nothing and Heather tried to sit patiently. After 30 seconds of silence, she almost got up as she concluded it was ludicrous of her to think she could learn anything from this obviously mentally challenged gnome.

"Why yes, my dear," Bernie finally said in his best Sean Connery voice, minus the "sh" for "s". "There has been a recent development that has resurrected this interesting case from the bowels of the archives."

It was Heather's turn to drop her jaw and gape wide-eyed, but she recovered quickly. "Oh, do tell." She flashed a gorgeous smile at the little man and gazed into his eyes. God, I'm so glad no one else is in this room to see me, she was thinking while holding the smile.

Bernie leaned in towards Heather and lowered his voice. "One of the subject babies, now 50 years old, has died. Murdered, to be exact." As Bernie slowly emphasized the word *babies* he held up and curled the first two fingers of each hand, gesturing parenthesis signs.

"Oh dear!" She exclaimed. "Which of the three was it?"

Bernie hesitated and Heather interpreted the pause as uncertainty as to whether he should tell her what he knew. But apparently he couldn't remember the name, for he reached in his pocket and pulled out a piece of paper, which he unfolded and held in front of his face. "Michael Ray Michtenbaum," he read. "His father found him dead in his home. I have the news article right here." He handed it to her. Heather noticed as he handed her the paper that his face and voice had changed once again – from the confident, smooth voice of a few moments ago to the timid, strange, squeaky voice of the file clerk.

Hmmm, thought Heather. Bernie may be a handy little guy to have around after all. The on-line news article was from the Journal News in Hamilton, Ohio. Hamilton, recalled Heather, was the same city where Michtenbaum and the other subjects were born. So he never left home, or he left and returned. It was at Mercy Hospital in Hamilton, Ohio, where Michael Ray Michtenbaum was born and had implants placed in his right eye and right ear on the night of his birth.

The article didn't state much – only that local resident Michael Ray Michtenbaum was found dead in his home Wednesday evening around 8:30 by his father who went to check on him when he didn't call two days in a row, a deviation from his normal routine. There was no apparent cause of death, police stated. The article went on to talk about Michael's law practice, his parents and his role in the community.

"You said he'd been murdered," Heather queried. "This article says there was no apparent cause of death."

"Yes." James Bond was back, eyes twinkling. "But that was yesterday's article. Here is this morning's."

Heather was slightly amazed at this guy. She took the second article and read, "Michael Ray Michtenbaum found dead...Medical Examiner Rachel Curry initial findings state he was victim of a homicide...pending final autopsy results...police not releasing details."

Heather read both articles twice and handed them back to Bernie. "So what do you know about this case?" She squinted her eyes as she looked at him and asked the question.

"Um, well." He glanced up at the clock on the wall. "Oh, my gosh! It's past my break time. I'm late!" He was so flustered he knocked his chocolate milk carton to the floor, spilling the remaining contents. "Oh, dear!" he cried, turning and waving his arms.

"Bernie, go on back to work. I'll clean it up," Heather offered. "Go."

Bernie hurried out without a word. Heather ran to the door

and called to him, "Bernie!" He turned to look at her but kept walking. "Meet me here at lunchtime. I need you to take me to the file room!"

Mary Beth Singer had her suitcase packed and everything in order to make the two-hour drive to Hamilton, Ohio, her home town. She had received the news late yesterday morning of her former classmate's death and she wanted to go to the visitation and funeral to be held on Saturday. She knew Michael well when they were in school; they had grown up together and were in most of the same classes from kindergarten through high school.

Although they didn't stay in touch on a regular basis, Mary Beth visited Hamilton at least three or four times a year to see her own family, and she always visited Michael's parents when she was in town. The Michtenbaums had been good friends of her parents, and good friends of hers, her entire life. She often ran into Michael when she was there and saw him every five years at their class reunions. She couldn't believe he had been murdered.

Mary Beth decided to take yesterday afternoon and today off work once she heard the news. She had planned to take her car to get new tires on Saturday, but she moved that up to Thursday afternoon. Today she had the oil changed in the car, ran several errands and planned to leave by early afternoon in order to take dinner to Michael's parents and eat with them this evening. She had already called them to make sure they were up to it. They were so glad she was coming and would be with them this evening. They needed the love and support of a dear friend right now and they insisted she stay at their house.

When Mary Beth learned that she and Michael had the same birthday – they were in first or second grade when she discovered this fact – they became even closer friends. When they were teenagers, and their two families were together for dinner one evening, Michael's dad Mitch told them the story of the night nurse who had been on duty in the nursery when they arrived at the hospital. She had disappeared that night and was never seen or heard from again. "It must have been you two screaming babies driving her crazy," laughed the older Mr. Michtenbaum, and the whole family laughed, but Mary Beth remembered thinking that story was very creepy.

Mary Beth was waiting for her husband to come home and have lunch with her. They had a tradition of always hugging and kissing goodbye before one left for an overnight trip. You just never know if it might be your last chance to say goodbye and I love you. Mary Beth and her husband were still very much in love even after 27 years of marriage. In fact, a few of her friends had told her she and Joe were the "poster couple" of a good marriage. Mary Beth thought so too. But she also knew of other couples whose marriages seemed perfect, and then one day their lives were shattered by an infidelity on the part of one, or the death of one. Life and love are fragile, Mary Beth knew, and she had decided long ago to savor every moment of each and to not take either for granted.

The phone rang. It was Lauren, Mary Beth's 22 year old daughter, who lived and attended college in Oxford, Ohio. She graduated three weeks earlier but was still living in Oxford until her upcoming trip to Europe for the summer, a graduation present from her parents. They talked for half an hour until Joe arrived for lunch, and both parents sent their love to their only child as they hung up the phone.

"Are you sure you can't come with me?" Mary Beth was playfully begging her husband as he walked in the door. He just grinned and shook his head. If the funeral had been of a close friend of his or a relative, or if he felt Mary Beth really needed him to be with her, he would have canceled his plans for the weekend and gone, but she had assured him that was not necessary and she was only teasing him now. He planned to golf most of the day tomorrow and then have dinner and go bar-hopping with his golfing buddies. He wasn't a big drinker, but he enjoyed the time with his friends and a few beers seemed to bring out the fun side of him. "Let's see," he scrunched his face as if trying to decide and held both hands in front of him, palms up, as if they were two scales weighing his thoughts. "A funeral, or golf and beer." He raised the left palm in the air as he weighed the option – "funeral of your old boyfriend" – he winked at her and then raised the right palm – "or golf, food and beer with my best buddies. Hmmm, tough decision." Mary Beth threw a piece of bread at him and laughed.

Joe pulled his wife to him, put his arms around her and kissed her. "You know I'm kidding. If you want me to go, just say the word. I know the Michtenbaums are good friends of yours." Mary Beth again assured him she didn't need for him to go with her. "Have you heard yet how he was murdered?" Joe asked as he let go of his wife and they sat back down at the kitchen table.

"No, the police didn't reveal that information. I don't know if they've told Mitch and Celia or not. I'll find out tonight when I talk to them, I assume. I probably won't bring it up, but they might."

"Well, call me tonight to let me know you made it okay. I'm going to take my sandwich with me and head back to the office. The Director called a meeting as I was leaving and I told him I'd be right back. I love you. See you Sunday," and Joe kissed his wife Mary Beth goodbye.

Heather spent the rest of the morning searching on-line archive records for any mention of Michael Ray Michtenbaum or the other two names mentioned in her dad's file. She found nothing, which is pretty much what she expected. With her mind now engrossed by this interesting case, she was resigned to getting very little actual work done today, so she simply decided to give herself permission to hold the work until she returned from vacation. One important and highly confidential task she had been told about by her boss yesterday was that the department was covertly checking into the actions of Director Dorgan, head of Intelligence and Analysis.

The Secretary would normally have assigned this task only to Heather so that no one else in the department was aware, but since Heather would be gone for the next week, the Secretary did not want to wait. She explained her reasoning to Heather, who was somewhat shocked at the fact that such a high level director was being internally investigated, and that the secretary had assigned the task to one of the director's own employees.

"It's unorthodox, I know," explained the Secretary, "but I know Jeremy James fairly well, and I trust him to do the job professionally and confidentially. However, I told him to come to me or to you if he needed anything, so there is a chance he might talk to you today before you leave. I just wanted to make you aware and also to explain why I wasn't having you do the investigation."

After this talk with her boss yesterday, Heather had done some investigating on her own into John Dorgan's personal life. She usually concentrated on financials, as money was often the motivator for someone to "turn". She found and reviewed all his bank accounts, real estate holdings, stocks and insured possessions.

She also checked to see what GPS devices were assigned to Dorgan. Four, the usual laptop, cell phone and car, and one memory stick, and it had only just been assigned minutes before she had checked yesterday. So far, all were stationery – three at Dulles Airport and one in Dorgan's office.

Heather had originally planned to leave work at lunchtime and meet Danny at 2 p.m. to head for the airport. She now knew she wouldn't be leaving at noon as that was when she was meeting Bernie for a second time. She needed to persuade him to take her to the archives and let her look at any files he might have on the Baby Case. Hopefully the persuading wouldn't take long and she could spend a half hour or so in the files.

A different-sounding ping on her computer brought her back to the present. Dorgan's memory stick was being accessed. She knew he was out of the office and the access was here in the building, so it wasn't him looking at it. She was able to pinpoint the location of the access, and then pinpoint the computer as being one of Jeremy James'. Well, that sort of made sense since he was investigating Dorgan, even though she didn't know how Jeremy got hold of the memory stick assigned to Dorgan. It was almost noon so she shut down her computer and cleaned off her desk as she would be leaving the building immediately after going to the archive room. She said goodbye to her boss, Rhonda Watterson, and told her to call her cell phone if she needed anything over the next week. The Secretary told her to have fun and that it would have to be a major catastrophe before she would interrupt her and Danny's romantic vacation in Fiji. Heather thought she detected just a hint of jealously in her boss's voice. Most people would love to be in Heather's shoes right now...she wished she was one of them.

It was five before noon and Heather decided to walk by Jeremy's office just to make sure it was him accessing the memory stick. She glanced through the glass door that led into the Intelligence and Analysis area. Jeremy had a large area to himself to the left of the door, with Dorgan's office right behind it. All of the other technicians had cubicles to the right of the door. Jeremy's spot was empty. It had been at least five minutes since she had identified one of his computers as the one accessing Dorgan's assigned memory stick. Perhaps Jeremy had left for a bathroom break or lunch. She went inside.

Jeremy's eight laptops were arranged in a partial semi-circle with their backs to anyone walking up to his workstation. A person would have to walk around the row of computers to be able to see any of the screens. Heather walked up towards the row of computers just as Jeremy raised up from behind the desk. They both gasped and jumped as the close and unexpected presence of the other person startled each of them.

"Oh, you scared me!" Heather laughed. "I didn't think you were here."

"Ditto," Jeremy said. "I knocked a cord loose with my foot from one of the power strips and I was crawling around fixing it. Sorry to startle you." As he talked, Heather noticed that he pressed a button beneath his desk that apparently caused all his monitors to go to screen saver. She was close enough to see the two screens on each end of his desk and they all changed appearance at once. Heather studied him for a moment and decided to just ask him what she wanted to know. "I know about the assignment you're working on currently – the one given you by Rhonda." She waited for him to acknowledge her statement, which he did. "I'm leaving on vacation in about half an hour so if you need any resources, please go directly to her, okay?"

Was it disappointment she saw on his face?

"Going anywhere fun?" he asked. "On vacation?" he added.

"Oh, yes, to Fiji Island. I hear it's beautiful."

"You don't sound that excited about it."

"I'll be fine once I get there. I just have so much to do and so much on my mind right now, it's hard for me to be excited about it yet."

Jeremy nodded as if he understood.

"One thing before I go," Heather leaned in a bit so as not to be heard by the others across the room. "I hope Dorgan's memory stick is helpful to you in your investigation of him. Be sure and put it back where you found it." She smiled at him.

Jeremy's surprise showed on his face, but only for a second, then he broke into a grin. "Of course."

Heather turned to leave and rather absent-mindedly added, "I actually wish I had this assignment," to which Jeremy replied "I wish we could work on it together." As Heather walked out the door, he added, "I hope you have a great time in Fiji." She smiled at him and headed quickly for the break room.

Bernie wasn't there when Heather walked into the break room and she hoped he was on his way. It was already five minutes past noon. She bought a bottled water from the vending machine and sat down to wait for him. Perhaps she'd overestimated his crush on her. She had believed he would help her even though he knew he wasn't supposed to. She was impatient and headed for the door to go look for him. As she reached the door, Bernie walked in. He looked different than earlier today. A different shirt? she wondered. He looked more nicely dressed. His thinning hair looked better as well. Nope, she thought, I didn't overestimate.

She did, however, underestimate his loyalty to his boss and his dedication to his job.

"I just came to tell you I can't let you in the archive room. It's against the rules." He looked down at his feet.

"Do you always follow the rules, Bernie," Heather snapped.

A pause as he looked at her, "Y, yes." he stammered.

She glared for only a moment and then her face softened and she smiled softly and genuinely. "That's good, Bernie. So do I."

Heather sat down and motioned for Bernie to sit as well. "I'm sorry I asked you to do something that could get you into trouble. I shouldn't have done that. I just have a bad feeling about this case – I can't explain it – and I wanted to dig a little deeper to find out what's going on."

Bernie had one of his silence episodes of several seconds, then said, "Me too," and reached into his pant pocket and pulled out a memory stick. He handed it to Heather. "This is everything I could find about it."

"Bernie!" Heather was truly surprised and elated. She

laughed and started to hug him but caught herself.

"So what do you plan to do?" Bernie asked. "With this information I mean."

"I'm not sure yet. I am supposed to be leaving this afternoon with my boyfriend for vacation in Fiji, but now I'm seriously considering going to Ohio instead – to Michael Ray Michtenbaum's funeral. Nice vacation, eh?"

Bernie gave her a weak smile. He looked dejected and disappointed.

Oh, what the heck, she thought. She held out her arms to him and said "May I?" His face lit up as he jumped up from his chair. The top of his head reached her at shoulder level. Heather leaned down and gave him a hug, careful not to hug too hard, but just enough to let him know she truly appreciated the brave act he had just done.

"Thank you very much, Bernie."

For Bernie, the hug was enough to fuel his fantasies for many years to come.

Heather called Danny from her car as soon as she was on the Dulles access road. She hated to ask him over the phone to change his plans, but she didn't want to wait until they were at the airport before she sprung it on him.

"Hi baby," Danny answered, "I'm so ready to go. How about you?" His voice exuded the excitement he was feeling.

"Of course. Can't wait." Heather tried to sound excited, but her response was too quick, too curt. She slowed down when she said, "Hey, I have a *huge* favor to ask. I'd rather ask you in person but I don't want to wait."

"Sure – shoot."

"I would like to make a detour on our trip for the first couple of days."

"Uh, okay. Why? And where?" He wasn't upset yet, she thought. So far, so good.

"To a city in southern Ohio called Hamilton. I want to attend a funeral in the morning and stay and talk to a few people the rest of the day Saturday."

"Geez, Heather, who died? I'm so sorry. Of course we can go to the funeral. It wasn't a family member I hope?"

"No, no. It was no one close actually." Oops, perhaps she should have let him think it was a close friend, she realized as soon as the words were out of her mouth.

"So who is it then?" He didn't sound quite as sympathetic now.

"Well, it's a long story but it's tied to an old case at work."

"Work. I see. Did your boss ask you to go?" Danny used the phrase "I see" when he either didn't see at all or saw the truth all too clearly. She wasn't sure which it was in this case but assumed the latter.

"No," she stated quietly. "I just want - need, actually - to find out something."

Danny was quiet. Heather knew she was damaging their relationship by even asking him to change their plans, but more so by not giving him a better explanation and by not approaching him differently with her request. *Danny, sweetheart, I love you and I want to be with you, please, please do me this huge favor and come with me on this adventure and I will really make it up to you, I promise!! Please baby please!!* But she only said "No, I just need to find out something."

"I see," said Danny finally, his voice so full of hurt that Heather almost changed her mind. This time, she knew he didn't see at all.

"Well, what do you think?" she sounded impatient.

His voice was quiet and even. "You obviously don't care what I think, but what I'm going to *do* is go to Fiji and probably get drunk. If you decide you want to give me a little of your precious time, you're still welcome to join me. Goodbye, Heather," and he hung up.

Heather shook her head and thought, there is truly something wrong with me. I have one of the greatest guys in the world and I'm purposely pushing him away. While she was somewhat relieved that Danny wasn't coming with her to Ohio, she felt strangely empty and alone. Although he said she could still join him in Fiji, his voice sounded as though it was over between them. She had expected him to pout but still come with her. He didn't usually reject her like this. Of course, I completely deserve it, she thought.

But she pushed the thought of Danny out of her mind and called the airline to change her flight from Figi to the closest airport to Hamilton, Ohio, which the customer service person said could be either Dayton or Cincinnati. Cincinnati had the first flight so she booked it. She was ready to go so continued towards the airport. She was anxious to read what was on the memory stick that Bernie had given her and would do that while waiting for her flight.

After the fiasco with the voice-mail converted to e-mail of yesterday afternoon, which Dorgan knew could be discovered, Dorgan told his hired agent that they would meet regularly in person to discuss business. They had met at 5 p.m. the day before and set pre-arranged times and places to meet and decided if something extremely important came up that needed to be communicated in between meetings, they would talk or text by disposable cell phone only – no voice-mails and no e-mails. They arranged to meet at a park at 8 a.m. to review once again how the agent was to remove the implants from both the eye and ear of Michtenbaum's body.

Following his 8 a.m. meeting, Dorgan planned to make a stop at the home of Michael Michtenbaum's parents and show them a photo of the man who killed their son. He didn't intend to tell them the man was the murderer, only that he was a person of interest. He needed to find the killer and know the reason for the murder. Did the murder have anything to do with the experiment? How could it? Dorgan could not think of any way that Michtenbaum's murder could be connected with the implants in his head, but he had to be sure. He had to find the man in the photo, captured by the eye of Michael Michtenbaum right before he died.

While still sitting in the park, having sent his hired agent on his task, Dorgan checked on the whereabouts of his two other subjects – Mary Beth Singer and Jonathan Moore. He saw that Mary Beth wasn't at work but at a garage having work done on her car. He then logged into Moore's live video. While Dorgan seldom watched any of the subjects for more than a few minutes at a time, he had noticed that in the last several months Jonathon had been acting differently. He was more depressed and more irritable and Dorgan watched and listened to him as he argued with someone at his place of work. He's probably having marriage problems, thought Dorgan. That will certainly depress and irritate the hell out of you.

There were a few times over the past twenty-six years since Dorgan had been monitoring the three subjects that he watched private moments of each of the subjects. He had caught them at a time when they were dressing in front of a mirror, or in bed with their spouse or lover, or some other extremely private situation, and he had chosen to watch a little longer instead of leaving their site. But those times were few as Dorgan had neither the time nor the inclination to invade these subjects' private lives any more than was absolutely necessary. His task was to ensure that the implants continued to work successfully and that the subjects and everyone else remained unaware of their existence. Since coming to Homeland Security as the Director of Intelligence and Analysis, he accessed the subject videos much less frequently. Since this project was technically discontinued, and since it was not a DHS project at all, he couldn't risk someone in IT or elsewhere catching him logging into the secret information. Therefore, he had tasked his employee Jeremy James to keep an eye on them – just a few minutes a day – to make sure each subject was alive and well. Jeremy always had access to at least two satellites, so it usually was not difficult, or suspicious to others, for him to use these satellites on a daily basis.

Although unexpected, the murder of Michael Michtenbaum was an opportunity to utilize the experimental technology to perform one of its many purposes – identify the perpetrator of a crime committed against the subject, or against someone else where the subject is a witness. With a built-in video camera and audio recording of every second of a person's life, it was possible to view everything that happened to that person and to those within view of that person. What a wonderful crime-solving, and crime-prevention tool!

The purposes were limitless. With every word spoken by the subject and those around him or her having been recorded, tapes of conversations could be replayed for use in court proceedings, or to resolve disputes. There would be few or no missing persons as they would be videotaping where they were at all times, even after death. Eyewitness accounts of crimes or events would now be one hundred percent accurate.

If the new technology, which had long replaced these initial and archaic implants of the sixties, was accepted by people, it could have even more uses. GPS devices were also imbedded in the smaller, more versatile, undetectable implants. Parents would not only know where their children were at all times, they could see who they were with and what they were doing. Miscommunications and misunderstandings could be more easily resolved when all parties could review exactly what was said as many times as they needed to hear it. Ninety-nine percent of murders, rapes, assaults, robberies and the like could be solved and many would be prevented if perpetrators knew for certain that they would be caught.

But, Dorgan knew, the public was not yet ready for such an invasion of privacy. Therefore, the test cases were still relatively few, highly confidential and the government was the only group monitoring the various subjects.

But perhaps I'll live to see the ultimate outcome of this project, thought Dorgan. It helps that people are naïve and complacent. It makes my job so much easier, he smiled to himself. It helps as well that people will give up a lot of their personal freedoms in exchange for perceived, or even real, security. Travelers will allow a stranger to see them totally naked through a full body scanner in the hope that viewing a terrorist totally naked will stop the plane from being hijacked. It's the citizens who think too much, who question everything, who believe too much in individual liberty to understand the price of national security, that cause the problems, thought Dorgan.

GPS for example. Most people love the GPS, or global positioning system, technology that they use in their automobiles for navigating. Just plug in the address you want to visit and Bambie, or Dundee, or whatever voice you choose, tells you exactly where to turn to reach your destination. Introduced to the general public in the late 1980's, most people do not know that GPS was actually invented by the Department of Defense in 1949 at the cost of twelve billion taxpayer dollars. It has been well worth it, of course, to both the taxpayers and government. GPS has been used to pinpoint any ship or submarine in the ocean. It can track your employees on the road, your dog when he's lost, a parolee on the run and, well, anything. Today the GPS receiver is so small it can be implanted almost anywhere. If the common citizen only knew where these tiny GPS receivers are hidden, most would be outraged. But that is the price of freedom.

The Director had provided all of his employees with cell phones and laptops, each of which contained a GPS tracking device. With many employees, he also ensured that their automobiles contained the same device. Field agents were required to have a micro GPS receiver implanted in their shoulder muscles. They knew about it of course.

Other people do not know, thought the Director. They don't know that they've been the subjects of numerous government experiments testing the newest implant technology. They don't know that the government can, and does, see and record their every move, and every sight they see and sound they hear. Talk about invasion of one's privacy! Of course, unless there's a threat to national security or other reason to view these recordings, the government certainly has better things to do than to watch private citizens' private moments. Unless the government employee is bored and has nothing else to do.

While Dorgan felt that such personal privacy invasion was necessary when it was conducted in the cause of national security, he did not want his own privacy invaded. He would even temporarily remove the GPS tracking device placed in his laptop when he was on a covert operation such as the one in which he was currently engaged. If anyone checked that GPS, his laptop would show as being in his car right now. And when he didn't want anyone to find him, he made sure his laptop was not traceable by its IP address either.

He usually carried his phone with him at all times, but he couldn't remove the GPS device without causing suspicion and he didn't want to be found, so he left it in his car, now parked at the Dulles Airport. He was going to use the excuse that this little vacation with his wife was a second honeymoon and she insisted he not be disturbed with work.

Dorgan entered the address of the elder Michtenbaums' home into Mapquest on his laptop to find his way to Michael's parents' house.

Linda Jayne

"Gotcha!" exclaimed Jeremy and a by-passing co-worker from a cubicle across the room just laughed, knowing Jeremy was at his best tracking the many terrorists and other threatening individuals that plagued the country's security.

Dragon had entered an address in Hamilton, Ohio, into his computer and was now making his way to that address. Jeremy's suspicions that Dragon had gone to the home town of Michael Michtenbaum were correct. He had hidden his tracks pretty well so far but just made another grave mistake.

Jeremy had read most of the information and viewed most of the photos on the memory stick he had stolen from Dragon's desk drawer and was sick to his stomach at the gall of the past and present leaders of his country. He was incensed that such an experiment could ever have been sanctioned. He tried to remember his historical dates and realized it must have been John F. Kennedy who had given the go-ahead for this project. Wasn't he in office at that time? Jeremy thought. No, wait, he was assassinated in 1963, so perhaps it wasn't him. Lyndon Johnson then. The President would have had to have known and given his blessing on the project.

Jeremy was only 24 years old but knew his American history quite well. He had his own theories and beliefs as to who actually killed JFK and why, even if he wasn't around on that horrific day of November 22, 1963. His dad had told him the story of how, like September 11, 2001, everyone old enough to remember that day could tell you exactly where they were and what they were doing at the moment they learned of the beloved President's mortal wounding in Dallas, Texas. Jeremy's father had been in the fifth grade and his teacher had left the room for several minutes and when she returned she was crying. She told her students, while sobbing and trying to control her tears, that President Kennedy had been shot and was dead. His father went on to say that JFK's wife Jackie died 30 years later and their son Jon Jon only five years after his mother. Kennedy was a President whom most Americans' loved, or so it seemed to Jeremy, especially since they even knew the dates of other major events in that family's lives.

Hmmm, Jeremy's conspiratorial mind thought. I've often

wondered if there were other reasons besides the Cuban missile crisis or Texas political climate that could have contributed to the decision to assassinate Kennedy. Perhaps he didn't agree to this project.

Dragon arriving at his destination caused Jeremy to curtail his outrage and anger for now and focus on the immediate task at hand. *Dragon is involved in this up to his eyeballs and I can at least bring him down,* fumed Jeremy, channeling his anger towards his traitorous boss.

Jeremy took still photos of Dragon's rental car and license number, as well as the man himself walking towards the Michtenbaum front door. He wondered what Dragon was up to – why he was meeting with the parents of the dead man. They invited him in. He wished at that moment that Dragon had the experimental implants in his eye and ear so that he could be a fly on the wall of the Michtenbaum living room, seeing and hearing everything.

Dorgan's burner cell phone rang while he was sitting in the living room with Mitchell and Celia Michtenbaum, parents of Michael Ray Michtenbaum. He knew it was his hired agent Johnson calling, but he couldn't answer at the moment so put the phone on vibrate. *Johnson must have important information,* Dorgan concluded.

Dorgan had flashed an FBI badge to Mitchell Michtenbaum when he answered the door and asked if he could have a few moments of his time. He apologized for having to bother him during his time of grief. The badge was real, although the name was fake on the ID. Dorgan used it for just such occasions.

Mitchell called his wife into the room and they sat on the couch, holding hands, across from the FBI agent who said he needed to ask them a few questions about their son's murder. Dorgan could tell Celia was barely functioning, the redness and swelling of her eyes an indication of constant crying, the strain on her facial features an indication of constant pain. He could tell she made an effort to smile at him – a person who was trying to help them find their son's murderer – but her mouth simply couldn't pull itself up from the trembling position of grief that held it down.

Mitchell's eyes were red as well. They held a look of loss and pain unlike any other Dorgan had seen. The two had to hold on to each other for support to even be able to function enough to talk to him. He truly felt sorry for them. He knew Michael had been their only son and a major part of their daily lives.

"I apologize again for having to bother you at this very sad time, but we've identified a person of interest. I wanted to see if you know this person," and Dorgan stood and walked the few feet to hand the black and white computer printed photo of the murderer to the Michtenbaums.

"Is this who killed our son?" Mitchell began to sob uncontrollably as his fragile emotional state crumbled further.

"We don't know that," lied Dorgan. "We just want to find and talk to him. We know he saw your son shortly before Michael died. Have you seen this man before? Do you know him?"

They both looked at the photo for several seconds and shook their heads in unison. "No," they said together. "I've never seen him," stated Mitchell softly. "Neither have I," murmured Celia.

"Do you know of any reason, any business dealings, or personal relationships, or any reason at all, that anyone would want to harm your son?" Dorgan knew the police had surely already asked this question, and he didn't expect to get any usable information from them in their current state, so he asked one final question before he left them. "Can you give me the names, and phone numbers and addresses if possible, of any of Michael's close friends. I'd like to show the photo to them as well."

Dorgan had fully expected them to question why the FBI was involved in this murder, which it wasn't, but the Michtenbaums were obviously so grief-stricken that their minds were not thinking straight. He was glad he didn't have to use his usual explanation since occasionally he would run into those few questioning, thinking individuals who would actually call the FBI and ask why an Agent Marcus Stone had been involved in their case.

As soon as Dorgan pulled out of the Michtenbaum driveway, he called Johnson. There was no answer, so he drove a few blocks and found a small café, parked and went inside for coffee and to log into his laptop. He entered Michtenbaum and his 25 letter password, hoping that the video he saw and the audio he heard verified that the implants were now in the safe possession of agent Johnson.

The video on his screen was the black box indicating a view of the inside of the dead eyelids of Michael Michtenbaum. The audio he heard was the voice of a woman whom he assumed was the medical examiner, Rachel Curry, that Agent Johnson had told him about. Apparently Ms. Curry was examining the fresh dead body of someone else lying close to Michael's dead but listening ear.

So Johnson hasn't been able to remove the implants yet, thought Dorgan. He was frustrated but not overly so. There's still plenty of time, he thought. Apparently, that's why Johnson was calling me earlier, to let me know there was a snag in the plan. Possibly the coroner recognized Johnson from their meeting the day before, even though he had changed his appearance for today's assignment.

Dorgan spent the next several minutes looking up directions to the two close friends of Michael's, the names and addresses of which were supplied by Celia Michtenbaum. As the waitress brought him the breakfast sandwich he'd ordered, Dorgan asked her the address of the café in which he sat.

"313 Main Street," she said, and Dorgan quickly entered his starting coordinates to use later. His phone rang.

"Yeah," he answered.

"Minor problem. They've already moved the body to the funeral home. Do you want me to go inside and just do what I came to do, or wait? It could get ugly if I run into anyone, and I assume they're prepping the body now or plan to soon." Johnson awaited Dorgan's reply.

"Where are you right now?" Dorgan asked.

"I dumped the ambulance and came back to my car and changed clothes. I'm about a block from the funeral home, just watching it right now."

"Sit tight for a few minutes and I'll call you right back." They hung up and Dorgan tried to temper his impatience with wanting to get the implants now with the reasonableness of waiting for a more opportune time.

The body was scheduled to be buried the next day, and worst case, they could retrieve the devices after the graveside funeral service. There was still time and means to secretly complete this mission. Today's plan had been for Johnson to intercept the body, disguised as the ambulance transport driver who was to move the body from the morgue to the funeral home. For some reason, Curry had changed the schedule and called a different transport service to move the body. Why? The question made Dorgan a little uncomfortable as he always questioned coincidence. But now, he could simply have Johnson disguised as the grave closer who would bury the body, but not before removing the implants. In fact, in this scenario, he could just bury the casket and take the body if need be. It's the better option than having Johnson go into the funeral home right now and....

"Shit! Oh shit!" Dorgan's mind was whirling as the realization just hit him. The hair on the back of his neck stood on end. *The body is at the funeral home and yet I just heard the medical examiner's voice, in the morgue, from Michael's ear!*

Does this mean what I think it means? He was trying to consider all the possibilities. It's possible that Johnson is wrong and it wasn't Michtenbaum's body that was moved. Perhaps it is still in the morgue. There's a slight possibility that Curry was at the funeral home, but no, she was recording information about a new body being autopsied. She had to be at the morgue. The only explanation, the one that he didn't want to believe, was that Curry had found the small implant behind Michael Michtenbaum's ear and had removed it. His body, and the implant in his eye, had been transported to the funeral home. His ear implant was still in the morgue, very close to where medical examiner Rachel Curry was currently working.

"But not for long," Dorgan spewed aloud as he dialed Johnson.

Jeremy continued to trail Dragon, keeping a close eye on him. While Dragon was in True West Coffee Shop on Main Street, Jeremy allowed himself a short bathroom break and a quick run to the break room for more coffee and junk food from the snack machine, all of which he brought back to his desk. He had already finished his thermos of coffee and most of his donuts.

He was also keeping watch over his six other computer monitors. He still had Michael Michtenbaum's screen running – not the satellite surveillance he had done for the past four years – but the implant video and audio that he'd recently discovered. He figured there was probably the same video and audio for Mary Beth and Jonathon, but Jeremy did not have the time or comfort level to invade the privacy of these two individuals by pulling up their implant recordings. He still watched them via satellite.

Michael Michtenbaum's live coverage was turning out to be pretty interesting for a dead guy. Jeremy could tell by the changes in light and the slight vibrations on the dark video screen that Michael's body was being moved and had gone from a very dark area, most likely a vault in the morgue, to a light area, probably the autopsy with fluorescent overhead lighting, to other various shades of semi-darkness. He now knew he was actually seeing Michael's closed eyelids. But the interesting part was that the audio did not reflect a change in the environment. It was either quiet or it was the same woman's voice, sometimes talking to a second person. He assumed it was the coroner. Perhaps it was she moving the body to different parts of the building? He didn't think anything significant had changed since the evening before, and he wished he had the time to pull up and review the recorded coverage from 7 p.m. of the day before until 6 a.m. when he arrived at work, but he simply could not add any more tasks to what he was already doing.

"Oh, Christ!" Jeremy yelled and spilled his large coffee on himself and his desk, some of it splashing onto two of his keyboards. He had been looking at Michael's computer screen and suddenly a huge face appeared on the screen, sufficiently freaking Jeremy out to the point of dropping his coffee.

"How does a dead man open his eyes?" Jeremy's eyes were glued to that screen. He forgot about the hot coffee on his shirt and pants, and everywhere else, as he looked at the male face that had to be only a foot or so in front of Michael's face. Then it was gone and the screen was back to semi-blackness.

Jeremy grumbled as he started wiping up the coffee and as he thought for a moment, he realized someone had opened the right eye of Michael. It was most likely a morgue or funeral parlor employee. But the audio was still that of a woman. How could that be?

When Dragon came out of the restaurant, Jeremy focused his attention back to him. The computer to the left of that laptop brought up the keystrokes of Dragon's computer and Jeremy had been watching that one closely as well. Dragon had entered two other addresses, one in Hamilton, Ohio, and one in Trenton, Ohio, and Jeremy had to scroll down the screen to make sure he hadn't missed any other key information while he had run to the bathroom and break room. The two addresses seemed to be the only key information entered. Jeremy quickly did a search for the names of the owners of these properties.

Dragon drove to a McDonald's in downtown Hamilton where he met up with his hired help, whom Jeremy recognized from other assignments. They sat outside the restaurant away from other people. Jeremy wished he could hear what they were saying, but he had to settle for watching and following them, and watching and following Dragon's computer.

Dragon was showing something to the other man on his laptop. Jeremy zoomed the satellite in for close up photos of the men and the computer screen. At the same time he watched the keystrokes of Dragon on his other screen. The Project website had been accessed and the Michtenbaum screen projected on Dragon's screen.

How convenient, thought Jeremy. I can just watch and listen to my own Michtenbaum screen. But he didn't know what the two men were saying to each other, which annoyed Jeremy greatly. He guessed that perhaps Dragon was having the same thoughts as he himself was - why is the voice from the morgue always nearby when the body seems to have moved. They stopped talking and seemed to be listening intently to what was being said by the woman. Jeremy turned up his earphones - there was no doubt that the voice was that of the medical examiner. She was performing an autopsy on another body and verbally documenting the process. There was also no doubt that Michael Michtenbaum's ear implant was close by, listening to and recording every word.

The job of medical examiner, or coroner as many counties call it, is an elected position, and one that Rachel Curry had desired for several years before her goal was finally realized two years earlier. She had been a physician in a large surgical medical complex for five years but was not happy there. While she related well with her patients and most of them loved her for her empathetic and personal bedside manner, she did not like the politics of working with the other doctors. Perhaps it was more that she didn't like two of the doctors in particular who treated her differently than they treated the older male doctors.

Although Rachel missed the relationships she'd developed with her patients, she now developed relationships with the families of her deceased patients. Her same empathetic and sympathetic qualities caused the families to trust her to treat their loved ones with care and respect, even when she had to dissect their bodies. When anyone else entered the room where she was examining a body or performing an autopsy, Rachel would cover the body as she herself would want to be covered if her naked body was lying on a table. She would inflict as little damage as possible to the outside tissues of the body and carefully sew up the incisions made to remove and examine internal organs. She was once even overheard by a family member who was standing outside Rachel's lab door, talking to the deceased in a soft and loving voice, telling the body that she was sorry the accident had happened to him and that she hoped he would now have a wonderful sleep and afterlife.

Rachel was performing her third autopsy of the week. She had completed Michael Michtenbaum's the afternoon before and was now thinking of the incident that had happened after the autopsy.

It was the strangest thing, and she still didn't know what to make of the very tiny, round piece of man-made metal she had removed from behind Michael's right ear drum. It was around 6:30 the evening before, and she had already called Michael's parents and the police to inform them of the autopsy results. As she finished the second phone call, one of her former patients from when she worked at the surgical medical group came to the morgue to see her, complaining of heart palpitations.

"Mr. Ritchie, you know you're supposed to be seeing Dr. Wright." This was the third or fourth time the 84-year old man had come to see her at the morgue over the past two years. While she would always tell him to go to his new doctor, she knew he just wanted a little attention from her, and she didn't mind at all having a live person to examine every once in a while. She pulled her stethoscope out of her desk drawer and listened to his heart and lungs as he took deep breaths as instructed. She jokingly told him that she thought his heart palpitations were caused by looking at too many pretty women. He winked at her and said, "Yep, that's my diagnosis as well 'cause it's jumping all over the place right now."

They talked a few minutes and she told him she needed to get back to work. She had a lot of documentation to complete in her office on both the Michtenbaum case and her autopsy of the day before, but she needed to get her taped notes from her lab. She walked Mr. Ritchie to the door and then entered her lab. Her autopsied patient of the day before had already been transported to the funeral home, and Michael would be moved soon as well. She had called another transport service that could come that evening instead of waiting until morning.

She opened the heavy stainless steel door where Michael now rested on a cold table. She pulled it out and looked at the man once again. The bruise from the needle injection on his neck was the only visible evidence of trauma to the body. He otherwise looked healthy and peaceful. As she looked down at him, the stethoscope still inserted in her ears from her "examination" of Mr. Ritchie picked up a slight buzzing sound. Rachel looked around to see if she'd left on any equipment but nothing was on. The room was deathly quiet. She turned back around towards Michael's body and stood still. Again, she heard a slight buzzing sound. She looked to see where the chestpiece diaphram of the stethoscope was resting. It was near Michael's head. She lifted it away from Michael and the buzzing was no longer audible. She lowered it by Michael's head again and heard the buzzing again. Very strange, she thought. She used the stethoscope to find the exact source of the buzzing. It seemed to be coming from his right ear.

She removed the stethoscope from her ears and put her ear up against Michael's to listen for the sound. Nothing. Whatever the source, it could only be heard when amplified by the stethoscope. She quickly turned on her portable x-ray machine and took several pictures of the right side of Michael's face. The developed film showed a tiny foreign object located behind the right ear drum. She wondered if Michael had ear problems as a child and the object had been placed there to help with hearing. She knew she could get to it easily and made the decision to remove it. She would ask his parents about it later.

She cleanly closed the small incision, placed the small object in a sterile tray on a lab table nearby, and went back to her office to work. She thought about the FBI agent who had visited her earlier that afternoon, claiming to be investigating Michael's death. He seemed more interested in whether or not she was doing an autopsy than in the actual cause of death. She wondered why the FBI was involved in the case, although she didn't ask. Something about him gave her the creeps and she just wanted him to leave.

That had been yesterday. Rachel completed the autopsy she was now performing and was ready to sew up the 62-year old man who had dropped over dead two days ago. She was reaching for her tools to sew the man's chest when the door to her lab suddenly opened and a masked man charged at her. He was on her with a hand clamped over her mouth before she was able to scream. He was strong and held her with a vice grip that would not allow her to move her arms or upper body, so she tried to kick him. He was behind her, and with a quick swipe took her down to the floor with a blow to the back of both knees. She screamed in pain.

"Do not make a sound," the man whispered into her ear in a low and gravelly voice. "I am going to remove my hand and if you make a sound, I will snap your neck. If you understand, nod." Rachel nodded, terrified.

The man removed his hand from her mouth. He maintained his grip on her arms while now kneeling behind her on her legs which was causing severe pain to her calves. "Yesterday you removed a small device from Michael Michtenbaum's ear. Don't waste my time by denying it. I need that device right now."

Rachel was too terrified to attempt to distract the man by saying the device was in another room. Her mind wasn't thinking at all, except that she knew she couldn't move and that her legs were starting to cramp. She didn't think that he might still kill her if she gave him what he wanted. She just wanted him gone and nodded that she knew where the device was. "It's on the counter over there," and she pointed her head in the direction of the table on which the small tray held the device.

The man lifted her effortlessly from the floor and carried her by her upper body to the table. Rachel saw him look at the small implant in the tray. He then turned and carried her towards the dead body cold storage units.

The man carrying Rachel, Agent Johnson, saw the small implant in the tray, but he had to get rid of Rachel before he could pick it up and place it in the small container in his pocket. He carried her towards the metal doors that housed the dead bodies in cold storage. He planned to snap her neck and leave her in one of these compartments so that it might take a while for anyone to find her. As he reached to open one of the doors, two police officers burst through the door into the lab. "Police! Let her go and put your hands on your head!"

As the man swung around at the sound of the police entering the room, he dropped Rachel to the floor and had his Glock readied and firing before he even saw their faces. He was striding towards them as he fired and after cleanly hitting each mark, he took only a moment to look at the two young faces. Rookies, he thought. I'm truly sorry you were on duty today. He meant it...he didn't like killing innocent people. He could see the terror on their now dead faces. He turned to finish the task he had begun. As he turned, Rachel swung her metal stool and hit him square in the chest, knocking the wind out of him for a second. She needed only that second to run past him and out the door.

Agent Johnson cursed loudly once he regained his breath and with only a second's hesitation, retrieved the implant before running from the lab to follow the medical examiner. "Damn!" he kept saying, so frustrated with not having killed the person who now knew something about his assignment, and for having to kill the two young officers who knew nothing. He tried several doors until he found her locked office door. He pushed hard but the door wouldn't budge. He could hear her on the phone with the police, her voice frantic. Within seconds, he heard the sirens of several more police cars close by, very close by. How could they have gotten here so quickly, he fumed.

He fired three shots into the door, hoping at least one of them hit his target. "I know about your daughter," he yelled to the door, "so keep your mouth shut." He then ran the opposite way down the hall to a back exit he knew would take him to a side street. He pulled off his mask and black jacket as he exited the door, stuffed them in a plastic bag he was carrying, and began walking down the street as calmly as his infuriated mind would let him.

Jeremy followed Dragon's hired hand from McDonald's and saw him park a block away from the morgue. He was wearing all black and as he entered a side door of the building, he slipped a mask over his face.

"That can't be good," and Jeremy again wished he had the use of satellites Samuel or Delilah with the capability to see and hear what was happening inside the building. He immediately called the Hamilton, Ohio, 911 and reported a masked intruder entering the morgue and said he thought the intruder might be after the medical examiner. They asked his name and wanted to know where he was and how he knew this information, but Jeremy told them to hurry or the woman could end up dead. He hung up.

He saw the police cruiser with two officers arrive three minutes later. As he waited for them to come out with prisoner in tow, he focused on following Dragon who was driving somewhere else now. He didn't want to lose Dragon, and it was getting more difficult following both of them with satellites when they were on the move. Fortunately, he had two addresses that Dragon had entered into his laptop, so Jeremy assumed he was headed to the Trenton, Ohio, address since was leaving the city of Hamilton and heading into the countryside.

Two more police cruisers pulled into the morgue and with guns pulled, two officers went in the main door. The other two officers split up, each walking slowly in different directions around the building. Jeremy saw a door open on the back side of the building and a man in a red shirt hurried out – could it be Dragon's man? He was carrying something and walking at a normal pace across a parking lot and down the street. Neither of the two police officers surrounding the building had seen him yet as they were proceeding slowly.

As he zoomed in, Jeremy was sure the man in the red shirt was the man working with Dragon. He dialed the Hamilton police again and stayed on the phone this time as he relayed step by step where the man in the red shirt was headed. If the dispatcher had been more interested in getting the information to the police instead of quizzing him on how he knew this information, the police would most likely have caught the man. As it played out on his computer screen, however, by the time Jeremy saw the two outside police officers sprint off in the direction of the man in the red shirt, the man had already climbed in his car and left. Jeremy gave the dispatcher the make, model, color and license number of the car, as well as a good scolding for her inefficiency.

As Jeremy glanced at his other monitors, there was not a lot of activity at the moment. Dragon was pulling into the driveway of a modest brick ranch home in Trenton, Ohio. Mary Beth was nowhere around and Jonathan had not gone to work that day. Michael hadn't opened his eyes anymore.

Three more police vehicles arrived at the morgue, as well as an ambulance. Not good, Jeremy thought. Hopefully, the medical examiner was only wounded and not dead.

He followed the man in the red shirt through many small residential streets. So far, no police were following him.

Jeremy signaled one of his co-workers and asked if he would mind getting him a large coffee. He had spilled his last one, he explained, and needed more caffeine. The co-worker was happy to oblige, and Jeremy knew he would not be able to leave this spot except for an extreme bladder or intestinal emergency.

The outside of the morgue was now completely filled with cars and people. Both police and sheriff vehicles were there, and another ambulance arrived as the one left. Damn, I wish I could see inside, thought Jeremy. The morgue was located between a busy four lane highway and a small two lane street almost parallel on the other side. Cars had begun to turn off the highway onto the small street and park to watch the growing throng of law enforcement vehicles crowding the small driveway and parking lot of the morgue. Cars on the highway were slowing, and one rubber-necker caused a minor accident as he slowed to a crawl, causing the car behind to rear-end him.

Jeremy hoped there were a lot more police in the city of Hamilton out looking for the car description he had given them, for it seemed they were all in the parking lot of the morgue at the moment.

A woman came out of the morgue with two police officers. Jeremy wondered if she was the medical examiner. Perhaps she wasn't hurt after all. Surely, someone was newly dead inside to have attracted this much attention.

Jeremy pulled up the on-line headlines of the local Hamilton paper, The Journal News, but there was nothing about this incident. He didn't expect it to be there yet, but he wanted to have the site up and ready for when the story hit. "In the meantime, let's see if we can hear what's going on in the morgue through Mikie's ear." He slid across the few feet of space from one end of his semicircular desk to the other on his comfortable stool made specifically for him. He turned up the volume on Michael Michtenbaum's streaming recording and heard a man's voice. "Answer the damn phone, Dorgan."

"What!" Jeremy knew he was listening to the man he was following. He looked at his screen where he continued to move the satellite to keep up with the moving vehicle. He must have gotten the implant from Michael's ear, Jeremy surmised.

He kept the volume up high enough to hear but low enough that others in the room couldn't hear unless they were standing right by his desk. His co-worker appeared with his coffee and Jeremy quickly thanked him and looked away, indicating to the man *now get lost*.

Dragon was on the move again, leaving the ranch house in Trenton. As he was watching Dragon pull out of the driveway, and watching the man in the red shirt pull his car behind a building and park, he heard the phone dialing from Michael's ear. Good, it was on speaker phone. "Thanks, bad guy," smiled Jeremy.

"Better be good news," answered Dragon.

"Well, the bad news is the woman got away. Somebody tipped off the police. I have no idea who or how. I had to kill two police and while I was shooting them, she got away. I went after her, but then more police arrived. I barely got away. There's a snitch somewhere. Somebody knew I was going to be there. Any idea who?" It was said accusingly.

"How the hell would I know?" snapped Dragon. "And that's a helluva lot of bad news for less than half an hour. Any good news at all?"

"I got the chip."

There was a moment of silence before Dragon replied "Where is it?"

"I have it here with me."

"Hang up the phone, you moron."

Jeremy heard some additional expletives and turned the sound down a bit. Now that Dragon knew someone else might be listening through Michael's ear, he didn't expect there would be any further conversation between those two until they were outside earshot of the device.

Jeremy called the police again to let them know where the man who had killed two police at the morgue was currently hiding.

Heather purchased a bottle of water and an apple and was now seated in the waiting area for her flight to Cincinnati. She chose a seat against a wall so no one could look over her shoulder and placed her carry-on suitcase in one seat beside her and her purse and bottle of water in the other seat. Men had a tendency to sit close to her and she wanted to discourage that as much as possible.

She had her laptop balanced on her lap and inserted the memory stick Bernie had given her. He had logged it in her name, which she hoped that neither he nor she would get into trouble over at a later date, and he had titled it simply Requested Files. She began reading the 150+ pages as she ate her apple.

This file was much more complete than the one she had viewed at her father's house. It included the names of some high-level agency officials involved in the project. It also included the Project Outline detailing the purpose of the project, anticipated results, containment and exit strategies should the project become public, present and future cost analyses and more. This document had also not been in her father's file. She read it carefully.

All of the baby photos were the same ones she had seen before, but this file also contained some photos of the three "babies" when they were older. The most recent appeared to be when they were in their late teens or early twenties. So this file had not been updated in almost thirty years. Why, she wondered, if there was still an active interest in it. Perhaps because she was looking at an old archived paper file. Perhaps there was a more up to date file electronically.

She was only partially through the file when the boarding call started. She shut down her laptop and put her phone on airplane mode, planning to turn them on again once she was in the air. However, a man who insisted on talking to her was her seating neighbor and she decided not to view the document with him sitting so close, so passed the time in polite conversation with the attractive man. At a lull in the conversation, she began thinking of Danny. He would be on a plane soon as well, headed for the beautiful island of Fiji. Would he be sitting next to a pretty woman and also making polite conversation?

She wished it was him next to her so she could close her eyes and lay her head on his shoulder, have him hold her hand in his lap and occasionally raise it to his lips for a kiss. They could be quiet or they could talk, but only because they wanted to, not because it was uncomfortable to do either. Right now, she really missed him. What am I doing on a plane to Ohio? she thought, closing her eyes and laying her head back on the seat, hoping the man next to her would get the hint and shut up.

She woke with a start and looked at the man next to her. His eyes were also shut, so apparently he had granted her wish. She wondered how long she had been asleep. She pulled her phone out of her purse and looked at the time. They had been in the air for over an hour, so she had slept at least forty-five minutes. She was tired from the little sleep she had gotten the night before, and the short nap refreshed her somewhat. The flight attendant was approaching with a cart of beverages and she asked for hot tea and cookies when he reached her seat. The man next to her was apparently sleeping and didn't wake for refreshments. Good, she thought. I really don't feel like talking to him.

She thought about continuing to read the confidential file on her laptop but at that moment the pilot announced they were making their initial descent into the Cincinnati airport, which the pilot stated was actually located in Kentucky. She munched her cookies and drank her tea and watched the scenery out of the window. There were rolling hills in the area and it looked quite picturesque from

30,000 feet.

Twenty minutes later they were on the ground and soon Heather was making her way to the rental car area. She took the map they offered even though she had her trusty GPS app on her i-Phone and didn't worry about getting lost. By the time she arrived at the Marriott Hotel in Hamilton, Ohio, a little over an hour later, she had been in three midwestern states. The airport was in Kentucky, and in taking the route indicated by her app, she crossed the Ohio River into Indiana instead of Ohio. She was a little panicky at first that she had made a mistake, but when she looked at the directions, she saw that the route took her across a corner of Indiana before going into Ohio.

Heather's room at the Marriott had a view of a river, although she didn't know what river. The nearby bridge and Monument building were very nice, she thought, and she took a few pictures on her phone. She changed into some comfortable sweats and plugged in her laptop. She wanted to finish reading the document on the memory stick.

Bernie couldn't stop thinking about Heather. She had hugged him! She had talked to him! And he had helped her by giving her a confidential file that could get him fired. He didn't try to cover up the fact that he'd committed this dastardly deed – he had used an agency-issued, GPS-tracked memory stick, assigned it to Heather's name and titled it. He at least felt good about the fact that he'd followed all the proper rules in breaking one major rule.

But overall he felt good. Heather had finally noticed him. And he'd finally come across a truly confidential, CIA and Homeland Security top secret, James Bond worthy, kick-ass file and he was part of it. Not officially part of it, but he had decided to become part of it, especially since Heather was now part of it.

Bernie pulled up the news site that had written the two articles about Michael Michtenbaum's death to see if there was anything new to read about the case. The top headline caught his attention. *Two Hamilton Police Dead – Attempt on Medical Examiner's Life.* The headline was posted only ten minutes ago.

"Two Hamilton police officers were fatally wounded in a

shootout with a masked intruder who also attacked Butler County Coroner Rachel Curry, according to Hamilton Chief of Police George Davies. The shootings took place at the Butler County Morgue on Erie Highway at approximately noon today. The first two officers on the scene were gunned down as they attempted to help the coroner.

"The gunman escaped the building but police have an eyewitness description of the man and his vehicle.

"The names of the police officers killed this morning are not being released pending notification to families.

"The coroner, Rachel Curry, escaped unharmed."

Bernie was trying to process what this news could mean. He had read both of the previous articles on Michael Michtenbaum and knew Rachel Curry was the coroner who had now been attacked. Was it because of the implants in Michael? he wondered. The person who attacked her has shown that he will kill anyone in his way. He killed two police officers. Police! The guy must be crazy!

Heather! he thought. Could she be in any danger? Did she go to Hamilton, Ohio, or did she go with her boyfriend? As much as he hated the thought of her playing in the sand and surf with another man, he hoped now that she hadn't gone to Ohio. It might be dangerous.

The memory stick. It has a GPS in it. Perhaps I can track and see where she is. Bernie's mind was reeling as he thought of Heather. She had hugged him. They were now in a relationship, at least the closest thing Bernie had had to a relationship in a long time, and he was going to make sure he took care of her.

I have no idea how to track the GPS in the memory stick, he thought dejectedly. Only the technical people know how to do that, and I can't tell anybody else about this. He sat depressed for several minutes, then an idea started to form in his mind. Maybe the tech guy Jeremy could help him. He had heard that Jeremy James was the one who found the Florida terrorist cell almost single-handedly. He was also the one who had helped find the world's number one terrorist leader. And most importantly, he liked Heather too. Bernie decided he could make up some story about working on a project with Heather and he needed to find her. He wouldn't have to tell Jeremy what it was about. It could work.

He had already taken his break and shouldn't leave his work

area, but Bernie decided this was an emergency and he had to go talk to Jeremy right now. He wasn't getting much work done this afternoon anyway. His mind was on Heather and on this case.

When he entered the office of Intelligence and Analysis, he could see that Jeremy was hunched over several laptops, intently scrutinizing whatever was on the screens. He walked quietly up to the desk and stood, waiting for Jeremy to notice him. It took a full minute before Jeremy moved and saw Bernie standing there.

Jeremy jumped slightly. "Geez Dude! Don't you know better than to sneak up on me like that!" He seemed irritated, but Bernie didn't move.

"What, already!" he shouted at Bernie. "I'm busy, dude. What do you want!"

Bernie didn't like to be yelled at. It made him very nervous. But this was for Heather so he took Jeremy's verbal abuse and said firmly, "I need you to track the GPS on this memory stick," and he handed Jeremy a piece of paper.

Jeremy stared at him a moment. "Since when do I report to you. I told you man, I'm busy, and if you make me lose track of my targets, I'm going to be major pissed."

Bernie audibly swallowed. "It's Heather. She may be in danger. You have to see where she is."

"Heather?" Jeremy seemed truly surprised at the mention of her name, and narrowed his eyes as he scrutinized Bernie. Bernie could tell that Jeremy was wondering what he, a lowly file clerk, could possibly know that would make him think Heather was in danger.

"I just saw her a few hours ago...she's fine," Jeremy emphasized the word fine, most likely in an effort to get rid of him, Bernie knew.

"That was a few hours ago. She may not be fine now."

"Okay, okay, I'll check on her. Just leave before you ruin all the work I've done today." Jeremy waved his hand towards the door, indicating he wanted Bernie to leave.

"Here's my extension. Let me know." Bernie handed him another piece of paper and left the office.

Jeremy made certain his satellite still had Dragon's rental car in his sight. It did, and Dragon was heading for the second address he had entered earlier this morning as far as Jeremy could tell.

Dragon's hit man must have known the police were on his trail, as he left his car where it was parked behind a building and took off on foot. He changed into a black shirt and Jeremy was pretty sure he had put on a wig – his hair looked longer and darker. But he was talking to Bernie while trying to watch the screen and the man took off running before Jeremy could get a close look. He was now trying to locate him by moving the satellite in the direction he last saw him running.

Jeremy spent the next fifteen minutes trying to find the hit man, to no avail. He concentrated on the residential subdivision behind the building where he parked the car as that was the direction he headed. When he didn't see him on any of the streets, he broadened his search in the other directions. He didn't see a man in black on foot in any direction. He could possibly have gone into a house or stolen a car. He had turned up the sound on Michael's ear hoping to hear sounds that would tell him where the man had gone, but the low sounds he heard were so muffled he couldn't distinguish what they were. Jeremy was furious with Bernie for taking him from his surveillance of this cop killer. Now he'd lost him.

He tried to calm himself by eating a donut and opening a Mountain Dew. He checked all of his other laptops. They were all under control at the moment. He took a long drink of Mountain Dew and again wondered why the file clerk would think Heather was in trouble. And he didn't need to track her via a memory stick. She had her agency cell phone with her, which was also equipped with GPS. He quickly checked its location. She was at the airport. Just as she said. Soon, she and her boyfriend would be in the air, heading for Fiji. Lucky dog, that boyfriend. Perhaps I'll check on her again later and make sure her plane is heading in the right direction, he noted to himself.

Jeremy noticed that Dragon was not heading for the other address as he originally thought. He pulled his stool up closer and watched the car. It was on Route 4, the same highway that the Butler County morgue was on, though the road had different names in different areas. Ah, he's going to pick up his partner, figured Jeremy.

He could see police cruisers everywhere as well, still looking for the fugitive. They had found the abandoned car and had crime scene investigators carefully going over the vehicle. Some police were on foot, going door to door in the neighborhood behind where the car was found.

Dragon drove past the morgue and another half mile or so to High Street, where he turned right and headed towards downtown Hamilton. Dragon picked up his partner in a restaurant parking lot and they drove back to their hotel, the Marriott.

Before taking a much-needed bathroom break, Jeremy called Rhonda Watterson. Dragon was now murdering people and she needed to know.

Jonathon Adam Moore didn't know it, but he was one of three babies born at Mercy Hospital in Hamilton, Ohio, who had two implants placed in his tiny head within the first 24 hours of his birth. His parents didn't know it either, although they knew he was unavailable for several hours when they wanted to see him. What tests were they running on their baby?

Jon was now 50 years old, married with two grown children, and self-employed with a local lawn care and landscape business that employed 23 people and provided a good income for Jon.

For the past couple of years, Jon had been experiencing tinnitus, or buzzing and ringing in the ears, and it was growing worse. At first, it was infrequent and not loud enough to bother him during the day when he was busy and distracted. At night when lying in bed and all was quiet, it always seemed louder. But lately, the past six months or so, the buzzing was becoming louder and was now constant. It was extremely annoying and he was becoming more and more agitated due to lack of sleep and the constant and irritating noise in his head.

He had already visited two ENT doctors, and neither could find any cause for the buzzing other than the tinnitus many people experience as they grow older. One doctor cleaned the excess wax from his ears, the other conducted a hearing test, and both gave him a thorough examination. They found nothing unusual.

While the buzzing was incredibly annoying, it was the other

sound that truly sent Jon over the edge. A high pitched screech inside his head that started about a month ago was driving him mad. It was not constant like the buzzing, but was becoming more and more frequent. He described the sound to his wife and to the ENT as similar to screeching nails on a chalkboard. It was so loud one day that he left the customer's home where he was planting a tree and drove straight to the doctor, hoping the sound would continue long enough for the doctor to hear it. Surely it is so loud someone else can hear it!, he thought. He was holding his head for fear it would explode as he ran into the doctor's office. "Please! I have to see him right now!" he begged the receptionist. Within the next two minutes the screeching subsided and the doctor could not find the cause.

Jon was exhausted. He had slept very little the past several weeks, and none at all the past two nights, and the more frequent high pitched noise coupled with the ever louder, constant buzzing caused him to be so stressed and irritable that he couldn't relax at all. He had come home from work early today after getting into a shouting match with one of his employees. He knew it was his own fault – he was just so tired – he needed to get some rest. His wife was at work and the house was quiet, which made his head even louder.

I can't go on like this much longer, his exhausted mind told him. Jon had always been a relatively happy and positive person, and he wasn't yet to the point of seriously considering suicide, but the thought had crossed his mind more than once. I definitely can't live the rest of my life like this, he had told himself several times in recent weeks. If I can't get some relief soon, I would rather be dead than this miserable.

Jon hated putting any kind of drug into his body, but he was definitely to the point of not caring about that anymore. He took three sleeping pills which he washed down with a beer and hoped the combination would knock him out for the rest of the day and night. The two sleeping pills he had taken a couple of nights ago were not strong enough so he was upping the dosage.

The screeching started again as he lay on the couch and Jon held his head between his hands and tried to withstand the actual pain it caused. He looked at the clock on the cable box below the TV and timed this episode. The screeching lasted eight long minutes before it stopped and he was able to try and relax again. He was sweating from the strain that his body just went through. All of his muscles were tensed, his head felt as if it was going to explode, and he was extremely frustrated with not being able to help himself get rid of this terrible problem.

Perhaps I have a tumor or something, Jon thought. I should get a CT scan and x-rays or other tests. Why haven't I done that already, he scolded himself. He decided to call his general practitioner when he got up and make an appointment to have tests done at the hospital. As it turned out, he didn't make the call that day as he finally fell into a sleep that lasted sixteen hours.

Heather finished the memory stick document and her outrage surfaced again. She simply couldn't believe that such devices were being used unknowingly on ordinary citizens. She was somewhat amazed that the eye implant technology was invented in the 1950s, although she knew of much more amazing technology through her affiliation with the Science and Technology division.

She knew this invasion of citizen privacy had to be unconstitutional and illegal, defying a citizen's most basic right to privacy. Not even including the bodily functions and personal hygiene scenes no one would want broadcast in color and surround sound on a monitor, she thought about the many other private things she did every day that she wouldn't want anyone, not even Danny, to see or hear. Writing in her journal, for example – Big Brother would now know everything in there as he could see it through her eyes as she wrote it. Talking aloud to herself, usually in her car, was meant for her ears only – everybody does that, right? She smiled as she thought about some of her self-talks. The little visit to her dad's house last night. If she had these implants then Big Brother would know that *she* knew that *he* knew....

"I'm getting a little crazy....and hungry!" Heather realized, her anger subsiding. She ordered room service as the hotel had a nice restaurant downstairs. She didn't feel like dressing and going down to eat and wanted the privacy, perceived though it may be, she mused, of continuing to read and research in her room.

She was now on the hotel's wifi and decided to look up the Privacy Act and how, or if, these implants violated that law. There really was no law that she knew of that addressed a person's privacy rights. The Privacy Act focuses on records, providing US citizens and permanent alien residents the right to access information concerning themselves that is maintained by any agency in the Executive Branch of the federal government. It established controls over what personal information the federal government collects and how it uses or discloses that information.

And with the onslaught of social networking and increasingly sophisticated computer, smart phone and other technology, privacy issues are becoming more and more prevalent and serious. "But not nearly as serious as what *you're* doing, Uncle Sam."

Heather already knew a lot about the law and about the general records management requirements for Federal agencies. She reviewed the five basic requirements that are most relevant to individuals.

First, each agency must establish procedures allowing individuals to see and copy records about themselves. An individual may also seek to amend any information that is not accurate, relevant, timely, or complete. The rights to inspect and to correct records are the most important provisions of the Privacy Act.

Second, each agency must publish notices describing all systems of records. The notices include a complete description of personal data recordkeeping policies, practices, and systems. This requirement was included as a means to prevent the maintenance of secret record systems.

Third, each agency must make reasonable efforts to maintain accurate, relevant, timely, and complete records about individuals. Agencies are prohibited from maintaining information about how individuals exercise rights guaranteed by the first amendment to the U.S. Constitution unless maintenance of the information is specifically authorized by statute or by the individual or relates to an authorized law enforcement activity.

Fourth, the act establishes rules governing the use and disclosure of personal information. The act specifies that information collected for one purpose may not be used for another purpose without notice to or the consent of the subject of the record. The act also requires that each agency keep a record of some disclosures of personal information.

Fifth, the act provides legal remedies that permit an individual to seek enforcement of the rights granted under the act. In addition, Federal employees who fail to comply with the act's provisions might be subjected to criminal penalties.

Heather liked to talk aloud to herself when she was alone and did so now. "I'm sure all of the audio and video recordings of these three Freedom Project subjects are maintained by the government, making them records that fall under the Privacy Act. And wow, are they ever violating the law!"

Bernie made himself do some work but couldn't stop thinking about Heather and wondering whether she had gone to Ohio or to Fiji. He realized that this was the first day in his working life that he hadn't given one hundred percent to his job. It was also the first day in his working life that he recalled doing something that he was not supposed to do. While these revelations bothered him a little, he quickly realized that they didn't bother him a lot. This is so unlike me, he thought, then smiled. It's about time I did something unlike me.

Bernie wondered why Jeremy had not called him to let him know the whereabouts of Heather. He knew Jeremy was very busy but he should have been able to take a few minutes by now to check on her. Suddenly it occurred to him that he could just call Heather on her cell phone and ask her where she was. He was sure Heather would tell him now that they were close friends. One minor problem, he thought. I don't know her cell number.

Bernie was pretty sure the list of agency issued cell phones and numbers was on one of the internal drives available to Homeland Security employees. He began searching for the list, excited about the prospect of calling her. His desk phone rang and he saw that it was Jeremy calling so grabbed it.

"How the hell did you know she wasn't on her way to Fiji," snapped Jeremy when Bernie answered the phone.

"I have my ways," replied Bernie, for once feeling superior to the brilliant young man who had been rude to him today. "Is she going to Hamilton, Ohio?"

"Yes," said Jeremy, sounding suspicious. "Do you know why

she decided to go to Hamilton?" he continued. "And why do you think she is in danger?"

"Yes, and she probably isn't in danger right now, but could be soon." Bernie stopped with that, not sure what Jeremy knew and what else he should tell.

Jeremy sighed. "I take it you read the file material that you gave to Dorgan yesterday on the memory stick. And I guess Heather knows about it also."

Bernie was shocked that Jeremy knew about the file and what was on it. Then it hit him that Jeremy was probably the internal person assigned to monitor the recordings of these three subjects. Somebody must be doing it, so it must be him. The thought disgusted him as images of what Jeremy would see flashed through Bernie's mind and his tone of voice changed from tentative and querying to harsh and firm as he answered.

"Yes, we both know. Heather decided to change her vacation plans and go to the funeral. Since there was an attempt on the medical examiner's life today, and two police officers killed, I thought Heather might be in danger too if she started asking questions. That's why I wanted to know for certain if she went to Ohio." Bernie felt he was holding his own with Jeremy and was proud of himself despite his anger.

"I believe you're right. She could be in danger." Jeremy sighed once again and continued. "I'll keep track of her from here."

Bernie made a decision right then and there. It was definitely the most spontaneous and outrageous decision he had ever made in his life, but he was ready to be spontaneous and outrageous. He would leave work right now, thirty minutes before quitting time, go home and pack a bag and some food, and drive to Hamilton, Ohio, tonight.

Dorgan was frustrated. Nothing was going according to plan and now his hired agent was wanted for the murder of two Hamilton police officers. That definitely limited Johnson's visibility and usefulness to him. Rachel Curry, who knew about Michtenbaum's ear implant, was still alive due to the botched attempt on her life. His trips to the elderly Michtenbaums' home and to a close friend of

Michael's had revealed nothing as to who the killer was. And, if there was someone else listening to Michael Michtenbaum's ear implant, he or she might have overheard a conversation that could finger both himself and Johnson.

Still, he'd had missions much tougher than this one, where a lot more had gone wrong. He kept telling himself that there was still time to finish this job with little or no fallout. He had Michtenbaum's ear implant, neatly and securely wrapped so that it was now undetectable. That was certainly a plus.

Dorgan told Johnson to lay low in the hotel for the rest of the day while he went to talk to the other friend of Michael Michtenbaum, hoping to get an identity of the guy in the photo who had killed Michael. He was also going to Michael's workplace, a law firm located in Middletown. He was driving there first since it might be closed if he waited too much later in the day, especially on a Friday.

The law firm where Michael Michtenbaum had worked for seventeen years was relatively small with only six attorneys, four paralegals and a legal secretary. Michael was one of the three partners in the firm of Daise, Shultz and Michtenbaum. The other two partners were now in a meeting trying to decide how to divide up Michael's legal cases. They would worry about the partnership issues later. They both looked tired when the legal secretary escorted Dorgan into the meeting room after she had informed them an FBI agent was there to talk with them.

Dorgan flashed his badge and introduced himself as Marcus Stone. They shook hands all around as the other two men introduced themselves. Dorgan already knew who they were. Not only had he checked up on them before coming, he had seen them before in past years through Michael's eye. "I'm very sorry about your partner," Dorgan offered.

"Thanks," the one named Daise mumbled. Since the elder partner offered nothing else, Shultz spoke up. "His death was so unexpected – we're still in shock around here." He offered Dorgan something to drink, which he declined. "May I ask why the FBI is involved in this case? I know the local police are working on it."

"Yes, it's still actually their case as of now. The FBI is doing a preliminary investigation based on a tip we received that could change the status of the case to federal."

"Really?" Shultz looked at Daise who still said nothing. "What was Michael involved in that could make his death a federal case? Was it one of the legal cases he was working on?"

"Well, I'm not at liberty at this point to give any details of the investigation – I'm sure you understand." The standard reply.

"Of course. How may we help you?"

"We have a photo of a person we are trying to find that may be able to help us identify Michael's killer. Have you seen this man before?" and for the third time that day, Dorgan handed over the 8 ½ by 11 sheet of printer paper containing the black and white photo. Both men studied the photo but shook their heads. They had no idea who the man was, they both said. Dorgan asked if he could show the photo to the rest of the staff, and Shultz asked each of the others to come in to look at the photo. One paralegal and one attorney were out of the office at the moment but the other six staff members came in. None of them knew or had ever seen the man.

Dorgan asked a few more questions, thanked them and left, then headed for the home of Michtenbaum's other close friend. He had called the man earlier to arrange a time that he could meet him at his home. The results were the same – the man had never seen the face in the photo.

Irritable and worried about what the Medical Examiner was probably telling the police and the press about what she had found and why she was attacked, Dorgan headed back to the hotel to plan his and Johnson's next moves. He first stopped at a favorite barbecue restaurant in Hamilton, Walt's Barbecue, and picked up two slabs of ribs, extra barbecue sauce and cole slaw for their dinner.

Since it didn't appear that Dragon's hit man was going anywhere right now, Jeremy decided to move that satellite to Heather for a brief time. Perhaps she would be outside and he would get to see her in all her tall and gorgeous glory. He pinpointed her phone GPS and punched in the coordinates. The satellite didn't move at all, and the aerial photo of the Marriott Hotel continued to show on the screen, at only a very slightly different angle.

"Oh, don't tell me!" Jeremy groaned out loud. "They're in the same hotel!" Now he *did* believe she was in danger. He dialed Heather's cell phone. He knew she wouldn't recognize his cell phone number but hoped she would answer anyway. If necessary, he would use his land line. She would recognize the main number as being that of DHS. She would also want to know why he was tracking her, and he planned to tell her the truth – that Bernie told him to.

Her phone went to voice-mail, so Jeremy hung up and dialed her number again from his land line. She still didn't answer and he left a message this time. "Heather, this is Jeremy from work. I know you're in Ohio and you may be in danger. Dorgan is in the same hotel with you, as well as a hit man working with him that just attacked the coroner there and killed two policemen. If you get this message, please call me on my cell phone and I'll explain everything." He left his cell number for her and hung up.

Jonathon Moore's wife Carol arrived home after work around 5:30 p.m. and saw her husband sleeping on the couch. She saw the sleeping pills and the empty beer bottle and at first was frightened that he might have taken a lot of pills, but upon examining the bottle, she saw it was still full. She was glad he was finally getting some rest. She tiptoed quietly around the house as she changed clothes and made herself some dinner.

She finally settled with a good book in a reclining chair next to the couch where Jon was lying. His breathing was even and he seemed to be sleeping well. The house was quiet and she was enjoying her book and a glass of wine, glad to have this time of peace, which had been infrequent in recent weeks.

Suddenly, her peace and quiet was disturbed by a sound, not loud, but shrill and screeching and close by. She looked around instinctively, but realized that this was the sound Jon had described to her...the sound in his head. It did seem to be coming from the couch where his head lay. His face now had a grimace on it, and he moved slightly but didn't wake. She moved from her chair to the couch and, on her knees in front of where he lay, she listened with horror at the shrill noise emanating from her husband's head.

After reading in her hotel room for several hours, coupled with her lack of sleep the night before, Heather was growing tired. Her large and delicious meal of grilled salmon, broccoli, wild rice, a glass of wine, and dessert of teramasu (she was on vacation, after all) didn't help matters either. She found herself yawning and her eyelids heavy. She usually watched the evening news but decided to go to bed early. She turned out her hotel room light at 9 p.m. and rested, but thoughts of the past two days would not let her sleep.

Were these the only three subjects who were in this experiment, or were there more people with such implants in their heads? This is very old technology. Is the government now doing the same thing but with newer technology? She suddenly sat up in bed. Yes! She knew of a study started about eight years ago with convicted pedophiles where implants were used to track and watch them. She thought at the time that the implants were similar to what many of their own agents had - a GPS tracking device implanted in their shoulder muscles. But now that she thought about it, that was not what the confidential report that she had seen had said. She was aware of video and audio recording devices so small they could be injected into a person intravenously. The devices, like specific medicines, target a particular area. She wondered if they could attach themselves to a retina or eardrum and never be detected. She wasn't sure, but believed it was possible.

Heather lay back down, closing her eyes and again trying to sleep. She wondered if the pedophiles knew about the implants. Perhaps they were given a choice of staying in prison or having the implants. She, like most people, wanted all pedophiles off the streets by almost any means possible, but she was still uncomfortable with the thought of anyone, criminal or not, having foreign objects placed in their bodies without their knowledge, not to mention having every minute of their lives subject to viewing.

There were so many other new technologies and advances to current technologies in recent years, most of which Heather had some exposure to in her previous role in the Science and Technology Department and in her current role assisting the Secretary of DHS, that now made Heather's mind think of the possible uses to which they were being put. The medical field, for one. She knew there was experimentation with vaccines that inserted molecular sized devices that could monitor internal organ functions.

Heather was finally able to slow her mind by thinking of Danny and Fiji. Is he sitting at the outdoor bar right now, feeling the cool breeze off the ocean as he sips a tropical drink, watching the beautiful moon over the water? Why do I have such mixed feelings about him? Why can't I love him unconditionally and love my job as well?

Speaking of her job, Heather felt like she was on a business trip instead of on vacation. She thought of what she wanted to accomplish in Hamilton, and it wasn't much, really. She hoped to get a chance to talk to the parents of Michael Ray Michtenbaum, Mitchell and Celia Michtenbaum, although she didn't know what she would say to them other than her sincere condolences. She couldn't very well walk up to them and tell them that their son had been under government surveillance his entire life, meaning that they themselves had been recorded many times, every time they were with their son. No, she definitely couldn't tell them. She felt so torn between what she believed was right and her love and loyalty to her job, her boss and her country. She was angry that she felt she was now having to choose between doing the right thing or betraying the government and country she loved.

She also wanted to talk to the Coroner Rachel Curry tomorrow. Perhaps the woman has found the implants and perhaps she has already told Michael's parents. She was sure that the articles Bernie had shown her had said there would be an autopsy on Michael's body. It's possible that these devices have already been found, although most autopsies would not include the eyes and ears. Chances are, they've not been discovered.

How can someone have two implants in his head and no one ever know about it? Wouldn't they show up on a CT scan or MRI? Heather was so tired and knew she must stop thinking and try to sleep. She tried to stop new thoughts and concentrated on her breathing.

Finally, Heather was able to fall asleep.

The assassin Agent Johnson had begun watching the six o'clock news in his hotel room when Dorgan returned with some dinner for the both of them. They had separate rooms but Dorgan sat down and ate in Johnson's room so that he didn't miss any of the headline story about the killing of two Hamilton police officers and the attack on the Butler County Coroner.

The television coverage of the story was 20 minutes long with an on-the-scene reporter standing near the morgue building. Behind the reporter could be seen dozens of city police, county sheriff personnel and numerous other people in the morgue driveway and parking lot. Several times, photos of the two young police officers were shown, and information about their families and their heroism reported. Taped video of the rental car of the perpetrator and where it had been hidden was shown. When a sketch artist drawing of the suspected killer came on the screen, both Dorgan and Johnson grimaced. The likeness was uncanny. There was no doubt it was Johnson, and Dorgan was cursing silently that he would never again be able to use this assassin. Johnson was thinking that he would now have to have major plastic surgery to alter his appearance if he didn't want his career, and possibly his life, to be over after today.

Johnson wondered how the coroner knew that her attacker was the same man who posed as the FBI agent the day before. He had worn a mask and different clothing when he attacked her and killed the police officers and he had disguised his voice. He never wore cologne to give off a recognizable scent. How could she be so sure that the two were the same guy – him.

Dorgan was wondering the same thing. He asked Johnson how she knew it was him and he said she couldn't have known. They didn't want to talk much for fear of missing important information on the news report, but both were thinking that perhaps someone else was watching and listening to them and that someone else had given the description to the police.

The reporter then interviewed the Chief of Police, who gave an update on the search for the killer. He said that while he was confident they would apprehend the killer soon, he wanted to urge all area residents to be very cautious and on the lookout for the fugitive who was armed and extremely dangerous.

Both Dorgan and Johnson stopped eating to listen more

closely when the reporter then turned to interview the coroner, Rachel Curry. Rachel relayed much of the horrific events that happened that morning but said she didn't know why she was targeted by this killer or what he wanted. Dorgan and Johnson looked at each other. The woman didn't say a word about the implant.

Perhaps she was afraid to admit anything that she knew for fear of another attempt on her life, Dorgan thought, or perhaps the police had asked her not to reveal the reason she was attacked. They often wanted to keep certain information confidential as part of their investigation. Johnson knew he had threatened her as he left, and assumed that was the reason. Whatever the reason, Dorgan and Johnson were both grateful for that small omission of information in their favor. While they both felt the Coroner had told the police about the implant, at least the whole greater Cincinnati viewing area wouldn't be aware of it....yet.

After they'd eaten, Dorgan went over Johnson's job for the next day. As they had discussed once as a possible scenario, Johnson would disguise himself as the grave closer. Immediately after the graveside service, once everyone was gone but before the real grave closers arrived, Johnson would remove the eye implant from Michtenbaum's body. He could be quick and messy now with the removal of the eye and the implant since the body would be forever six feet under ground. Johnson would close the grave and get out of town immediately.

"What about the coroner?" Johnson asked. "I can still get her, I'm sure of it." Dorgan shook his head. "No, I'll have to take care of her some other way. She's probably under police protection now and it will be much harder to get her alone. I need you to concentrate on this one very important task of getting the eye implant." Johnson nodded his agreement and looked somewhat relieved and more relaxed. Dorgan knew if he had told Johnson that he would let him try again to kill the coroner that the assassin would have been very suspicious. Botched jobs were not reassigned to the botcher. As it was, Dorgan let Johnson believe he was still going to use him for part of the job.

It wouldn't matter for much longer. The arsenic Dorgan had put in Johnson's BBQ sauce was already working, he could tell.

Johnson would be dead before Dorgan finished cleaning up the rib bones scattered on the table where they sat. He would give Johnson the professional courtesy of waiting until he died before calling in his replacement.

Jeremy tried calling Heather several more times and left another message for her. He hoped she had simply forgotten to take her phone off airplane mode and didn't realize she was getting incoming calls. He also sent her a text message in case that was her usual mode of communication. At 7:30 p.m., after thirteen and a half hours at his desk and eating only junk food, coffee and Mountain Dew, he decided to call it a night. He was tired from very little rest the night before and wanted a good meal and a good night's sleep.

Even with all systems visibly shut down, his satellites were recording in the position he left them, and he planned to come in early in the morning and view the night's recordings on high speed, especially any comings or goings from the Marriott Hotel in Hamilton, Ohio.

Before he left, however, he made another call to the cell phone of the Secretary of Homeland Security.

Linda Jayne

SATURDAY

It took Bernie ten hours to drive from his apartment near downtown Washington, D.C., to Hamilton, Ohio. He arrived at 5 a.m. and ate breakfast at a 24-hour Waffle House on High Street. He wanted to wash his face and brush his teeth, but he was not tired from the long journey. He was too excited about the crazy adventure he was on and the thought of seeing Heather. Would she be happy to see him, he wondered.

He had a map of the area that he'd picked up at a gas station, as well as information as to where the funeral home and cemetery were located. He also wanted to look up the addresses of the morgue and Michael Michtenbaum's home. He felt like he was on vacation and these were his sight-seeing spots. He didn't know what hotel Heather was staying in, and he was mad at himself for not asking Jeremy that question yesterday. Jeremy probably knew. He really wanted to see her hotel and maybe even see her coming out of the hotel. What if it had a pool and she went swimming? It was too much to hope for, and Bernie found himself drooling a bit on his waffle.

Bernie missed payphones. He liked the old fashioned ways of communicating. Waffle House Restaurants, and of course many locations, used to have them, but not anymore. Bernie did not own a cell phone and while he had to use a computer at work, he had no use for one personally. He didn't Google, text or tweet. He wasn't on Facebook, LinkedIn or any other social site. But once in a great while, like now, he could use a little technology since an old-fashioned phonebook wasn't available and he needed address information.

Bernie looked around. There was only one other customer in the restaurant at this early hour and the sole waitress on duty was not busy right now, unlike the waitresses at the café near his home where he ate dinner every day. So although he had finished his waffle and milk and had his money out and ready to pay, he decided to order some coffee. He wasn't a fan of coffee, but it was a drink, unlike milk, that could be refilled many times, therefore giving him the time to ask questions of the waitress.

He sat back down and ordered coffee, and the waitress

looked at him with a bit of a surprised look, but then smiled. "Not quite ready to go to work?" as though she knew the feeling.

"Oh, I'm not working today." Then he realized he had an opportunity here, and rephrased. "Well, actually I'm here on an assignment having to do with yesterday's murders of the police officers." He could tell she wasn't sure if she believed him, and then she even got a bit of a frightened look, so he pulled out his Homeland Security badge, held on a lanyard which was usually around his neck. He showed it to her and she relaxed a little.

She wasn't exactly pretty but she wasn't bad looking either, thought Bernie. She was shorter than he, and even rounder, and had a beautiful smile.

"I'm not an agent with Homeland Security; I'm just here to do some research." He decided to be honest, well, somewhat honest, instead of trying to impress her with a fake title. Women never seemed to be fooled anyway. It worked. She asked if he wanted a free donut to go with his coffee and put her elbows on the counter to listen to him.

"I drove all night to get here from Washington, D.C. Where is the nicest hotel in Hamilton?" He wasn't asking for himself. He figured Heather would be at the nicest place.

"Washington, D.C., how exciting! Have you been to the White House?"

Bernie couldn't believe he had found a woman who was so easily impressed. He silently vowed to do more road trips. "I've been through the White House seven times actually," he beamed.

"Oh my gosh, that's so neat!" she was actually staring at him. Bernie was dumbfounded. They were both startled when the other customer shouted to get the waitress's attention. "Can *I* get some coffee as well?" The cook glared at the waitress and she ran to serve the other customer.

"Um, I probably shouldn't keep you from your work," Bernie apologized when she returned. He was so used to his 45-minute time allotment at his local café and getting chastised for monopolizing the waitresses' time. "Um, about that hotel? Is there one that's really nice in Hamilton?"

"That would be the Marriott – used to be called the Hamiltonian. Just keep driving that way," and she pointed west down High Street, "til you get to Front Street. Turn right and it's just one block up. You can't miss it."

"Also, can you tell me where the county morgue is located?" The waitress gave him the easy directions, then used her hand to tell him no payment was necessary when he tried to pay for his coffee.

"My name's Bernie by the way."

"I'm Sheila," she continued to smile at him. "I'm here from midnight to 9 a.m. every day but Monday if you want to stop back in."

"I'll try to…thanks…and nice meeting you, Sheila."

This has already been the best day of my life and it's only 6 a.m., thought Bernie as he got into his car.

Even though it was Saturday, and the third Saturday in a row that Jeremy had to work, he arrived at 6 a.m., anxious to find out exactly what else Dragon was up to, and to make sure Heather was okay. The fact that she hadn't responded to either phone or text messages had him worried about her. He also wanted to spend time today researching the identities of both the hit man helping Dragon and the man who had killed Michael Michtenbaum. His quick searches for them yesterday, done in the usual, a.k.a legal, databases had revealed nothing.

He turned on the recorded video footage from Audrey, one of the two satellites watching the Marriott Hotel. He kept it on live coverage until he had his other seven laptops up and running. He turned on his program that tracked Dragon's keyboard strokes and saw that there had been no activity since last night at 9.

Michtenbaum's live video and audio recordings yesterday had held some surprises, so Jeremy wanted to keep that program up and running even though he didn't expect anything unusual to happen today. The man would be buried and his video screen would stay black forever. His ear implant had been removed but was contained so that any sounds it received were no longer audible. Still, you never know.

He had been considering utilizing the implant video and audio coverage of the other two project subjects, Mary Beth Singer and Jonathon Moore. For the past four years, he had tracked them almost daily via satellite, just to make sure they were alive and well. Now he knew he could access the implants in their eyes and ears to see and hear everything that they saw and heard, just as he had done with Michael Michtenbaum, and just as Dragon was apparently doing with all three of them, and probably had been for many years.

He had an ethical and moral issue with accessing this information, which surprised even himself. He had no ethical or moral issue with illegally hacking into computers or picking the lock to his boss's office.

But this infringement was different, much different. No one should have their privacy violated to this extent, in this manner. He decided to check on them in the usual manner – via satellite. He would reserve the use of the other method if, and only if, he was unable to locate them by satellite, or if he felt that their lives were in danger in some way. He did not believe that was the case right now.

On one of his computer monitors he set up a split screen and began accessing private and confidential databases, looking for the identities of the two killers. He accessed military, CIA, FBI, MI6 and eightten other similar databases housing photos and information on spies, intelligence operatives, assassins, special ops and a variety of other good or bad, but primarily unknown, individuals. This program, which simultaneously hacked into all databases, was another that he had developed himself at the age of eighteen and the one that had gotten him arrested and subsequently hired by Homeland Security. They "hired" his custom hacking program as well. He was only to use it in times of extreme need, and this was one of those times, he decided. He fed several photos of Dragon's partner into the program, from different angles. He was fairly certain he already knew the identity of this man – he had seen him numerous times – but it was possible that he could be wrong. Last year, a rogue agent had plastic surgery to make himself look like another agent in order to disguise his own identity. Jeremy didn't want to make a rookie mistake by not confirming the man's identity.

Jeremy had only the one point-of-view photos of Michtenbaum's killer. Still, he ran three slightly different facial expressions of the man into the computer program. He also had a blurry side view of him walking past a window. He expected this identification to take a little longer.

Heather's GPS showed that her phone was still in the hotel. He truly hoped she was as well, and that she was sleeping peacefully. He would try calling her again in an hour or so. If she was sleeping, he didn't want to wake her quite this early.

Dragon and his hired killer's cars were both in the hotel lot. He zoomed in just to make sure the men weren't in their cars. He knew Dragon was an early riser as he was often at work when Jeremy came in. He thought he remembered Dragon saying something about running in the morning as well. He decided to view the recorded footage that the satellite had taped of the parking lot and area surrounding the outside of the hotel. He backed it up to 5 a.m. and began watching at six times the normal speed. After almost six minutes of watching, he saw a figure leave the front door of the hotel, walking, then running. He immediately stopped the video and backed up one minute. Since the video was recorded, all he could do was slow it down, speed it up, and zoom in or out. He couldn't change the angle of the view of the person. But a close up of the person leaving the building at 5:35 a.m., at the angle shown by the satellite, proved that it was indeed Dragon. Once the runner was out of view of the satellite, he sped the recording up to six times the speed again and watched until the present time. Dragon had not yet returned to the hotel.

A ping on one of his computers told him that he had a hit on one of the photos fed into his special program to identify spies and other operatives who were basically invisible to the rest of the world. Two more quick pings...probably the same person, different photos, thought Jeremy. He looked and saw a different photo of the same man he had followed yesterday – the man who had attacked the coroner and killed the two policemen – Dragon's hit man. He was a former CIA agent, now rogue assassin, real name Nathan Johnson. Just as he thought. The program was still searching all databases for the other killer.

Jeremy's own e-mail chimed and he saw that the sender was rwatterson. The brief message already displayed on his screen. "Samuel would like to see you."

"Thanks, big boss," laughed Jeremy. Samuel was the newest and greatest satellite that could not only hear a whisper inside a building, but could see through concrete, brick, wood, steel or almost any barrier substance. Jeremy had used Samuel much of the past two weeks to track the terrorists plotting to attack the Orlando theme parks, but once that assignment ended, he no longer had use of the extremely expensive and versatile satellite. Jeremy had called the Secretary again yesterday evening to update her on the status of his surveillance of Dragon and to request the use of Samuel once again.

Jeremy was somewhat surprised that the "big boss," DHS Secretary Rhonda Watterson, did not decide to intervene to stop Dorgan now. Jeremy had informed her about the attack on the coroner and the shooting of the two police officers. "As tragic as those events are, we must find out what Dorgan is really up to...we need more information to do that. Therefore, we must just watch him with little or no interference," she told him. Jeremy interpreted that statement as she might not have wanted him to call the police when he saw Johnson escaping from the morgue.

Did the Secretary know about Heather's change in vacation plans? If not, should he let her know? No, he thought. If Heather wanted her boss to know, she would tell her. For now, he would leave it alone.

Jeremy was once again giddy with excitement at the surveillance possibilities offered by Samuel. He would have to contain himself to not use the multi-billion dollar gadget to spy on innocent individuals, such as Heather, although he really wanted to check on her and make sure she was alright. It's for watching and listening to the "bad guys," he reminded himself. This satellite does what the invasive implant devices do – it can see and hear everything.

Suddenly Dragon entered into Audrey's view and Jeremy focused his attention on him. Did I see another guy with him a moment ago? He stayed on live video a little longer until Dragon entered the hotel, and at the same time positioned his favorite toy, Samuel, over the hotel to now find and watch Dragon inside the building. As soon as Dragon entered his room, he started removing his clothes and heading for the bathroom. Uh, no thanks, thought Jeremy and left Samuel viewing the bedroom only.

He went back to Audrey and pulled up the recorded three minutes before Dragon entered the hotel. "There!" Jeremy pointed to the computer screen. There was definitely another man talking with

Dragon on the very edge of Audrey's view. The other man then turned and walked out of view. Jeremy played it over three times and though he couldn't see the other man very well, he felt certain it wasn't Nathan Johnson, Dragon's partner. What else are you up to, boss? He took several still shots, poor as they were, of the mystery man and fed them into his facial recognition software.

Jeremy was out of computers – all eight were in use now – so he shut down one of the other satellites watching the hotel. He had Samuel and Audrey, which was enough. That freed up a monitor. He needed to check the local Hamilton on-line news to refresh his memory as to where the funeral and graveside services were being held so that he could move his satellites there in case he happened to lose any of the cars that would be heading towards the service in a couple of hours.

Dragon was dressing and watching television so Jeremy decided to use Samuel to look for Heather and Johnson. He moved room by room on the same floor as Dragon. 30 seconds and three rooms later, he found Johnson, dead on the floor of his hotel room. Jeremy frantically began searching for Heather. She wasn't on the same floor with Dragon and Johnson, which was some relief to Jeremy. It took him a few seconds to remember how to move up and down floors with the satellite and he was soon one floor higher. After six or seven rooms of zooming in so close on sleeping faces that he could almost feel their breath, he finally found Heather. She was safe, standing in her room with a towel around her and drying her hair with another towel. She was watching the news and he could tell from her exclamations and expressions that she was hearing for the first time about the killings the day before. He decided to call her now since he knew she was up. He dialed her cell number but he didn't hear it ring and neither did she. It was either turned off or the battery was dead, as he knew from his GPS tracking that the cell phone was definitely in her room.

I can call the hotel and have them ring her room, but at that instance Heather let her body towel drop to the floor as she yawned and stretched her nearly six foot body. Jeremy couldn't take his eyes off her. She was magnificent.

"I am so going to hell for this," he murmured as he and Samuel zoomed in and could practically count the pores on parts of

Heather that no man had ever seen so vividly.

Jeremy's MyBackdoor program pinged again and he tore his eyes away from Heather to view the identity of Michael Michtenbaum's killer. "Holy shit! I need to let the Secretary know about this right away," and he picked up his desk phone and dialed her cell number, at the same time minimizing the screen on which Heather was still naked as if the secretary would be able to see what he was doing.

Dorgan had already met with his new agent, Johnson's replacement, following his morning run. The man had flown in late last night and they had prearranged to meet at 6:15 a.m. between the monument building and art center on the path by the river. Dorgan reviewed the man's assignments for the day. The new agent then left to complete his first assignment while Dorgan went in the hotel to shower, dress and eat breakfast.

Dorgan had breakfast in his room and turned on his laptop to briefly check on his other two subjects, Mary Beth and Jon. Jon was still sleeping as Dorgan could hear his even breathing and his video screen was dark, indicating shut eyelids. He entered a different username and password for Mary Beth – she was still sleeping as well.

Dorgan had not had any luck finding Michael Ray Michtenbaum's killer, either from his earlier database searches or from showing the man's photo to Michtenbaum's family, friends and co-workers. He needed to learn the man's identity, and soon. He knew Homeland Security owned a facial recognition software program that could undetectably search the databases of all major intelligence, military and high level law enforcement agencies around the world – the program written by his own employee, Jeremy James. While the program could be accessed and used by several persons with clearance within the agency, Jeremy was the most adept at using it and was the one most often called upon to find the true identity of a foreign spy, a Gitmo detainee or a dead military special forces operative. He needed Jeremy and his special program to find out if Michtenbaum's killer was in that database.

Dorgan dialed Jeremy's cell phone number. It was only 7:30

on Saturday morning and he was sure he would be waking Jeremy from a drunken sleep, but it couldn't be helped.

Jeremy answered after the third ring. "Sorry if I woke you. This is Dorgan. I apologize for having to ask this since you've worked the past two Saturdays, but I need for you to go into the office and do a job for me this morning." Dorgan was used to giving orders, although politely, but still in a tone and manner that did not allow for refusal.

Jeremy sounded as though he'd just woken up. "Uh, okay. What time is it?"

"7:30. How quickly can you get to the office?" While Dorgan felt certain that Jeremy still had illegal software programs on what he was sure was some serious hardware at his residence, Dorgan also knew that part of Jeremy's agreement with Homeland Security in both keeping his job and staying out of prison was that Jeremy was not to recreate the program or ever use it anywhere or for any reason other than at the Homeland Security office and under the orders of a superior.

"I need to shower. I can be there in less than an hour. What do you need me to do?" and Dorgan heard a loud yawn.

"I'm going to fax a photo to you on the private fax to run in your facial recognition software program. I need this guy's identity a.s.a.p. Got it?" Dorgan wasn't sure Jeremy was awake enough to get it.

"Yeah, I got it," said Jeremy sleepily.

"Good. I'll check in with you later to see what you've found." Dorgan hung up the burner cell phone he had picked up the day before.

Dorgan then used his other untraceable cell phone to call his new partner. "I have an extra task for you to do. Come back to the hotel right away."

Jeremy yawned for real and took a gulp of his now cold coffee as he maximized the screen of Samuel watching Heather's room. "Oh, I haven't called her room yet!" He reached for his phone, looking around for her on the screen. She wasn't there. He moved Samuel to the bathroom but she wasn't there either. "Crap! How could she have gotten dressed and left so quickly!" She still might not know that Dragon was in the same hotel as she, and that Dragon, his now-dead partner, and a new partner, were on a murdering spree.

He moved Samuel downstairs to the lobby area and to the restaurant looking for Heather. Perhaps there was still time to catch her. He tried her cell phone again but again, no answer. Audrey was still watching the hotel parking lot and Jeremy kept one eye on Dragon's car in case he left. He figured he had at least an hour and a half before Dragon called him back to check on the status of finding the identity of Michtenbaum's killer. Jeremy thought he did a good job of convincing Dragon that he was home in bed still asleep. So Dragon would probably wait an hour before sending the fax.

Jeremy checked Heather's room again as well as the hallway. She was nowhere to be seen. How could he have missed her leaving the hotel? Surely he would have seen her in the parking lot. Wait, he thought, perhaps there's a gym or indoor pool. He continued moving Samuel throughout the first floor looking for her. He found an indoor pool and there, sure enough, was Heather, her long body taking only a few seconds to swim the length of the small pool before expertly turning and gliding the opposite way.

"While I'd love to keep watching you," Jeremy said to Heather, "I need to look and listen in on what our friend Dragon is doing."

Dragon was still in his room, looking out the window. Samuel moved over a bit to peek over his shoulder and look out the window as well. Dragon's room was on the front corner of the hotel overlooking a portion of the main parking lot.

Are you waiting for someone? Jeremy wondered.

Heather hoped to be able to talk to the county coroner, Rachel Curry, before the visitation service for Michael Michtenbaum started. After watching the morning news, she felt certain that the attack on the coroner which led to the deaths of the two police officers was directly related to Michael Michtenbaum although she couldn't prove it. She just knew in her gut that it was. She assumed the woman was at home today, not work, but she would find both addresses and go visit Rachel with the hope that the woman would talk to her.

After her swim, Heather returned to her room and changed into a black skirt, white blouse, black and red scarf, and black flats, suitable for walking around a cemetery. She needed only mascara and lipstick, ran her fingers through her still-wet hair, and grabbed her purse. She would look up the addresses on her i-Phone while having a muffin and coffee downstairs.

As Heather approached the elevator and pressed the down button, another man was coming towards the elevator as well. He was quite attractive, she noticed. He smiled and nodded at her as he waited with her for the elevator. Once inside, he made polite conversation, asking if she was in town on business. She replied that she was just in town for the funeral of a friend to which he offered his condolences.

The man continued to walk with her to the restaurant where they each bought coffee and a blueberry muffin. Heather then excused herself, saying she needed to leave, and took her items to go. The man touched her lightly on the arm and sincerely wished her a good visit in Hamilton despite the circumstances. Heather thanked him and headed outside to her rental car.

Once in her car, Heather pulled her phone out of her purse. It's dead, she realized when she tried to turn on the phone. She had brought both a car charger and the regular charger with her, and was scolding herself for not plugging in the phone last night. She rummaged in her purse for the car charger and pulled it out. No wonder I haven't gotten any texts, e-mails or calls. Her phone normally pinged, chimed, sang, rang or vibrated every few minutes but she had been so engrossed in her thoughts and reading last night that she hadn't noticed that she'd heard nothing from her phone.

After a few minutes of charging, she saw that she had three voice messages, four text messages and twenty-seven e-mails. None were from her boss or Danny, so she connected to the internet to look up the work and home addresses of Rachel Curry. Rachel's address was listed but not her home or cell phone number.

Heather spoke the address into her phone to activate the turn by turn GPS system. As she drove to the west side of town, she again began questioning herself. What am I doing? Am I really going to reveal a top-secret government study, *and* to someone I don't even know? What if there's more to this than I'm aware of....perhaps everything was not in the file. I should talk to my dad first. As Heather turned into the attractive community where Rachel lived, she was still uncertain. What if yesterday's tragedy had nothing to do with Michael Michtenbaum? I've jeopardized my career and ruined my relationship with Danny for nothing. No, I can't blame this situation for my ruined relationship....I did that completely on my own.

She was driving down Rachel's street and saw two police cruisers in front of the coroner's home. At first Heather thought another attempt had been made on the coroner's life but then realized that it was most likely a precautionary measure. Rachel had a protective detail watching out for her.

Heather was uncomfortable with stopping so continued to drive. If she stopped and asked to speak with the coroner without an appointment, the police would question her and perhaps even search her. No, she needed to call the coroner first and make an appointment. She stopped a street away and checked the internet once again for Rachel's phone number. The number of the morgue was shown, but she couldn't find a personal phone number for Rachel Curry.

She sat and ate some of her blueberry muffin. She wasn't sure of the county name she was in so looked up Hamilton, Ohio, morgue and found her way to the Butler County website and some information about the coroner, Rachel Curry. It stated that she was unmarried and did not mention children, so Heather assumed the other phone numbers with the last name Curry, while perhaps family members, were not of a husband or child.

Finally, she tried calling information. "I'm sorry, we have no listing for that name," said the operator, which was what Heather expected. If the number isn't published, they can't give it out.

She then had another idea and drove to the morgue, which took about twelve minutes. If someone, anyone, was working there today, perhaps they would call Rachel for her. She was in luck. Although the door was locked, she rang a doorbell and a man in a white lab coat answered. He introduced himself as the Assistant Coroner and he was instantly enamored with Heather. He offered to get her coffee, asked how he could help her, offered her a seat, and she hadn't even introduced herself yet.

After he stopped fussing over her, she was able to ask him if he could call Rachel. She needed to speak with her urgently but didn't have her personal number. "I know she is traumatized after what happened yesterday, and I won't take much of her time, but I really need to speak with her about the attack. I think I may be able to shed some light as to what happened."

"Really?" The Assistant Coroner now scrutinized her a little more closely. "You know who did it?"

"No, but I think I know why, which will help lead us to who. But I need to ask the coroner a few questions and tell her what I know. Would you at least call her and see if she's willing to talk to me?"

"Okay." Heather noticed that he now spoke more cautiously, and his eyes had changed from adoration to suspicion, an emotion she didn't usually evoke in men.

He continued to look at Heather as he spoke into the phone. "Rachel, hi, it's Bill. Sorry to bother you, but there's a young woman here who says she knows something about yesterday's attack – why it happened – and she wants to talk to you." There was a pause as he listened, then he directed his question to Heather. "She wants to know why you just don't go to the police with your information."

"Because I need to ask her something first. I think it may have to do with one of her cases, but I could be entirely wrong, in which case I don't want to bother the police." The Assistant Coroner, Bill, relayed Heather's response to Rachel, and a few moments later he handed the phone to Heather.

"May I ask your name first?" was Rachel's response to Heather when she thanked Rachel for speaking with her.

"Heather Barnes. I'm with Homeland Security." Bill's eyes widened and the adoration returned. "I think the attack on you had to do with Michael Michtenbaum," Heather offered, and then waited a moment. If Rachel had found an implant in Michael Michtenbaum, she might know that the attack could be related, even though she stated on her television interview that she didn't know why she was attacked.

"Yes, it did." Rachel hesitated, then spoke again. "Can you

stay at the morgue. I can be there in fifteen minutes and we can talk."

"Of course," replied Heather.

When Dorgan saw his new agent, Jones, pull into the parking lot, he sprinted down the stairs to meet him at the side door. Now that he had seen Heather Barnes, assistant to the Secretary of Homeland Security, at the hotel, he knew he was probably being watched and planned to take more precautions. He handed a small package and written instructions to the man and left without a word. He was back upstairs in his room within two minutes, looking out the window again to make sure his man tailed the right car. He hoped one of the cars within his view was Heather's, although it was possible she had parked elsewhere.

Why would they send Heather? She isn't a field agent. Intelligent, yes. Trained, no. Was she here to spy on him? No one knows I'm here, do they? Or was she here to also make sure Michtenbaum was put in the ground? Just how many others were involved in this project? Dorgan hated uncertainty and he hated what he now might have to do to this beautiful woman. He didn't know her well, although they'd spoken on numerous occasions. But he always noticed her. In a different time, a different place, perhaps he would have hit on her. Most women found him attractive, although most didn't like him once they got to know him. He was too cold...too distant. His wife had told him that for years until she finally stopped talking to him all together. But he had to be cold and distant...it was a job requirement and he had learned at a young age, in his early 20's, to discipline himself in all areas of his life, although his temper often got the best of him at times. He could now look at a woman like Heather and not feel the stirrings that would cause most men to lose their self-control, and if he did feel something, he could turn it off quickly.

He recalled his shock of earlier this morning when he had first seen Heather. He had gone downstairs to buy a newspaper and cup of coffee. While he got his news on-line or via television, he still enjoyed the feel of holding a newspaper and a hot mug of coffee in his hands...one of his few pleasures. As he was leaving the lobby, he saw the backside of a tall, beautiful woman walking towards the pool. He had seen that backside before, that elegant walk, the short messy blond hair – it was Heather Barnes from work. He followed her to the pool area just to be sure. He couldn't believe it. And now he had another problem that he had to eliminate.

Jones would have planted the device in her purse by now and Dorgan had his computer up and running to listen in to her. He unfortunately didn't have another listening device he could plant on Heather other than the implant from Michtenbaum's ear, so he used that. She would never find the tiny device now at the bottom of her large purse, and he needed to know what she was up to. He had called Jones back from his initial task of ensuring that he would be one of the grave closers – he said he had been successful in making that arrangement already – to plant the device in Heather's purse and then follow her. So far, so good.

Bernie found the Marriott Hotel without any trouble – Sheila was right, you couldn't miss it. He sat in his car in the parking lot with a good view of the front and side entrance for forty-five minutes before deciding to drive around and find the other key spots. It was still quite early. Heather probably wasn't even up yet since she wasn't going to work, assuming she was even at this hotel. The visitation for Michael Michtenbaum started at 10 a.m. and the funeral was at noon, both being held at the Webb Noonan Kidd Funeral Home on Ross Avenue. The burial would then be at Greenwood Cemetery on Greenwood Avenue, with the graveside service starting at 1:30 p.m. He would go find these places, as well as the morgue. There was still plenty of time to find Heather before the visitation began.

Bernie stayed seated in his car in the hotel parking lot while he looked at the map of Hamilton he had bought. Ross Avenue was just on the other side of the river, within walking distance even. Greenwood Cemetery wasn't too far either, a couple of miles perhaps, and according to the address, the morgue was located right by the cemetery. This shouldn't take long, Bernie said to himself and left the hotel lot to check out these other three locations.

Following the map, he crossed the High Street Bridge then

saw that a left turn wasn't allowed onto B Street which led to Ross Avenue. He continued on Main Street and turned left on the next street, C Street. He loved orderly streets. C ran into Ross Avenue, but to his dismay Ross was one way only and he had to turn left, taking him back in the direction he had come to B Street. He went around the block and back to Main Street, turning left and this time going further down Main several blocks before turning left again. This time when he turned onto Ross Avenue he passed the funeral home on the left. It was a gorgeous red brick building with a huge wrap-around porch. It looked as though it was once the mansion home of a wealthy resident.

Bernie continued down Ross to head back across the bridge to find the cemetery on the other side of town. He began to think of Sheila whom he had just left a little more than an hour before. Perhaps he could spend the night in Hamilton and go to breakfast again in the morning at the restaurant where she worked. He wanted to see and talk to her again. She was very nice.

Bernie turned left off of High Street and followed it to Heaton Street, which his map indicated would take him by the cemetery. The cemetery appeared quite large on the map and was surrounded by three different streets. He could either turn onto Greenwood or continue on Heaton a little further before going left. That way would take him near the morgue so he chose it.

It was a beautiful morning and the air was still cool although the forecast for the day was temperatures in the high 80s. Bernie drove around the cemetery several times, as well as through it, to become acquainted with the various entrances and sections. He saw two tents set up for graveside services and assumed one of those would be for Michael Michtenbaum later today.

He then drove onto Route 4 and past the morgue. It was across from the Butler County Fairgrounds. He turned around and drove through the driveway of the morgue where he could view the cemetery. He felt he now had a good understanding of where everything was – the hotel where Heather may or may not be staying, the funeral home, the morgue and the cemetery, some or all of which she would eventually visit. He parked his car under a large shade tree near the peaceful cemetery and decided to catch a nap before the visitation service began.

Jeremy watched Dragon sit in the upholstered chair in his room, still reading a newspaper and sipping what now had to be cold coffee. Earlier, Jeremy and Satellite Samuel watched Dragon run downstairs and Jeremy had a hard time keeping up with him. In fact, he lost him for about five seconds but found him at the side exit of the building on the main floor. He was already leaving the man he had met at the door, but Jeremy got a couple of shots of the man who he believed was Dragon's new agent, the one he had met early this morning while on his run. He hadn't received any hits on the earlier photos he had fed into his software program…perhaps he'd have better luck with these photos since he got a fairly clear facial shot.

Is Dragon aware that he's being watched? wondered Jeremy. Is that why he ran down the stairs and met with the man for only a second or two? He didn't catch any of the conversation between the two men, if indeed there had even been any conversation. He supposed that a man like Dragon, a field agent with the CIA for seventeen years and allegedly still involved in covert operations, was always cautious and suspicious. Jeremy hoped Dragon wasn't overly suspicious now or it could make Jeremy's job much more difficult.

There were voices coming from Dragon's room and Jeremy quickly turned down the sound on his other laptops to listen. He zoomed in even closer. The voices were coming from Dragon's computer and Dragon, too, was leaning in to listen. The laptop screen was partially closed as if Dragon knew someone might be watching over his shoulder.

"Well, hello," said a man's pleasant voice. "And how may I help you?" There were some sounds of a door opening and closing and feet moving. "I'm Bill Simmons, the Assistant Coroner. Would you like some coffee?" Finally a woman's voice said yes, thank you and there were more noises of coffee pouring and other such sounds. "Please, have a seat. I don't usually get such lovely, and living, guests." He laughed and asked again, "What can I do for you?"

"I need to speak with the coroner, Rachel Curry, on a very urgent matter but I don't know how to contact her other than here at work. I was hoping you would be able to call her for me."

Jeremy knew that voice – it was Heather's. When did she leave the hotel? He hadn't seen her leave. How could he and Audrey have missed her! He quickly accessed her phone GPS again and sure enough, she was at the morgue.

Jeremy noticed the look on Dragon's face…one of recognition as well. Dragon knew it was Heather's voice.

"I know she is traumatized after what happened yesterday, and I won't take much of her time, but I really need to speak with her about the attack. I think I may be able to shed some light as to what happened."

Jeremy watched Dragon as they both listened to the conversation between Heather and the assistant coroner.

"Okay," the assistant coroner said. There were sounds of the man dialing the phone.

"Rachel, hi, it's Bill. Sorry to bother you, but there's a young woman here who says she knows something about yesterday's attack – why it happened – and she wants to talk to you." There was a pause. "She wants to know why you just don't go to the police with your information."

"Because I need to ask her something first. I think it may have to do with one of her cases, but I could be entirely wrong, in which case I don't want to bother the police."

"She says she needs to ask you something first. She's not certain that the attack involves one of your cases, and she doesn't want to bother the police until she is certain."

"Thank you for speaking with me. Heather Barnes. I'm with Homeland Security. I think the attack on you had to do with Michael Michtenbaum."

It was obvious the coroner on the other end of the line was talking but neither men could hear what was said. Jeremy could tell Dragon had turned up his laptop volume to as high as it would go and was straining to hear. Whatever device he is using to record Heather's conversation, thought Jeremy, at least it isn't in her ear.

"Of course," came Heather's voice again.

There wasn't an alarm clock in the room where Mary Beth slept and when she woke, she was afraid she had overslept as the sun was pouring into the room. For a moment she didn't know where she was, then remembered she was in the home of Mitch and Celia Michtenbaum, the parents of her childhood friend, Michael Ray Michtenbaum, whose funeral was today. She had arrived at their home late yesterday afternoon and the three of them had spent the evening together. They had cried together, reminisced about the many memories they each had of Michael – Ray, as his parents called him - held each other, and met with other friends who stopped by throughout the evening to offer their condolences. They had also gone to the funeral home so that Celia and Mitch, together and separately, could spend some last time alone with their son.

Mary Beth had never seen Mitch or Celia in the state they were currently in – one of total devastation and grief. Celia managed to smile a couple of times during the evening when she thought of a particularly happy moment with her son, but it wasn't the radiant smile that she normally wore.

Her heart ached for them. Michael was their only son and he had always been such a good son. He hadn't given them any grandchildren, and Mary Beth knew Celia was heartbroken over that more than ever now. Grandchildren and great-grandchildren would have given them something of Michael to keep with them forever and ease the pain somewhat in the years to come.

Mary Beth checked the time on her phone and relaxed somewhat since it was only 8:30. She had overslept but there was still plenty of time before the visitation service started. She wanted to fix breakfast for her friends so jumped in the shower and hurredly dressed and put on her makeup. She was one that could be ready to go in 20 minutes.

She was surprised to see Mitch and Celia already in the kitchen with breakfast prepared. They weren't eating, but wanted her to do so. Mary Beth was going to apologize for sleeping late and for not having breakfast prepared for them, but quickly realized Celia needed to be doing something such as fixing breakfast for a guest, so she kept her mouth shut other than to thank them for the wonderful spread of fruit, bacon, eggs, pancakes, orange juice and coffee sitting on the table.

They were already dressed in their best black. They were going through the motions of sipping a little coffee, setting a plate for

Mary Beth, trying to make a little conversation, but Mary Beth knew it was going to be an extremely difficult day for them. She glanced out the patio doors at the beautiful sunny day and thought it just wasn't right that the day should be so bright and lovely when the hearts of her friends were so overcast and gloomy. She remembered the words of an old song "Why does the sun go on shining? Why does the sea rush to shore? Don't they know it's the end of the world...." She guessed that's how Mitch and Celia were feeling right now.

The funeral home personnel had been so helpful. One young man had stopped by the house the evening before to get a few remaining photos that Celia wanted to use in a collage of Ray's life that would be displayed at the visitation and funeral service. They had taken on every duty they could to spare Mitch and Celia the pain of having to do it, and the couple were grateful, although they were clearly in too great a state of grief to really understand the amount of help they were being given. The same young man had apparently come to their home the day before as well and gone through the many albums of photos, suggesting ones the couple might want to select. If he had not taken the initiative to gather the photos himself, they would not have had the strength to do it. Celia could clean and cook right now, but she couldn't look at smiling photos of her handsome son whom she would never see again, and there were no other relatives to help them.

Mary Beth helped Celia clear the table and the three hugged and cried once more before they left for the services.

Bernie woke from his nap to the sound of his little travel alarm clock that he had set for 9:30 a.m. He was lying back in the driver's seat of his car, parked near the Greenwood Cemetery and the county morgue. He sat up slightly and saw that there were now three cars in the parking lot of the morgue where there had only been one before. One of the new additions was a police cruiser. He also noticed another car parked inside the cemetery near the entrance and within view of the morgue. A man was outside the car placing flowers on a nearby grave.

Bernie decided to stay low. James Bond would in this

situation, he was sure. Keep out of sight and keep your eyes and ears open. You're on a mission, perhaps a very dangerous mission, perhaps an impossible mission. Your mission, should you decide to accept it, which I have already accepted, is to protect Heather Barnes. This tape will self-destruct in five seconds. Five...four...three... Bernie was also a Mission Impossible fan.

Bernie was certain the man in the cemetery was watching the morgue as well. He was squatting by a grave, but his face was up and looking in the direction of the morgue. Bernie then saw the man make a phone call. I think I really am involved in something here, thought Bernie, and he felt both excitement and fear as he crouched back down out of sight.

When his heart stopped pounding, Bernie slid up enough to see the man and the morgue again. He looked at his watch as well. 9:50 a.m. The visitation service would be starting soon and he wanted to find a good spot near the funeral home to stake out the building and watch for Heather. She might arrive on time or perhaps sometime after ten – the visitation lasted two hours and many people, he knew, would come later and stay for the funeral at noon. So he decided to stay where he was and see what happened.

A few minutes later, several people came out of the morgue. There were two police officers and two women. One of them was Heather. Bernie tried to contain his excitement at seeing her, and almost jumped up but caught himself in time. He didn't know if the man in the cemetery had noticed his car parked on the street not far away, but he might notice if there was movement in the car. Heather got in a car by herself and the other woman got in the police car with the officers. They left and Bernie noticed that the man in the cemetery got in his car as well and followed after them down Route 4 towards High Street.

"Let's see just how good of a secret agent you really are," said Bernie aloud. He made an assumption that the cars were heading for the funeral home, and took an entirely different route, hoping to arrive and park before the other three cars got there.

⌒〜⌒〜⌒

"Hello," Jeremy answered his desk phone.

"You got the fax I assume," said Dragon. "Have you found

anything yet?"

Jeremy had expected the call from his boss an hour ago, but he knew why he hadn't had time to call – both of them had been listening to Heather's conversation with the coroner Rachel Curry about Michael Michtenbaum. There was now no doubt in Jeremy's mind that Heather was in danger. He wondered if she had listened to her cell phone messages or read the text he'd sent to her. He hoped so, for her sake.

"Yes, I've found the man. He's Russian, former KGB, real name Viktor Andronikov. He's apparently been in the U.S. for ten or eleven years, and no one has seen or heard from him during that time, until now I assume?" He was baiting Dragon.

"Really?" Dragon sounded surprised and perplexed, but didn't seem to have heard the question at the end of Jeremy's recitation.

No not really. Jeremy was thinking so loudly he thought Dragon might hear. This is just the story the Secretary wants me to tell you, so to you the killer is Viktor Andronikov. To the Secretary, he is Collin Reuth, code name Raptor.

"Spell the name for me."

Jeremy spelled the Russian name, which was of an actual former KGB operative who looked somewhat like the photo of Michtenbaum's killer.

Dragon hung up and Jeremy watched him shut down and close his laptop, taking it with him as he left the hotel.

He stayed on Dragon with the satellite Samuel and simultaneously queued up then played back the recorded video from Audrey of the hotel parking lot from 7:50 a.m. to 8:30 a.m. to see when Heather had left and to hopefully discover how her departure had evaded him. On the recording he saw her leave, dressed beautifully in black and white with a splash of red at her neck, and get into a red sedan. The sedan was parked in the very first spot outside the front entrance of the hotel so she was only visible two or three seconds at most. He zoomed in and got the plate number, make and model of the car. Then he noticed the second car, a tan sedan, leave the lot immediately after her, following in the same direction. He backed the tape up again to get a look at the man even though he already knew it was Dragon's second hired killer. He got a few still shots of that car as well showing the plate number.

Jeremy logically could understand how he missed seeing Heather walk from the canopied front door only a few yards to the red car – and he did remember seeing the red and tan cars leave the Marriott parking lot - but he was still mad at himself. How many other important things have I missed? he thought. He prided himself on having one eye focused on four screens at all times, with the other eye on the other four screens. He was incredibly disgusted and had to talk himself into letting it go before he missed something else important while in the process of beating himself up.

Dragon was not driving towards the funeral home and Jeremy kept an eye on him. He no longer needed to watch Jon Moore today so moved that satellite over the funeral home for the time being. He hadn't seen Mary Beth yet this morning and checked her office to see if she'd gone in to work since she had taken off a day and a half. Her car wasn't in the parking lot so he checked a few other common places, but realized he didn't know her common places on a Saturday besides home. He didn't usually check on her on Saturdays. Maybe it was time to invade her privacy and check on her through her own eyes and ears. After all, Michael Michtenbaum had died without him knowing it. He would be mortified if a second subject met the same fate on his watch. He had documented Dragon's keystrokes equivalent to the user name and password to access Mary Beth's implant recordings and entered them on the computer where her satellite forlornly watched an empty house.

He turned up the sound just a bit on Michael Michtenbaum's ear, as he was now calling the implant that was in Dragon's possession. He could hear muffled sounds, such as car noises, as he had heard before, but nothing that could help him, as he suspected.

Jeremy was still wondering how Dragon had listened in to the conversation of Rachel Curry and Heather. Had he planted a bug in Rachel's office at the morgue? That would make sense since Johnson had been there twice. How did he know to listen at that time? He had sent his new guy to follow Heather, but if the man had followed her to the morgue and then called Dragon to let him know, Jeremy would have known – he would have heard Dragon's cell ring. Maybe he texted him? Jeremy didn't recall Dragon even looking at his cell phone all morning, but of course I could have missed it, he bitterly reminded himself.

The funeral home parking lot was filling with mourners coming to pay their last respects to Michael Ray Michtenbaum. Jeremy searched for the red sedan and was pleased to see it pull in right at that moment, behind a police cruiser. They both parked near the rear of the lot. He decided to try Heather's cell phone again and quickly punched in the number before she was out of her car. This time she answered it.

"Hello?" A pause. "Hello? Is anyone there?"

Jeremy hung up the phone as if it had stung him and stared at the computer screen of Michael Michtenbaum. He was trying to make sense of what he had just heard. Heather's voice saying hello was being transmitted from Michael's ear. How is that possible? How did Dragon manage that? Is it on her person some way? How?

Her purse? Maybe the guy who followed her slipped it on her or in her purse. Jeremy was stunned.

He felt terrible that he still didn't warn her of the danger she was in, but he couldn't let Dragon hear him talking to Heather and give away his covert operation. He had an assignment from the Secretary herself and he never jeopardized an assignment, especially for personal reasons. He wasn't sure if these would be considered personal reasons or not. Heather wasn't supposed to be in Ohio, at least he didn't think so. He wasn't supposed to know she was there, and he wouldn't have known if it weren't for Bernie. Again, he wondered if he should let the Secretary know about Heather in case she wasn't aware.

The assignment might have already been compromised. If Heather listens to my voice-mails on speaker, or has already done so since Dragon planted the Michtenbaum ear implant on her, then he will know that I am watching him. Still, Jeremy decided to send her another text message. He knew that her phone was now working.

Mary Beth's new screen, the one that showed live video and audio from the viewpoint of her right eye and ear, had come to life and she was alive and well. She was in a room full of people. He could hear all the voices of the many people in the room, as if he himself were there. In a way, he was. He was seeing exactly what Mary Beth was seeing and hearing exactly what she was hearing. It was quite amazing.

He could also hear many voices, although quieter, coming from Michael Michtenbaum's ear. The transmitter was definitely with Heather and she had entered the funeral home as he could see via the satellite positioned there. With both Heather's audio and Mary Beth's audio, there was quite a lot of talking going on, but the loudest and clearest voices were that of Heather and the coroner, Rachel Curry, and that of Mary Beth and the people right by her. It was too much to listen to, so he turned off Mary Beth's audio in order to concentrate on Heather's.

"Come and I'll introduce you to Michael Michtenbaum's parents." It was Rachel's voice talking to Heather, Jeremy knew.

He heard another familiar female voice quite clearly. "Celia, I'm going to the ladies room. I'll be right back." It was Mary Beth's voice! He looked at Mary Beth's screen and saw Heather off to the side. Mary Beth was at the visitation as well! So she must have known Michael. Of course that's possible. They were born in the same town, were the exact same age, probably went to the same schools.

The woman in front of Mary Beth, apparently Celia, Michael's mother, replied "Okay Mary Beth."

As Mary Beth turned to walk, her eyes viewed, even though she didn't really see, Heather Barnes, who had a look of extreme surprise and then alarm on her face. Heather quickly turned from Mary Beth's view.

She realizes she's just been recorded by Mary Beth's eye implant. Jeremy was impressed at how quickly Heather understood what had happened. Maybe now she'll get out of there and go to Fiji where she belongs.

Bernie had a clear view of Heather's car in the parking lot from the street where he was parked. He had not seen the tan sedan anywhere so was beginning to question whether the man in the cemetery really was following Heather and the police car.

People were coming and going from the parking lot as the visitation service continued. Bernie sat and watched for more than half an hour. Then he saw him. It was the same man, he was certain of it. The man was at the far end of the lot where both Heather's car and the police cruiser were parked. He was on foot so must have parked on another street and walked there. He was carrying a small duffle bag.

Bernie had brought his spy kit with him that he bought at the Spy Store on F Street in D.C. So far he hadn't had any occasion to use it. It included a tiny pair of binoculars, but they were quite powerful. Putting the glasses to his eyes, he watched as the man swiftly and expertly slid under Heather's car, stayed about ten seconds and then repeated the process with the police cruiser. He was gone in under a minute. It happened so fast and Bernie was so shocked that he forgot to use his spy camera to take photos of the deed, which Bernie felt sure was the placement of car bombs beneath the two cars.

What should I do? Bernie got out of his car and as he waited for traffic to ease in order to cross the street to the funeral home, he saw Heather, the coroner and the two police officers come out a back door of the building and walk towards their cars. They were now much closer to their cars than if they'd come out the front door.

There was no time to wait for traffic. "Stop!" Bernie screamed as loud as he could and he ran across the street, with one car barely missing him and giving him a long blast of its horn. "Stop! Heather!"

Hearing her name caused Heather to turn and look. The police were also looking. "Don't get in your cars!"

He was running and was out of breath by the time he reached them, more from the drama of the situation than from the length of the run.

"Bernie?" Heather was staring at him as if he had two heads. "What are you doing here?"

"You're in danger." He was leaning over with his hands on his thighs, breathing heavily. "So are you," he nodded at the coroner.

"What's going on here?" one of the police officers asked Bernie, putting a hand on his sidearm.

"I just saw a man plant bombs under both of your cars." Bernie stood now and could breathe a little better.

One officer immediately went to the cars and looked underneath. He nodded affirmative at the other officer.

"Which way did he go?"

Bernie pointed and started telling the story, but the officer stopped him for a moment while he called in the report and the bomb squad.

Soon, the funeral parking lot and surrounding area was overrun with police vehicles and a bomb squad van. Mourners were notified to stay inside the funeral home until further notice and those arriving were turned away from the parking lot. The area around the affected cars and several other cars was taped off and Bernie, Heather, Rachel and the two officers were placed protectively in an armored vehicle that arrived on the scene within three minutes of the called report.

Bernie told his story several times about the man at the cemetery and then seeing him here. The police showed Bernie the sketch artist portrait of the man who had attacked Rachel the day before, but he shook his head – it wasn't the same guy.

"Are you sure? Perhaps he changed his appearance?" the police questioned.

"I don't think so." It was a firm statement of certainty from Bernie. "This man has a lot more hair than the man in the picture, and it's darker. He is better looking than the guy in the picture as well. His face is more..." he was looking for the word, "chiseled." He was pleased with that word.

"Tell us again what he was wearing." Bernie wondered why they kept asking him the same thing. "As I've already told you," he wanted to make that point clear, "he had on dark slacks, a medium blue shirt, and a dark sport coat at the cemetery but didn't have the coat on when he planted the bombs."

Bernie wanted to talk to Heather, not the police, and he turned around to look at the women in the back of the armored van. Heather was visibly shaken as was Rachel. They were being consoled and questioned by a female officer. Rachel had asked for a tranquilizer to calm her down. Almost being murdered twice in as many days will rattle you a bit. The two police officers whose cruiser was targeted were a bit nervous as well. They would soon be attending the funerals of their two fellow officers who were murdered and were now feeling the effects of the knowledge that they, too, had almost met that same fate.

"Are you alright, Heather?" Bernie still had his head turned and was looking at her. The questioning officer felt certain the little man was telling the truth and allowed him some time to check on his friend.

"I'll be okay," she said, hardly looking at him and then, as if it hit her at that moment, she looked straight at him, "Oh, Bernie, I haven't thanked you. You saved all our lives. Thank you so much!"

Dorgan couldn't believe his bad luck. Not only had Michael Michtenbaum been murdered, but he had been murdered by a professional killer, which strengthened the likelihood that Michtenbaum's death had something to do with the Freedom Project. In addition, another attempt on the coroner's life had failed, as well as the one on Heather's. Who was this Bernie guy who had seen Jones plant the bombs *and* saw him earlier tailing Heather. Were two agents sent to watch him? What the hell was going on?

This Bernie guy would now be able to identify Jones and was on his way to police headquarters right now to give a description to a sketch artist. "I can't keep killing off my agents, even though I'm getting pretty sick and tired of incompetency," Dorgan grumbled angrily to himself.

Was Bernie also aware of the Freedom Project? Wait a minute. Bernie. Surely this isn't the same Bernie that works in the archives room. At least I think his name's Bernie. Couldn't be. He's a file clerk! Dorgan felt as though he was in some kind of strange dream. How many people know about this? If the coroner hadn't told the police before, she's sure to do so now. Perhaps it's better to go with Plan B where the project is revealed, but those currently behind it are protected. Otherwise, the body count is going to be very high.

Plan B was still not his first choice. He wasn't ready to concede defeat yet. If I can still get the implant from Michtenbaum's eye, there will be no evidence on that body. The only other evidence is in Mary Beth Singer and Jonathan Moore. Is that the better way to go? End the project and let the conspiracy theory nuts who want to claim the experiment ever existed try and prove it? Some files would need to be destroyed as well, but that's the easy part.

Dorgan burned the note that he was going to leave under the park bench for Jones. He would let the agent proceed at the cemetery later today. Surely the man would have the intelligence to disguise himself adequately and pay better attention to any possible stalkers. If not, he deserved to be caught.

Dorgan continued to sit on the bench with his computer on his lap and listen to what was being said by Heather and those around her. He selected this park as it was quiet and uninhabited, and he preferred the beauty of the park on a day like today. He definitely needed something soothing to calm his nerves. All five of the passengers of the armored van were moved to the police station, both for their own protection and to question them further, hoping that they might know some additional piece of information that would help identify the bomber, or yesterday's killer.

So far, neither Heather nor Rachel had mentioned Michael Ray Michtenbaum's name to the police. Of course, they were still recovering from their trauma and hadn't been questioned thoroughly so perhaps they still intended to do so. Bernie was apparently with the sketch artist away from Heather and Rachel as Dorgan could no longer hear his voice. Heather asked to use the restroom and Dorgan could hear her footsteps going down a hallway.

Dorgan looked up at the beautiful sky and the serenity of the nature around him. He so seldom took the time to notice or appreciate it. His entire adult life, for the past 34 years, had been in service to his country but in a way that most people wouldn't understand. He would never be considered a hero by the masses, not only because they would never know of his service, but also because most wouldn't approve if they did know. He was not a bad man – he was a good man who did bad things when necessary for the greater good. The Freedom Project was definitely an example of that fact.

He had only been a CIA field agent for three years when he was appointed to the top-secret Freedom Project committee and assigned the on-going monitoring of the three project subjects. He, like everyone who first hears of the project, which he now grimly reminded himself was a lot more people since Michtenbaum died, was appalled by the audacity of his government to monitor private citizens and violate every core value relating to personal freedom and privacy that we have.

But as time went on, he grew to accept and even justify the project in his mind as a critical step forward in protecting the freedom of his great country. He personally did not overly invade the privacy of the individuals he monitored, although he didn't know about his predecessor or anyone else who had access to the special site, which was actually within a Central Intelligence Agency's server. He knew that many homeland experimental projects such as the Freedom Project and MK-ULTRA tasks were the clandestine assignments of CIA.

He knew that since the inception of the Freedom Project, a few more, similar, technologically advanced projects, involving larger groups of people, had been initiated and were still on-going. He was involved in those as well, up until nine years ago when he made the move from CIA to DHS. He had grown tired of constantly being on the road on undercover missions…extremely dangerous missions. Two bullets in his gut that grounded him for six months helped him make the decision to retire from field work and take a quiet, safe desk job for the next three years as a high level director at the agency. However, a change in directorship at the CIA and conflict in personalities forced him out. He used his connections and was soon working again in a high level position at Homeland Security.

The only top secret project that the CIA asked him to maintain was the initial Freedom Project. It was his to oversee until his death or the death of all of the participants. It was his to protect and ensure its continued secrecy or die trying, and that's what he intended to do. He would never give up the commitment he made to his former boss, the Director of the CIA, and to those in the highest posts of government who depended on him to keep the country's, and their, most critical political, military and technological secrets.

Dorgan heard the flushing of a commode, quickly followed by "Oh no!" as Heather cried out. He heard the clatter of items and listened more closely. She had to still be in the bathroom and he didn't hear any voices, only scuttling noises as if Heather was picking up or moving items on a shelf or the sink. Perhaps she dropped her purse, he guessed, and he hoped the tiny receiver/recorder that he was now listening to wasn't one of the items that fell out. He heard water running and he envisioned her pretty tear-stained eyes staring into the mirror as she touched up her makeup before returning to the other room.

Jon Moore awoke feeling rested. The three sleeping pills and beer had done the trick. Even though the buzzing in his head was as loud as ever and the piercing screech started within minutes of his waking, he at least could bear the stress much better with a rested body and mind. The screeching stopped after a few minutes.

He looked at the clock and realized that he had been asleep for sixteen hours. He could never remember a time in his entire life that he had slept sixteen hours straight. He was glad. He really needed the rest.

His wife left him a note on the coffee table by the couch saying that she had run to the grocery store and would be back shortly. She put a P.S. – I have something important to tell you! and drew a little smiley face. Hopefully she's not pregnant, and he smiled at his little joke.

He was also smiling because, even though it was Saturday, he was going to call his doctor and ask him to admit him to the hospital for tests. If the doctor wouldn't, or Jon couldn't get hold of him, he would go to the emergency room. One way or the other, he was determined to take steps today to find out the cause of this unbearable problem.

He went to the kitchen where Carol had already made coffee. He poured himself a cup and a bowl of raisin bran. He was looking up his doctor's number when Carol walked in the back door with groceries in her arms.

"Here, give those to me," and he reached to take the bags from her arms. "Are there more in the car?"

"Yes, but I'll get them. You finish eating." She smiled at him. "Feeling better this morning?"

"Yes, at the moment at least. I really got a lot of needed sleep."

"I'm so glad." She sat down at the table instead of going out for the other groceries. "When I came home yesterday, you were asleep on the couch. Later I was sitting and reading in the recliner, the house was quiet, and I heard a noise."

"What kind of noise?" he asked, not sure where she was going with this.

"*Your* noise – the screeching noise in your head. I heard it!" His mouth was full of raisin bran and although he started to talk, Carol continued, "I wasn't sure what it was at first, because it was not very loud, but I walked towards the couch, and it grew louder. I crouched down and put my ear up to yours…it was definitely coming from your ear. I still can't believe it!"

The two got up from the table and hugged each other. Both felt strangely happy about this discovery. Jon never doubted his wife's love and sympathy for his growing problem, but now he felt there was a closer bond between them and that she would fight harder with him to fix his pain. He told her about his decision to call the doctor and get the tests. She hugged him again and said she would call – he should finish eating.

Heather needed to get Rachel alone to talk to her. They couldn't go in the restroom as Heather had just dumped her purse to find and get rid of the small device that had been planted there. The device was now out of her purse and well hidden in a corner of the bathroom behind a trash can. She searched her mind as to how the device was planted in her purse and she remembered the man she met in the elevator that morning. He was the only person she could think of with whom she had come into close contact, besides Rachel, the assistant coroner and the police. She thought of all the people in the funeral home, but realized that Jeremy's text was sent as she was entering that building, so it had to have already been there.

When first entering the bathroom stall, she had checked her text and phone messages, which she hadn't had a chance to do all morning. She had two text messages from that Jeremy guy at work and read them first, after which she immediately checked his two voice messages. Her mind was still reeling from the messages, which she reviewed, then deleted. She had read the second text message first, sent to her only an hour ago:

"*Heather, it's Jeremy from work. I don't know if you've gotten my other messages yet, but you're in grave danger. Dorgan and his hired assassin may be after you as well as the coroner. He has a bug planted on you or in your purse and can hear everything you say. Find and get rid of it. If you haven't listened to my voice-mails yet, don't put them on speaker or he'll hear. Delete all messages."*

The other text was from yesterday at 7:15 p.m. Yesterday! How could she have not checked her phone!

"It's Jeremy from work. I've left two voice-mails for you. You may be in danger. Dorgan and man who attacked coroner and killed two policemen are in your hotel. Be careful."

Dorgan was here in Ohio and was the one who just tried to kill her, Rachel and the two police officers with the car bombs. He was behind the other attack on Rachel and the killing of the two policemen, meaning he was after the implants in Michael Michtenbaum. Would he go after Mary Beth Singer as well? Did he know she was here? Of course he would if he was the one viewing Mary Beth's eye and ear implants. Maybe Jeremy was the one who was responsible for monitoring Mary Beth and the other two. How had Jeremy known she was here?

Heather walked slowly back towards the room where Rachel was seated, dozens of questions running through her mind. She, Rachel and the two police officers who had been assigned to stay with Rachel were still waiting for instructions as to what they should do. They were all still distraught over the fact that they'd almost died only half an hour ago. The bombs had now been removed from her rental car and from the police cruiser, she had overheard the bomb squad leader state.

She continued to stand in the room and look about at the various glass-encased rooms around her. She saw Bernie in a room beyond the one where she was now standing, and he looked up and waved to her. She smiled and waved back. She wanted to talk to him as well and find out why he was in Hamilton.

She was still trying to figure out Jeremy's role in all of this. He was assigned to watch Dorgan, so perhaps in that surveillance he had seen her at the hotel. Which satellite is he using, she wondered, and groaned at the thought of Samuel or Delilah in the hands of a horny 20-something year old kid.

Had Dorgan heard her conversation with Rachel at the morgue? Yes, of course he had if the device had been planted in her purse by the man in the elevator. Then he would know exactly how much each of them knew. That's why he tried to kill her as well. Since when was Homeland Security in charge of this project? She knew about most project and mission names, even if she wasn't always up to speed on the details. In her years at DHS, she had never heard of the project before. She only knew about the file that her father had – a CIA file. Dorgan had been CIA for 20 years. But Bernie did have the old file in DHS archives. How was that explained?

The two police officers left Rachel for a moment, and Heather walked over to her. "I need to talk to you alone when we can. Don't say anything to the police yet about the implant until we've talked, okay?" Rachel nodded as the two officers came back.

Heather tried to recall exactly what she said and what Rachel had said a couple of hours ago while at the morgue. The two police officers who were with Rachel wanted to sit in while the two women spoke, but Rachel said that it wasn't necessary – they could stand guard outside her office door. Bill, the Assistant Coroner, also offered to stay with Rachel, but she dismissed him as well.

So they had been alone in Rachel's office for over half an hour before leaving for the funeral home. But they weren't really alone as Dorgan had apparently listened to everything they said. Jeremy perhaps as well, and he might even have been able to see them.

Heather closed her eyes and thought of the conversation that had taken place.

Suddenly, the room in which Heather was sitting and waiting became noisy and chaotic. Something had happened and police were scrambling to leave. "What's going on?" Rachel shouted to whomever might answer. The Police Chief motioned her into his office and her two detail officers, and Heather, followed. The Police Chief frowned at Heather and was going to stop her from entering his office, but Rachel said it was okay to let her hear as well.

"A man has been found dead - at the Hamiltonian – I mean the Marriott." He looked at Rachel when he said, "We believe the deceased may be the man who attacked you and killed our two officers. I'm going to call Bill right now to go over and check the body."

"I can go." Rachel's statement wasn't very convincing.

"No. Under the circumstances, I think it's best if Bill goes. I'm going to have these two take you home now. We'll have two other officers take their place later at shift change. Stay home and get some rest. Your cars," and he nodded to the police as well as to Heather, "are both clear and under guard by the way. We may need for both of you to come back later," he said, looking at the two women, "but for now you can go."

The ear-piercing scream that emanated from the hallway of the second floor of the Marriott Hotel woke the only guest on that floor still in his room at that hour, and he ran in boxer shorts and a T-shirt to the hallway to see what was wrong.

"Socorro! Socorro! El esta muerto! Auxilio!" The man ran towards the screaming woman, which frightened her even more. She pointed into the room and backed down the hallway, moving behind her cleaning cart, to stay away from the half-naked man approaching. He saw the dead body as soon as he entered the room and moved halfway across the room to stare at it a moment, then quickly retreated, as the Hispanic maid had done as well. "I'll call the police! *Policia,*" he shouted to her, holding his hand to his ear as if it were a phone, and running back towards his room. The dead man looked like the face they had shown on the news last night – the one wanted for killing two cops.

Hotel security arrived within a few minutes and the police weren't far behind. Even the hotel security person didn't enter the room more than a few feet, so he told the police he was sure the crime scene had not been disturbed by any of the three people now standing there who had seen the dead man.

An Hispanic officer questioned the maid, while another officer focused on the guest who had called in the death.

The police secured the scene, not certain whether the man had died from natural or unnatural causes, but overly cautious due to the fact that he might be their cop-killer. The Assistant Coroner arrived within 20 minutes and began examining the body.

"Bag the food items in the trash over there," he told them. "This appears to be a poisoning from the amount of saliva and the odor of his mouth. At first glance, I would say this is a murder." He checked the victim's liver temperature and estimated the time of death to be between 6 and 8 p.m. the evening before.

Dozens of photos of the body and the room were taken and the victim's hands were bagged to preserve any possible poison, skin cells or other residue that might be on them.

A few other hotel guests had gathered outside in the hall once word of a death on the second floor got around. When the rumor spread that it was the cop killer who had died, someone called the newspaper and a reporter and photographer arrived breathlessly on the second floor as the paramedics and coroner were removing the body from the hotel room. There was a click, and a flash, as the photographer captured the covered body on a gurney and Assistant Coroner Bill Simmons walking towards the elevator.

Jeremy read the three-word text that Heather sent back in response to his second text message. "Got it – thanks."

Finally he had been able to warn her about Dragon and about the transmitter hidden somewhere on her, most likely in her purse.

He was still trying to figure out why Bernie had gone to Ohio. He was sure it was the same Bernie – he recognized his voice. From his satellite view it looked like him and Heather knew him. The little gnome must have gone last night. Why? Was he that concerned about Heather? Well, look what happened. If Bernie hadn't been there, Heather and at least three others would probably be dead right now. Just when you think you have someone figured out, he goes and does something to totally change your belief system. Go figure!

Jeremy really needed to use the facilities after six plus hours of drinking coffee. Dragon hadn't moved from his park bench for two hours, even after he realized that Heather no longer had Michtenbaum's ear in her purse. He had not only lost the implant, probably for good, but he'd also lost the ability to listen in on Heather. That realization was definite only ten or so minutes ago. Jeremy could see the dejected look on Dragon's face and Dragon still hadn't moved. He had closed his laptop and was just sitting there.

Audrey showed that there was a lot of commotion at the Marriott with several police cars and an ambulance arriving, and Jeremy assumed they had found Johnson's dead body.

Mary Beth was still at the funeral home and the actual funeral was just now starting. She apparently was good friends with the Michtenbaums as she stayed by their side every minute. Jeremy kept the sound down on that computer as it was too distracting.

He fidgeted on his desk stool. "Can't wait any longer." Jeremy hit the button that shut down all of his screens and ran to the restroom down the hall.

When he returned, Dragon was gone. So was his car. "Just great!" and he slammed his fist on the desk. He moved Samuel out to a view of 4 or 5 square blocks. "He couldn't have gotten far – I was only gone two minutes." He didn't see any car resembling Dragon's. He followed what would be the most likely route back to the hotel, thinking that may be where Dragon was headed, but he didn't see his car anywhere. "My timing is really off today," he grumbled.

Would Dragon go to the funeral, Jeremy wondered. I wouldn't think so. He might go to the cemetery to make sure Michael is put in the ground, but that service doesn't start for another hour and a half, and they won't actually bury him until after the service. Maybe he's just going to get something to eat. Don't panic man, you'll find him soon.

Jeremy had gotten a hit almost immediately on the photos of the man Dragon had talked to this morning at the side entrance. He knew he had some good facial shots of the guy. The man was an independent mercenary for hire and was best known in the mercenary-for-hire circles as an integral part of JSOC and Blackwater. Jeremy called and told the Secretary, as he hadn't had a chance to do it earlier. She had requested to remain informed of Dragon's movements and contacts. He didn't mention anything to her about Heather or Bernie, or the device planted in Heather's purse.

Jeremy no longer had Heather in his sight or audio, and although he knew she was okay, he wanted to keep track of her just the same. He checked the GPS in her phone and saw that it was moving, which surprised him. She's in a car? Maybe the police are taking her back to her car now. They should give her a protective detail too since she was targeted with a bomb specifically for her. Perhaps she's in the car with her police escort.

Jeremy loved GPS. The original Global Positioning System was formed by eighteen satellites, six in each of three orbital planes. Young as he was, Jeremy remembered when he was only able to calculate a geographical position to an accuracy of a meter using one of those satellites. Now, the GPS advances allowed him to pinpoint a location to within half an inch or even less. "Heather, I'll know not only which car you're in, but which seat, where your purse is, and which part of your purse your phone is in."

Since he lost Dragon, Jeremy moved the satellite Samuel to follow Heather for now. He would much rather see her in person than as a blip on his screen which is all her phone GPS allowed. Samuel and Jeremy quickly found Heather's red rental car crossing the river heading west on Main Street. A police cruiser was behind her so perhaps the police were watching out for her. He hoped so. It was difficult to get specific audio on a moving target such as a car since there was so much other outside noise. He could do it, but it took a lot of effort and he would have to follow very closely. He simply didn't have the luxury of doing so right now, so just watched the two cars from a comfortable 50 foot view.

Whoa! Jeremy saw an elbow stick out of the passenger side of Heather's car and zoomed in, trying to get a side angle to see who was in the passenger seat. It's only Bernie, surmised Jeremy. His car must still be at the funeral home.

Heather's red car made a left turn, but the police cruiser continued straight on Main Street. He assumed the police detail was still with Rachel and they were heading for her house. Heather must be taking Bernie back to his car.

Jeremy's cell phone rang – the caller ID said private but he answered. "Jeremy, it's Dorgan. Are you still at the office by any chance? I need another favor."

Jeremy's suspicion meter zoomed to high. He got goosebumps on his arms when Dragon said "by any chance." He decided it was best to tell the truth. "Actually, I am still here. Thought I might as well work a little since you have to pay me for the day anyway."

"Good. I need you to watch someone for me for a little while. He will be at the graveside service of the man who died the other day – the coordinates are 39.404090, -84.542601. He'll be one of the grave closers so may not get there until the service is over. I don't know what the other grave closer looks like, but it doesn't matter...watch them both. This is critical - I also need for you to watch at enough distance to see if there is anyone else around. If anyone is watching them, I want to know. Look all around the surrounding streets, inside the cemetery, anywhere someone could be hiding and watching, okay?"

"Sure, okay. How do I let you know?"

"Feed the live video to my computer. Any questions?"

"No, I got it. By the way, sorry you're not able to enjoy this vacation time with your wife." Jeremy wondered if Dragon even remembered he was supposed to be "vacationing" with his wife.

"Who says I'm not enjoying my vacation?" Dorgan replied without missing a beat.

Jeremy now had the creepy feeling that Dragon might actually be watching *him.* Dragon's office was situated right behind his desk and the top two thirds of that wall was glass. When sitting or standing in his office, Dragon was able to see Jeremy and his eight computer screens. There were screen covers on some monitors that greatly cut down any peripheral viewing, but nevertheless, he would be able to view any screen with which he had a straight line of sight. Jeremy knew this and for the most part didn't care – it was part of the job for the boss to watch his work.

Jeremy also knew there was a camera on the ceiling of Dragon's office that focused on Jeremy's workspace. Could Dragon be accessing that camera right now and watching him? If so, he would have to be using another computer as he definitely wasn't accessing it from the laptop that he had with him. I would have known from the keystroke monitoring he was constantly running on that computer if it was being accessed from his own computer, Jeremy thought. Has he been able to see that I've been watching him? Does he now know that I can access the Freedom Project videos? If he's watching, he can see that Mary Beth's and Michael's are both running. Has he watched me run two different men through the facial recognition software?

Or am I just feeling very paranoid today?

On an impulse, Jeremy located the Hamilton Library and moved Michtenbaum's satellite over it, careful to keep his body in front of the computer screen. As he suspected, there was Dragon's car parked on the street in front of the Lane Public Library. So you *are* there, and I'm *not* paranoid. You're on another computer. He quickly moved that satellite to the cemetery coordinates given to him by Dragon and then checked on all his other computers to assess how much Dragon now knew.

It's now a whole new ballgame. Dragon knows I'm watching him.

Jacob Barnes arrived home from New York in the early evening on Saturday. He brought his new girlfriend Susan to spend the week with him at his house and stay until his daughter Heather came back from vacation so that the two of them could meet. He hoped Susan liked his house as he wanted her to live there with him soon. And he hoped that the two women in his life would like each other as well, for he wanted to spend more time with both of them. He had focused solely on work for 4o years and he had now given notice that he would be retiring in three months, right after his 62nd birthday. It was time he had a life and some real happiness. He hadn't felt this happy since he had asked Heather's mother to marry him and had built this house for their family.

"It's beautiful!" exclaimed Susan as Jacob pulled the car into the driveway of the large white colonial. The lawn and shrubbery were meticulous and Jacob was glad the lawn service had recently cut the grass and edged the driveway and sidewalk. He continued up the drive and through a carport attached to the side of the house leading on to a separate three-car garage at the rear of the property. A glimmering pool took up a small portion of the expansive back yard and expensive but virtually unused patio furniture was strategically placed on the deck, patio and in the pool area.

"I love the yard, especially the back." Susan squeezed his hand as she said it. Jacob knew that Susan was used to an elegant New York townhome, but no yard. He hoped she was the pool and patio type, because he had never been, not because he didn't want to be - he just never took the time. He only remembered getting in this pool three or four times, when Heather was fairly young. But he vowed to change all that. "Let's go for a swim this evening. It's in the 80's so it will feel good."

Jacob watched Susan marvel over the kitchen. She loved to cook and this was, indeed, a kitchen fit for a five-star chef. It had a large granite-topped U-shaped island with a built-in stove top and grill on one side, a sink and built-in chopping block, and room for a dozen or more tall stools to seat friends and family. This room was surely the heart of the house. Another two walls totaling at least 30 feet in length had three built-in ovens, one over-sized, as well as another stainless steel stovetop. The cabinets went on and on above and below the endless counter space. The stainless refrigerator door was huge and when Susan opened it, she gasped to see that it was actually a walk-in with a freezer door inside the refrigerator. It looked like an appliance a large restaurant would own. "How many hundred people do you plan to feed, Jacob?" Susan asked lovingly. "It's as large as my spare bedroom." There was a large table with eight chairs on the other side of the island, with four more chairs lined along the completely windowed wall with a view of the back yard and pool. This was indeed a party house in need of a party.

Jacob found Heather's note and smiled, although he thought it a little odd that she would drive to his house just to get a suitcase. He knew she had plenty of luggage. Perhaps it was for Danny, he thought. He saw the broken wine glass in the kitchen trash, as she had said. He was a little disappointed that she had drunk the bottle of wine that he had bought specially for this evening with Susan, but it wasn't a big deal. He had more wine.

Jacob gave Susan a tour of the house, even his office, which he told her usually remained locked. He could tell that she was sufficiently impressed and she hugged him when they came back to the kitchen. "Thank you for inviting me here. I know I'm going to have a wonderful time this week."

"Make yourself at home. I'll fix us some dinner in a bit, but I'm going to go to my wine cellar in the basement and pick us out a special bottle. "

"Oh, let me fix dinner, Jacob. Please! You know I love to cook and it would be a dream to cook in this kitchen. " It was almost as if her cooking in this kitchen would be a rite of passage. He wanted her to be the woman of this house, soon, and he was happy that she loved the kitchen and wanted to cook the first meal of her visit there.

He put his arms around her and pulled her close. "Of course you can, sweetheart, as long as you're doing it because you want to and not because you feel you have to."

"I feel like a kid in a candy store in this room. I really want to try everything out. Just come find me if I get lost in the refrigerator." They both laughed.

"Don't worry if the door closes on you. It opens automatically with just a slight touch...freezer door too." He moved away from her to look in a cabinet. "I know I have pretty much stocked, but if you need me to run buy anything, let me know."

He left her happily flitting about the kitchen, opening cabinets and drawers, lifting down pots from the hanging rack above one portion of the island, and he went to the basement in search of wine befitting this wonderful occasion.

Jacob was alive today because he noticed the smallest details, paid attention to everything around him and was constantly on his guard. He had been one of the best and brightest of the CIA agents and had spent more than ten years of his career training other agents. Never trust anyone, he drilled into their heads. See that young mother with a baby stroller to your right, he used in one training exercise. Odds are great that she's just a young mother with her baby out for a stroll. But you can't let yourself dismiss her as harmless when your life is at stake. The woman pulled an automatic weapon out of the stroller and riddled the trainees with fake bullets. He put the trainees through that exercise numerous times - sometimes the woman was an innocent young mother with her baby; sometimes she ran screaming into the trainees' line of fire at the real enemy; other times she was part of the terrorist or other group they were fighting. Jacob rarely selected as agents any trainee who accidentally shot the innocent young mother or her baby or who didn't shoot or disable the woman who was a threat.

Watch every movement – everyone around you. Notice every detail – anything out of place, be it ever so slight.

Jacob froze when he noticed a tiny shard of glass outside the door to the basement safe room. Had Heather been down here? He picked up the shard to see if it appeared to be part of the shattered wine glass and was satisfied that it was. Why was she down here?

She didn't mention it in her note.

He punched in the code and opened the door to the safe room. He smelled a faint bleach odor and noticed the unusually clean spot on the floor by the couch. The boxes were in order but slightly askew from how he had left them. Although unmarked, he knew the boxes well enough to note that one box that had been on the top of the third column was now switched to the second position.

What were you looking for in here, Heather? And was it just you? He pulled down the two boxes that were misplaced and looked through them. The old Freedom Project file folder was in one of the boxes and he remembered that evening when he caught Heather in his office looking at the folder. He had never forgiven himself for his explosive reaction towards his young daughter, but he also knew that his emotional reaction was due to being terrified of her having any knowledge of that project. He had chosen to simply never talk of it again in the hope that she hadn't seen much and that she would forget about it, which had seemed to be the case.

Until now. He opened the folder and saw that the papers were not in the perfect alignment as he had left them. She had looked at this file. The terror he had felt for her fifteen years ago returned in that instant. Has she told Danny? Has she told anyone else? My sweet little girl, do you know what you've done?

Jacob ran back up the stairs. He tried to sound as normal as possible as he spoke to Susan. "I just remembered a critical project I need to finish for work. I'm so sorry. I've been having so much fun with you," and he gave her a little smile and kiss, "that I forgot all about this and it's overdue. I'll be in my office. Just call me when dinner's ready, okay. Sorry."

"Sure, honey, that's fine," she replied, but Jacob didn't hear. He was already into the next room and headed for his office.

Heather dropped Bernie off at his car which was still parked in front of the funeral home. The lot and street were full of cars as the funeral was now in progress. They both got out of Heather's car and looked under Bernie's car as well as under the hood, just in case. They agreed to meet later according to a quick plan they had devised while driving from police headquarters, which was only a few minutes away. There was not time to put much of a plan in place, but Heather had been thinking about it while still at police headquarters and quickly included Bernie in on her thoughts. He was more than happy to be included in whatever she asked of him and he waited to meet up with her later.

Heather had two important errands to run before attending the graveside service for Michael Michtenbaum, which would start in an hour. She had to hurry. She found a BoRics hair salon that accepted walk-in customers and asked them to take off almost all of her already short hair.

"I need to look like a man for a prank I'm pulling today and I'm in a huge hurry. There's a $100 tip in it for you if you can quickly darken my hair and then use a little of it to give me a fake mustache." Heather slipped the edge of a $100 bill out of her wallet for the hairdresser to see.

"How much time do I have?" the hairdresser was determined to get the $100 and was already cutting Heather's hair.

"Twenty minutes, twenty-five tops." She made a funny and apologetic face. "Sorry."

"Don't be," laughed the middle-aged woman . "A hundred bucks for twenty minutes work! I'll take that any day!"

The woman asked another hairdresser to mix up the hair color for her – she was using the comb-in kind that would wash out. The young hairdresser assisting her took some of Heather's hair from the floor and began brushing the dark hair dye onto it.

"Now run next door to Kroger and buy some clear glue or paste – make sure it's clear and make sure it isn't super glue!" Heather smiled appreciatively at the woman, who not only was making quick work of her unusual request but also seemed to be thoroughly enjoying it.

"Right! No super glue!" Heather added.

After twenty-two minutes in the salon, Heather had paid the woman the amount of the hair cut and dye, plus the $100 tip, and gave another $20 to the young woman who helped. "No, I'm going to give her some of this money," said Heather's hairdresser.

"That's okay. Keep it. And thank you both!" She ran to her car and headed across the street to Walmart. She laughed at her face in the car mirror. The mustache looked so real. She would need to remove the mascara from her eyelashes, which still looked way too feminine. Her lipstick was already gone. She hoped once she dressed in the men's clothing she was about to buy that she would be able to fool everyone at the graveside service, especially Dorgan or anyone else who might be looking for her.

She was self-conscious about walking through the store in women's clothing wearing a mustache. What must people think! She first picked a pair of men's shoes and had to try on several pair before finding ones that fit. She then picked out a pair of dark trousers and quickly grabbed socks to match. An oxford cloth collared shirt and sport jacket completed the ensemble. It was too warm for the jacket, but she needed to hide her breasts with more than just the shirt. She took the men's clothes to the women's changing area and received a look of surprise from the Walmart attendant.

"I know it looks strange, but I have to dress as a man and I'm in a huge hurry. It's really important. Can you help me?" The woman's look of consternation softened. "What do you need me to do?"

"While I'm trying these on, could you please buy me a pair of men's sunglasses. I'd greatly appreciate it. Here's $20...if they're more, I'll pay for them shortly."

The attendant gave an approving smile at Heather when she came out of the dressing room. "How do I look?" Heather asked as she put on the sunglasses the woman had bought. "I still need to remove my mascara."

"You look like a beautiful man," the attendant laughed.

The sunglasses were only $12 and the woman handed $8 back to Heather. "Keep it for your help," said Heather. "And thank you." She headed towards the check-out lines with her other clothes and the price tags for the new ones.

The graveside service was starting in ten minutes. She would be late, but only by a few minutes. It couldn't be helped. She was so glad that the first pieces of men's clothing she had selected fit her and she didn't have to try on more. She would never have made it before the end of the service otherwise.

As Heather walked out of Walmart, she saw Bernie waiting for her in his car. He didn't know it was her until she opened his passenger door and got in. "Let's go Bernie...we're late!"

The graveside service for Michael Michtenbaum was delayed a few minutes as the long line of cars that had driven to Greenwood Cemetery from the funeral home were still parking, one behind the other, along the narrow road within the cemetery. The people in the cars at the end of the procession had quite a way to walk to get to the area where a hundred or more chairs had been set up on three sides around the grave site. The casket was positioned above the open grave and a tent covered the casket as well as the first several rows of chairs where family and closest friends would sit.

Jeremy watched as the mourners continued to take their seats or to stand behind or near the chairs. He was sending the live video to Dragon's computer as he couldn't think of any other choice he had. A plan was forming in his mind, however, to possibly help whomever Dragon was going to touch with his fiery breath of death. He didn't know if his plan would help and he didn't even know what Dragon planned to do. He only knew that Dragon had a plan and he had to do something to stop it.

Jeremy had used a trick once when playing in an on-line Halo 3 tournament. At the time, it was called cheating, which he regretted afterward and vowed not to do again. Now he would call it a lifesaver, and he hoped he would have no regrets. By programming the video feed to run at a slightly faster speed, he could play the video, in almost real time, but in reality one second out of ten, or six seconds per minute, would be "lost" in the playback. And the effect was cumulative, meaning a half hour later, the viewer, Dragon in this case, would be watching "live" coverage of events that had happened three minutes earlier.

If the service lasted thirty minutes, and it took another thirty minutes for everyone to leave, Jeremy could delay what Dragon was seeing by six minutes. If the grave closers were even later than that in getting started, there would be even more of a delay. Whatever Dragon was planning, his action would be taken three or more minutes after whatever or whomever caused him to act. Jeremy hoped that would be enough of a lag in time to allow the intended victim to be in a different location.

It was too risky to speed the satellite video up any more than one second out of ten. The "live" coverage would then look abnormal, sort of like the characters in an old silent movie who moved a bit too fast.

It wasn't a fool-proof plan by any means, but it was all he had.

Jeremy's monitor that was visible to Dragon's office camera would also show the sped up version of the satellite coverage. But Jeremy fed the real live coverage to his iPad, which he placed at an angle between two of the end laptops so that it was not visible from the window behind him. He was careful to use his body as a shield to cover what he was doing as he removed the iPad from the backpack he always carried with him and placed it in its hiding spot on his desk.

Jeremy wasn't certain what Dragon was able to see on the eight monitors situated in a semi-circle on Jeremy's desk. He would proceed by assuming that all of them were, and had been, visible, but it could very well be that Dragon had only just checked on him within the past half hour while at the library and perhaps could not see most of the monitors very well. He looked at each of them now as if Dragon were seeing them.

The first one, which had been Michael Michtenbaum's screen before, now showed the cemetery from above, per Dragon's request. The second monitor was Mary Beth's implant video screen, now showing the cemetery as well, but through her eyes on a personal and close up level. If Dragon hadn't known Mary Beth was at the Michtenbaum funeral before, he would know now. He would also now know that Jeremy had access to the usernames and passwords to view these private videos.

Jeremy wasn't overly concerned that Dragon now knew he had access to the Freedom Project subjects' implant videos. Jeremy always went above and beyond, or insubordinately outside of, an assignment's boundaries to find out everything he could about it. Dragon knew Jeremy would have found out as much as he could about the three subjects he had been watching via satellite for four years. Was it that much of a stretch that he should find out about the implants? Especially now that one of the subjects had died? Maybe, but at least it didn't prove that he was watching Dragon, which was

Jeremy's main concern.

The third computer was the satellite that normally watched Jonathon Moore but was now hovering over the funeral home. So Dragon may know I've seen the attempted bombing of Heather and the police officers' cars, thought Jeremy. Positioning himself in front of that monitor, he moved the satellite the milli-distance needed to watch the library – and Dorgan's rental car. He then minimized the screen and would check on it only when he could block it from Dragon's view.

The fourth was the facial recognition software program, which was only showing the program name, MyBackdoor, on the screen. It had been at least forty-five minutes since the last face had shown on the screen, so he could be okay on that one unless Dragon had been watching for a longer period of time than this particular visit to the library. Jeremy had no reason to believe that was the case.

The next monitor was Jeremy's Outlook and whatever else he needed to look up. It had been a little while since he had viewed any incriminating information.

The sixth screen was the one monitoring the keystrokes on Dragon's laptop. Most of the time the screen was empty, but even when it was showing keystrokes, Dragon might not be able to tell what it was, or even be able to read it depending on the zoom capabilities of his camera. Of course, why have a camera there at all if it can't zoom in and read the print on all of these monitors, Jeremy mused.

The seventh screen was Audrey's view of the Marriott Hotel and parking lot where Dragon was staying. That and the next and final monitor, he knew, were the most incriminating of all. The final one was Samuel, which usually was watching Dragon but now was following Heather and the live video was currently of the Walmart parking lot. Heather was apparently disguising herself, as she had her hair cut and dyed, and was wearing a mustache when she came out of a hair salon about fifteen minutes ago. Samuel followed her to Walmart and even into the store where she tried on men's shoes and picked out some men's clothing, but then Dragon's phone call, and Jeremy's subsequent tweaking of the satellite to speed up the video, took Jeremy away from following her for several minutes. He checked to see if her red car was still in the parking lot. It was.

Jeremy wanted to take Samuel back inside Walmart to watch Heather but decided the better use of his time would be to keep a close eye on his iPad that was showing the live coverage of the graveside funeral service at the cemetery where Michael Michtenbaum's body, with an incriminating eye implant still intact, would be buried soon. Unless Dragon is purposely trying to lead me in the wrong direction, thought Jeremy, this should be the video that shows me his next move.

This screen was unfortunately at the other end of his desk, and small, and somewhat hidden, so he would not be able to keep as close an eye on Heather, or the hotel, or Dragon at the library. He inconspicuously changed a setting on the computer running the keystroke software so that it would let him audibly know if Dragon was typing on his computer, but not show the keystrokes on the screen until such time as Jeremy pulled it up. And on the off-chance that Dragon hadn't seen him monitoring the Marriott Hotel, he had minimized that screen.

A car was entering the cemetery from a back entrance and taking an internal road behind the area where the Michtenbaum funeral was taking place. There was a long row of tall evergreen trees that would obscure the view of the funeral service from that car. It pulled over and a man got out of the passenger side. He walked through the gravestones in a large grassy area, towards the trees. Jeremy knew Dragon would be watching this soon as well – his video was only about seventy or seventy-five seconds behind. The man hid in the trees, and the car drove on. Could that be who Dragon is looking for? Jeremy wondered, and he was glad he wasn't in that man's shoes.

He had to find a way to stop Dragon from seeing this portion of the video as he felt certain the man in the trees was in grave danger. He had only a minute or so to prevent these ten or twelve seconds of the video from streaming to Dragon's laptop. Jeremy replayed and timed exactly how long the car and man were in view before the man disappeared into the trees – 11.2 seconds. He then quickly copied the previous 11.2 seconds of the video, immediately before the car arrived, and re-fed it to the delayed video that would soon appear on one of his own, and Dragon's, laptops. He didn't have time to watch the result of this spliced video before it hit his screen, so he watched it at the same time he was sure that Dragon was watching it. Would Dragon be fooled? Would the video still look real or would Dorgan be able to tell that there were two millisecond glitches in the coverage and that the same 11.2 seconds of the graveside service had repeated itself.

Mary Beth held on to one of Celia's hands and Mitch held on to the other as the last service for the Michtenbaum couple's beloved son began. They were all sitting in the front row of chairs, under the awning, which was a blessing as the sun had warmed the May day to over 80 degrees. From her vantage point, Mary Beth could see the road and the long row of cars to her left, the expansive cemetery in front of her and a row of thick pine and spruce trees about 50 yards away to the right.

The somber occasion made Mary Beth think about death. Her own, in particular. I could be gone tomorrow, she thought. She felt at peace with the fact that her family knew she loved them as she told them so almost every day, and they did the same. She hoped they would not feel any guilt about not having said goodbye or that they loved her should she die suddenly, and she felt the same would be true if one of them met an untimely death. She knew she, and they, would be grief-stricken of course, but not harbor feelings of guilt.

She and Joe had not made their final arrangements and here they were, 50 years old. It was time to do so, and she would talk to him about it when she got home tomorrow. Recently she'd thought about cremation instead of traditional burial. What would Joe think of that? Would he agree? She thought about Michael Michtenbaum and what his wishes would have been. He'd probably never made them known to his parents, thinking he would outlive them. Would he have preferred cremation? She knew he was an environmentalist and had once fought a legal case against a city that was dumping refuse in an environmentally unsafe manner. Not that fighting for a clean environment would mean he wouldn't want to be buried in the ground. Well, it didn't matter now…he was already in a box and going in the ground soon.

Mary Beth planned to stay with the Michtenbaums tonight as

well. There would be neighbors at their house preparing food right now for the gathering of people that would come throughout the afternoon and evening. Tomorrow would be the day when the activity ended and the quiet but harsh reality would return for Mitch and Celia. Mary Beth wished she could stay with them longer, but she needed to get back to her home and her work. She had promised them this morning that she would return the next weekend and see them and would bring Joe with her this time. They were grateful.

A soft breeze blew through the crowd and Mary Beth turned to look at the many faces behind her. A man was walking from her right to the back row of seats and took an empty one. Most everyone else was seated except for the few funeral home personnel, the pastor who was still speaking, and a few teenagers who were probably forced to come but talked quietly off near a shade tree.

Mary Beth's mother and both maternal grandparents were buried in this cemetery as well. She wanted to buy some fresh flowers and visit their graves a little later when she could be alone. Her mother had died only two years earlier of breast cancer and Mary Beth missed her terribly.

The funeral home personnel were now handing out single red roses to all of the mourners. Once the service concluded, everyone would walk by the casket and place their roses on it.

The pastor asked everyone to bow their heads as he offered the final prayer. Mary Beth listened to the sounds around her as she had her eyes closed. A few sobs and sniffing could be heard from the crowd, the pastor's voice, several chirping birds, cars driving in the distance, a dog barking, a distant lawnmower and the rustle of tree branches in the slight breeze.

The prayer concluded and the funeral home personnel directed those in the last row of seats to get up and walk by the casket with their roses. They were followed by the second to last row, and a steady stream of solemn people walked by and offered their flowers and prayers to Michael. Many turned to hug or offer additional condolences to Celia and Mitch.

Finally, it was their turn to stand and walk the few feet to the casket. Celia leaned against it as if to hug her son once last time and kissed the mahogany box. She laid her rose on top of the many others that were on the casket.

Cars began to leave and the Michtenbaums headed for the limousine provided by the funeral home. Mary Beth lagged behind a bit as Mitch put his arm about his wife and walked with her.

"Excuse me," said a man's voice beside Mary Beth. "Are you Mary Beth Singer?"

Mary Beth turned to see the man she had seen earlier arriving late and taking a seat in the back. He was about 6 feet tall with short dark hair, dark glasses and a mustache. He was wearing a sports jacket and dark slacks.

"Yes," she replied. "I'm sorry, I don't know your name," and she held out her hand to shake his. The hand was soft, feminine. He definitely had a feminine air about him, Mary Beth thought, but that never bothered her. Everyone was equal in her eyes.

"Danny. Danny Wheatley. I know you're in a hurry, but I just wanted to meet you. Michael had mentioned your name to me several times as being a good friend. I was hoping you would be here today."

Mary Beth's eyes may have widened a bit, she wasn't sure. She had the impression that this man, Danny, was gay, and it now made her wonder about Michael. Was that why he was married only a short time and never had children? It would not have changed anything about her own relationship with Michael, and she wondered if his parents knew. And she had another brief thought – if he was gay, did that have anything to do with his murder?

"It's so good to meet you Danny. Why don't you come over to Mitch and Celia's house. There will be plenty of food and we can talk some more. I do have to go right now though. They're already in the car waiting for me."

"Of course, I'll be there shortly, thank you," Heather said.

Dorgan sat in a quiet and secluded corner of the public library in a cubicle set up with a computer. He had his laptop with him as well but hadn't used it yet. He had been disappointed when he first came into the library and saw that their public computers were all together on one long table – there was no privacy at all. Anyone could look over his shoulder or listen in to any phone calls he would make. It wouldn't do at all.

He asked a library attendant if there were any quieter study cubicles and the young man said yes, there were two on the upper floor. He was kind enough to show him to the one furthest from the public areas, and Dorgan thanked him.

When he had been sitting on the park bench, after he knew that Heather had accidentally or on purpose gotten rid of the "bug" in her purse, he knew that he needed to get a handle on what was happening. Two Homeland Security employees, one a low level, low security clearance, uneducated clerical person, and one much higher level, intelligent and resourceful employee, were here in the same town as he. Why? There was absolutely no logical answer to that question that he could perceive. Although he originally thought they were sent there to watch him, he knew that made no sense whatsoever. Why would they send those two? He knew them – he would recognize them. They weren't field agents – they wouldn't be trained to follow and watch someone. No, he simply couldn't believe they were trying to watch him. In fact, he didn't even think they knew he was there.

They wouldn't have been sent by DHS or CIA regarding the Freedom Project either. Again, that made no sense. Unless these two are the best-kept government secret ever, thought Dorgan, and Bernie's simpleton behavior and appearance is a stroke of master genius to fool the likes of me and everyone else, these two have no reason to be here. Dorgan was stumped.

But he couldn't deny the fact that Bernie had followed his agent Jones from the morgue to the funeral home and had watched Jones plant the bombs under Heather's and the police cars. And someone had also foiled Johnson's attempt to kill Rachel Curry in her lab at the morgue yesterday by calling in the police. Could that have been Bernie as well? Who is this guy anyway? Perhaps he *is* an undercover agent, and better than both of my guys it seems.

Okay, that would explain Bernie. But what about Heather? Why is she here? Is she also a trained agent? Why would they send someone so obviously conspicuous and known to me? Perhaps these two were *so* good that it didn't matter. Perhaps these two truly were DHS's best kept secret.

What about Jeremy? How much does he know? Could he be watching me and my guys and relaying that information to Bernie and Heather? Could he have told her about the bug in her purse? He certainly has access to all of the technology to do it. I've never really trusted that kid.

It was then that he decided to go to the library and check in on Jeremy from his office camera to see if he was helping Bernie and Heather, and if so, why? What is their mission?

He could see Jeremy at his desk and it appeared that all of his computers were in use. Dorgan was aware of three current projects that Jeremy was working on, none of which were of the same urgent nature as his two most recent assignments. That would soon change, he was sure. There were always new terrorists to track in the US, politicians to watch, suspected spies and double-agents to follow. But Jeremy had been working non-stop for the past month, most recently identifying the large terrorist cell in Florida and prior to that, assisting law enforcement in tracking and finding a school shooter that had killed 24 kids and gotten away. The killer had managed to elude capture for over six weeks. Once Jeremy was involved with helping find the young man, he was able to locate him within a week by sending himself and the task force responsible for finding the man every purchase of ammunition in the country fitting the ammunition that the man had used in the school shooting. Immediate calls or dispatch of local police to the places of purchase soon led to the man's capture.

Jeremy should be home now getting some much-needed rest, and probably would be, Dorgan reminded himself, if I hadn't called him in early this morning. But why hasn't he gone home? Two of his current projects were handled by other personnel when Jeremy wasn't there – they needed 24/7 surveillance. So someone else was currently watching the numerous Presidential candidates as well as the Maryland senator who had been receiving daily death threats for the past month. Jeremy was reviewing a great deal of riot video footage from recent protest riots, but he didn't have to do that on his day off. Jeremy alone monitored the three Freedom Project subjects, but that only took a few minutes a day. What exactly was he up to?

Dorgan could zoom in a little from the small surveillance camera located on the ceiling of his office behind his desk. It allowed a view of almost all of his office except right up against the back wall, as well as a view outside the front glass wall of his office, which was

Jeremy's work area. He knew he wouldn't be able to read any small text on any of the computer monitors on Jeremy's desk, but he should be able to see any larger photos or text.

He zoomed in as far as he could – Jeremy was moving back and forth along his desk looking at the various monitors. What was he so intent on watching?

Dorgan clearly saw the computer monitor with the MyBackdoor software, but nothing was running on it at the moment. He also saw Jeremy's e-mail and calendar page on another screen. He could see a view of the tops of a few buildings and a parking lot on one screen but didn't recognize the scene. The monitor next to that one was blank at the moment. The two computers on each end of Jeremy's desk, because they were in a semi-circle and not a straight line, were not visible to him. He would probably have been able to clearly see the two next to the ones on each end except they had security screens attached to the monitors that allowed viewing only from a close and direct angle. Still, he could slightly see one of them, which appeared to have an overhead view of a building, parking lot and surrounding area. The building and parking lot looked common enough. What caught Dorgan's eye was the river behind the building. While difficult for him to see, Dorgan believed this screen could very well be a satellite view of the Marriott Hotel where both he and Heather were staying. So Jeremy might be watching him, or watching Heather. But why?

Dorgan knew that Jeremy was the type who would investigate way above and beyond what he was instructed to do, so one explanation, he thought, was that Jeremy put two and two together, figuring he, Dorgan, had gone to the scene of Michael Michtenbaum's murder – Hamilton, Ohio. Or perhaps he is following Heather for whatever reason and has seen me here as well, Dorgan surmised.

He decided to call Jeremy. I might as well have him working for me if he's going to be there anyway. He dialed Jeremy's cell phone from the other untraceable cell phone he had purchased before coming to Ohio.

"Hello," came Jeremy's voice.

"Jeremy, it's Dorgan. Are you still at the office by any chance? I need another favor." He rather smugly accentuated the words "by any chance" as he could see him sitting there answering his phone.

Jeremy turned so that his back was to Dorgan's camera. "Actually, I am still here. Thought I might as well work a little since you have to pay me for the day anyway."

Heather had made up her mind that she was going to tell Mary Beth Singer and Jonathon Moore about their implants so that they could have them removed. She didn't care if it cost her her job. She truly hoped it wouldn't cost her her life. She had the opportunity right now to tell Mary Beth, but there were several problems. First, she preferred to <u>not</u> be identified by whomever was watching through Mary Beth's eyes besides Mary Beth. Would this disguise be sufficient? Second, even if her disguise was sufficient, telling Mary Beth when she knew someone else, probably Dorgan, was watching and listening, wasn't safe for Mary Beth. If Dorgan had no present plans to hurt Jon or Mary Beth, he would definitely have reason to do so once they were aware of the project. Third, who else might get hurt if she exposes this project? Her father? Her boss? It really bothered her to think her dad might still be involved in some way. Fourth, Mary Beth might think she was a nut case. She might not believe her at all.

She wasn't sure why she cared about being identified herself. Dorgan had already tried to kill her. He already knew how much she knew. Still, she rationalized, perhaps it was his agent who had tried to kill her before Dorgan knew who it was, or maybe he wouldn't make a second attempt if she let it go. It's possible, Heather, she tried to convince herself.

But problem number two was enough to make Heather decide not to approach Mary Beth directly. How can I talk to her, either as a man or a woman, when everything we say can be heard by the government that doesn't want the subject ever mentioned? I'm sure they could have us dead very quickly indeed. I can't write it down and give the message to her to read, as everything she sees and reads can be seen and read by whomever is watching. How then can I communicate with her?

Should I expose the project publicly, going to the media?

Would they believe me?

But it's wrong. It's wrong on every level and it needs to be righted. I want to fix it for Mary Beth and Jon and stop any similar future government infringement of the people, without causing mass hysteria or further bloodshed. Can I do that? Is it possible?

Heather was driving Bernie's car. He was still hidden in the trees near Michtenbaum's gravesite, watching with his binoculars and instructed to take photos of the grave closers and anything unusual. She would pick him up in a couple of hours. She hoped he would be okay lying in the pine needles under the trees. They had switched positions in the car right before reaching the cemetery – Bernie got in the passenger seat and Heather took over as driver. She had parked the car away from the rest of the cars at the graveside service and walked across the cemetery to the service.

She drove back to the hotel to use the restroom. She didn't want to be seen going into a public women's restroom dressed as a man, and she definitely didn't want to go into the men's room. She still wanted to talk to Rachel – they had never gotten another chance to talk after the bomb scare. While everything she had told Rachel in their half-hour talk this morning at the morgue was the truth, she hadn't told her the whole truth – not even close. Rachel now knew the small implant she had taken out of Michael Ray Michtenbaum's head was placed there as part of a highly secretive government project. That was really all she had revealed to Rachel, and Rachel *may* have read into that statement that Michtenbaum knew about it.

Most of the half hour talk had been Rachel telling Heather exactly what had happened, word for word as she could remember it. She hadn't told the police about the implant and the killer's words to her because he had also made another threat. He somehow knew about her family; about her mother who cared for another child that she had raised as her own daughter. In reality it was Rachel's daughter, now 20 years old. The man had threatened to kill her daughter and mother if she told the police. He had yelled it at her after she had locked herself in her office and he had run away at the sound of more police arriving. His words had chilled her to the bone. And even though that man was dead, she knew he wasn't the one in charge.

Also, from their conversation, Heather had surmised that

Rachel didn't know that Michael also had an implant in his eye. That made sense as an autopsy would not normally reveal a foreign object behind an eyeball unless one was specifically looking for it.

Heather wanted to help Rachel, and herself, get out of this mess, but was uncertain of how much to tell the coroner. Telling her even more about the project could put her further at risk.

Heather checked her mustache in the mirror to make sure it was still on straight and securely. She wished she didn't have to wear the sports coat on such a warm day, but it couldn't be helped. With the sunglasses covering her long lashes, she felt the disguise was pretty effective. Her hands were her biggest giveaway. She rarely polished her nails and didn't have any color on them now, but her slender hands and fingers didn't look masculine at all.

Heather had the elder Michtenbaums' address and spoke it into her phone as soon as she left the hotel. She still didn't know how to approach Mary Beth and hoped that an idea would come to mind on the ride over. It was way too risky to just tell her, risky for both of them. But how do you communicate with someone when it can't be verbally or visually communicated? What else was there?

Heather imagined Mary Beth's reaction as well. It would most likely be disbelief at first, especially coming from a stranger, but once she was convinced that it was true, how would she react? How would I react?, thought Heather. How would anyone react who knew every moment of his or her life was recorded and subject to viewing by strangers? It reminded her of the movie "The Truman Show," where a man's entire life, from birth, was shown worldwide on a reality television program. He was the only person in the world who was unable to view the show. I would probably react with rage, thought Heather. I would want to get back at those who did this unconscionable thing to me.

Her phone told Heather to turn right ahead and she did. She only had a few minutes before she would arrive at the Michtenbaum home. Suddenly, an idea struck her. Her husband. Heather recollected from the files that his name was Joseph Singer. If I could talk to him – explain everything – he could convince her. A plan was already forming in Heather's mind as she approached the Michtenbaum home. There were dozens of cars near the house and she had to park a block away.

It was well after 2 o'clock and Heather realized she hadn't eaten anything since early morning. She was hungry, so as soon as she entered Mitch and Celia's home, she headed towards the spread of food that covered the dining room table as well as a portion of the kitchen counter. The Michtenbaums were both on the couch, still holding hands, and talking with four other people seated nearby. Heather saw Mary Beth talking with a couple outside on the back patio. Dozens of other people milled about both inside and out.

Heather filled a plate with small finger sandwiches of turkey and cheese, tuna and egg salad, as well as a generous helping of fruit salad and baked beans. She chose a bottle of water over coffee or a soft drink, then retreated to a chair in the shade of a large tree in the back yard.

As she was finishing her meal, Heather saw Mary Beth walking towards her. She quickly reviewed her cover story in her mind, as well as reminding herself to use the same voice, as close to male as she could achieve, when talking with anyone, but especially when talking with Mary Beth, as others would be watching and listening to her as well – others that perhaps already knew her.

"Danny, right?" Mary Beth extended her hand to shake Heather's, who stood as Mary Beth neared.

"Yes, Danny Wheatley. Here, have a seat," and Heather put on her most gentlemanly act, nodding towards her chair for Mary Beth to sit. "I'll get another chair." She picked up a folding chair from the patio and walked back to the tree to sit with Mary Beth.

"You said you were friends with Ray," began Mary Beth. "I'm embarrassed to say that I don't remember him mentioning you, but as you know, he talked a lot and I have to say that I wasn't always listening." She grinned and chuckled slightly.

"Well, we weren't close friends. We worked together at the firm, or I should say I worked for him and Mr. Schultz and Mr. Daiz at the firm, several years ago. I was only there a little over a year as a paralegal, but we talked quite often about the cases I was helping with. As you said, Michael – Ray - talked a lot. He mentioned your name on more than one occasion as being a good friend. I just wanted to tell you that, even though I'm sure you knew he felt that way."

"Thank you very much…it does make me feel better to know

he considered me such a good friend that he would tell others. I can't understand why anyone would kill him. Have you heard if they're making any progress on finding the person who did it?"

"No, I haven't heard. I'm sure they'll find him though – I'm assuming it's a him. I heard about the attack on the coroner and the killing of two police officers as well. Is it always this violent in Hamilton?"

"I don't really know, but I don't think so. I live in Columbus now and have for over 25 years since Joe, my husband, and I married. Where do you live?"

"I live in Oxford, near the university." Heather had spent her time at the graveside service accessing the internet on her iPhone, gathering some information for questions she wanted to ask and questions such as this that she might be asked. "So, is your husband here with you today?" Heather didn't think he was since she hadn't seen a man with Mary Beth at the funeral home or the cemetery or the Michtenbaum home.

"No, Joe had a golf outing already planned for this afternoon. He would have come if I had asked him to – he's so sweet – but it wasn't necessary. The Michtenbaums are my close friends. He knows them, even though Joe usually hangs out with my dad when we come down and I visit Mitch and Celia. He was very torn about what to do about today and said he would cancel the golf outing but I told him no. I wanted him to have today with his friends. He doesn't get to play nearly as often as he'd like."

"I played once near Columbus – I think the course was called Champions Golf Course. It was nice." Heather was fishing for a course name to find out where Joe could be reached.

"We just joined a golf club last year, or I should say Joe joined. I don't play. It's expensive but now that our daughter is through school, we felt we could spend a little on ourselves. Have you heard of Brookside Golf and Country Club?"

Danny admitted that he hadn't heard of it, and Heather memorized the club name.

"Joe loves it and hopes to play a lot more this summer." Mary Beth glanced at her watch. "If you'll excuse me, Danny, I am going to head back over to Greenwood Cemetery. My mother and my grandparents are all buried there and I want to put fresh flowers on their graves. I miss my mother terribly and spending a little quiet time with her always makes me feel close to her again. It was so nice talking with you." Mary Beth stood and so did Heather.

"It was nice to meet you, Mary Beth. I'm sorry to hear about your mother." They shook hands again and Mary Beth headed into the house. Heather followed not far behind and heard Mary Beth tell Celia and Mitch that she would be back in an hour or so. She walked up to introduce herself to the Michtenbaums and Mary Beth did it for her, just as she had hoped. "Celia, Mitch, this is a friend of Ray's that used to work at his firm a few years ago – Danny Wheatley. Danny, these are Ray's parents, Celia and Mitch Michtenbaum." Mary Beth hugged Celia and left.

"Oh, so you know Mary Beth as well?" Celia asked, mostly just to have something to say to the young man.

"Yes, and I'm hoping to play some golf with her husband Joe now that he's joined the Brookside Golf Club. Oh, I meant to ask Mary Beth for Joe's cell number." Heather pretended to excuse herself to look out the picture window to see if she could still see Mary Beth, "but she's already left. I guess I can just call the club and try to reach him."

"I think we have Joe's number in our book," said Celia and she stood and walked into the kitchen, returning a minute later with an address booklet. She opened it. "Yes, here is his new cell phone number that Mary Beth gave us," and she read the number to Heather, who typed it into her phone.

"Thank you. It will be easier to track him down this way." Heather then told the Michtenbaums how sorry she was about their son, and that he would be greatly missed. They thanked him and began talking to other friends and neighbors waiting their turn to speak with them. Heather left the Michtenbaums' home, planning to call Joe Singer later that afternoon.

Bernie had never felt so alive. He was on a secret government mission, so secret not even the government knew about it. A real one, not just one of his fantasies. And he was really working with Heather Barnes! He would have pinched himself, but the pine needles sticking in his arms were enough to remind him that he was really here. He was really on a covert mission, spying on a bad guy. He had his binoculars and spy camera, which also took short videos.

Per Heather's earlier instructions, he was to stay hidden under the trees throughout the graveside service and afterwards until the grave closers arrived, which would be soon after the service. He was to watch them carefully to see what transpired and get as many good photos and videos as possible.

Bernie's breath caught in his throat when the first man arrived 20 minutes after everyone left the service. He didn't recognize the man at all – stout, bearded, with thinning hair; he did, however, recognize the car. It was the same tan car that had been in the cemetery this morning near the morgue. This man was most likely the same man who had tried to kill Heather and Rachel at the funeral home, concluded Bernie, only in disguise. Bernie felt somewhat frightened when he came to this realization and the knowledge of what this man was capable of doing.

His spy camera was small and hardly made any noise when either the button or the shutter clicked. He was grateful for that. He took a dozen photos of the man, as close up as the zoom lens would allow. While the face didn't look the same to him as the one he had described to the sketch artist earlier, perhaps computer software that removed the beard and added hair could see the match.

The man used the equipment holding the casket in the air to lower it into the grave. The man looked around in all directions then jumped into the open grave of Michael Ray Michtenbaum. "Oh, man," Bernie whispered.

Bernie could no longer see the man and waited expectantly for him to climb out of the grave. In the meantime, another car arrived and a second man walked towards the gravesite. Bernie took several photos of this man as well. Suddenly, the second man squealed and jumped as if he'd seen a ghost. Bernie took the camera away from his eye and saw that the man had reached the open grave and was now bending over and looking in.

"What are you doing!" Bernie heard the second man shout. He switched to video, hoping to get some audio recording of what was being said between the two men. The video captured a hand reaching up out of the grave and grabbing the second man's leg, pulling him down into the grave. The man's scream was captured on tape.

Bernie found that he was holding his breath and tried to let it out slowly and quietly. His heart was pounding. He realized he was truly frightened and wished the men would leave and Heather would come and get him.

He stopped the video while nothing was happening, waiting for one or both of the men to emerge. Two minutes later, a hand appeared out of the grave. Bernie turned the video on again and captured the first man climbing out of the grave. He bent over, seemingly picking up something off the ground, then threw it down again.

The man quickly filled in the open grave with the nearby dirt which had been covered with a tarp. He stopped momentarily and looked at his cell phone. Bernie's hands shook as he continued to videotape another murder – that of the second man now buried with Michael Michtenbaum.

Then Bernie froze. The man was looking right at him. The camera was still to Bernie's eye and he didn't dare move it for fear any movement would give him away. Could the man see him? He had just looked at his phone. It was almost as though someone had sent him a message that Bernie was hiding in the trees.

Bernie heard a noise to his left and proceeded to wet his pants.

The man finished filling in the grave and jumped down from the backhoe. He pulled a gun from inside his shirt and began walking through the gravestones towards Bernie.

Jeremy used his body to shield any monitor that held incriminating information that Dragon could possibly see; in some cases he would minimize the screen. This method of viewing the eight monitors meant that Jeremy was frequently moving back and forth in front of his desk, and couldn't leave all monitors on for a quick glance from the other end of the desk. It was frustrating, and much less efficient, but he had to proceed as if Dragon was watching and could see everything.

He occasionally maximized Mary Beth's implant video and audio for moments at a time only, making it look to the camera behind him that he had only paused in his seat for a moment. He usually took a sip of coffee at the same time so it wouldn't appear he was viewing a screen.

In the cemetery Mary Beth looked around once and Jeremy could see a man arriving late to the service and sitting in the back. Dragon's keyboard pinged at that time and Jeremy quickly minimized Mary Beth and moved with his coffee cup to sit in front of that monitor, pushing a key to bring onto the screen what Dragon was typing into his laptop. Jeremy sipped his coffee and pretended to be reading his incoming e-mails on the next computer over.

Dragon was accessing Mary Beth's implant software so he could see and hear what was going on at the service. He's going to figure out very soon that I've tampered with the satellite feed, Jeremy worried, but it's a chance I have to take. Jeremy glanced at the monitor showing Samuel, who was dutifully still watching Heather's car in the Walmart parking lot.

Jeremy decided to work on one of his other projects as well so it would appear to Dragon that he was legitimately working. He picked one of the laptops that would be in clear view of Dragon's camera, so selected Jonathan Moore's satellite which had been watching the funeral home. He targeted the home of the Senator who was receiving death threats. He left the video of the house on the screen and shot an e-mail to one of his intelligence-gathering colleagues, asking for the Senator's schedule so that he could track him by satellite.

The live coverage of the cemetery on his iPad showed a few men handing out long-stemmed roses to the seated mass of people. The delayed screen of the cemetery, the one that Jeremy was certain Dragon was still watching at the public library, showed the man that had arrived late and was now sitting down in the back row.

A reply to his e-mail came almost immediately. The Senator was at home or at least was not on the road this weekend. Good, thought Jeremy. I really don't want to watch that one right now. He zoomed into the front door to make it look as though he was doing something other than what he was really doing.

He listened in briefly to Michtenbaum's ear. A toilet flushed. Nothing new there.

Jeremy checked Samuel once again – Heather's car was still in the Walmart parking lot. OK, there's no way she's still in there, he thought. He knew she was disguising herself so he could easily have missed her if she came out and got into a different car. He toggled one of his monitors in order to check to see where her phone was. Not at Walmart, but right smack in the middle of the cemetery, at Michael Michtenbaum's graveside service.

"That's it! Jeremy, you're an idiot!" he yelled at himself and smacked the palm of his hand on the side of his head. It now occurred to him that the car he had seen earlier in the cemetery could have been Bernie's. Jeremy had avoided zooming in to see the person in the trees as that would have alerted Dorgan to the man's presence. As it was, Jeremy thought he had done a good job of doctoring the video so that Dorgan had not seen the car or the man.

But now he wondered if that "man" could have been Heather in disguise? His satellite view was from 200 feet up and he could not see details very well. He knew she had darkened her hair. He had seen that when she came out of the salon. She was obviously trying to alter her appearance. At the time he saw the car in the cemetery, he thought Heather was safe and sound inside Walmart, so it didn't occur to him that she and Bernie could have met up again and driven to the cemetery. How the hell do I manage to find terrorists when I can't even track a beautiful woman and her beasty sidekick. He was again afraid for her life and beating himself up considerably at the same time.

Jeremy pinpointed where Heather's phone was. It wasn't in the trees but sitting in the crowd of people. It has to be Bernie under the trees, surmised Jeremy, so he situated himself in front of his far right computer and pulled Samuel from Walmart to Greenwood Cemetery. He zoomed in along the treeline. From this vantage point he could see the back and legs of a man lying on the ground, facing towards the Michtenbaum gravesite. He zoomed down through the tree cover to see Bernie's short, paunchy body lying there, binoculars to his eyes.

Jeremy watched the remainder of the graveside service on his iPad while moving the Senator's satellite around, pretending to look for him. The crowd was leaving and Mary Beth and the Michtenbaums were walking away from the casket and heading for their car. Mary Beth stopped and a moment later she was talking with the man who had arrived late to the service. Jeremy turned up the volume on Mary Beth's designated computer.

"I know you're in a hurry, but I just wanted to meet you. Michael had mentioned your name to me several times as being a good friend. I was hoping you would be here today."

Jeremy looked closely at the man standing and talking in front of Mary Beth, the man who had Heather's phone in his pocket. The short dark hair and mustache were very familiar. It was Heather. Jeremy grinned. "Even as a man, I still want to jump your bones."

"It's so good to meet you Danny. Why don't you come over to Mitch and Celia's house – there will be plenty of food – we can talk some more. I do have to go right now though – they're already in the car waiting for me."

"Of course, I'll be there shortly – thank you."

Jeremy minimized Mary Beth as she walked towards the limo and he watched Heather from 50 feet up as she walked off his screen to the right. As much as he wanted to use Samuel to follow Heather, he knew he wouldn't be able to follow her in her car without drawing Dragon's suspicion, so he settled for finding her later at the Michtenbaums. For now, he would continue to watch the cemetery, and Bernie, who was in the greater danger now.

Jeremy's stomach rumbled and he decided while the cemetery was clearing of people, it would be a good time to quickly take a bathroom and snack break. He hit the button to shut down all screens and left his office.

Dorgan had his small command center set up in a corner of the top floor of the library, partially surrounded by four-foot high partitions. He had his computer screens angled so that anyone who might decide to invade his personal space by walking right up to, or inside, the entrance to his cubicle could not see the screens.

Now that he was suspicious of being watched, he accessed fewer sites on his agency-issued laptop and used the library computer and the iPad that he had brought with him. It was now coming in handy. The small desk space in the cubicle barely had room for the three computers set up there, but he was able to see all of the screens if he stayed close to the wall.

On his agency-issued laptop, Dorgan watched the live satellite feed from Jeremy of the cemetery. On the library computer, he was watching Jeremy from his office camera. On the iPad he hacked into a CIA database. He had been in this database many times, legally, when he was with the CIA. This was one site to which he knew every back door and had found out after he had left their employ that he could still get into the site. He wasn't a hacker, but this was definitely considered hacking. He had only hacked in a few times in the past seven years, but now he felt his own team might have turned against him.

The original Freedom Project was officially listed as *Terminated.* He knew that. He was the Project Leader and remembered the day the Director himself told him the project was officially ending. Dorgan would no longer get financial support for surveillance and he was not to discuss the project again. But then the Director indicated that unofficially it was still his project. How could it ever be officially over until all three of the subjects were dead and buried? He was still charged with protecting, with his very life if necessary, the continued secrecy of the project as well as the anonymity of everyone involved, past and present. The project had served its purpose and had paved the way for larger scale and more technologically improved Freedom Projects, all of which were still active.

It was a crappy job but someone had to do it. Dorgan had been disenchanted with his CIA job and the added disappointment of being tasked with a job that received no internal support or recognition pushed him to leave that agency and join another. The Project still went with him, as the CIA would not reassign a terminated project to someone else. Dorgan took his assignments seriously. He would fulfill his pledge to the CIA, to his President, to his country, and would do his job. At least at DHS, he could unofficially use some of the resources he had at his disposal to babysit this project that would be his until he died.

The original organizational structure for the Freedom Project, FP-I as the initial project was called, had a chart structure showing the President/Commander in Chief at the top. The block below the President was The Director, Central Intelligence Agency and reporting to the Director was the Freedom Project Leader. In 1963, before the first project had even taken place, it had been a man by the name of Robert Duley, a twenty-year CIA veteran. Reporting to Duley in matters relating to this project was a Project Committee. Project Committee members were from different agencies and organizations. The by-laws of the project stated that there had to be at least two members from the CIA, one member from any organization appointed by the President of the United States and at least one member from the NSA or DHS, added when the by-laws were updated in 2002. The committee, not including the high level leaders, could be as small as four members and as large as six members.

Duley led and oversaw the project until 1995, when he retired at the age of seventy-one. He was replaced by Jacob Barnes, also a twenty-year CIA veteran at the time. Dorgan knew that Heather was Barnes' daughter and had been wondering today, in light of her involvement, if Barnes had discussed this project with her. It was absolutely forbidden and Barnes could lose his job, his pension and more if it was discovered that he had told Heather about the Freedom Project.

Dorgan didn't know why at the time, but in 1995 he was assigned as Project Leader for Freedom Project I. Jacob Barnes had recently been promoted and perhaps had requested to be removed from the responsibility. Later, Dorgan came to know that Barnes was leading the committee of all of the newer, active, Freedom Projects. Barnes was the leader who got the recognition and the resources. But Dorgan never let his bitterness interfere with his work.

Dorgan couldn't believe the CIA file he was now accessing. He had never seen it before. It held the highly confidential file contents for eight subsequent Freedom Projects, each identified by a Roman numeral. The most recent was Freedom Project IX. Dorgan read through portions of the file and felt his patriotism wane a little. He checked to see who the Project Leader was – Barnes.

"And they think I'm ruthless," Dorgan mumbled.

Dorgan shook his head and returned his attention to the live cemetery feed on his laptop. Everyone was now gone. He hadn't seen Heather at the graveside service and now he couldn't hear her either. He still wondered if it was truly accidental that she spilled her purse and lost the transmitter. He wanted to believe that, but didn't. Not at all. Someone else was listening and had tipped her off. Maybe Jeremy? Maybe Jacob Barnes?

Heather's most likely under protective custody as well since this morning's bomb threat on her life, thought Dorgan. She might still be at the police station. When he was ready, he would find her. But for now, the primary mission was to get the eye implant from Michael Michtenbaum's dead body.

Dorgan saw Jones park his car near the gravesite and walk to the equipment used to hold and move the heavy casket. He knew it was Jones even though the man had disguised himself as an overweight, bald guy with a heavy beard.

Dorgan watched Jones lower the casket into the hole and then jump in to do his assigned job, which was to remove Michael's right eye and get the implant imbedded on the back side of the eyeball. While Jones was still in the grave, Dorgan saw a slight movement in the tree line about thirty yards away. Since he was receiving his video feed from Jeremy, he couldn't zoom in to take a closer look. But he felt certain those were legs showing on the back side of the tree line, attached to a person who was watching Jones.

Dorgan wondered if the man was undercover Hamilton police that Heather had asked to watch the proceedings. His determination to follow this project through to the end returned. The man in the trees would be sorry he decided to spy on this particular operation…dead sorry.

At that moment, another car parked near Jones' car. The man approached the open grave and Dorgan assumed he was the real grave closer arriving to do his job. Damn! Why can't we catch a break! thought Dorgan. A few more minutes and the man could have lived to work another day.

Dorgan picked up his cell phone and dialed Jones. He wanted to warn him about the arrival of the other grave closer and to tell him about the man hiding in the trees. Jones didn't answer. Dorgan tried again with the same results. Dorgan watched as the arriving man was pulled into the grave, and Jones climbed out a couple of minutes later.

Dorgan didn't see any other choice but to send a text message and hoped Jones would check his phone very soon. "Eyes on you, thirty degrees southwest in trees – eliminate before too late."

He continued to watch as Jones removed a tarp from the pile of dirt put there when the hole was dug, then climbed up onto a backhoe to fill the grave. Several minutes later while still filling the hole, he saw Jones look at his phone and then look toward the trees.

Finally! thought Dorgan. He continued watching as Jones finished filling in the grave and jumped down from the backhoe, pulling his gun from inside his shirt and walking towards the trees. He knew Jones would be calling him soon and thought it best to take the call in the privacy of the men's room. Grabbing his laptop and iPad, he made a quick dash for the restroom only a few yards away.

Dorgan's phone rang as soon as he entered the men's room. "Is it done already?" he answered. He was surprised that Jones could have reached the trees and found the guy that quickly.

"No one was there," was Jones' reply. "I could tell someone had been lying in the pine needles though, and very recently. I could still smell his sweat and piss. I've gone up and down the treeline twice looking for him, but I haven't seen anyone. I'm almost back to my car. Should I continue to look for him? I don't know what he looks like, so it won't be easy unless I see someone running through the cemetery a little further out."

Dorgan was quiet. How could Jones have possibly had time to go up and down the treeline twice and be back to his car? He's barely had time to get to the trees from the gravesite. Why is he lying to me?

Dorgan said the words slowly and deliberately, "If you'd bet your life on the fact that he isn't there, then go ahead and leave. Put the package where we agreed and finish your first job. You're one for three and I'm not happy." Dorgan hung up, left the restroom and went back to his temporary workstation. He immediately started watching the cemetery again.

Jones must have decided to look further after their little talk as he was walking along the treeline, not far from where the man would have been. Dorgan watched him stealthily walk west along the trees. He lost sight of him for a few seconds as the satellite coverage ended but he then saw him on the other side of the trees, crouching and walking the entire length of the south side of the tree line. The trees ended at an access road within the cemetery and Jones circled around them and came back along the north side this time, back to the spot where he'd started. He did the same thing again, stopping periodically to look under the trees, then finally headed for his car once again.

Dorgan saw Jones pull out his cell phone and make a call. He waited for his phone to ring and for Jones to tell him he looked further and still couldn't find the man, but his phone never rang. It was obvious from the video feed that Jones was talking to someone. Someone other than me, cursed Dorgan silently.

Who is Jones talking to? What the hell is going on?

As Heather was leaving the Michtenbaums' home, her cell phone rang. It was Jeremy.

"Heather, you need to get Bernie out of the cemetery right away. Dorgan might know that someone is hiding in the trees so he could be in danger."

"How did *you* know Bernie was hiding in the trees? Never mind, dumb question. Is Bernie in danger right now?"

"I think he might be very soon. Dorgan's goon just arrived at the gravesite and Dorgan has a satellite over the cemetery covering a seventy-five yard radius in all directions of Michtenbaum's grave. I can see Bernie's legs sticking out from below the trees, so I'm sure Dorgan can see them as well. I've managed to delay Dorgan's satellite feed by a few minutes, so you won't have much time once you arrive before he sees you as well. Are you close to the cemetery? Perhaps you should call the police and let them help."

"I'm about ten minutes away but I'll hurry. I don't want to call the police in on this if I can help it. We'd have to explain a lot more than I want to right now. By the way, you do know I'm in Bernie's car and dressed as a man, right?"

"Of course," replied Jeremy dryly.

"And Jeremy," Heather added, "thanks for watching out for us."

Heather exceeded the speed limit and was glad she now knew the way to the cemetery. She arrived in eight minutes and parked near the west end of the pine and spruce tree line. She hoped it was outside the range of the satellite coverage, but she was more worried about getting to Bernie in time. She quickly walked to the trees then disappeared underneath them. She crawled under the trees towards where Bernie was hiding. She wasn't certain how far it was but it seemed forever before she reached him. He must have heard her coming and he turned to look at her with a terrified look on his face.

"Shhh, it's just me!" whispered Heather. "We need to get out of here right now!" They could both see a man with a gun headed their way. She turned and crawled on her belly, followed by Bernie, back to the car. Once in the car, Heather smelled urine and suggested they go to the hotel to freshen up and plan their next steps.

Heather figured Jeremy could see that they got away unharmed. The hotel was only a few minutes away and during the short ride Bernie talked non-stop about everything that had happened. As they got out of the car and headed into a side door of the hotel, she asked Bernie why he thought the man jumped into the grave.

"Well, he could have just been hiding from the other guy, the one he killed you know." Bernie paused to think, "but I don't think that was the reason. I think he was getting the implant out of Michael's eye."

Heather grinned at the stinky little man. "I think you're right."

As they walked towards the elevator, Heather dialed Jeremy. "Jeremy, can you see if the man is still in the cemetery?"

"Yeah, I think he's talking to Dorgan on his phone at the moment."

"We're pretty sure he cut the eye implant out of Michtenbaum. Did you have a close enough view to see?"

"I didn't have a close up view but he definitely opened the casket and messed with the body, so yes, it makes sense that he took out his eye."

"Can you follow the guy? Bernie said he's probably the same guy that tried to kill us with the car bombs, although he's changed his appearance."

"Yeah, I'll figure out a way. Dragon has a hidden camera on me and is watching my every move, so I have to be careful what I have visible on my screens."

"Really?" Heather exclaimed. "Geez, no one trusts anyone, do they?" She hesitated a moment. "He's not listening in to you also, is he?"

"If he is, I'm doomed." Jeremy said flatly. "But I don't think so. I have a bug detector which I use every time I leave my desk. It hasn't chirped at me. Hey, hold on a minute, my other line is ringing. It's probably Dorgan. He's actually been calling and giving me assignments to do."

Heather and Bernie reached her floor and her room. Bernie had brought his small suitcase in and she gave him use of the bathroom to shower and change while she waited on the phone for Jeremy to return.

"We're in luck," said Jeremy cheerily when he returned to the line. "Dorgan wants me to follow his guy as well, so now I can do it without having to worry about Dorgan seeing me!"

Heather laughed. "As I said, no one trusts anyone, do they?"

"You guys be careful," cautioned Jeremy softly and Heather could tell he was sincerely concerned. She smiled when she thought about her two new unlikely partners and heroes – Bernie and Jeremy. Two days ago, even yesterday for that matter, she hardly knew them. Now she was trusting them both with her life.

"Oh, Jeremy, can I ask one more favor before we hang up? I need access to some data and I think you're the guy to help me get it." She told him what she needed and then wrote down the information Jeremy gave her.

Heather spent her time planning their next steps while Bernie was in the other room. She needed to call Joe Singer and convince him to see her. He was probably the only one who could carry out the plan that was forming in her mind to let Mary Beth know about the foreign objects in her head. If that went well, she would do the same thing with Jon Moore's wife.

She also wanted to go back to the police station and get the implant that she had taken out of her purse and left in the women's restroom. It was evidence that may be needed later. And Dorgan surely must have figured out by now where it was – he may be planning to get it as well.

Bernie emerged from the restroom with his thinning wet hair plastered to his head. He stood nervously, not sure whether to sit on the bed since Heather was in the chair near the window.

"Have you eaten today?" Heather suddenly thought to ask, knowing he definitely hadn't eaten since before the bomb scare.

"Not since 6 a.m., so I am kind of hungry," Bernie admitted. Heather gave him the hotel menu and told him to order room service. She also told him that she would pay for a room for him at the hotel. She turned on the TV to see if there was any breaking news about the bomb threat, or someone seeing a man with a gun in the cemetery, or whether the police had found the man who killed the two police officers or Michael Michtenbaum.

She turned on her laptop as well to check the local newspaper for top stories.

"Oh my gosh! Dorgan's first hit man is dead!" Heather directed her announcement to Bernie, who walked over and sat on the bed in front of her. Heather went on, "Wow, looks like we made all of the top headlines." She didn't know whether to feel the excitement of the adventure or the extreme fear of the death that was happening around her. She realized it was both.

She read each brief headline story to Bernie.

"A second attempt was made on the life of Coroner Rachel Curry this morning as she exited the Webb Noonan Kidd Funeral Home on Ross Avenue after attending visitation services of a friend. According to Hamilton police, a bomb was found under the police vehicle in which Ms. Curry was being transported by two police escorts. An eyewitness to the placement of the bomb under the vehicle alerted Ms. Curry and those with her of the danger before they reached the car. Police have released a sketch artist drawing of the alleged bomber."

Heather read the rest of that article to Bernie and told him she was glad that their names weren't mentioned. The article also didn't mention that her car had been targeted as well. "Listen to this!" she then told Bernie.

"The body of a man found dead at the Marriott Courtyard Hotel in Hamilton today shortly after noon is believed to be that of the killer of the two Hamilton police officers yesterday and the man who attacked Coroner Rachel Curry. The identity of the man has not yet been determined. Assistant Coroner Bill Simmons estimates that the man died sometime Friday evening. An autopsy is being performed on the body to determine cause of death."

"You were right, Bernie," Heather added after she read the short article. "Today's guy that placed the bombs is different from the man yesterday."

"Do you think Dorgan killed him?" asked Bernie thoughtfully.

"Probably," stated Heather. "He botched the job. He didn't kill Rachel like he was supposed to but did kill two police that brought all kinds of attention to him and ultimately to Dorgan. My guess is that Dorgan killed him then brought in a new guy today."

Heather left the news stories and typed in the information that she had requested and received from Jeremy. Within ten seconds she saw video on her screen. She recognized Greenwood Cemetery and off in the distance could see the row of evergreen trees that she had just crawled under to retrieve Bernie.

"This is amazing," she said under her breath as she watched the scenery before her through Mary Beth's eye.

There was a knock on the hotel room door and both Bernie and Heather jumped slightly. "I'm sure it's room service," Heather said as she got up to go to the door. She peered through the peephole and saw a young woman holding a tray of food.

Heather tipped the woman with cash and told her to put the food charge on her room. Since she was still in disguise, she used her male voice. There was a burger, fries and Coke on the tray.

While Bernie ate, Heather continued to watch Mary Beth visit her mother's grave, talking softly to her mother about the many good things in her life, then telling her about Michael Michtenbaum's death and finally telling her she loved and missed her. Heather was uneasy listening in to this very private moment but needed to see and hear exactly how these implants transmitted on the screen. She entered a different time into the recorded data field and was able to view the funeral home through Mary Beth's eyes earlier today. The previous day's date with a time of 12:10 p.m. showed Mary Beth having lunch with her husband Joe.

Heather was amazed that this technology had been available in the early '60's and that implants were still working effectively 50 years later. And she was again enraged that poor Mary Beth had unknowingly had such private moments as the ones she had just witnessed invaded her entire life.

Heather returned the screen to live coverage just in time to hear Mary Beth scream. Bernie stopped eating and stared at Heather and her computer as if to say what in the world are you watching?

Mary Beth had pulled her hand back as something dropped out of it onto the ground. Heather assumed Mary Beth was still in the cemetery but couldn't tell exactly where she was as the woman was staring at something on the ground in front of her and making "ugh!" and "augh" sounds. Heather motioned that Bernie could come around and watch with her and they both looked at the ground as Mary Beth's eyes zoomed in on a human eyeball lying in the dirt.

They looked at each other. "He took the implant but left the eyeball!" Heather said to Bernie. They looked back at the screen. Mary Beth was taking a photo of the eyeball with her phone and then calling 911.

"This is better than reality TV," giggled Heather.

"This is better than James Bond!"

Heather and Bernie spent the next thirty minutes viewing some recorded footage of Mary Beth, and continually going back to the live scene in Greenwood Cemetery where the police had set up crime scene tape around the eyeball and Michael Michtenbaum's grave. At one point, Mary Beth had called the Michtenbaums to let them know she would be out a while longer, but she didn't mention the eyeball that had been found near their son's freshly closed grave.

Heather explained her plan to Bernie of calling Joe Singer and convincing him to "talk" to his wife. "It just all sounds so crazy that I don't think he'll talk to me. He'll probably just call the police."

Bernie was an unexpected voice of reason. "That's why you have to use the recordings we've just seen to make him believe you. If you can quote word for word, or better yet show him, what his wife said to him yesterday, he'll have to believe you."

"Or," Heather played devil's advocate, "he could think I'm a voyeur or stalker and call the police!" She threw her hands into the air.

"Well, you have to try. I can't think of any other way, can you?" knowing that she would agree.

"I know. I'm just not sure I should be doing this. Do you mind if I make the call alone. Here's some money. Why don't you go pay for a room for yourself for tonight." She handed him two $100 bills.

Bernie left with the cash and Heather dialed Joe Singer's cell phone number. She knew he had an early afternoon tee off time but thought he was probably finished playing golf by now and probably drinking beer with his buddies.

The phone was answered on the third ring. "Joe Singer."

"Mr. Singer. My name is Heather Barnes with the Department of Homeland Security. I need to talk to you right away, in person, regarding some very sensitive and critical information about your wife Mary Beth." Heather decided it was easier to meet with him as herself than dressed as Danny Wheatley. She waited for him to speak.

"What? Homeland Security? What would Homeland Security want with Mary Beth? What is this about?"

"Sir, that's what I need to talk to you about. I can't go into it over the phone. Are you able to come to Hamilton, Ohio, tonight?"

"That's where Mary Beth is!"

"Yes, sir, I know."

"Is she okay? She's not hurt is she?"

"No, sir, she's fine."

"Then what is this about? Is she in trouble?"

"No, she isn't in trouble." Heather hesitated. "She's in danger."

"In danger! From what? Please tell me what this is about."

"I plan to tell you everything, but I can't do it over the phone. Please, sir, how quickly can you get here? Every minute counts."

"I can be there in two hours. Where should I meet you?"

"There's an amphitheater next door to the Marriott Hotel on Front Street. Meet me on the bench in that park at 6:00 p.m. One other thing, Mr. Singer. Do not mention this conversation or anything about it to your wife. There are people listening to her right now and I wouldn't want either of you to be in any further danger. Do you understand?"

"Yes. I'll be there. Please make sure she doesn't get hurt!"

Heather was amazed that the conversation went as smoothly

and as quickly as it did. She had a lot to do. She went into the bathroom and carefully removed her mustache and placed it on a tissue on the counter in case she might need to use it again. She put on makeup and earrings and changed into white capri pants, white sandals and a white tank top with another pink tank over it. She was glad to be out of the hot jacket and men's long pants.

As she started out the door, she ran into Rachel Curry, Bernie and a female police officer walking towards her door from the elevator.

"I was just coming to see you," said Rachel. "I ran into Bernie downstairs and he was kind enough to show me where your room was. Also, I wanted to thank Bernie again for saving my life," and she put an arm around him and hugged him.

"Do you think we could drive and talk?" said Heather. "I need to run a quick errand; to the police station, actually," and she nodded towards the policewoman. "If the three of you would prefer to wait here for me, I can be back shortly."

"I can drive us," said the policewoman and they all headed to the elevator.

"You dyed your hair," stated Rachel, "and cut it." She didn't say she liked it, Heather noticed. Not the kind of woman who lied. She liked that.

"Remember I told you this morning that a man presenting an FBI badge came to see me Thursday evening?" Rachel was looking at Heather in a way that said *this is all of the story that the police know...please don't say anything else.*

"Yes."

"The man gave me the creeps. It was his eyes and his voice. Well, I don't know if you've heard the news, but a man was found dead here in this hotel just a few hours ago and it was him – the same guy. I've just come from the morgue to see the body."

"Yes, we heard. Do you think he was also the man who attacked you and killed the two police?"

"The police say it is. They had a photo of him and it's the same guy. I didn't see his face - he was behind me most of the time so I didn't see his eyes, and he had on a mask. And he changed his voice...made it deeper. They still don't know who he is yet, though."

"Have the police had any luck finding the man who tried to

kill us this morning?"

The police officer answered for Rachel. "No, we haven't any leads at all."

"Maybe we'll get lucky and this guy will end up dead as well." Heather was joking but the other two women looked at her strangely.

"And now we have another mystery to solve, possibly another murder. I simply can't stay at home and let Bill handle all of this work."

"What happened?" Heather feigned ignorance, but knew it was about the eyeball.

"A human eyeball was found in Greenwood Cemetery. They're taking it to the lab right now and I'm going to run some tests on it shortly. Since you've had some experience with such things, I was hoping you would join me to conduct the tests." Rachel's eyes were again pleading with Heather to go along with her. She and Heather had still not had an opportunity to talk alone and this was her way of making that happen.

Heather's eyes let Rachel know she understood. "I have to be somewhere else soon, but I can come by the lab for a half hour or so if that would help."

"Oh, yes, that would be a great help," said Rachel.

They walked out of the lobby door and into the parking lot, heading for the police car.

Bernie stopped in his tracks several yards before reaching the vehicle. He stared at a car with a man sitting at the wheel. The women saw Bernie staring and they stopped and looked as well, although they didn't know why or at what Bernie was staring.

No one said a word for a full minute. Bernie continued to stare, then started to back away, towards the entrance of the hotel. The women followed. The police officer had unlatched the cover to her revolver holster and had her hand on it, looking in the same direction as Bernie. The man in the car was the only person she saw.

"What is it?" Heather asked him as soon as they had retreated to the door of the hotel.

"It's him," said Bernie in a frightened voice. "It's the man from the cemetery."

"What man from the cemetery?" asked the policewoman.

Heather shot a look at Bernie that said she wished he hadn't said that in front of the cop. He shrugged apologetically and she nodded sympathetically that it was okay to go ahead and tell her. They both had felt the need to report the murder of the other grave closer.

They all watched the car with the man still sitting in it while Bernie explained what he had seen from the trees a short while earlier. He told Rachel and the policewoman about the man in the car jumping into the grave after lowering the casket into it, then pulling the other man into the grave and filling it with dirt.

The policewoman exploded at that point. "You saw him putting dirt on this other man, who may not even have been dead yet, and you didn't call the police right then! What if he was still alive? You could be considered an accomplice to his murder!"

Bernie began to tremble. He certainly never considered that he could be in trouble for trying to help. Heather interceded. "He didn't have a cell phone with him, and I think if you arrest this man, you'll find he's some kind of hired hit man. I greatly doubt the man he pulled into the grave was still alive when he began filling the grave. It was probably his eyeball that was found on the ground." Heather knew it wasn't but was trying to dissuade the policewoman. "I was on my way to the police station now to report the event." Another lie.

"Why did you wait until now?" The policewoman was calling in the report and asking for backup to approach and arrest the man who was still sitting staring straight ahead in his car. He hadn't moved at all. Heather was beginning to think the man was dead. Oh great, she thought, as she recalled her statement of just a few minutes earlier.

Jeremy watched all of the drama at the cemetery as Dragon's second hitman killed a man and buried him in the same grave with Michael Michtenbaum. The goon had apparently also ripped out Michtenbaum's eye in order to get to the incriminating implant. He then started after Bernie hidden in the trees, and Jeremy found himself quite nervous until he knew for sure that both Heather and Bernie were safe. Heather had pulled it off somehow...he wasn't quite sure how.

What Jeremy didn't know was how much Dragon had seen or now knew. Did he know that Jeremy had tampered with the video and that it was several minutes off? It wouldn't take a genius to figure out something was amiss if Dragon had called his guy and while talking to him could plainly see on the video that the man wasn't talking on the phone.

The call Jeremy had expected from Dragon was "what the hell is wrong with this video? Did you do something to it?" but what he got was, "Follow the guy in the cemetery. Keep feeding me the video."

There was no longer any reason for Jeremy to delay the video, but he couldn't switch it immediately to live coverage or Dragon would notice. On Dragon's screen it showed the man driving out of the cemetery. On the live coverage video on Jeremy's iPad, it showed the man already in downtown Hamilton, almost to the hotel, which appeared to be where the man was headed.

Jeremy reversed the process he had done earlier to start adding time back to the video. He decided to double the time in order to get it back to live coverage as soon as possible.

The door to Jeremy's office opened and Rhonda Watterson walked in. Jeremy immediately stood to talk to her. Was Dragon watching? Would he be suspicious of why the head of the country's third largest agency came in to talk to a lowly tech, and on a Saturday at that? Dorgan would not know that Jeremy had asked her to stop by and do him a favor.

Jeremy still felt certain Dragon couldn't hear him, so he told the secretary right away that he believed Dorgan was watching him from a camera in his office. The woman understood the implications of Dorgan seeing her standing and talking at any length with Jeremy, so she pointed towards Dorgan's office and asked if he was in. Jeremy shook his head, and the secretary walked around and used her keycard to swipe and enter Dorgan's office. On cue, Jeremy sat and turned slightly on his swivel stool to look through the window into Dragon's office.

The secretary saw him look and closed the blinds on the large windows. Dorgan would think she was snooping in his office. He wouldn't be happy about it but she had every right to do so.

That worked out nicely, thought Jeremy with a grin, and he

moved Samuel to the Lane Public Library and began searching inside for Dragon.   He found him and positioned the satellite right over Dragon's shoulder where he could watch his three computer screens and listen to any phone calls.

He made certain none of his other computers showed any evidence of Heather or Bernie, or of Mary Beth, until after the secretary left. He brought up the satellite of the hotel and parking lot so that he could keep an eye on Bernie's car that was parked there. Dragon's other hit man was parked in the hotel lot and was sitting in his car.

Jeremy checked the Hamilton headline news to see if there had been any new developments. They'd found Johnson's body in his hotel room. The story about the bomb attempt was there and he was glad that Heather and Bernie weren't mentioned. The fewer people who knew they were there, the better. That seemed to be it, so he left it on the screen in case the secretary wanted to look and see what he was doing when she came out of Dragon's office.

Jeremy watched Dragon sitting in the library cubicle watching his boss go through his desk and files. Jeremy was certain that she must be planning to fire Dragon as she would have to know that there could no longer be any trust between the two after this breach of Dragon's space. He would most likely be thinking the same thing.

Dragon was also watching his hired man driving down Heaton Avenue heading back towards the hotel.

The third computer, an iPAD, of which Jeremy had not been aware before now, had a screen full of verbiage. He zoomed in a little more to read it. "…utilizing vaccination of children in United States entering seventh grade. This vaccination should provide the …"

The Secretary came out of Dorgan's office, locking it behind her. He zoomed back away from the document on Dragon's screen. He glanced at all of his computer screens to ensure they were all acceptable.

"Thank you," he told her as she walked the few feet to stand behind his desk.

"Well, we can't have our spy-ee spying on our spy-er." She glanced across his desk. "Anything new?"

"He's in the library where he's monitoring three computers as you can see here," and Jeremy scooted over to his far right. "He's watching his office, which he'll probably change now, and he's watching his hired man that just left the cemetery, and he has another document pulled up but I haven't read it yet. I just pulled this up since I couldn't do that while he was watching." He was glad she didn't ask him to read it.

He filled her in on the other events of the day. Jeremy couldn't believe that she was not intervening to stop Dorgan since he was responsible for two more deaths. She thanked him and left and he breathed a sigh of relief that he could finally get back to some real surveillance now that he was totally alone again.

Jeremy started to read the rest of the document page that he could see on Dragon's computer when Dragon suddenly exited out of the program and began shutting down that computer. It surprised Jeremy. It was almost as if Dragon knew someone was looking over his shoulder. Dragon did the same with his other two computers and began packing his two devices into their cases.

Jeremy had wanted to move Samuel to make a quick check on Heather and Bernie, but now that Dragon was on the move, he couldn't afford to lose him so followed him out of the library to his car. Audrey showed that Bernie's car was in the hotel parking lot so he hoped they were safe and sound inside.

Dragon headed towards the cemetery then drove the back way out, following the same route as his agent who had left the cemetery only minutes before. Jeremy was listening in as well but Dragon hadn't made or received any phone calls.. He was heading for the hotel but driving slowly as if looking for something.

Jeremy activated Mary Beth's implant video and immediately saw that something exciting was happening. There were police around her and Jeremy realized the setting was the cemetery. Why was she back in the cemetery, he wondered. It was Michael Michtenbaum's gravesite area. Had the other body been discovered in the grave already? Had Heather or Bernie called the police? Why was Mary Beth there?

He watched for a while but the scene revealed nothing new as to what was going on. The grave was not opened so they must not have discovered the other body.

Jeremy stared back at Audrey's screen and realized Dragon's hit man had never gotten out of his car. He zoomed in to the car and saw the man sitting in the driver's seat. His eyes were open but he wasn't moving. Nothing had happened to him from the time he left the cemetery and drove to the hotel. Could he be asleep with his eyes open? Perhaps he puts himself in some kind of trance or meditative state. And yet Jeremy couldn't shake the feeling that the man was dead. How could Dragon have killed him? He hasn't been near him all day.

Jeremy zoomed out again to look at the front entrance and parking lot. Dragon was pulling into the hotel lot. He parked several rows away from his partner. What are they both doing just sitting there?

Jeremy saw several people walk out the front door of the hotel. He zoomed in. It was Heather, Bernie, a policewoman and the coroner, Rachel Curry.

They were walking towards the probably-dead hit man in the car but then stopped and headed back towards the entrance to the hotel. Bernie must have seen and recognized the man, Jeremy concluded. I don't think they can see Dragon from where they are, he thought.

Dragon was moving again and Jeremy followed him, watching his every move, keeping his other eye on the next monitor over, where police were arriving at the Marriott parking lot with lights and sirens.

Mary Beth finally left the cemetery and drove back to the Michtenbaums' home. She had calmed down considerably after finding the eyeball near Michael's grave, but the unsettling event was still on her mind. Surely it hadn't been there while the funeral service was going on. It had to have been placed there in the past two hours.

While in the car, her cell phone rang the familiar chime of her husband's phone. "Hi honey," she answered.

"Mary Beth, are you okay?" Joe sounded a little out of breath.

"I'm fine. You sound tense. What's wrong?"

"Nothing. I just felt like something was wrong and I wanted

to check on you."

"Well, I *did* just have a little scare, so maybe you're psychic," and Mary Beth proceeded to tell Joe about the eyeball in the graveyard.

"The police don't know whose eye it is?" asked Joe.

"No, not yet, but I'm sure a one-eyed person will show up soon. I don't mean to make jokes about it, I was so upset about it, but I'm much better now."

"You sound like you're in the car now."

"Yes, I'm on my way back to Mitch and Celia's. I should be there in about ten minutes."

"Good. Please be careful honey. Would it be okay if I come down and stay there tonight?"

"Joe, of course, but what about your friends! I thought you guys had a big night planned."

"We canceled after golf, so I thought I'd come be with my best girl tonight."

"Wonderful! I can't wait to see you, Joe. You remember how to get to Mitch and Celia's don't you? What time do you think you'll be here?"

"I remember how to get there, and I don't know exactly what time I'll get there, but it should be early – maybe 6:30 or 7:00. I'll call you when I'm getting close."

"Okay, honey. Drive carefully. I love you."

"I love you too, Mary Beth."

"Sir in the tan sedan, put both of your hands outside the window where we can see them!" The Police Chief was using a bullhorn and his voice traveled throughout the parking lot and into the next block.

The policewoman tasked with guarding Rachel was keeping Bernie, Rachel and Heather away from the lot, at the front door of the hotel, where they had been previously waiting. The Chief had spoken with them to get Bernie's story before calling to the man.

The man in the tan sedan didn't move. A half dozen police had the sedan surrounded from about twenty-five feet away with weapons drawn and aimed.

"Sir, this is Chief Davies of the Hamilton Police. You are wanted for questioning in a possible homicide. Put your hands out of the window now!" There was still no response.

The Chief motioned for two officers to approach the car from the rear, one on each side. Within seconds, they were on each side of the car with weapons trained on the head of the man inside the car. Two other officers with pistols aimed towards the windshield moved in closer to the vehicle. Still the man didn't move.

The officer on the driver's side of the tan sedan tested the door and it opened. With one hand holding a gun to the man's head, he reached with the other hand to take the man's pulse at his neck. He lowered his gun and turned towards his boss, shaking his head.

The Chief turned to the policewoman with Rachel. "Call in the wagon and crime scene unit for this one and then call and let the dispatcher know my team is headed for Greenwood Cemetery. Have her get someone from the cemetery there to help us open up that grave." He turned to the coroner, "Rachel, looks like you're going to have to go back to work. The dead bodies are piling up faster than we can keep up with them."

Rachel called Bill to let him know where she was and that she would be handling the dead body found at the Marriott. "But I have the dead body that we found at the Marriott," he corrected her.

"Oh, sorry, Bill, I mean the *new, second* dead body we just found at the Marriott."

"Holy Christ!" Bill exclaimed. "What the heck is going on?" He didn't really expect her to answer that. "Rachel, do you want me to do the tests on the eyeball that the police brought in here? I'm about finished with my autopsy and can do that for you if you wish."

"No, I don't think it's going to be necessary. The police are headed for the cemetery now and I think they're going to find the person that belongs to that eye. So we'll just wait before we do anything. I should be there pretty soon with this body, but you can go on home if you wish. I can autopsy this one."

"No way I'm leaving you here. I'll stay and help you."

Rachel thanked him and hung up, then set about the task of examining the dead body in the car. She quickly discovered that he had a fake bodysuit on under his clothes that made him appear fatter, as well as a false beard and other facial makeup to change his appearance. The police officer was still assigned to stay with Rachel and stood guard close by. She told Bernie and Heather that they needed to give formal statements at police headquarters but could go back inside the hotel for the time being.

Heather's plan to get to police headquarters to retrieve the implant from the ladies room was now postponed. Her meeting with Rachel was not going to happen yet either. She had little less than one hour before she was to meet Joe Singer. How could she get out of going to police headquarters until after she talked to Joe?

"What do you know about this Heather woman?" the police officer asked Rachel. It was obvious to her that Heather and Bernie were smack in the middle of whatever was going on with all of these murders and attempted murders.

"Not much," replied Rachel. "I just met her this morning. I know she works for Homeland Security. So does Bernie. And I also know they're the good guys. Whatever they may know about this, they are in just as much, maybe more, danger than I am."

"Good guys or bad guys, they need to tell the police what they know. And there's no excuse for waiting to report the probable death of the man at the cemetery!" She was still incensed about the fact that they hadn't called 911 right away.

"I know. I agree with you there. I don't know why they waited to tell the police about that." Rachel really didn't want to say anything more to the policewoman and set about helping the paramedics remove the body from the car and place it in the ambulance.

"We need to go inside and get those two, and I'll drop them off at the police station, then we'll head on to the morgue."

Heather and Bernie had stayed downstairs and were sitting at a table at the edge of the restaurant when Rachel and the officer came in. They hadn't had much time to talk but Heather had been able to quickly tell Bernie about an idea she had.

"We're ready to go," stated the police officer.

"Is it okay if I come in an hour or so? I have an appointment that I had arranged earlier and I can't miss it. Besides, Bernie is the one who saw the man. I didn't."

"This is official police business, ma'am. We really need for you to come now," stated the police officer firmly.

"And I'm on official Homeland Security business that can't wait either," stated Heather just as firmly, even though her statement wasn't exactly true. "I promise I will come to police headquarters as soon as I finish my business."

The officer hesitated but didn't think she could force Heather to come, and she remembered Rachel's statement that Heather was one of the good guys. The officer still believed Heather knew a lot more about the murders that she wasn't telling. "I will be waiting for you at the station."

Heather thought about her budding plan further – the one she had just explained to Bernie, albeit the CliffsNotes version. It was extremely dangerous for everyone involved. Everyone would therefore need to consent to the plan and how she was going to pull that off by the next day was beyond her at the moment. But it had to be done. She hoped she was doing the right thing. She ran to her room and accessed her laptop and the special program, entering username jmoore, password KJ156#%1478Dklm330JM00$er. She wanted to see what Jonathan Moore was doing right now.

After running through his kitchen and into his home office, Jacob Barnes had immediately checked several sources to find out what, if anything, was going on with Freedom Project I. He hadn't heard anything about that project since it was officially discontinued, and he hadn't been involved in it since 1995, when John Dorgan took it over as Project Leader. He knew Dorgan now worked at Homeland Security where Heather worked and wondered if there was some connection there. Had Dorgan talked to Heather about the discontinued project at some time? Surely not. If he did, thought Barnes, I'll see that he's fired.

It didn't take him long to find out that one of the original test subjects, Michael Ray Michtenbaum, had been murdered. So that what's started the ball rolling, thought Barnes. Even with a terminated project, the current project leader would be expected to oversee any possible problems that could arise and clean up any loose ends that might jeopardize any future projects and those involved. So Dorgan had initiated something. But that still didn't explain why Heather was involved. She didn't report to Dorgan and even if she did, she wouldn't be involved in a former CIA-led project.

He dialed her cell number. It went to voice-mail. He left a message for her to call him right away, stating that it was urgent. He then looked up Danny's cell number in his phone and tried it. It, too, went to voice-mail and he asked Danny to have Heather call him right away. He remembered their last phone call on Thursday evening. She had wanted to talk to him about something. Was it this? The Freedom Project?

Jacob continued to look up everything he could find about Michael Michtenbaum's death and found the local Hamilton, Ohio, news. He was even more concerned for his daughter when he read the several news articles of the past few days. While the articles didn't state that any of the murders or attempted murders were directly connected to the death of Michael Michtenbaum, Jacob knew they were.

Thank goodness Heather was in Fiji right now. She shouldn't be in any immediate danger. He would talk to her soon and find out why she looked up the old file on the Freedom Project. Perhaps she overheard Dorgan talking, or maybe even her own boss had said something about it and she remembered that file she had seen so many years ago.

He had calmed himself down by the time Susan called him to dinner. The table was beautifully set and Susan had picked a few spring flowers and placed them in a crystal vase as the centerpiece. She had prepared a fresh salad with mixed greens, feta cheese, strawberries and almond slivers. Beautiful bacon wrapped filet mignons sat in the center of two of his best china plates, with asparagus spears and small red potatoes on each side. A basket of hard rolls also sat on the table. Susan had changed into a red dress with a scoop neckline that extended around her bare shoulders. The dress tapered at the waist to hug her curves and stopped a few inches below her knees.

The old Jacob, when his mind was on a case, would have hardly noticed the beautiful scene before him, but the new Jacob, only three months from retirement and, he hoped, marriage, was once again drawn in by the lovely Susan and sat down to a wonderful meal.

Two minutes into the meal, Jacob's cell phone rang. It was

Danny's phone.

"I'm so sorry, Susan, but I really have to get this." He stood and walked towards the living room with his phone. "Heather?" he answered.

"No, Jacob, it's Danny. I got your message. I guess she didn't tell you, but Heather didn't come with me to Fiji. She said something about going to a funeral – something to do with work."

Jacob's heart stopped. This couldn't be happening.

"Jacob?"

"Thanks Danny," Jacob barely managed to say and hung up.

The amphitheater park was right next door to the hotel. Heather left her room at 5:50 p.m. to meet Mary Beth's husband, Joe Singer. She was nervous. So far, she hadn't told anyone about the Freedom Project except to let Rachel know that the ear implant she found in Michael Michtenbaum was part of a CIA top secret experiment. Now she was planning to tell this man almost everything about the experiment.

Once she told someone, there was no going back. She would no longer be able to change her mind, and she might never be able to go back to her previous way of life. She might not have a job or even a life to go back to. She was not only putting herself in more danger, but she was now putting anyone and everyone she told in extreme danger as well.

She had considered waiting until she talked with her dad but finally decided that he might be part of the problem and not want to help with her solution. She knew beyond a shadow of a doubt that he would try and talk her out of what she was about to do and she knew in her heart that she had to do something to help the two remaining victims of this experiment. No, she couldn't turn to her dad for help in this situation.

As soon as she left the hotel and turned towards the park, walking through the small parking lot, she could see a man sitting nervously on a bench. She had seen Joe Singer in the recordings of Mary Beth that she had viewed a little earlier, so she knew the man was Joe. Heather didn't bring her purse, but did have her laptop in its case.

"Mr. Singer, thank you for coming." Heather extended her hand for him to shake, which he stood and did hesitantly and briefly.

"Tell me what this is about. Why is Mary Beth in danger."

"Please, sit back down. I brought my computer so I could not just tell you, but show you." Heather took a deep breath and began telling Joe Singer how his wife was one of three babies born in Mercy Hospital who had been part of a top secret CIA experiment that implanted video and audio devices within the babies' heads on the night of their births. She ended with Michael Michtenbaum's murder and the events of the past couple of days, including Mary Beth finding the eyeball in the cemetery.

"She told me about the eyeball a little while ago," Joe said, sounding dazed. She wasn't sure he was buying any of the story until she came to the part about the eyeball.

"The man that removed Michtenbaum's eyeball only wanted the implant; the evidence that could incriminate him, the CIA and others. Five people have died since yesterday because of this, and the coroner has been attacked twice and is lucky to be alive. And I'm not even counting Michael Michtenbaum. We don't know why he was murdered. It probably had nothing to do with the project, but I'm not certain of that."

"So the government has been watching and listening to everything Mary Beth does? Is that what you're saying?"

"I'm not saying anyone is necessarily watching and listening all the time, but they can and definitely do sometimes. Let me show you." Heather kept her keyboard hidden as she entered the information to bring up Mary Beth's live video and audio on her laptop screen, then she turned the computer towards Joe.

Heather could hear water running, a shower, and Mary Beth humming softly. She leaned in to look at the screen. She could tell Joe didn't know what he was looking at. It was a bathtub with the shower going, and Mary Beth's arms and hands could be seen washing various parts of her body.

"She's in the shower?" He still seemed dazed.

"Yes, remember the implant is in Mary Beth's eye, so the view will always be from her point of vision. When she gets out of the shower, there will most likely be a mirror and you'll be able to tell it's her."

"I can already tell it's her." He was stunned at what he was trying to comprehend. "I just don't understand why the CIA would want to do this. Why would they want to watch a person taking a shower, or going to work, or eating at home. I don't get it!" He shouted the last sentence and angrily stood up, running a hand through his hair and bending over at the waist as if he was going to be sick.

"They don't want to watch those things, and hopefully they haven't been watching much of your personal lives."

Joe sat down and put his head in his hands when Heather made that statement.

"Oh, my God." he said.

"One purpose would be to be able to identify a killer, for example. The local police don't know it yet, but Michael Michtenbaum most likely recorded a video of his murderer, if the person was in Michael's sight. Law enforcement would be able to catch almost every criminal if they could watch a crime through the victim's, or through a witness's, eye."

"That doesn't make it right! It doesn't give them the right to horribly invade our private lives like they've done." Joe was distraught.

"I know. That's why I'm here talking to you. I can't have this knowledge and not do something about it. I can't just go back to work and know that I didn't tell the other two people involved."

"Why are you telling me? Why not just tell Mary Beth? You've seen her, right?"

"Yes, I've seen her. Think about it. If I talk to her, the government will hear me. If she looks at me, the government will see me. If I write her a note, they will read it. Now, the same is true for you, but there are two reasons you should do it instead of me. One, she knows and trusts you, and will believe you. Not so with me. The bigger reason, however, is that you have the ability and opportunity to be able to tell her without being seen or heard. And here's how."

Heather explained the rest of her plan to him. It involved, at the least, Joe telling Mary Beth in a way that could neither be seen nor heard through her implants. Then it was up to them if they wanted to take the next step. Heather explained the pros and cons of taking the action she was proposing, but the decision would have to be Mary Beth's.

"What about the other guy? Have you told him yet? What does he want to do?"

"No, I haven't told him yet. I plan to approach his wife just the same way I've approached you. It would be best if everyone is in agreement to do it the same way, but whatever each individual decides is okay. Just remember, after you "tell" her, it will most likely be obvious to whomever is watching and listening to Mary Beth that something is wrong. She will be upset and may be overly careful not to look at anything of a private nature. That may give her away. And she will want to talk to you about it, but absolutely can't. It will be difficult not to slip up. That's why it's important to think about the other step right away."

"How do I get in touch with you in the morning?" Joe asked.

"I'll call you. It will be from a different number than the hotel number I called from before." He looked at her with some fear in his eyes. "I'm just being cautious," she smiled.

But she knew that every word they had just said had been heard, and every movement they had made had been seen. If someone wanted them dead, they would be dead soon, cautious or not.

Heather hurried back to the hotel and retrieved her purse with a few extra items she had packed, then headed to the morgue in Bernie's car. She knew the police officer, Officer Davis, would be livid with her for coming to the morgue before going to police headquarters, but she needed to talk to Rachel first. And she didn't know how long they would detain her at the police station.

There were two police officers at the morgue with Rachel, one middle-aged man stationed outside the entrance to the building, who frisked Heather and called inside to make certain it was okay to let her enter, and Officer Davis, who was inside the lab with Rachel and Bill, both of whom were busy with autopsies on two of the three bodies found dead that day. The third body, the extra one in Michael Michtenbaum's grave, would be arriving for autopsy soon. Bill and Rachel were in for a long night.

Officer Davis was not happy to see Heather once she found out she had not yet been to the police station. "I have to talk to Rachel for a few minutes, then I'll head straight there," Heather promised her.

Rachel was cleaning the body of the man found in the car at the hotel parking lot. She had removed the body suit he was wearing, the false cap that made him appear bald, and the makeup and fake beard. She stopped spraying the body when she heard Heather say she needed to speak with her.

"Let's go in my office," Rachel offered while pulling off her gloves. Officer Davis started to follow but Rachel assured her they would be fine and that she could stand watch outside her office door if she wished, or stay in the lab. Officer Davis frowned and stood outside the office door.

"What a day, huh," Rachel smiled wearily. "With his disguise off, the man that I'm working on looks like the man Bernie identified as the bomber. It appears that both of the men who tried to kill me are dead. What do you think that means?"

"I think it means their boss is not happy with their performance," said Heather truthfully, then she wished she hadn't been so blunt when she saw the fear in Rachel's eyes. "Sorry, I didn't mean to frighten you further," Heather apologized.

"It's okay. I know this is obviously a very serious and dangerous matter, although I don't know why. Can you tell me more?"

"Yes, I want to tell you a lot more, but first I need to ask you if it's okay if I explain a portion of the story – the part about Michael Michtenbaum – to the police. I won't mention that you know anything about it, but I'll tell them that the assassins are trying to kill you because you removed, and therefore know about, the one implant. Hopefully, with these two assassins dead, your family is in less danger."

"I guess you're going to have to tell the police. You can't just refuse to say anything or they may hold you. What did you mean when you just said you'll only tell them a portion of the story – the Michael Michtenbaum part – you mean there's another part?"

"Yes, there's lots more." Heather gave as brief but as thorough an explanation as she could about the three subjects. She didn't mention the name of the project, or Jon Moore's name, but she did tell Rachel about Mary Beth Singer being another one of the subjects with implants in her ear and eye. She explained that Michael's eyeball had been removed because it, too, had a micro video camera imbedded on the back of it and the people assigned to keep the project quiet had to retrieve both devices.

"The dead man you're working on should have the eye implant somewhere on him or in his car. Did you find it by any chance? It looks similar to the one you removed from behind his ear."

Rachel picked up her desk phone and called the lab. "Bill, could you do me a favor and bring all of my victim's personal effects to my office please."

Officer Davis asked Bill what was in the bag before he took it into Rachel's office, then he left and the two women went through the man's clothing, wallet and other items. They found the small round implant, with eye tissue still attached to it, in a small clear plastic bag inside the man's wallet. "May I keep this?" asked Heather. "Here's what I'd like to do," and she explained the rest of her plan to remove the implants from both other victims and hopefully allow all of them to stay alive during and after the process.

"Do you think you could perform the surgeries to remove the eye and ear implants from Mary Beth and the other person?" Heather asked Rachel. "Since you already know about this, and you're a surgeon, it would be best if no one else was involved."

Heather watched Rachel as they spoke. She liked the woman. She could tell that Rachel was flabbergasted by the whole story and at the thought of removing the implants from two living people. But not once did she get the feeling that Rachel did not believe or trust that what she saying was the complete truth.

"The ear implants would be fairly easy. I'm very comfortable with those. I'm not so sure about the eye implants though. I've never performed surgery on an eye, and the eyeball would have to be disconnected and removed and reconnected. I really don't think I could do it. Not if they still want to see out of that eye," Rachel added.

"Okay. Well, I've already talked to Mary Beth's husband and he is going to talk to Mary Beth tonight, without talking of course," she added. "If I can get hold of the other guy, would you be able to remove the ear implants tomorrow?"

"Tomorrow! Why so quickly! And I greatly doubt these two people will just take our word for it without seeing their doctors, getting x-rays and CT scans, and what if they go to the press? I would be incredibly angry if this had happened to me. I'd want everyone to know about it." Rachel rambled on for a minute, but finally said, "If it's tomorrow, that's fine with me. I can even do the surgeries here in my lab. I'll need Bill to assist though, so he will need to know what's going on."

"I rather doubt either of them will want the procedure done tomorrow either," stated Heather, "but be prepared just in case. Go ahead and tell Bill what you think he needs to know. Obviously, neither of you can tell anyone else."

Heather rose to leave.

Rachel spoke to her before she opened the door. "So all of this conspiracy theory stuff you hear about is really true? Our government has really done this terrible thing to its citizens, and will now kill innocent people to keep it quiet? It's extremely scary to think about."

"Yes, it is," and Heather left for the police station.

Heather's first stop once inside headquarters was the ladies room where she went straight to the spot she had hidden the small ear implant. It was right where she left it. She immediately wrapped it in a small piece of aluminum foil then placed it inside a small round plastic pill case. She closed the lid on the pill case and placed it inside a small glass jar, tightening the lid. She slid the jar into a thick sock and stuffed it in the bottom of her purse, hoping her precautions were enough to keep any sounds she or anyone else made from transmitting through the small device.

She had taken the aluminum foil and small jar from Bernie's room service tray after he'd finishing eating earlier. The jar held the ketchup for his burger and the fries were wrapped in foil to keep them hot and fresh. The sock she had found in Bernie's car, and the pill bottle was her own.

She hoped the police interrogation wouldn't take too long. She had a lot of work yet to do.

When Heather walked into the large room where she had

been earlier that morning after the bomb scare, she could see Bernie in a side room giving his statement. She hoped he didn't reveal too much information about the Freedom Project but she couldn't worry about it. The Police Chief saw her and motioned her into his office.

"Miss Barnes," he started. "Welcome back to headquarters." He looked very tired and Heather could only imagine the weekend he was having so far. Two of his young officers had been killed the day before. There had been two attempts on the coroner's life in as many days and he therefore had one or two officers assigned to Rachel at all times. Three dead bodies had been found that day, all seemingly related to the attacks on the coroner. Michael Michtenbaum's murder was still fresh and unsolved.

"Officer Davis seems to think you know more about what's been going on around here the past two days than what you're saying. She said you stated that the dead man in the car was a hired hit man, and that you were aware of the dead body we just found in the grave with the Michtenbaum guy. Also, she said you seemed to know that the eyeball found belonged to one of the men in the grave." He gave her a tired but cold look. "I'd really appreciate it if you could explain all of this to me."

"The reason I've kept quiet is that anyone who knows the reason for these killings is in danger of becoming a victim as well. Rachel accidentally discovered something and is therefore a target. I know about it and a bomb was placed under my car today. Bernie knows about it and the man in the cemetery came after him with a gun. The fewer people who know, the better. But you need to know, so I'll tell you." She explained only about Michael Michtenbaum and stated that Rachel didn't know what she had discovered when she removed the implant from Michtenbaum's ear.

"So who was the other man in Michtenbaum's grave? What did he have to do with this mess?"

"Nothing. He was the real cemetery worker who had come to bury Michael's casket. He just arrived at the wrong time, and the man assigned to remove the implant from Michael's eye killed him."

"Who killed both of the hired killers?" The Chief asked.

"I don't know for certain but I am assuming it was whoever hired them. Neither one of them was able to kill Rachel as assigned, and both killed people they weren't supposed to kill. Their employer was most likely not very happy." Heather didn't like withholding information from the police. She was fairly certain Dorgan was the man who had killed his two agents, but Jeremy had warned her that the Secretary of Homeland Security, Heather's boss, did not want him, and therefore did not want anyone else, jeopardizing DHS's investigation and surveillance of Dorgan. But innocent people were dying and she didn't know how long she would continue to withhold Dorgan's name.

The Chief sat thinking for a moment. "You said that the eye implant can see whatever the person sees, and all data is recorded. Would Michael Michtenbaum's eye implant show who killed him if he saw the guy before he died?"

Good question Chief, Heather thought. She smiled at him. "Yes, but good luck finding out who in the government can and will give that to you."

The Chief started to say something else, but stopped. "A few more questions. Why did you and Bernie come here? You're both from Homeland Security, I understand. You're not CIA. I truly hope you're not involved in these murders. So what are your roles in this?"

Heather was thoughtful about her answer. She told the truth, although it wasn't the whole truth. She didn't mention anything about her dad and his secret file. "Word leaked out somehow among a few people at DHS about this whole experiment once Michael Michtenbaum died, Bernie and I being two that heard. I doubt my explanation for coming will sound plausible, because it doesn't even make sense to me, but I just didn't want to go on vacation with my boyfriend, and I was curious about this case, so I flew here instead. I don't really know why Bernie came except I know that he has a crush on me and he was probably worried about me and just wanted an adventure."

The Chief stared at her for a long moment as if he was considering the plausibility of her statement, but he didn't pursue the question further. "Will the two of you be staying in town a while? We may need to talk to you again."

"We'll definitely be here through sometime tomorrow. Bernie may be planning to head back tomorrow. He is supposed to be back at work. I'm on vacation so could stay longer if needed."

"Let me know if and when you leave."

Bernie was waiting for Heather when she came out of the Chief's office. Once in the car, they shared their stories given to the police and were relieved that they were remarkably similar.

"Great minds think alike," laughed Heather and Bernie beamed.

Carol Moore had convinced Jon's doctor to schedule a CT scan for Saturday afternoon. There would be an additional cost to bring in the technician for a non-emergency scan, the doctor told her, but Carol insisted that was alright. Jon needed to know as soon as possible what was causing the terrible mind-piercing noise in his right ear that was driving him crazy. Carol told the doctor that she heard it as well and he told her that was not possible. He began explaining the medical reason why she would not be able to hear Jon's tinnitus, no matter how bad it was, and Carol interrupted him. "Doctor, yesterday morning I would have believed you, but today I don't. I definitely heard the screeching noise coming from his ear."

"Okay, I'll order the test right now. Be at the hospital at 4 p.m."

Carol and Jon spent a quiet day at home, other than when the frequent bouts of pain were unbearable and caused Jon to yell out loud, but the couple passed the time alone until they went to the hospital. They arrived early, but it was 4:30 before the nurse called them in for the test. Several views of Jon's brain were taken, primarily on the right side.

They returned to the waiting room to wait for the scans to be read and for Jon's doctor to arrive to interpret them and talk to the couple. Jon was happy for the most part. He had a good feeling that this test would reveal something to help him get rid of the pain that was plaguing his life.

The doctor arrived a little before six and went to retrieve the scans. Carol and Jon stood up when he walked back into the room where they were. He motioned for them to follow him to a private office.

"Jon, were you in the service?" the doctor asked. "Did you ever get any schrapnel or other pieces of metal or plastic in your head?"

"What! No! Do the tests show I have metal in my head?" Jon was confused.

"Look here." The doctor held up an image for both Jon and Carol to see and pointed first to a small dot behind Jon's right ear. "This isn't supposed to be here. I'm not saying it's causing your problem, but it could be."

Jon was confused but excited. "So, if we take that out, the noise in my head might go away, right?"

"Maybe. I don't know what this object is, so I can't really say. But we can have it removed and see if that solves the problem."

Jon looked at Carol and she was smiling as wide as he.

"There's something else," continued the doctor.

"What?" Jon and Carol asked together.

"See this scan? There's another foreign object of the same size and shape behind your right eyeball. It shouldn't be there either."

This time when Jon and Carol looked at each other, their faces showed worry and confusion.

"You can't remember ever being in an accident, or having an operation, or anything that would account for these two objects being in your head?" the doctor asked again.

"No. I've never had an operation in my life. I wasn't in the service, or in a car accident. I have no idea how these things got in my head. Can you get the other one out as well?"

"Maybe, but it seems extremely close to your eye, so if it isn't bothering you, you may want to consider just leaving it."

The doctor told Jon to call or come to his office the following Monday to schedule the operation to remove the foreign object from behind his ear.

Jon was in a good mood when they arrived home. Surely it had to be this object causing the severe sounds in his ear, and soon it would be gone and he would be back to normal. He ordered a pizza and sat down on the couch with a beer to try and enjoy a movie.

The phone rang and Carol answered it. A woman's voice said, "Is this Carol Moore?" and when Carol answered yes, Heather continued, "My name is Heather Barnes and I'm with Homeland Security, the Washington D.C. office. I need to talk to you right away, in person, regarding some very sensitive and critical information about your husband Jon. If he is there with you, please don't say anything to him. Is he there?"

"Yes," Carol answered. "What is this about?"

"It might be best if you walked into another room or outside to talk so that he can't hear you." Carol didn't care if her husband heard her, and she wasn't in the mood to play games with this woman, but still, she walked into the kitchen and out onto the back porch. "Would you be able to meet me for about a half hour this evening and I will explain everything. I'm in Hamilton, Ohio, so I'm not far away."

"No," said Carol rather curtly. "I'm not meeting you anywhere unless you tell me now what this is all about."

"Okay, please just make sure you're somewhere where Jon won't be able to hear you talk."

Carol was annoyed, but replied, "I'm on the back porch. He's in the house, so we can talk."

"What I'm about to tell you is going to sound bizarre and one of the reasons I wanted to meet in person was to show you evidence that I'm telling the truth." Carol could hear Heather take a deep breath before she continued. "Your husband Jon, along with two other people, were operated on at birth as part of an experimental project by the government. They each have two implants in their heads – one behind the right eye and the other behind the right ear. Recently, one of the three…"

"Where should I meet you?" Carol interrupted Heather. "I can come right now."

"Oh, uh, okay, great," Heather said with a sound of surprise in her voice. "Where is a fairly quiet place away from crowds where we can talk. I'm not familiar with the Trenton area, so I'll let you pick."

Carol told Heather where they should meet.

Twenty-five minutes later they were both seated away from anyone else at an outside table at a restaurant.

"I was surprised that you changed your mind so quickly," Heather began the conversation.

"Well, your timing couldn't have been more apropos. In fact, it was a bit eerie. When you called, we had just gotten home from the hospital where Jon had a CT scan which found two implants in his head – one behind his right eye and the other behind his right ear."

"Really!" Heather exclaimed.

Carol went on to tell Heather about the buzzing and screeching noises in her husband's head which led him to get the CT scan. "We're scheduling surgery to get the ear implant out. We don't know about the eye one yet since it isn't bothering him and is apparently a much more difficult surgery."

"Well, what I'm about to tell you now will probably help you make up your mind to have that surgery done as well," and Heather explained the purpose and function of the two implants. She went on to explain that someone may have been watching and listening to Jon's meeting with the doctor and now know that he is not only aware of the foreign objects in his head, but plans to have them removed. "That could increase the danger to the two of you. I truly don't mean to frighten you, but these people have already killed several innocent people to get this other person's implants."

"Oh, my God! What should we do?" Carol was shaking.

"I would suggest staying somewhere else the next few nights as a precaution. Also, if you want to have the ear implant removed tomorrow, the surgeon who removed the one from the dead man can do it for you. She's the coroner, but she's an experienced surgeon. I'll explain to you why I think it would be good to have it done tomorrow if possible." Heather explained the rest of her plan and Carol agreed to talk to her husband.

"Obviously, you can't really talk to him, Carol. People are listening. If you could play a little game with your husband and get a blindfold on him, then uncover his left eye so that he can see. Make certain the right eye stays well covered. You can then communicate in writing. It will take a while, and you have to be extremely careful not to talk or have him ask questions out loud. If you can get him to the morgue in Hamilton tomorrow, we can have the ear devices removed and then we can all talk freely about the next step."

"We'll be there," said Carol Moore.

Even though Bernie hadn't slept much in over 36 hours, he wasn't able to do so when he laid down on the bed in his hotel room to rest. He closed his eyes hoping to get a brief nap, but his mind wouldn't rest long enough to allow sleep to come. Heather had left to talk to Jon Moore's wife. When she returned, they were going to buy several memory sticks to make copies of the Freedom Project file. Heather hadn't told him her plan in its entirety, but he knew she wanted several copies of the file, and Michael Michtenbaum's implants, in safe places should they ever need to use them as insurance.

Bernie was looking forward to spending time with Heather in her room, eating a room service meal at the small table and helping her put the three packages together. It was too much to hope that something more would happen between them, but Bernie lay on his bed with his eyes closed, thinking about the possibility anyway, and smiling. In this fantasy he was Pierce Brosnan instead of Sean Connery. He believed Pierce was taller, and Heather needed a tall man.

The phone by his bed rang loudly and Bernie jumped. "I'll be right there, Heather," he said and made a quick trip to the mirror to check himself out before heading down one floor to her room.

Heather filled Bernie in on how well it went with Carol Moore, especially since Jon's ear implant was apparently defective and was now giving him a lot of trouble. She told him about the CT scan and the fact that they were going to have the ear implant removed anyway.

"If Dorgan's been watching and listening to these three subjects for years, which I assume he has, why didn't he notice that Jon's ear implant has been having problems? Carol said she could even hear the awful screeching noises it was making. Why didn't Dorgan hear it? I would think one of the purposes in monitoring the subjects is to determine if the devices work for the 75 years they're supposed to."

"Maybe he *did* report that it wasn't working properly," offered Bernie. "I'm not sure what they would do about it. They couldn't very well fix it for them, right?"

"Yes, you're right. And, maybe they don't necessarily listen in most of the time. Perhaps they just watch and would only listen if something seemed out of the ordinary."

Bernie nodded.

"Well, we need to go buy the memory sticks and materials to sound-proof and protect any implants that are removed." She thought then added, "You don't have to go if you don't want to. You must be tired. I can put these packages together tonight."

"No, I really want to help. When we're finished, could we order room service again? That food was really good."

"Sure Bernie. We'll be good and hungry by that time."

She had barely gotten those words out of her mouth when a loud knock came on her door. She peered out the door peephole and saw two Hamilton police officers. She opened the door. "Heather Barnes?"

"Yes?" she replied.

The officers eyed Bernie, in his mid fifties, short and stout in the middle, with thinning hair, sitting on the bed, and tall, lean, strikingly exotic, young Heather. They looked at each other with that "it takes all kinds" look.

"Heather Barnes, you're under arrest for removing evidence from a crime scene in a murder investigation."

"What!" Heather and Bernie both knew what evidence they meant – Michael's eye implant – but both were truly surprised that she was being arrested for it. "No, please, I can't be arrested! There are lives at stake!"

"Turn around please," stated one officer who was removing handcuffs from his belt.

"Can't she just give back the evidence and you let her go?" Bernie was just as upset by the unexpected intrusion that was not only going to take Heather and his room service meal away from him but possibly stop Heather's plan for helping the Singers, the Moores, Rachel and themselves.

"The implant isn't here anyway," she lied and Bernie saw her look at him, then at her purse, and back at him to make sure he saw her look at her purse again. He understood her look indicating that the implant, both actually, were in her purse and she had no intention of handing them over to the police.

"We don't make those decisions. We're just here to arrest Miss Barnes." The officer who spoke clicked the cuffs on Heather and they guided her out the door.

"Call Rachel and Jeremy," she called to Bernie as she left.

Bernie was quite upset and wasn't sure what to do first. He looked up the phone number of the morgue and called it from Heather's room phone. He was pretty sure Rachel was still there doing an autopsy. It went to voice-mail and he left a message for her explaining what had happened. Would she please be able to help him get Heather out of jail?

He then called Jeremy and told him what had happened as well.

"I've seen Heather meeting with both Mary Beth Singer's husband and Jon Moore's wife. What exactly is she planning to do?"

Bernie quickly told him Heather's plan to have the ear implants removed from both people early in the morning by the coroner and what little he knew about her plan to safeguard the implants and copy the files.

They talked a few minutes more and Jeremy told Bernie about Dorgan's whereabouts at the moment. "I doubt if he'll come back to the hotel again. He probably figures you guys have told the police about him by now and that they're watching his room. Be careful, man," Jeremy added before hanging up.

Bernie began going through Heather's purse to find the eye implant. She had mentioned to him earlier that she had the ear implant, safely wrapped and sealed to keep it from receiving and transmitting any sounds, so he looked for that as well. He had dumped the contents of her purse on the bed and quickly found the sock, which he recognized to be his own, and found the ear implant in the jar, in the pill case, in aluminum foil. He wrapped and sealed it again carefully and set it aside. The eye implant, which had not been cleaned but still had eye tissue attached, was in an envelope. He placed it on the bedside table with the jar, then thought better of it. What if the police came back, looking for the evidence? He decided to move those to his room, but first he wanted to look at the items in Heather's purse. He couldn't resist touching her lipstick tube and holding her cell phone. He opened her wallet and saw a photo of Heather with a very good looking man. Must be her boyfriend, he thought, frowning.

He finally put the items back in her purse and took Heather's laptop and both Michtenbaum implants, as well as his car keys and the memory stick, and left her room to head for Walmart. He was going to do the project that Heather had initiated. He wouldn't let her down.

Bernie bought three small metal lock boxes with combination locks, three memory sticks, bubble wrap and tape. It only took him half an hour once he was back in his room to copy the files using Heather's computer. He ordered room service and asked for two jars of ketchup with his hamburger and fries. He saved the aluminum foil as Heather had and washed the two jars to use to hold the other ear implants that would be surgically removed the next morning.

Bernie combined both implants of Michael Michtenbaum into one secure and sound-proof container, wrapped it safely in bubble wrap, and placed it in one of the metal boxes with one of the duplicated memory sticks.

Bernie sat down on his bed. What was Heather planning to do next? How would having the implants and copies of the Freedom Project file ensure their future safety? What would James Bond do? A plan began to form in Bernie's mind as to how to inform Dorgan, and anyone else who might be out to harm them, of their plan to notify the press should the need arise. He moved to the desk and started writing.

Bernie hid the one completed, and two partially completed, metal boxes in the trunk of his car in the compartment where the spare tire was located. He hadn't heard from Rachel so decided to drive to the morgue. He was worried about Heather and wanted to see if Rachel could get her out. He wished he had thought to bring Heather's cell phone from her purse, but he couldn't get back into her room. And he hadn't even thought to take her room key.

When he reached the morgue, two police cars and two other cars were in the parking lot. Once he was allowed to enter the building, Bernie noticed that a new female police officer had taken the place of Officer Davis. He was looking through the window of the lab door where Rachel and Bill were working together on a corpse, and the officer started to pull her weapon when she saw Bernie at the door.

"It's okay," called Rachel when she looked up at the officer's rapid movement and saw Bernie. "He's a friend." Rachel motioned to Bernie to come in.

Prior to that day, Bernie had never seen a dead body other

than at a funeral. Now he was surrounded by them. Three bodies lay on stainless tables in the room, two partially covered with sheets. The third, the grave closer who had innocently come to work a little early and ended up dying because of his good work ethic, was lying naked on a table with Rachel on one side of him and Bill on the other. The man's chest was laid open like the pages of a book.

Bernie looked at the other two men. One was apparently the man who tried to kill Rachel the day before and did kill the two Hamilton police officers.

"Arsenic poisoning," Rachel said when she saw him looking at the body. "It was apparently in the barbecue sauce. He was most likely murdered by whomever ate with him or served him his meal."

Bernie knew who that probably was. Why not tell the police? I know who killed two of the three men in here – the two who deserved it. And I even know where he is right now.

The other man Bernie recognized. He was the man who had planted the bomb under Heather's car, the man who in disguise had torn out Michael Michtenbaum's eyeball, killed an innocent man and buried him and ran after Bernie with a gun.

"How did this one die?" asked Bernie weakly.

"Poisoned as well, but with a different substance and in a different method. His poison was airborne. It's quick acting, so it must have been planted in his car and he breathed it in. The crime scene people are looking at the man's car right now to see what they can find. Keep all this to yourself, Bernie. The police may not want the information released, okay?"

"Sure, of course." Then Bernie remembered why he'd come there. "Did you get my message?" He directed the question towards Rachel.

"No, I haven't even been in my office. What is it?"

"The police arrested Heather for taking evidence - the implant from Michael's eyeball." The new policewoman gave them both a quizzical look as she had no idea what they were talking about.

"What! When did this happen?" Rachel stopped taking samples from one of the man's organs and laid the blob on his stomach.

"About two hours ago." Bernie was going to say more, but stopped. Rachel knew about Heather's plan for the next day, but Bill might not know, and the policewoman definitely didn't.

"Bill, we're almost positive of the cause of death. Do you mind terribly confirming that and then finishing up while I go and try to get Heather out of jail? Then, please go home and get some rest. We have an early day tomorrow." Rachel scrubbed her hands and arms with antibacterial cleanser and removed her lab coat.

Bernie drove separately to the police station. Rachel was still being driven everywhere by her police body guard. It was after 10:30 p.m. on a Saturday night and the police station was quite busy. It was several minutes before their inquiry into the status of Heather Barnes was answered and that quick response was only because Rachel was the coroner.

"She's been released. Her lawyer made bail."

Joe Singer had to stop his car on the way to the Michtenbaums and pull over to the side of the road. He wept uncontrollably for almost five minutes. He wept out of rage that his beautiful wife and their wonderful daughter had been spied on in the most intimate way their entire lives, and he for the past twenty-five years since he had married Mary Beth. He wept out of sorrow for what he knew would be Mary Beth's most traumatic night of her life once he managed to get the message of her implants across to her. He wept out of anxiety for Mary Beth having to undergo surgery to have the implants removed, but mostly he wept out of fear for their very lives. Would they ever have a normal life again, or would they always live in fear?

He waited a while until the redness left his eyes before he called Mary Beth and told her he would be there in a few minutes. She sounded so happy to hear his voice, he thought. He was almost glad that he didn't have to use his voice to tell her the terrible news. She might not ever be happy to hear his voice again if it brought such bad news.

Joe hugged Celia and Mitch when he entered the Michtenbaum home. There was still a spread of food on the dining room table and two neighbor women were in the kitchen keeping the dishes washed, the food available and the drinks poured for any new visitors who came by. They offered to make Joe a plate of food.

"Thanks, but no, I'll get something in a little while."

"Betty, Jan, why don't you two go on home. You've done enough for today." Celia seemed to finally notice that the women were still there. "Thank you so much. I don't think many more people will be by today."

"Are you sure?" they asked, and Celia assured them that they would be fine, especially with Mary Beth and Joe there to help them.

Mary Beth hugged her husband and he could see in her eyes that she knew something was wrong, that something brought him here tonight. She knew him so well. He had never been able to hide anything from her.

After an hour of talking and eating, Joe and Mary Beth excused themselves and went to the guest bedroom. Joe closed the door to the small room and stood behind his wife of 25 years, wrapping his arms around the front of her. "Mmmm," she said.

"I love you honey," Joe whispered in her ear.

Mary Beth turned around while still in his embrace. "I love you too, sweetheart. And I know you well enough to know that something is wrong. What is it?"

"You're right, and I'll tell you later, but can we play a little game right now?"

"A game!" she laughed. "You don't plan to get me all hot and bothered with people right outside the bedroom door, do you?"

"Well, we'll just have to see, won't we," and he pulled a handkerchief out of his pocket and wrapped it around her eyes.

"Oooh, this is different," she cooed. "Good thing I trust you."

He kissed her, then placed one hand over the handkerchief portion of her right eye, but removed the cloth from her left eye. "Shhh," he said softly and held a finger to his lips. He then folded the entire handkerchief over her right eye and tied it in place around her head with a shoestring he had taken out of his sneaker earlier.

"What in the world are you doing?" She was grinning at him but with a look of confusion.

"Shhh," he said again and once again held his finger to his lips. "There's no talking in this game, okay? Only kissing and moaning." He kissed her again and sat her down on the bed.

"Joe, this isn't the time or the place. Really, honey!"

Joe pulled his phone out of its holder on his pants and typed the text. "Please don't talk. I need to tell you something important and someone is listening. Please don't say anything."

He showed her the text and she opened her mouth but shut it again and nodded at him. He again held his finger to his lips as he got her phone out of her purse. He made sure both phones had all sounds turned off.

"Mmmm," he said out loud as he was typing the text and did a circular arm motion in front of him telling Mary Beth to go along with the game.

She frowned at him, but played the game. "Yes, mmmm." Her arms were crossed in front of her and she continued to frown at him.

He handed her phone to her and he typed his next text for her to read. "What I have to tell you is almost unbelievable, but it is the truth. I just found out a few hours ago and I am still in shock about it myself." She just sat there, so he kept typing. "Apparently you have a small implant in your right eye and in your right ear, placed there at birth, with which the government can see and hear everything that you see and hear. That's why I'm typing, so they can't hear us. And that's why the cloth is over your eye, so they can't see."

"What are you talking about!" she typed back. "That is ridiculous! Who told you this?"

"Mmmm, keep that up, baby....that feels good," he said, rolling his eyes.

"I know it sounds crazy, but it's true. I saw the video and heard you myself. A Homeland Security agent who is trying to help us called me today and told me. I saw the video of you in the cemetery today."

"Anybody can take a video! That doesn't prove anything."

"Mary Beth, she asked me when Lauren was born and entered that date and time in the computer. She showed me the birth of our daughter through your right eye, and I heard everything that was said." Mary Beth's face now showed some shock and fear, and Joe continued typing. "She showed me lunchtime yesterday in our kitchen when we kissed goodbye and you left to come here."

Mary Beth gasped out loud, and he rushed to hold her, but first motioned for her to try and remain quiet.

She gently pushed him away and typed, "Why? I don't

understand why they would do this?"

"Me either, but apparently you were one of three people that the government decided to use as guinea pigs for their experiment." Joe was afraid to tell her that Michael Michtenbaum had been one of the other two. He had been murdered. Was this the reason why?

"What can we do? Can't we tell someone and get the government in trouble for this?" "Mmmm, you're so good to me," she said out loud, with real tears in her eyes.

He smiled a sad and sympathetic smile at her, and kissed her again.

"We can get the implants removed, for one thing. Then we can at least talk about it with each other."

"Won't they know if we remove them? What would they do?"

"I don't know. The woman from Homeland Security is going to help us. She has arranged for a surgeon to remove the ear implant tomorrow morning if you wish. The eye surgery is more difficult and will have to wait. In the meantime, you can wear an eyepatch to keep your right eye covered."

This was too much information too quickly for Mary Beth and she began sobbing. She covered her mouth with her hand and tried not to make any noise, but she couldn't stop herself. She buried her face in Joe's chest and they laid down on the bed, holding each other and crying. He gently removed the handkerchief from her eye.

Dorgan slowly drove the route from the cemetery to the hotel looking for Jones' car. Surely the man could not have breathed in the highly poisonous gas and lived long enough to drive all the way back to the hotel. His car had to be wrecked or stopped in route along the side of the road. As Dorgan got closer to the hotel, he thought perhaps the man had taken a different street and circled back to follow a different route as well. The car was nowhere to be seen, so he finally checked the hotel.

Jones was there, sitting dead in his car. Dorgan was stumped as to how that could have happened. He thought back over the past ten minutes. While in the library, he had seen the video of Jones leaving the cemetery in his car after getting the eye implant from

Michael Michtenbaum's dead body. From his computer, Dorgan had remotely released the vial of highly toxic and deadly gas that he had placed as an air freshener in Jones' rental car earlier. It was a trick he'd learned in one of Jacob Barnes' training classes. The gas kills within seconds. Even if Jones had the car windows down, which it did not appear that he did, the gas was placed to aim directly at the driver, so most of it would hit the nose and mouth of the driver. He should have died on Greenwood Avenue, not in the hotel parking lot.

Jones had betrayed him. He wasn't sure how, or why, but he had lied to him. He was working with someone else. There was no other explanation. I saw him talking to someone else on the phone. He lied and told me he had already looked for the man in the trees, when he hadn't. Dorgan had truly hoped he wouldn't have to use the vial of gas, but his second assassin turned out to be worse than the first. From here on out, he would take care of business himself.

He needed to get the implant from Jones' car, but at that moment he saw a group of people, including a police officer, heading across the parking lot towards Jones and him. It was Heather and Bernie. He quickly ducked down and once the group retreated, he pulled out of the side entrance to the parking lot and headed for High Street.

Dorgan was trying to make sense of what was happening. His boss, Rhonda Watterson, had snooped in his office. He didn't know what she could be looking for. The CIA folder and files he had just accessed were unbelievable. He needed to read more to understand if what he thought he had just read about the Project Leader and Freedom Projects was correct. If so, God help us all. Both of the undercover agents he had hired had missed in their attempts to kill the Coroner and one of the men may have purposely messed up the job. They both killed innocent people, which might be overlooked if they had accomplished their primary objective, but that wasn't the case. Bernie and Heather had shown up unexpectedly, and he strongly felt that someone was watching him and his agents and warning the intended targets. At first, he thought it might be Jeremy, but now he was thinking CIA. And now, he had lost both of the implants from Michael Michtenbaum that he had come to retrieve. Not one of my better days, he groaned inwardly.

With at least two dead bodies that could possibly be traced to him, Dorgan decided not to return to the Marriott. He had his laptop and iPad with him and he could buy a change of clothes and more toiletries. He drove south on Route 4 and checked into a motel in Fairfield. He was getting hungry and got back in his car to find a store where he could pick up some sandwich ingredients and cold beer. He found an enormous grocery store close by called Jungle Jim's that was like a shopping mall with various other stores within the huge compound.

He would have liked to have spent more time roaming the huge store as he was fascinated with the variety of international foods and entertaining displays, but he had a lot of work yet to do that evening. He bought a pint of chicken salad, bread, cole slaw and a six-pack of beer and headed back to his new headquarters to finalize the details.

Heather was mortified at being arrested. She was fingerprinted, which wasn't a big deal since her fingerprints were already on file as a condition of her employment at DHS. Her mug shots were of a pretty woman with extremely short black hair, very man-ish looking. She was actually glad she didn't resemble her normal self in these photos. She hadn't taken her purse with her, purposely, and she wasn't wearing jewelry, so there were no personal items to take from her.

She was placed in a holding cell with two other women. One of the women was very chatty. "Hi honey. My, you're tall! Why do you wear your hair so short? You're so pretty, you should wear it long then you'd be beautiful. I used to be beautiful and have long hair, but that was before," she stopped, sighed and took another breath. "What are you in here for? You look too good to be a druggie or prostitute. Did you kill you husband or boyfriend? I'd like to kill my boyfriend, he's such a jerk." She laughed at her own statement.

Heather smiled at her but told her she didn't really feel like talking, so the woman directed her conversation to the other woman in the cell, who also ignored her.

Heather closed her eyes and leaned back against the wall.

She couldn't believe she was in jail. She thought of one of the Bridget Jones movies where Bridget, played by actress Renee Zellweger, was arrested in a foreign country and was in a large cell with a lot of women. They sang Madonna songs, danced and told stories. She wished she had the personality that Bridget had, and that this woman talking incessantly had, that would allow her to sing, and make friends, and actually enjoy her time in jail. But no, she would fret and worry and stew and be angry and remain totally dejected.

Heather hoped Bernie would get in touch with Rachel soon and that the coroner would be able to pull some strings and get her out of there. She wasn't sure what, if anything, Jeremy could do to help, but she felt better knowing that he and his electronic eye knew where she was. She didn't have her cell phone with its GPS on her, or any other way to track her, so she wanted him to know her whereabouts.

Heather thought about the Singers and the Moores. She liked all three of the four she had met so far. And both couples seemed to have such good marriages – to be so much in love. Would Joe Singer and Carol Moore be able to convince their spouses to come to the Butler County morgue early in the morning and have a device surgically removed from their ears? Jon Moore, maybe, but Mary Beth? Why would she do that? Would Joe and Carol be able to keep their spouses' right eyes covered and present the message to Mary Beth and Jon in writing? Heather was now having doubts about this crazy plan. Who would believe this conspiracy theory story under the best of circumstances, let alone under the circumstances in which these two couples found themselves. I wouldn't believe it, thought Heather. She put her head in her hands. What have I done?

Thirty minutes passed and Heather wondered if and when the police would let her call someone. She wasn't certain of who else she would call. An attorney perhaps? She had never been arrested or even gotten a speeding ticket before.

"Heather Barnes!," a voice called.

"Here!" Heather called back.

An officer opened the door to the small cell and Heather was escorted back into the main room of the police station.

A tall man in an expensive suit was standing in the room and talking to another officer, the one in charge of the evening shift.

They both looked at Heather when she walked in and the tall man smiled broadly, extending his hand to her. "Hi, Miss Barnes. I'm Dan Jackson, your appointed attorney. Are you ready to go? Do you have a purse or anything?"

"Uh, no," Heather wondered how she got an attorney so fast, especially when she didn't ask for one. "I don't have anything with me."

"Okay, great." He started walking towards the door and waited as she followed. "I've posted your bail," he continued. "Your hearing is set for Tuesday morning. You'll need to be there by 8 a.m. We'll go over everything in the car."

"Thanks," Heather told him. There was a shark-like quality to the man. He was too fast, too slick, she thought. "How much was bail? I can pay you for it – well, once I get my purse. It's back at the hotel."

"We'll worry about that later. For now, I need you to tell me the whole story from start to finish. You were arrested for confiscating key evidence in a police murder investigation, right?"

"Right." She really didn't want to tell him anything.

"So where is the evidence?" he asked as he opened the car door for her. Heather hesitated getting in. "Can we meet tomorrow and talk about this? I'm very tired. I just want to go back to the hotel and rest."

"Well, I suppose so, but we can talk for a few minutes, can't we? I'll drive you to your hotel and you can give me a brief version of what happened."

His request was certainly reasonable and although Heather was hoping to postpone talking to the man, she couldn't think of a good excuse to not have him drive her to the hotel. She got in his car.

Heather realized immediately the man was driving in the opposite direction of the hotel. The police station wasn't far from the Fitton Center and the hotel was only two blocks from there. Her attorney was driving the other direction along the river.

"The hotel is the other way," she said with a strange feeling starting in the pit of her stomach.

"Well, I'm just taking the long way around so we can talk."

"Let me out. I'll walk." Heather tried not to sound frightened.

He looked at her and pulled the gun out of his jacket. "I think you know I can't do that. Now just relax and you'll be fine." He didn't speak again and Heather wondered why he was not grilling her about the whereabouts of Michael Michtenbaum's implants. Surely that is what he wanted - why he kidnapped her.

She offered the information. "The implants that you're looking for are in my purse, back in my hotel room."

"Implants?"

Heather could tell he did not know what she was talking about, although he tried to hide that fact quickly. "Noooo, they're not." He steered the car with his knees for a moment as he held the gun in one hand and reached into the back seat and brought Heather's purse to the front. "I've already checked there. And everywhere in your room. Try again." He pointed the gun at her face. "And this time make it the truth."

The man had crossed the river over another bridge and turned left, heading out into a less populated area.

"I swear to you, they were both in my purse when I left." Heather assumed, hoped, Bernie had taken them out, and also hoped this man didn't know about Bernie. "Someone else must have gotten into my room and taken them. Who else is looking for them?" Heather knew who else but wanted the man to admit it.

The man actually seemed bored with what she was saying, as though he didn't care at all whether he retrieved the implants or not. Perhaps they were still in her purse and he was just taunting her since he now had them in his possession. Or perhaps this was about something else all together, something much more sinister than obtaining the implants of Michael Michtenbaum.

"Please, I'll give you the implants. Just take me back to the hotel."

The man looked at her. "Implants. Small ones I guess."

"Yes," Heather replied.

"Well, I guess I'll just have to do a cavity search," and he gave her a look that scared her to her core.

Dorgan skipped a lot of the 4000 page CIA document that appeared to belong to Jacob Barnes. There simply wasn't time to read it all, and he wanted to read the most recent entries. In the last five pages of the document, he learned what he had suspected. He was being set up by someone, or several someones, in the CIA. His death warrant was written in black and white, to be carried out that very evening. For what reason, he had no idea. This entry was dated before Michael Michtenbaum's murder, and therefore before his screw-ups of the previous two days.

He had finished his dinner and two beers long ago. He now felt the need to drink the remaining four beers. He would need a lot of courage for what he had to do. Not that he ever lacked courage. It was always there when he believed in his cause, always there when he had an assignment that was for the good of his country. Neither of these scenarios was the current case – not any more. So he needed some artificial courage to complete his mission.

He gulped down two more beers, hid his electronic devices in a safe place close to the motel and returned to his room. He dialed the number of his boss, Rhonda Watterson. A half hour later, he had finished the final two beers and began speaking out loud.

"Jeremy, if you can hear me, listen carefully."

It was 9:45 Saturday night and instead of drinking beer and playing in the tournament game he had scheduled, Jeremy was still at his desk at Homeland Security's Nebraska Avenue complex. His team mates were pretty annoyed with him for canceling at the last minute, but he told them it couldn't be helped.

Dragon had gone to another hotel and had been in his room for hours. He was lying on the bed reading from his laptop screen. It was the same document Dragon had been reading at the library, the one that mentioned implants being injected into seventh graders through their vaccinations. Dragon had been reading for a couple of hours and Jeremy hated wasting Samuel's talents on such a boring and unproductive task.

He began thinking of Heather. My God, she's beautiful, thought Jeremy, and his pulse quickened as he remembered seeing her naked in her hotel room that morning.

He propped his head on his left hand and closed his eyes. His tired mind began to drift. He imagined himself and Heather at his place. No, he thought, it's a mess. Let's go to her place, and he pictured a tidy, spacious apartment with large windows overlooking a scenic park with water.

Across the room stood Heather, her back to him, naked except for a pair of red high heels that further tightened her shapely calves and buttocks. She leaned over and lay on her stomach on the dining table, her legs slightly spread, her luscious bottom an invitation to him. She raised her head slightly to turn and look at him, her smile and her eyes seductive.

Jeremy's right hand moved involuntarily from his desk to his lap.

Heather raised herself slowly from the table and turned towards him. She sat on the edge of the table, lifting one red heel to rest on a nearby chair. Jeremy remembered every square inch of the front of this beautiful body. Her breasts were perfect - large and white, round and smooth, their perky chocolate centers pointing slightly upwards.

Jeremy's breath was now coming in small, quick bursts.

"Let me help you," Heather offered and she strode to stand in front of him. Sitting low on the couch, Jeremy's face was directly in front of her neat, black triangle of hair, and he moved his face forward towards it, his hands reaching around for her firm bottom.

"Next time," she breathed. She went to her knees, pushing him back onto the couch. She wiggled herself between his legs and unzipped his jeans. He lifted himself slightly to allow her to pull them off. His boxers showed that it was going to be difficult for him to enjoy her foreplay for any length of time.

She took him into her mouth, her lips and tongue sweet and skilled in their quest.

Jeremy cried aloud as his hand finished its task.

"Geez!" he hissed. He wiped his hand on a rag pulled from a drawer and examined his shorts. "Crap!" He wiped them as best he could for now and pulled up and zipped his jeans. He checked on Dragon to make sure he was still reading in his room and took a few deep breaths to refocus his mind.

Jeremy had both Mary Beth's and Jon's videos running, with the audio turned low. Since both of Michael Michtenbaum's implants had been removed and the ear one was apparently well-insulated now so that little or no sound was being recorded, Jeremy moved that satellite over the Marriott Hotel where Bernie was. He had moved the satellite Audrey to follow Heather when she was taken away by police, and Audrey was now dutifully watching the Hamilton police station. Jeremy couldn't see inside the police station, or hear anything, but he knew Heather was still there.

The last few hours had been eventful with Jon and Mary Beth. Jon and his wife had gone to the hospital and had a CT scan performed on Jon's head. Jeremy knew that Jon and Carol were now aware of the two implants in Jon's head and that Jon was planning to have his doctor remove the ear implant very soon. What are the chances of this event happening at the same time of Michael Michtenbaum's death, thought Jeremy. Crazy!

Mary Beth's husband had shown up earlier. Jeremy wasn't sure what had happened between the couple a short time ago because Mary Beth's eyes were covered and he couldn't see through her implant, but he had the feeling that whatever they were doing, it wasn't of the relaxed nature they were trying to convey. Their voices sounded distraught, not playful as the words would have indicated. He suspected Heather told Joe Singer of the implants since she had met with him earlier that evening. Heather had also met with Carol Moore. Did Heather tell Joe and Carol to tell their spouses about the implants? Heather was getting herself deeper and deeper into this mess and Jeremy was afraid for her.

Jeremy ordered a large steak hoagie and fries, to be delivered. He would have to go downstairs and pick up the delivery once it arrived, and told the restaurant to have their delivery person call him when he was close to the building. He planned to spend the night in his office and needed something different to eat than the snack foods in the machines. He stood and stretched. His lower back was starting to hurt from sitting on the computer stool for sixteen hours straight.

Jeremy had watched Bernie leave the Marriott and travel to Walmart, back to the hotel, and then to the morgue. Jeremy wished Bernie would stay put as it was difficult to keep track of him when he kept moving and didn't have a phone or other device with which to track him.

Suddenly Jeremy's attention was drawn to the screen

showing the Hamilton police station and he sat down quickly to watch. Heather was leaving the police station with a man in a suit. He zoomed his satellite in for a better look. Probably an attorney. They were talking and getting into a car. Jeremy snapped a photo of the license plate number and make of car, as well as two facial shots of the man. He began running the facial shots through his MyBackdoor database as well as the more common law enforcement databases, just in case.

They were heading in the opposite direction of the hotel and Jeremy wondered where they were going. Jeremy's gut was telling him something wasn't right. Heather might be in trouble. Could this man be another of Dragon's assassins, posing as an attorney, hired to get the implants and kill Heather? Could it have been Dragon or his hired man that contacted the police and had Heather arrested? Jeremy wondered.

He wanted to wait for the facial recognition software to tell him who the man was, if indeed he was a hired assassin, but the software could sometimes take hours to come back with an identification. Heather might not have that long.

He called Heather's cell phone. The GPS tracking showed that her phone was in the car with them. It went to voice-mail. Jeremy took that as a bad sign.

Bernie was on the move again, this time following Rachel and her police escorts. Jeremy watched them leave the morgue and drive to the police station. Perhaps he could get Bernie to follow the car that Heather was in. He knew Bernie didn't have a cell phone so he called the Hamilton Police Department.

The car with Heather in it had crossed a bridge on what Jeremy's map identified as Columbia Bridge and then turned left onto Route 128. It was dark and Jeremy was thankful for the phone GPS tracking since it would be difficult to track the car in extreme darkness.

"Yes, my name is Jeremy James and I'm calling from Homeland Security in Washington, D.C. I believe a man by the name of Bernie Kossack is there in your station, with the coroner Rachel Curry, most likely inquiring about a woman by the name of Heather Barnes that you just released from custody. I need to speak with Mr. Kossack. I know he doesn't carry a cell phone and I desperately need to speak with him if you could please find him."

Usually speaking kindly but authoritatively and throwing out the agency's name would get him what he wanted.

Not this time. "I'm sorry sir, but we're very busy and I can't have this person tying up my phone line. If he is here, I will find him and ask him to call you from some other phone. Good evening, sir," and she hung up.

His cell phone rang almost immediately. It wasn't Bernie, but the delivery man letting Jeremy know he was only minutes away from the building. Jeremy asked if he could please meet him at the front door and he shut down all of his screens, took his cell phone with him in case Bernie called back, grabbed some cash, and headed downstairs to retrieve his food.

Jeremy was away from his desk only three minutes. He had run down the hall and taken the stairs two at a time. The delivery person was standing at the door and Jeremy had his money ready to make the transaction quickly. He didn't wait for his change from a $20 bill, so the delivery man got a nice $8+ tip.

He pressed the button that brought all his monitors back to life simultaneously. He checked Heather's phone GPS and saw that it was now stationary. They had stopped 1.7 miles down Route 128. He positioned Audrey there but didn't see the car. The man could have picked this spot because of the heavy growth of shrubbery and trees along the side of the road – they were hidden under the canopy of trees where Audrey couldn't see them.

Rachel and Bernie both left the police station. Hoping Bernie would be heading for his hotel room, Jeremy called the hotel and asked for Bernie Kossack. Jeremy left a message for Bernie to call back right away. He wasn't going to count on the woman at the police station having given Bernie the message.

The hell with it. He knew he shouldn't use Samuel to look for Heather as Dragon was his assignment, but Dragon was sitting there reading and had been for hours. Heather could be getting murdered at the moment. He had to see through the trees and hear what was going on. He slightly adjusted Samuel to be able to find Heather six miles away.

He then moved Audrey over Dragon's hotel in Fairfield. He could at least keep an eye on Dragon's car in the lot for now, and

Jeremy had access to Dragon's laptop via the keystroke software. It shouldn't take too long to find Heather. He could switch the satellites back soon, he hoped.

Jeremy's cell phone rang. It was Bernie.

"Bernie, I think Heather might be in trouble. Hold on a minute. I'm trying to find her by satellite."

"I think she's okay," offered Bernie. "She was just released from the police station a little bit ago and went with her laywer. I thought maybe they came here, but I knocked on her room door and she isn't here."

"I know she isn't there," snapped Jeremy. "She's with her attorney, or maybe he's Dorgan's hit man, I don't know, but something isn't right. He's taken her out in the woods and I'm trying to find her. Wait! I just found her phone. Crap!"

"What!" cried Bernie. "What is it? Is she okay?"

"I found her phone and her purse, but that's all. No car, no people. He must have thrown her purse out of the car when he realized her cell phone was in it and that she could be tracked." There was a moment of silence, and then Jeremy muttered, "Oh, crap."

"What is it?" Bernie sounded frantic.

"I tried to call her about eight or ten minutes ago. The phone was moving then so it was definitely still in the car. He must have thrown it out right after that. This pretty much proves he isn't her lawyer."

"What should I do?" asked Bernie hysterically.

"Call the police. Tell them Heather has been kidnapped and you think her life is in danger. I have the license number and make and model of the car. Let them know the car was headed south on Route 128 towards Ross. Also, I think it's time we turned in Dorgan. I'm not supposed to and may get fired for it, but this has gotten way out of hand." Jeremy gave Bernie the name and address of the motel where Dorgan was now staying.

Jeremy zoomed out with Samuel to look for the car carrying Heather and a man in a suit who was most likely the third assassin hired by Dragon in the past two days. He calculated how far they would have gotten in the past ten minutes if they continued to drive on that same road and began looking closely at every car he saw. He moved further down the road, past where they could possibly be, and looked at every car coming in that direction. He couldn't find them.

Twenty-five minutes passed and he knew they must have stopped somewhere between the spot he was now in, a place called Miamitown, and where Heather's purse had been found. He turned up the sound on his other monitors to alert him of any activity, then concentrated solely on checking every inch of both sides of the road along a fifteen mile stretch of Route 128 leading out of Hamilton. It could take all night.

"I'm so sorry, Heather," Jeremy said softly, and he felt a heavy sense of guilt. If he hadn't left for those three minutes to get his food, he wouldn't have lost her. If she died tonight, he would never forgive himself.

The police told Bernie to stay where he was so they could question him further, but he said, "No, I have to go look for Heather!" He had told them everything he knew – that John Dorgan of Homeland Security was the one who was hiring the assassins and that they should arrest him at the hotel in Fairfield – and that there was probably now a third assassin, the one who had Heather.

"I can't just sit here! I'm going to look for her!" and Bernie hung up on the police. He knew getting Dorgan would take precedence over finding Heather for the police.

Based on Jeremy's excellent directions and landmarks guiding him to the exact spot, Bernie found Heather's purse rather quickly despite the extreme darkness of the wooded area. He then drove on slowly, letting other cars pass him. There were very few cars on the road. The night was dark and he knew he wouldn't be able to see any tire tracks that might signal that the car carrying Heather had pulled off the road into any of the fields or treed areas that flanked the road on both sides. There were occasional houses and businesses and Bernie looked for the tan sedan that Jeremy had described.

It was after midnight before he gave up and started back for the hotel. He was devastated. He had a terrible feeling that something awful had happened to Heather. He tried to think what else he could do but fatigue was starting to set in. Other than a very brief nap in his car Saturday morning, he hadn't slept in 42 hours and he was suddenly exhausted. He should sleep a while and then figure out what to do.

No, he thought. I can't sleep while Heather is missing. He needed some caffeine. That would help. He looked at the clock in his car and realized Sheila would be on duty at Waffle House so he headed up High Street to the restaurant.

Sheila was happy to see him and waved him over to sit at the counter so she could talk to him more than if he was at a table or booth. "You look tired," she said as he sat down.

"I am. I haven't slept since Thursday night, so I need lots of coffee." She had already poured his first cup. "On me," she said. Both of them were glad there was a different cook on duty who wouldn't know about her free cup of coffee to him eighteen hours earlier.

There were several other customers in the restaurant so Bernie had to share Sheila's time with them. The other waitress had gone off duty at midnight and Sheila had the graveyard shift alone, except for the cook.

"I watched the eleven o'clock news before I came in," Sheila whispered to him. "Three murders today and another threat on the coroner with a bomb! Was any of that related to your case here?"

"All of it was related," stated Bernie tiredly, "which is why I've had no sleep." He could see her eyes widen, not in fright but in awe and excitement. Bernie couldn't believe that he wasn't even in his James Bond persona and he was impressing the hell out of this woman.

Sheila wanted to hear all about it and Bernie told her bits and pieces without revealing anything about the Freedom Project or its subjects. He tried to be matter-of-fact when he told her it was he who saw the bomber placing the bombs and was able to stop Rachel and the police from getting into the cars. Sheila was swooning. Bernie made a mental note to act as tired and matter-of-fact as possible in the future when talking to women. He told her about hiding in the trees and seeing the man kill another man in the cemetery. Then he told her that his partner had been kidnapped and might be dead right now. He was truly upset and Sheila came around the counter to stand beside him and give him a hug.

"I wish there was something I could do to help," she said sympathetically. Bernie hadn't told her his partner was a beautiful woman he was madly in love with. She might not have been as sympathetic.

"Just listening to me and keeping my coffee cup filled is helping a lot, really it is," and Bernie smiled weakly at her.

"Since my partner is gone," and he choked slightly, "I must finish our mission alone." Bernie wasn't trying to impress Sheila at this point. He was talking from his heart, as much to himself as to her. He had to finish what Heather was going to do, even though he didn't know exactly what that was. The implants would be removed from Jon and Mary Beth, if they both showed up, in less than six hours. It was up to him to finish what he had started the night before, even if this wasn't the plan Heather would have used. All she had said was that they needed to prepare an "insurance plan" utilizing both the Freedom Project file document and the implant evidence they had from Michael Michtenbaum, that would be revealed to the press and others if and when the need arose. Then she was taken away by the police.

So it was left up to Bernie to complete the task. His plan was to prepare three packages and give them to their respective keepers. One would go to the Singers to entrust to whomever they wished and the second would go to the Moores to do the same. The third one - the one that was already completed and held both Michtenbaum implants, a computer memory stick holding the complete original Freedom Project files and printed instructions for the package's trustee - was ready to go. Heather was going to give it to someone, he supposed, but Bernie didn't know to whom. So now he had to decide who to give it to. It had to be someone completely trustworthy and someone who would not be associated with any of the project subjects or with Heather, Bernie or Rachel. These were the people who needed protected from anyone looking for the implants or the files.

"Did you ever see the movie The Firm?" Bernie asked Sheila after she'd checked on each of her other customers.

"Yes, loved it!" she replied.

"Well, I've done something similar in that I made copies of

some very confidential files that I now have to find a safe place to keep – forever hopefully – as insurance that the bad guys don't come after us." Bernie was too tired to realize that this scenario was exactly what he had wished for years to be able to say to Sheila or some other woman at the diner back home. Only now he wasn't saying it for Sheila, he was just thinking out loud and trying to stay awake.

"Kind of like the boat in the movie." Sheila giggled.

"What?" Bernie wasn't sure he knew what she said.

"The boat, you know. They put all the mob files on the boat that Tom Cruise's brother and Holly Hunter were going to sail away on."

"Oh, yes, of course." Bernie was distracted as he tried to get his tired mind to think of someone he could trust with the metal box. "But we don't want to use a boat."

Sheila looked at Bernie closely and leaned on the counter in front of him. "I thought you said you weren't an agent. It sure sounds like you are. This is dangerous stuff, right?"

"Right," was all he said.

"Well, how about a Priest? My Priest is the most trustworthy person I've ever known."

He looked at her blankly for a second and she clarified for him. "You could give the confidential files to a Priest to keep locked up in the church."

A look of understanding crossed Bernie's face and he grinned at Sheila. "That's actually a very good idea!" he said with the most excitement he had mustered since coming into the restaurant.

She smiled happily back at him, glad that she could help. "I'm going to mass at 10 a.m. if you want to join me," she said, topping off Bernie's coffee once again.

Bernie was thoughtful for a moment, then said softly, "If my partner doesn't show up before that time, I will meet you a little before ten to go see your Priest."

Sheila gave Bernie the name and address of her parish, and Bernie finally decided he had done all he could for the time being and headed back to the hotel to get a few hours of much needed sleep.

Carol Moore was trying to think of the best way to cover Jon's right eye and then write down what the woman from Homeland Security had told her, but it just seemed so silly to her. She and Jon had a wonderful marriage and a good sex life, until recently, since Jon's ear problem had caused him so much pain and anxiety. However, it would be totally out of character for her to blindfold her husband. They had never played such games before and she would feel utterly ridiculous doing so.

Were they really in danger right now? Was someone watching and listening to their every move and word and did they know Jon was planning to have the foreign object removed from behind his ear? If so, things couldn't get much worse for them and Carol decided to just *tell* Jon what had happened with her meeting an hour ago with the woman named Heather Barnes. She would whisper it into his left ear with the hope that the buzzing noise in his right ear would prevent her whisper from being heard by anyone but Jon.

He was on the couch and had his sleeping pills on the table. He wasn't tired, he said, but the screeching that was happening more and more frequently drained him and he couldn't enjoy watching television or reading a book, so he planned to take three sleeping pills around ten o'clock and hoped to get another good night's sleep.

Carol walked behind the couch and leaned in to whisper into Jon's left ear.

"Jon, don't turn around and don't say anything, just listen carefully to me."

"What! Speak up," and Jon turned around to look at Carol. She gently put both her hands on his head and turned it back towards the TV.

"Shhh, just listen to me okay?"

"Okay," he said.

Well, this is going great so far, thought Carol sarcastically.

"Honey, when I went out a little while ago I met with someone who knows about the two implants in your head." She immediately held her hands on his head and whispered, "Shhh, don't say anything and don't move, just listen, please!"

He had struggled a little and started to say something, but was then quiet.

"This is going to sound hard to believe, and I'm not one hundred percent sure I believe it, but the woman said you and some other people were part of an experiment by the government 50 years ago. When you were born, the implants were placed in your eye and ear. Right now, someone may be watching us through your eye and listening to us through your ear. Apparently, your ear implant is defective in some way, which is why you're now having the buzzing and other problem. Getting it out will definitely stop the noise."

She went on. "I know you have a million questions and so do I, but for now, she is recommending we get the ear implant out tomorrow, at the Butler County morgue, by the coroner Rachel Curry. Please listen honey. I know you want to ask questions. Let me try to answer everything I can think of first and if you still have questions, we'll try something else. They may be able to hear us even with me whispering in this ear, but I'm hoping the buzzing in your right ear will keep them from hearing what I'm saying. Rachel Curry is the woman that we saw on the news that someone tried to kill, twice. It has to do with this very case. A man who died also had these implants and she found them which is why they're trying to kill her. We may be in danger too if they know that we know about this experiment. Heather said we might be in danger anyway. I truly don't know what's going to happen to us but I think we both know you have to get the things out of you and the sooner the better. Do you agree with that? Just nod if you do."

Jon nodded. She hugged him and told him what little else she knew. She said it would be best if they waited until tomorrow to talk about it further, after the implant was out, but if he wanted to talk to her now, they would need to cover his eye and then type on the computer to each other. Jon liked that idea and acted as though he was laying down to rest and closed his eyes. He then kept the right eye closed and taped a patch over it. He turned on their computer and started typing.

"What if the meeting tomorrow is a trap? Shouldn't we just wait and let my doctor remove the thing from my ear?"

"I guess it could be a trap," typed Carol, "but I don't think so. Whoever is behind this already knows who we are and where we live. They could kill us at any time if they wanted to. Why lure us to the morgue and kill us there? Besides, I believe Heather – she seemed truly concerned about us. Also, what if Dr. Malley can't do the operation for a week or so? The sooner the better, right?"

"I guess so. This is too weird. How could the government have implanted chips in my brain without my parents knowing about it, or without the hospital personnel knowing about it?" Jon then gave Carol an odd look, and he kept typing. "My parents told me that on the day I was born that dad went down to the nursery to look at me and I wasn't there. He said I was gone for several hours in fact. When he asked a nurse where I was, she said there was a problem and they were checking me out more thoroughly, but no one could ever tell them what the problem was, or where I was. And, the nurse in charge of the nursery that evening mysteriously disappeared after that day. That all seems like a strange coincidence, doesn't it?"

"Yes it does," Carol typed.

They sat there without typing for a while as the full impact of what these implants meant started to sink into their minds. How could a person even begin to comprehend such knowledge, let alone believe it. They both instinctively knew there was some truth to it, although they had no idea to what extent. The joy Jon had felt of knowing he would be rid of this terrible pain that was plaguing him was now greatly overshadowed by a deeper, darker fear of the unknown. How would this knowledge change their lives?

Jon didn't take his sleeping pills that night. Even though Heather had recommended they stay somewhere else that night, they didn't. The couple stayed close together, talking some via their computer, but mostly holding each other on the sofa and waiting for 5:30 a.m. to arrive when they would leave their home and drive to the Butler County morgue.

Jacob had finally found true love and happiness again, something he had had only briefly in his life many years ago, and now he was going to do what he said he would never do again – put work before her.

Well, this wasn't just work, this was his daughter's life that he was putting before her. Surely Susan would understand that.

"Susan, I just found out my daughter may be involved in something very dangerous. I am so sorry, but I just can't eat right now. I have to find out where she is and get her back home."

Jacob could see the concern on Susan's face. "Of course, honey. I thought she and Danny were in Fiji?"

"So did I, but that was Danny on the phone and Heather didn't go with him. She's gotten involved in something dangerous and I might need to go get her. I'm so sorry. I wanted your time here to be fun and relaxing and now I'm going to spoil that."

"Don't you worry for a second about me. I'm fine. You go do what you need to do to find Heather. Is there anything I can do to help?"

"No, I don't think so, at least not right now. Thanks so much for asking. I'll be in my office for now, but will probably need to go to Ohio tonight." He hugged and kissed her and vowed silently to make it up to her later.

Jacob turned on his laptop again. Only once in his life had he ever accessed this specific subject's site that he was now accessing. He pulled up the program that he had used many times before with other subjects and then typed in username barnesheatherm17225 and his 25 digit password. Within a minute, Heather's implant video and audio would come to life on his screen.

The technology of the video and audio implants used twenty years after the original Freedom Project were much more advanced. Both picture and sound quality were better. The implants were so tiny that they would not appear as more than a speck of dust on an x-ray or CT scan and they were virtually indestructible. They were also trackable via GPS, which the originals were not. Still, they weren't even close to today's technology, which utilized vaccinations to implant the devices. They were undetectable and targeted both eyes, both ears and attached to portions of the brain and organs that provided data for research on a variety of functions including short and long term memory, organ function and detection of any virus or bacteria in the body. Freedom Project IX was sending this brain and organ function data on a regular basis to several highly funded research laboratories located throughout the world.

If Jacob had it to do over again, he would not have used his daughter as a test subject. His wife had died within six hours after giving birth to Heather, and he had been in an angry and precarious state of mind. Briefly, he had blamed his new baby for his beloved Claire's death and had agreed to let his predecessor, Robert Duley, use his baby girl as a subject as long as her name was not listed on the official project subjects list. Only the two of them, besides the doctor, knew that Heather was a test subject and she had not been monitored frequently as the others had been.

Once, when she was 7 years old, Heather had gone missing. She had not gotten off the bus in front of her house as she usually did when returning home from second grade. Jacob didn't know for several hours as he was in a remote training facility, unreachable while in the desert teaching survival techniques. The housekeeper responsible for ensuring Heather was safely home tried to reach Barnes, then called the local police who contacted the FBI. When the FBI finally reached Barnes, his daughter had been officially missing for four hours. He was frantic, more so because he wasn't home to help look for her. It was then he decided to use the implant technology to search for her. The GPS told him she was not far from their home – only about four blocks away and stationary. Terrified to actually access her implants, afraid of what he might see through Heather's eyes, he knew he had to do it.

She was playing with a friend at the other little girl's house.

Jacob was brought back to the present when his computer screen came to life.

The video through Heather's eyes appeared on his laptop screen and Jacob could see that she was in a bedroom and someone else was there with her. He turned up the volume.

"If Dorgan's been watching and listening to these three subjects for years, which I assume he has, why didn't he notice that Jon's ear implant has been having problems? Carol said she could even hear the awful screeching noises it was making. Why didn't Dorgan hear it? I would think one of the purposes in monitoring the subjects is to determine if the devices work for the 75 years they're supposed to."

It was Heather talking, and it was about the Freedom Project. She was looking at a short, balding middle-aged man whose large stomach was slightly showing beneath his t-shirt. Who was this guy?

"Maybe he *did* report that it wasn't working properly. I'm not sure what they would do about it. They couldn't very well fix it for them, right?" It was the man talking.

"Yes, you're right. And, maybe they don't necessarily listen in most of the time. Perhaps they just watch and would only listen if something seemed out of the ordinary."

"Well, we need to go buy the memory sticks and materials to sound-proof and protect any implants that are removed. You don't have to go if you don't want to. You must be tired. I can put these packages together tonight."

"No, I really want to help. When we're finished, could we order room service again? That food was really good."

"Sure Bernie. We'll be good and hungry by that time."

There was a knock on the door. Jacob could tell that Heather was approaching the door to open it. "Heather Barnes?"

"Yes?"

"Heather Barnes, you're under arrest for removing evidence from a crime scene in a murder investigation."

"What! No, please, I can't be arrested! There are lives at stake!"

"Turn around please." Heather was looking at a police officer and apparently the second officer was handcuffing his daughter.

"Can't she just give back the evidence and you let her go?"

"The implant isn't here anyway."

Jacob noticed Heather looking at her purse and then at the small man. She was signaling him that the implant was in her purse.

"We don't make those decisions. We're just here to arrest Miss Barnes."

"Call Rachel and Jeremy."

Jacob continued to watch as the officers took Heather to the police station, booked and fingerprinted her, and put her in a holding cell with two other women.

He wondered who Rachel and Jeremy were, and he remembered that the name Rachel Curry was mentioned in more than one of the news articles he had read from the on-line Hamilton newspaper. That must be the Rachel Heather was talking about. But who is Jeremy? And who is the man in the hotel room?

At least Heather was safe and sound in the police station for now.

Jacob was going to need some expensive resources and, unfortunately, the use of such resources for personal or unauthorized tasks was frowned upon by his employer. Hiding the use and utilization cost of so-called "non-existent" agents, as well as multi-million dollar equipment, required special skill and, fortunately, Jacob had that skill. He logged into several CIA sites to check availability of the resources he needed. He made a phone call, then logged off his laptop and gathered what he needed from his office to take with him to Ohio.

Heather, Heather, Heather, why did you have to get mixed up in this, he thought. Why are you making me do what I don't want to do?

Several hours later, as his helicopter neared Hamilton, Ohio, Jacob fired up his laptop from his front passenger seat and logged in to see if Heather was still at the police station.

"Where do you want to set down, sir?" the young pilot asked him.

"Hold on a moment and I'll let you know."

It was very late and dark outside, but there were plenty of lights from the streets and buildings below them. "Oh my God," mumbled Jacob when the video through Heather's eyes appeared. She was looking at a man seated in front of her, outside, in the dark. There was a cage of rats in front of him and Jacob could hear Heather crying softly. He turned down the sound so the pilot couldn't hear and quickly determined her location.

"Get to these coordinates and hurry!" Jacob fed in the coordinates of 39.343732, -84.597831 for the pilot.

The small aircraft moved forward at an increasing speed heading straight for the coordinates. It took only a few minutes to arrive near their destination. Jacob was watching his daughter's captor on his computer screen which distracted him from seeing the Blackhawk helicopter in front of them until it was too late.

"Watch out!" he shouted at the young pilot, who had not seen the quiet stealth vehicle coming from his right. The helicopters almost collided, but the huge Blackhawk maneuvered quickly away from the small aircraft and sped off. However, the relative wind from the Blackhawk and Jacob's young pilot's overcorrection in trying to maneuver caused their helicopter to begin spinning out of control. They were going down.

Eight squad cars, sixteen officers and the SWAT team van with six sharp-shooters were dispatched in record time to the Fairfield motel address that Bernie had given the Hamilton police. He had also told them the color, model and license number of Dorgan's car, which was in the lot when the entourage arrived quietly without sirens or lights. They didn't want Dorgan running.

It had taken only twenty minutes for the Hamilton Police Chief and the Fairfield Police Chief, who was immediately called, to completely coordinate the surprise arrival which they hoped would lead to a smooth arrest. The two Chiefs approached the desk clerk in the motel, a young man of about 30, to ask how many rooms currently had guests. Fifteen. Where was John Dorgan? No one registered by that name. This is his car make and license number. Oh, yes, John Johnson. Room 204. Are you sure it's him? Oh yes, I told him he had a car just like mine. Either rooms on each side of 204 occupied? No. Good. Give us keys to those rooms, and to 204. Please don't shoot them up.

Within five minutes, four SWAT team members were in position, one on the roof, one on the ground in front of the second floor room and one in each of the adjoining motel rooms. Other police were positioned in various locations throughout the parking lot and walkways to keep any gawking guests inside their rooms.

Dorgan was not given the courtesy of a knock on his door. He was wanted for the murder of five people, two of them police officers and one an innocent man with three children. The key card was swiped and within seconds two SWAT police, followed by the two Police Chiefs, were inside Dorgan's room.

Dorgan was lying on the bed, sleeping the peaceful sleep of the dead. Four guns were trained on him as the Hamilton Police Chief felt for a pulse on Dorgan's neck. There was none. "Damn!" he shouted.

All but two of the Hamilton officers and one of the Fairfield officers were dismissed. Both Chiefs stayed at the scene. Two officers were assigned to guard the door to Room 204 up and until the crime scene people were through and the body moved. The Fairfield officer patrolled the motel and parking lot on foot, sending the police chasers and other hotel guests on their way.

The Hamilton Chief made the now-too-familiar call to the coroner. "Rachel, you're not going to believe this but we have another body. Looks like it could be poison again."

"Oh my goodness!" responded Rachel to the news. "When is this going to stop?"

"The good news is that we believe this is the main guy we've been looking for, the one who tried to have you killed." The Chief hoped that news would make Rachel feel a little safer. "But, that's still to be proven."

"Do you need for me to come there or can you just bring the body here? If it's okay with you, I'd like to wait until Tuesday to do the autopsy. Bill and I are just now finishing the last one, and I have some other work to do in the morning. And we're all exhausted."

"Of course. Tuesday's fine, and we'll have the bus bring the body to you shortly. Can you wait for it?"

"Yes, I'll stay here until it arrives. Thanks, and try and have a good holiday."

"You too. Hey, Rachel, I'm still leaving one officer with you until we sort this whole thing out. I'm not sure the threat is over."

"Okay, thanks George." Rachel had returned to the morgue after she and Bernie found out at the police station that Heather had been released. As much as she wanted to go home and sleep, she felt guilty leaving Bill with all the work, so went back to help him finish up.

"We have another one, Bill." She actually laughed when she said it, shaking her head. "But I'm saving him for Tuesday so we can have Monday off; and, we're going to be busy again in a few hours. Go on home and get some rest and I'll see you here at six, okay?"

Bill left and Rachel waited forty-five minutes for the ambulance that transported the body of John Dorgan to the morgue. She completed some paperwork in her office as she waited. The paramedics wheeled Dorgan into the lab and lifted the body onto one of the cold storage slabs Rachel had opened and ready. She wasn't doing anything to the body tonight. This monster could wait. She pushed Dorgan's body into the wall, closed the steel door and left to get a few hours of sleep.

Heather's cell phone rang. The loud noise caused both of them to jump slightly; Heather, because she was being held in a car at gunpoint by a man who probably planned to kill her, and the man because he was deep in thought as to what he was going to do to this gorgeous woman. "Well, we don't need that interruption now, do we?" said the man, and he reached into the back seat once again and lifted Heather's purse off the seat. He slowed the car and moved over into the oncoming lane since they were alone on the road at the moment, rolled down his window and threw the Coach bag with the ringing phone into some trees.

Heather immediately regretted not returning her father's call from earlier that evening and letting him know where she was.

She had no idea where the man was taking her. After only a few minutes of driving on Route 128 he turned off the road and drove a short way into the cover of trees. She could hear gravel under the tires as he parked in a spot completely hidden by trees. The night was dark. Did he know about this spot ahead of time?

Heather tried to remain calm and rational. There was no need to panic until he gave her a good reason to do so. She needed to be able to think to get herself out of this situation. She truly hoped Jeremy was still watching and following her and that he had figured out something was wrong. Surely if he saw them driving out of town and into the woods, he would call the police or someone to come help her. Please Jeremy, send help!

The man stopped the car and got out. With the car lights off, it was almost pitch black both inside the car and out. The man didn't seem to be in any hurry to have her get out of the car as he walked slowly around its perimeter like a pacing animal, eyeing her inside her cage. Could he really see her, Heather wondered. It was so dark. She couldn't see him clearly, just a shadow passing by and moving around and around her. The window on the driver's side was down just slightly, and she could hear his shoes on the gravel, walking slowly.

If he was trying to unnerve her, it was working. He had circled the car at least ten times when he suddenly pushed his face

231

up against her window, pressing a horrible, wild grin onto the glass. Heather screamed and tried to move away from the window, sitting on the console between the seats. What little light there was caught the white of his eyes and their mad glow terrified Heather.

What Heather didn't know was that this man was no ordinary assassin; not the typical trained and disciplined killing machine. This man was a psychopath – a criminally insane killer who enjoyed the foreplay of killing – the teasing, the torture, the terror he caused. Killing the victim ended all of the fun. This madman didn't like the killing part at all, but it was a job requirement.

He moved his face away from the window and checked his watch. He clapped his hands and jumped up and down gleefully, opening the trunk of his car.

Heather watched through the darkness as the shadow moved back and forth from the trunk of the car to a place 25 feet away under more trees. He was carrying something from the trunk each time. She could tell he was setting up equipment under the trees. She just couldn't see what it was.

She checked the glove compartment for a weapon she could use. Only the car manual was in there. She felt under the seat for an ice scraper, anything she could use. There was nothing. She had already locked the doors although he had the keys so that was rather silly, she thought.

She was a strong runner and could probably outrun this guy. In the dark he might not be able to see to shoot her. However, in the dark, in the woods with no clear path, she wouldn't be able to run fast. If only he didn't have the gun, she would have a fighting chance. She was as strong as most men and could throw a good boxing punch.

The door beeped and as Heather realized the man had just unlocked it, she was jerked out of the car by both her arms. He placed a large plastic tie around her wrists, holding them together in front of her, before she even comprehended what had happened. He then put wide gray tape across her mouth and swiftly kicked her feet out from under her, sending her abruptly onto her back on the gravel, then tied her feet together in the same fashion as her hands.

Heather couldn't believe how quickly the man had

immobilized her. It took him only a few seconds. He had obviously done this before. He squatted down next to her. He just looked at her, starting at her feet and slowly working his way up until his black, crazy eyes reached hers. He straddled her and pulled her tank tops up over her arms, covering her face, and held her arms above her head. She screamed into the tape.

"We have eight hours to play," he whispered into her ear. He let the full weight of his body rest on her and the sharp gravel cut into her back. "I don't usually have such a beautiful victim to torture, I mean play with," he laughed as he licked her armpit.

Heather shuddered in disgust and in fear. The madman continued to whisper in her ear. "My victims are usually old men. Yes, I still have fun in case you're wondering. But I prefer women, especially beautiful women. And I have hit the jackpot with you." He was running his hands and tongue over her and wiggling his body on top of her. "Tonight is going to be special. My best night ever!"

He then jumped up and dragged her by her arms off the gravel and in the direction of the trees where he had taken the items from the car trunk. He clamped a wide, heavy leather harness around Heather's waist. Her tank tops were still over her face and she couldn't see the nylon ropes attached to the harness which were threaded through a series of pulleys. He used two of the trees as anchors for the pulleys. He pulled Heather up off the ground to show her how it worked.

It hurt to try and hold her back and shoulders up as she was being lifted from the waist, face up. Her waist was the highest point in the air with her legs and torso falling downward towards the ground. Her back began to hurt almost immediately.

Heather again tried to scream into the tape when his two hands pulled her sports bra up and began roughly squeezing her breasts. She then felt his tongue and teeth on her breasts, like a savage, sucking and biting her. He must be on his knees, she concluded, as he was pulling her upper body, which was upside down at the waist, down towards him. He placed her head within his crotch and held it there with his legs as he continued to lean in and bite her. She could feel his hardness on her face which hurt as he used it to press her lower to the ground.

Suddenly, he released her and for several minutes she hung in the same position, her back screaming in pain, her breasts sore from his bites. She could hear him walking around her, breathing on her, making sadistic licking and laughing noises.

Just as suddenly, he jerked her capri pants down. They stayed around her ankles as her feet were strongly bound together.

"Oooh, I LOVE thongs!" She could hear his hands clapping and his crazy giggly laugh. She felt him get beneath her, again on his knees, his head beneath her waist. She felt her buttocks being pulled apart slightly and the sadist's tongue and teeth searching for the thin piece of material of the thong imbedded within her buttock cheeks. His tongue and fingers probed, playing with the material, twisting it and then sticking it within his mouth, which chewed and sucked on the material as if it were a delicacy to be savored.

His fingers then began to probe her, both front and back, slowly at first, and then with increasing viciousness. "This little piggy went to market," he said softly as one finger went into her vagina. "This little piggy stayed home," and he shoved two fingers in as far as he could. At "this little piggy went wee, wee, wee," he stood suddenly and shoved his entire hand into her vagina, groping inside, scratching her fragile tissue with his nails. Heather's screams of pain were muffled beneath the tape on her mouth.

He dropped to the ground beneath her and pulled her bottom towards his face. Heather felt something hard and cold being pushed into her anus. She knew he could feel the resistance so he shoved harder. The pain was unbearable as a metal tag of some sort on the steel rod caught and ripped her rectum. She realized as she nearly passed out that he was probing her with his revolver. He wiggled it around and then pulled the trigger. Heather barely had the strength to scream into the tape once again. He pulled it twice more, laughing hysterically.

"Way too early to kill you my pretty, so no bullets!" and he ripped the gun out of her. He then jumped to his feet and flipped Heather over in her harness so that her legs and arms hung down, her face towards the ground, her waist and bottom in the air. She could hear him removing his clothing, and with her ankles still tied, he stepped between her legs. He pushed her lowered head and hanging torso against a tree and lifted her legs apart at the knees as far as he could, inserting himself into her bleeding anus. Holding her knees apart with each hand, he shoved himself into her, harder and harder, slamming her body against the rough tree with each violent push. "I like the sound of that," he said as he finished and exited her. "Your head hitting the tree." He giggled and pulled her body back as far as the nylon ropes would allow, and pushed her as if pushing a child in a swing. Her body flew into the tree, her right shoulder bearing the brunt of this first hit. He continued several more times pulling her back by her feet and letting her go with a push. She used her shackled hands and arms to protect her head as best she could.

After half an hour of her agony and hanging in the air, the kidnapper lowered Heather slightly so that her feet and head touched the ground. She was grateful for the slight increase of comfort.

The comfort didn't last. The man turned her face up once again, cut the ties to her feet and lifted one of her legs high into the air, quickly harnessing it and tying it to a tree limb. He repeated the process for her other leg, spreading it as far apart from the other leg as he could, giving him total access to her body.

"Would you like to watch?" The man pulled Heather's tank tops down from her face but left them, and her bra, above her breasts so that he had access to them as well.

Heather tried to talk – to plead with him – but he put his hand over the tape on her mouth and told her "no talking allowed at this time. I need to concentrate."

"Now, I want to show you some of the fun things we're going to do tonight." He jerked her head to the side so she could see the display of torture tools he had laid on the ground.

Heather looked, terrified, at the items in front of her. There were two large rats in a cage, mangy and hungry looking, sniffing and frantically trying to reach a substance outside the cage. There was a large dildo with metal spikes protruding from all over it. There were six or seven other items but Heather closed her eyes and started crying. She should have run. Getting shot in the back would be greatly preferable to what was going to happen to her now.

"Oh, come now. You have to look at everything. You need to pick what you want to do first. I saw you eyeing my little pets here." He put his hand on top of the cage and one of the rats jumped at it.

When his engorged penis was ready to burst, he moved from Heather's legs to her head which was almost touching the ground. He grabbed her by her short hair and pulled her head up. He ripped the tape off her mouth and shoved his thumbs into each of her jaws so that she couldn't bite down. He then inserted himself into her mouth. He held her head tightly by her jaws, angled in such a contorted fashion that she thought she would choke to death as he pushed himself as far into her throat as he could.

She smelled the sickness of him. Her nose was shoved in his scrotum and she couldn't breathe. Then she felt her mouth and throat fill with his venom and she wished for a quick death.

He collapsed on top of her, releasing her head which fell towards the ground. His weight was unbearable on her contorted back and fragile insides which continued to be punctured and ripped by his weight against the dozens of items within her cavity walls. Heather could finally breathe again. She gagged and spit as the man stood and walked back around to her legs.

Heather passed out for several minutes when the man used forceps to open her wider. She was unconscious while he retrieved his treasures from their warm nesting place. He stuffed a diamond necklace into Heather's mouth, bringing her to groggy consciousness. He ordered her to suck the necklace clean, and repeated the process with each item he removed from her. He placed a few in his own mouth as well.

Heather started vomiting and the man jerked her upside down so that she wouldn't choke on her vomit. The swift movement brought her back to her senses to some degree. She tried to think how long they had been here. Definitely several hours. How many more hours until daylight? She knew he didn't want her dead yet. He wanted to torture her for the rest of the night before he killed her. She wished he would just go ahead and shoot her. She had no means of escape and no strength left to run even if she could.

He made her finish sucking his toys clean. She vomited again when he tried to push the small, slimy, squealing mouse into her mouth.

"Clean him off!" he demanded.

"No!" Heather screamed and she clamped her mouth shut.

He held the mouse by its tail, hanging within an inch of

Heather's face. The tiny creature grasped at her lips with its small front feet. Heather didn't dare cry out as she knew the man would push the frightened mouse into her mouth if she opened it even a little.

He bent down so that his own face was in front of hers, the mouse hanging between them. "Fine," he said abruptly, standing up. "I'm hungry anyway." And within a second he raised his head and dropped the tiny mouse into his open mouth, swallowing it whole.

Heather squeezed her eyes shut, willing herself not to be sick again.

The man released her legs from the tree limbs and re-tied her ankles with a heavy duty plastic tie.

He let her sit on the ground for a few minutes while he put on his clothes and sat in front of her, putting his souvenirs back in their box.

Heather felt the strong breeze from above and behind her but didn't hear the helicopter. She was looking at this horrible, sickening face in front of her and saw his hair and shirt blowing back slightly. A second later, she heard the barely audible thud and saw the red patch appear on his shirt over his heart.

She knew that he had felt the breeze as well and had looked up slightly to see what was causing a wind on this still night. He apparently felt something and looked down at the blood on his shirt. He never moved again.

What happened? Heather was thinking, tears streaming down her face. She looked at the man. He was sitting on his blanket on the ground, his eyes were open and he was looking down at his shirt. Is that blood? she thought, hoped. She didn't hear anything and the breeze had stopped. His hair and shirt were no longer moving.

Is he dead? Please, let him be dead. Please God, let him be dead.

She looked up and around trying to see something, anything. She now heard a helicopter nearby and listened intently. Were they coming to save her? They must have been the ones who shot the man. Maybe Jeremy had seen what was going on and sent someone to shoot this man.

She then heard a different noise. It sounded like a playing

card in bicycle spokes – click, click, click, click – very fast and repetitive. Surely it was the helicopter blades in contact with something. Then the sound stopped and the darkness and quiet enveloped her again. She kept looking back at the man, expecting him to look up and grin his sadistic grin at her. Was this just another one of his games? The thought made her cry even more.

Minutes went by and the man didn't move. The rats had moved from one side of the cage to another – the side facing the man. Did they sense something? Heather thought. Do they sense he is dead? She was suddenly more hopeful. Perhaps she was not going to die tonight after all.

She reached up with her tied hands and slowly pulled her bra and shirts down to cover her. The man still didn't move so she continued. With great effort, she managed to get her pants pulled up. She fumbled with the belt around her waist. It was clasped in the back and she couldn't reach around with her wrists fastened together. She gnawed at the heavy-duty tie holding her wrists but she didn't even leave teeth marks in the strong plastic.

She made herself look at the items in front of her, the items meant for torture and eventually, for killing. Surely there was something here she could use to cut the ties around her hands and feet. The gun! Perhaps she could shoot the ties, at least the one on her feet. But in examining the ties closely, she realized there was no space at all between her feet or her wrists – the ties were too tight and she couldn't shoot them off without shooting herself.

She didn't see a knife of any kind. What kind of crazy, psychopathic killer doesn't have a knife? Perhaps there's one in the trunk of the car, but of course I can't get to the car until I can cut the ties and get out of this belt.

Frustrated and exhausted, Heather began to sob again. Her back ached terribly, and she was extremely sore, perhaps even bleeding internally from the gun, piece of wood and other foreign objects he had shoved into her. She wanted to lie down and rest but was afraid to take her eyes off the man. She still wasn't certain that this wasn't a sick trick on his part.

She rolled onto her side to get into a more comfortable position. A thick fallen tree branch was nearby and she rested her head on it. She didn't remember falling asleep.

Jacob awoke to the sound of sirens. His head hurt and he touched his right temple. Warm, sticky blood was on his head and now on his hand. He was still in the helicopter but it was sideways. He was hanging from his seatbelt towards the pilot. "Rick," Jacob called to the pilot. "Rick, are you okay?"

Jacob tried to reach Rick's neck to see if there was a pulse but he couldn't quite reach from the position he was in. He didn't see any blood on the pilot but he also couldn't tell if the man was breathing. He released his seat belt and fell on top of him. The entire helicopter dropped several feet from the force of Jacob's shifting weight. Through the pilot's window which was right below him, Jacob could see that the small helicopter was precariously balanced in the top of several trees. They were at least 30 feet in the air. Jacob also realized the window was no longer intact. It was broken out by the tree branches and he was being held in the chopper by the pilot, who was being held in by his seatbelt as well as a large tree branch.

The sirens were closer. Jacob presumed they were meant for him and his pilot. He felt for the pilot's pulse now that he was right on top of him. It was weak, but the man was alive. He tried to move so that his full weight wasn't on the young man, but each movement caused the helicopter to shift, so he finally remained still.

He looked about for his laptop. He didn't see it anywhere. He checked for his phone, which was gone as well. They both most likely fell through the broken window to the ground.

He wondered how close he was to Heather's location. Would the rescue units arriving find her and the man also?

It was a Blackhawk helicopter that they had almost collided with. Was it just arriving or just leaving from its mission when they almost ran into each other? Were they its target? Jacob wondered.

Jacob felt certain that he wasn't injured except for the nasty bump on his head and he considered climbing over the pilot and out the open window but decided against it. The helicopter was too unstable in the tree and he didn't want to risk killing the pilot by climbing over him and possibly causing him to fall.

However, Jacob did not want to be detained by paramedics or anyone else looking for the crashed helicopter. He needed to get out.

He could tell the vehicles with the sirens were trying to find them. They were close but there were probably no roads beneath him and since the helicopter didn't explode and burn, there was no smoke to guide them.

Jacob pulled a small pistol from a strap near his ankle and shot out the passenger window above him, careful to shelter the pilot from the falling debris. He doubted the gunshot was heard over the blare of the sirens, which were getting closer. Positioning one foot on a tree branch stuck in the open window below him, he stood on one leg and reached up through the now-open window above him, grabbing another fairly large branch. Most men his age would not be able to pull themselves up in this manner, but Jacob could still do so although it was much more of a struggle to do now than thirty years ago.

Once out of the helicopter and balanced on the only substantial tree limb in the near vicinity, Jacob looked down. It was extremely dark, but he felt sure there weren't any tree limbs below him for at least fifteen feet. He cursed softly, then looked around. He could go up and then over to another tree. In the dark it was hard to tell if he could safely cross to another tree, but at this point he hadn't much choice. He began to climb.

Ten or twelve feet higher, Jacob was getting close to the top of the tree and the branches were too small to hold his weight. He could barely make out a larger branch from another tree crossing a few feet in front of him and he jumped to it, landing on the branch on his stomach in order to grab it with both arms and legs. It hurt, but at least he was now in a larger tree with heavier branches. He scooted towards the tree trunk.

He saw the spotlight hit the tops of the trees before he heard the whining engine of a small aircraft. Unfortunately, Jacob twisted around a little too sharply to try and get a look at the source of the spotlight and engine noise and lost his grip on the limb. He fell, smacking forcefully onto another limb ten feet below him, before falling the remainder of the way to the ground. He hit hard, with his left side taking the brunt of the fall. He thought he could hear voices in the distance as he passed out.

The Man watched the live video being fed to him. The woman on his screen was terrified and in extreme pain and he watched her brutal rape with little emotion. What did that say about himself, he wondered. Not that he cared. He was a powerful man who could have whatever he wanted, including hiring a psychopath to torture a beautiful young woman in front of a video camera because he ordered it. Had it been anyone other than this particular girl he might have enjoyed watching the rape, enjoyed getting off at the sight of her legs spread wide and tied to tree limbs, her sweet womanly center bigger than life in front of his face, and being stuffed with everything from a diamond necklace to a live mouse.

He continued to watch. He knew if he let it go on that the rape would get worse, much worse, as the psychopath had a plethora of torturous instruments and devices on the ground beside him. The rape and torture would end in her death.

He was making her pay for not obeying him, but he didn't want her dead. So he would stop the torture. Just a few minutes more to properly teach her a lesson.

SUNDAY

Jeremy had screwed up big time. This mistake would cost him his job. Samuel, the two-billion dollar satellite that the Secretary of DHS had requisitioned for his use, was to watch Dragon, and Dragon only. He had done that for several hours straight. But then he lost Heather and knew she was in trouble. Dragon was sitting and reading in his hotel room, so Jeremy had temporarily moved Samuel to find Heather. And wouldn't you know Dragon goes and dies while I'm not watching him. What are the chances of that? Either he committed suicide, which is highly doubtful, reasoned Jeremy, or he was murdered. And if I had done my job correctly I would know who murdered him, how and when. But I know none of the above. The only consolation I will have when I'm out on the street without a job is that I found Heather.

Jeremy knew he should call the Secretary and give her the news of Dragon's death, but he couldn't yet bring himself to do so. It had been six hours since Dragon's body was found and he should have let her know immediately. He was trying to think of a good excuse, but he had nothing other than the truth.

In the meantime, Samuel was still watching Heather where Jeremy had found her only minutes earlier. He had searched all night for her, meticulously moving Samuel mile after mile along each side of State Route 128. He might never have found her had it not been for the helicopter crash in the area, which he went to investigate. Even though he suspected the crash might possibly be related to Heather in some way, when he didn't find her within a mile radius of the crash site, he returned to searching closer to the road. Only half an hour ago did he finally go back and expand his search around the crash site. She was only another one hundred yards beyond the scope of his last search.

Heather seemed to be sleeping and Jeremy hoped she was not unconscious or hurt. Jeremy picked up his phone to call Bernie to let him know where Heather was so that he could pick her up. He was calling Heather's cell phone as he knew Bernie had it, along with her purse. He hoped the call would wake Bernie and he would answer the phone, but it went to Heather's voice-mail. If he couldn't get hold of Bernie soon, he would call the police to go and pick up

Heather.

At one point in time during the night, Jeremy had gone to the break room and bought five sandwiches, five soft drinks, three coffees and several bags of snacks. He also brought out of a storage closet three gallon sized containers with lids to use as portable potties. He didn't plan to make the mistake of being gone from his desk again if something important happened. He was now stocked with food and something to pee in. Thank goodness no one else was working anywhere close to him. And hopefully he wouldn't need to take a dump.

There was a ping on one of Jeremy's other computers indicating activity and he jumped and stared at the screen when he saw which one. It was the keystroke software - someone was on Dragon's laptop! Good thing he hadn't shut down that program yet in light of Dragon's death. It had to be either the police on the laptop, who would have confiscated it from Dragon's hotel room, or Dragon's murderer, who would have done the same.

Jeremy watched as the familiar username and password was entered for Mary Beth Singer's secret monitoring video. Those keystrokes were followed by Jon Moore's video information. Well, this rules out the police, thought Jeremy. He wondered how many CIA or other agents had access to this confidential data and which of them had killed his boss.

Dragon had removed the GPS tracking device from his laptop so Jeremy couldn't track the whereabouts of the computer that way. Since someone else was now using Dorgan's computer, Jeremy began searching for its location by its IP address.

He watched Mary Beth and Jon's monitors closely so that he could see the same thing being seen by the person now accessing Dragon's computer. Both of them, and their spouses, were up and dressed even though it was not yet six a.m. Jon and Carol were driving in their car, and it appeared that Mary Beth and Joe were planning to leave in their car as well. Jeremy was pretty sure they were headed for the morgue.

The next keystrokes entered on Dragon's computer were different than any Jeremy had seen before. He quickly re-typed onto his own laptop everything that was just entered. The user was accessing a highest security level CIA folder, belonging to Jacob

Barnes. Jeremy wondered if Heather knew about her dad's association with this project and whether Jacob Barnes knew where his daughter was right now.

The file, entitled Freedom Projects I-IX, was 4000 pages long. "I'll get right on that," Jeremy groaned.

He was having no luck finding the location of Dragon's computer. Whoever had it was using a VPN proxy chain.

Jeremy heated one of his now cold cups of coffee in a small microwave he had behind his desk and opened a turkey sandwich. Was his assignment officially over? He was supposed to track Dragon and report back to the Secretary as to his whereabouts and activities. With Dragon dead, Jeremy had now done all of that, with the exception of reporting back that he was dead. Minor detail.

But the assignment didn't feel over yet, not by a long shot. Someone was on Dragon's computer, Heather's father perhaps? Someone had kidnapped Heather last night about the same time that Dragon had died – did Dragon order the hit, or was it his murderer that ordered it? Others may still not want these implants to come out of Mary Beth and Jon and that was going to happen soon. Did these others know that, or would they know soon?

Jon had closed or covered his right eye several minutes ago and Jeremy could no longer see where they were headed, even though he already knew. Both couples had talked very little in route since they knew someone, possibly several someones, might be listening.

From the satellite Audrey that Jeremy had moved to follow Bernie, he could see that Bernie had slept in his car most of the night near the morgue. When he awoke a half hour ago, he had driven to McDonald's and quickly returned to the morgue. The others should be arriving soon. Since Bernie wasn't answering Heather's phone, he would try him again soon at the morgue.

Jeremy started to peruse the secret 4000 page file, glancing at the table of contents first. He couldn't believe it. There were nine separate Freedom Projects listed. He quickly looked at the contents of Freedom Project I which held no major surprises. There was more information in this document than in the one he had read on the USB drive he borrowed from Dragon's office, including the names of every CIA and other agency members involved in the project. And

Jeremy had been right - Lyndon Johnson was in office at the time.

He skimmed through pages of the next several projects, numbers II, III and IV. In each case, there were more subjects and the technology improved each time. In only the first two projects were the eye and ear devices actually implanted surgically.

Jeremy fully intended to read the entire document at some point in time, but right now was not the time. He continued to skim through pages, when he heard a familiar voice to his left which caused him to look at another computer screen.

"To whomever is watching and listening, my name is Bernie Kossack and I work for the Department of Homeland Security in Washington, D.C." Bernie's voice, although quite faint, was coming from Mary Beth Singer's implant video. There was no video, only faint audio.

He listened to the short speech, and truly hoped no one else was listening. If anything would get Bernie and the others killed, it was that speech. He certainly hoped that Heather and Bernie knew what they were doing. They were both revealing a lot of this secret project to a lot of people.

Another computer pinged. It was the facial recognition software returning the identity of the man who had kidnapped Heather. It had been eight hours since Jeremy had entered the photos of the man and he had all but forgotten about it. "You piece of crap software!" Jeremy yelled at the computer. "Eight hours! Really? I'm going to have to re-write you, even though you deserve to be deleted entirely!" He laughed at his little joke since no one else was around to laugh.

The man was bad news. Thank goodness he was dead. At least 30 deaths from various torture techniques had been attributed to this assassin. He had been caught once and served three months in an institution for the criminally insane but had escaped by capturing and torturing one of the floor guards who, according to the report, was a huge bear of a man - 6'6", 275 pounds of solid muscle. The report that accompanied the man's identity went into detail as to how the guard was bound and tortured, but Jeremy had just eaten and stopped reading in the middle of the report to prevent the return of his sandwich.

Jeremy had both Jon's and Mary Beth's audio turned up as

loud as they would go. They were both in the same room, along with their spouses, as well as Bernie, Rachel Curry and Bill, the assistant coroner. The two audios were therefore of the same muffled conversation.

The coroner didn't waste any time and began prepping Jon for his surgery. The conversation almost ceased for the next 15 minutes and Jeremy heard very little until the implant from Jon's ear began its horrible screeching. Jeremy jumped as the noise was incredibly loud.

"I don't know how he lived with that thing right next to his ear drum. It had to be excruciating." It was the coroner talking and Jeremy could hear her voice quite plainly now, even with the screeching noise, so he assumed the device was now out of Jon's ear.

"Hopefully wrapping it, putting it in the jar and then into the metal box will keep anyone from being able to hear it, but I'm not sure. It's so loud!" This time it was Carol's voice.

Jeremy's cell phone rang. It was Bernie.

"Are you still at the office?" Bernie asked him.

"Yes, I've been here all night, looking for Heather, and I've been trying to call you."

"Did you find Heather?" Bernie's voice was hopeful. "I didn't stay at the hotel last night. I'm sorry, I should have called you earlier."

"I've been calling Heather's phone . I thought you had it?"

"Oh yeah, I forgot about it. It's in my trunk."

"I found Heather, and she's okay but she's tied up and needs help. Can you go get her?"

"Of course!" Bernie was ecstatic. "Just tell me where she is."

Jeremy calculated the 3.5 miles out 128 from the Columbia Bridge at New London Road, and then gave Bernie explicit instructions from there on how to find Heather. "And take a knife or some heavy duty scissors. I think she's tied up."

As Jeremy hung up his phone, his eye was drawn back to his laptop where the secret file of Barnes was displayed. Something was being entered onto the screen. Jeremy looked at his laptop that showed whether there were any keystrokes being made from Dragon's computer. There were none. Someone else was entering the information into Jacob Barnes' folder while both Jeremy and the stranger on Dragon's computer watched.

"Oh my God!" cried Jeremy. An unmanned drone with warheads was being requisitioned. The destination was the Butler County Morgue, Hamilton, Ohio, coordinates 39.403408, -84.536859. The mission was to destroy the building and all inhabitants.

"Oh my God!" he screamed again and grabbed his phone. Dragon's keystroke software pinged. Jeremy's blood went cold as he read the words being typed into Dragon's laptop.

Jeremy...call and warn them...now!

Jeremy tapped on the most recent incoming call to re-dial the morgue. Hopefully Bernie or someone was still close to the phone and would answer. It rang and rang. No one answered.

He tried Heather's number in hopes that Bernie had made it to the car and taken the phone out of the trunk.

No answer.

"Crap! Crap! Crap!"

He started to dial the Hamilton police when his phone rang. It was from the morgue number. "Bernie!" he answered.

"Yeah, I heard the phone ring but wasn't close enough to answer it. But when I saw who..."

"Never mind! Get everyone out of there, now! You're going to be attacked very shortly. Do you understand!"

"Uh, yes. I'll get everybody out. Where should they go?"

"It doesn't matter...the police station maybe...just get out now!" Jeremy hung up to discourage Bernie from asking more questions.

With Audrey positioned over the morgue, Jeremy saw Joe and Mary Beth leave the morgue right away. It was more than a minute before he saw Bernie, Rachel and Carol leave. Bernie took his car and was most likely headed to pick up Heather, and Rachel and Carol left together in another car. That left Jon and the assistant coroner inside. Oh, God, Jeremy thought. Jon was still passed out under anesthesia. Perhaps Bill is giving him something to wake him up and they will then leave. Hurry!

Where would the drone come from? How quickly could it get there? Jeremy knew there was an air force base close by in

Dayton, Ohio. Would they have a drone capable of carrying missiles? If so, it could be there in a matter of fifteen or twenty minutes, maybe less.

As he waited, willing Jon to wake up and Bill to get him out of there, a truth hit Jeremy like a lightning bolt. Dragon is still alive! It was him on his laptop. He sent me that message to warn them.

Jeremy watched the morgue but his mind was on Dragon. He's not the one who ordered the drone. It was someone else, probably Heather's dad. Dragon knew I'd be watching. He wanted me to see that CIA folder. But why would I still be watching if I thought he was dead? "Because, you idiot," he said out loud since no one was around to hear, "he thought you were watching him when he faked his death, but you were too busy watching Heather."

The door to the morgue was opening and a man was coming out. Jeremy knew it must be Bill since it wasn't Jon. Where was Jon? Was he coming right behind Bill?

It didn't matter. The silent drone was there and then it was gone. And so was the morgue and the men.

Heather awoke to extreme cold. She was shaking and heard a scuffling sound close by. What was it? She couldn't move very well. She ached all over and couldn't move her legs at all. It was dark and she didn't know where she was.

Then she remembered. She focused her eyes. The man was still sitting there, looking down. The rats were scuffling in the cage. She eyed the man's blanket. She had on only her two sleeveless tank tops and her short capri pants. The night had gotten cool from the previous day's heat.

With painful effort, she was finally able to sit up, then stand with her back against a tree. Holding onto one of the ropes attached to the belt around her waist, she jumped around the display of torture devices to the back of the man. Most of the blanket was behind him. She reached down to try and grab the edge of the blanket and fell hard onto her elbows. Her face almost hit the man's back and she cringed in disgust and fear. She managed to back up and pull the blanket from a kneeling position. She jerked hard and the blanket came from beneath the man, toppling him over onto his rat cage. Heather managed to wrap the warm blanket partially around her and went back to sleep.

When Heather awoke a second time, the sun was up. She guessed it to be 7 or 7:30 a.m. Her plan was now in shambles. She was supposed to have been at the morgue by 6 a.m. and was to have called Joe Singer before 6 this morning to tell him when and where to meet to have Mary Beth's implant removed. The Moores had most likely come to the morgue at 6, but would they have gone ahead and let Rachel remove the ear implant if she wasn't there? They would all be wondering where she was and perhaps thinking it was all a setup or a lie. The Homeland Security agent who had set this all up didn't even show up. Bernie would be truly worried, she knew, wondering where she was.

Why hadn't Jeremy sent someone to get her? He must have been the one that sent the sniper to kill the man who had kidnapped her? Who else could it have been? And if whoever it was knew the psycho assassin was here, they had to know she was here as well. Why had they left her here?

She had another thought. Did Jeremy see what happened? Had he watched? She couldn't bear to think that anyone had seen what had had happened to her last night.

Perhaps she would die after all, stuck out here in the woods, tied up and unable to get food or water.

"Stop it Heather," she said aloud and instinctively looked at the dead man. He didn't move. His hand was lying next to the dildo of death and she wondered if the nails would cut the ties binding her hands. She would have to find a way to secure the object so that it didn't move while she scraped the tie across the nails. She would most surely scrape her hands and wrists against the nails as well, but at this point, she was determined to find a way to get away from this place.

One of the other objects lying on the ground was a stainless steel rod about an inch in diameter and about eighteen inches long. She picked up the rod and pushed it into the ground about 8 inches, to anchor it well. She carefully picked up the spikey hollow cylinder and slipped it over the steel rod. It was way too loose and when she tried to move the tie on her wrists up and down on the nails, it moved with her and wouldn't cut the tie.

She looked around again and saw the tape that had been pulled from her mouth last night. She carefully unwadded it and wrapped it around the base of the nailed object, securing it somewhat to the steel rod. She doubted if it would be strong enough to hold it though. Did he have more tape? She didn't see any. She tried the nails again anyway but the tape didn't hold – as soon as she rubbed the tie up and down against the nails, the device pulled free of the tape.

Heather screamed as loud as she could, mostly out of frustration but also in hopes that someone might hear her. She couldn't be too far from the road.

Heather looked at the rats in the cage. They were quiet now, sleeping. Heather gasped as she realized the rats were no longer starving. They had been feeding on the man's fingers and his face, both of which had fallen onto the top of the cage. "Serves you right!" she screamed. She continued to sob and scream, venting her anger and frustration.

Then suddenly she stopped and listened. A car was approaching. She didn't know whether to be happy or afraid.

Bernie had set his spy watch alarm for 5:30 a.m. As much as he wanted to sleep in his bed at the hotel, he had decided to sleep in his car in case the police sent an officer to the hotel to bring him in after he called in the report about Dorgan and Heather. He couldn't risk being unavailable to go to the morgue at 6 a.m., especially since Heather was probably not going to be there. He had parked his car on the road near the morgue and the cemetery as he had done early the day before.

He woke at the sound of the alarm from a deep sleep, but was immediately alert. Had Heather been found? was the first thought that came to his mind. Does my breath smell like a garbage can?, was his second thought, and he breathed into his hand. "Ugh, yes," he grimaced. His toothbrush and change of clothes were at the hotel, so scrubbing his finger over his teeth would have to do. He was hungry and wondered if he had time to drive through McDonald's since there were no cars at the morgue yet.

He drove the mile and a half to the downtown McDonald's

where he spent $3.00 of his remaining $75 to buy two sausage biscuits and a small Coke from the dollar menu. He would need every penny of his remaining money for gasoline for the drive home, even though he had no intention of leaving until Heather was found.

By the time he returned to the morgue, there were three cars in the parking lot. He parked by them and walked to the door. It was locked and he pushed the doorbell. Rachel came and let him in.

"Are you not under police protection anymore?" Bernie asked her since he didn't see a police cruiser in the lot.

"I didn't want the police to know what we're doing here this morning, so I sent the officer home this morning and drove here myself. Besides, I think the guy that's been trying to kill me is dead now."

"No, the two dead guys that tried to kill you aren't the ones in charge. But the police should have picked up the guy in charge, Dorgan, by now, so maybe you are safe."

"They did pick him up, but he's dead. He's in one of my vaults now."

"Dorgan's dead!" Bernie exclaimed. "What happened to him?"

"I don't know yet, poison probably. But I'm not going to worry about him for a while. Today we have a bigger task to do." Rachel looked around realizing Heather wasn't there and asked, "Isn't Heather with you?"

"No," and Bernie choked a little as he continued, "the lawyer that picked her up last night wasn't a lawyer at all, but kidnapped her. I don't know where she is or what has happened to her." He had tears in his eyes as he finished.

"Do the police know?"

"Yes, I told them when I called them about Dorgan. I don't know if they've found her or not. I know she would want us to finish what she started so I came here with some stuff I put together. Oh, it's out in the car, I'll be right back."

Rachel waited so that she could open the locked door for Bernie. Bill arrived right then and walked in with Bernie. The Moores and the Singers were already in the lab, waiting. Jon and Mary Beth both had patches over their right eyes. Rachel had the forethought to pick up some earplugs as well and had them each put an earplug in their right ears. It would only muffle the sound, but that would help.

With Heather not there to lead the group, everyone was nervous and uncertain as to what to do. Bernie told the others what little he knew about what had happened with Heather and that made Mary Beth even more nervous. "Joe, I don't think this is such a good idea. Perhaps we should go."

Rachel intervened. "I know that the past few days have been the most traumatic and nerve-wracking ones in my entire life and I can only imagine what is going through each of your minds as well. Whoever is behind this has tried to kill me more than once and has now kidnapped and possibly killed Heather."

Rachel continued. "These attempts on my life and the several killings and murders that have happened in the past few days, are all related to these implants – the ones that were in Michael Michtenbaum and the ones that are in you."

"Ray had these implants too!" Mary Beth interrupted loudly, very distraught now. "Joe, did you know that? Oh, my God! Did they kill him because of the implants?"

"I don't know," Rachel confessed and looked at Bernie, who said he didn't know either.

Bernie told Mary Beth, "The eyeball you found was Mr. Michtenbaum's. The man who planted the bombs at the funeral home parking lot was the same guy who took Michael's eye and took the implant off of it. He was trying to get rid of the evidence."

Mary Beth had her head in her hands now and was crying. Jon, Carol and Joe all looked extremely nervous as well.

"And I found and removed the implant from his ear," said Rachel. "The first attempt on my life that left two officers dead was another hit man that was after that implant. Heather managed to get both of them back and we have them here."

Bernie held up a silver steel box.

"Okay, we all know we're in a lot of danger now," said Joe, holding onto his wife. "I think we're all in agreement that these devices need to come out of their heads if we ever want to have another private moment in our lives." Jon nodded and Joe continued, "but how are we ever going to feel safe again? How do we know they won't they come after us tomorrow, or the next day?"

Bernie took over. "You don't, really. But that is what we're going to do with these boxes – hopefully provide us all some protection. Heather had the idea that if we threaten to reveal the Freedom Project to the press if something happens to one or more of us, that whoever is behind this will leave us alone."

"Freedom Project?" questioned Jon. "Is that what they call this experiment?"

"How ironic," added Joe. "They take away your most basic freedom – of privacy – and call it the Freedom Project."

"Anyway," Bernie continued, "I don't know what Heather had in mind to do, but since she isn't here, I thought we could use what I put together; that is, if you all agree." Bernie explained about the three boxes, which would each contain a set of implants, a USB drive of the Freedom Project file and instructions for whomever was entrusted with the box. "Initially, only your ear implant devices will be in the box until a surgeon can remove the ones in your eyes." He went on to tell the group that he planned to give a speech in front of either Mary Beth or Jon, so that whoever might be watching and listening to them at the moment would know what he and the others intended to do.

"I don't think it's a good idea to tell them, whoever THEY are, about what we are about to do. It may give them more of an incentive to kill us." It was Mary Beth speaking and her husband Joe agreed.

"What are you planning to say?" Carol asked Bernie.

They were all speaking softly, hoping that the ear plugs fitted securely in Mary Beth and Jon's ears would be sufficient to keep anyone from hearing what was being said. Bernie began reading the speech that he had written the night before.

"To whomever is watching and listening, my name is Bernie Kossack and I work for Homeland Security in Washington, D.C. I, and others, recently became aware of the Freedom Project that was started by the CIA 50 years ago. With the murder of Michael Ray Michtenbaum this past Tuesday, who was one of the three subjects who had implants placed in his head at birth, the project was brought to my and several other people's attention. Since that time, at least three totally innocent people have been killed and all three of their killers are now dead as well. There have been attempts made on at least two other people's lives that have knowledge of this project and one of them may now be dead.

"We are obviously afraid for our lives as well, but not enough to do nothing about this atrocity that has taken place against these three human beings. Therefore, here is what we are going to do.

"One: the implants are going to be surgically removed from the other two subjects' heads this morning."

Bernie chose not to mention that the eye implants were not being removed.

"Two: these implants, along with Michael Michtenbaum's implants, will each be placed as evidence in separate containers. The entire Freedom Project file, naming names, dates and everything else known about the project, has been copied onto several memory sticks and will be included in each of the separate containers.

"Three: separate trustees have been identified and notified that they are to hide and maintain these boxes, forever, unless and/or until anything happens to one or more of the Freedom Project subjects or any member of their families, and you know who they are, or to the Butler County Coroner Rachel Curry, or to myself Bernie Kossack."

A look of fear came over Rachel's face at the mention of her name. Bernie could see that Mary Beth was very uncomfortable as well and her husband spoke up. "Stop right there, Bernie. Maybe it's not a good idea to let anyone know what we're doing."

Everyone in the room was silent for several seconds. "I agree," said Jon.

Bernie's feelings were hurt. He had spent hours writing his speech and thought it was pretty good, but this wasn't the time to be upset over it. "OK," he said.

Rachel began prepping Jon for his surgery. He was going first and said she expected the surgery to take only ten minutes. Even so, he would be placed under general anesthesia which would keep him asleep for at least forty-five minutes. Bill would be assisting Rachel and the others were asked to step outside the lab. Carol put on a mask and stayed with her husband.

Bernie sat in the lobby area for fifteen minutes, mostly thinking about Heather. He held one silver steel box on his lap, the one with Michael Michtenbaum's implants. He planned to take it to

Sheila's Priest later. Heather would be proud of me, I'm sure, he thought. He watched Joe and Mary Beth Singer but tried not to listen in to their conversation. They were a nice couple. They didn't deserve this huge problem in their lives.

Bernie thought he should call Jeremy and looked around for a phone. He saw one on a desk in an adjoining room. He dialed Jeremy's cell phone number, which he had memorized.

"Are you still at the office?" Bernie asked him. When he finished his conversation with Jeremy, he told Joe and Mary Beth the good news about Heather and that he had to leave right then to get her. "I'm going to run tell Rachel and the others," and Bernie ran down the hallway and into the lab.

Rachel walked with Bernie back to the front door as she wanted to tell Mary Beth it was her turn to have her ear implant removed. As they walked down the hall, the two could hear a phone ringing. Bernie knew it was the same phone on which he had just talked to Jeremy. "Do you mind checking that?" Bernie nodded toward the ringing phone. By the time Rachel got to it, the ringing had stopped. "Bernie, it's a D.C. number."

"It's Jeremy again. Must be important," and Bernie called Jeremy once more.

"Yeah, I heard the phone ring but wasn't close enough to answer it. But when I saw who...." Rachel, Joe and Mary Beth watched as Bernie's face took on a worried look.

"Uh, yes. I'll get everybody out. Where should they go?"

Bernie hung up the phone quickly.

"Everybody needs to get out right now! Jeremy said someone is going to attack us very shortly!"

Bernie was shaking as he left the morgue. Joe and Mary Beth had already left and Rachel and Carol left when he did. Bill, the Assistant Coroner, had insisted that everyone else leave and he would get Jon out. Carol wouldn't leave without her husband, but Bill convinced her that if he couldn't wake Jon, he would put him in one of the cold storage trays and he would be safe there. No one would think to look in there for a live person and any flying bullets wouldn't penetrate the steel. Still, she was crying as Rachel helped her out to the car. The four of them were headed for the police station, Bernie knew. Maybe the police would get back there before the attackers arrived. Or, better yet, there would be no one at the morgue when the assassins arrived and their plot would be foiled.

Bernie once again drove south on route 128. He watched his odometer so that he turned off the road at the precise mileage that Jeremy had said and again when he needed to turn into the heavy tree growth on a graveled path. He was relieved to know that Heather was okay and he couldn't wait to be the one to rescue her. He saw a car ahead but no one was in it. He proceeded slowly.

He pulled his car to the right of the other parked car. He could see Heather sitting with a blanket around her and when she recognized that it was him, he saw a huge smile come across her face. He also saw a man slumped over on the ground He grabbed the scissors he had stolen from the desk at the morgue and got to Heather as quickly as possible.

"Bernie, I have never been more happy to see anyone in my entire life!" She shrugged off the blanket. "Can you unbuckle this belt?"

Bernie saw the dead man, a sight he was now becoming used to, and the three-foot wide area of horrid looking instruments as well as two caged rats. "What kind of sick guy was this?" and he unbuckled Heather from her harness. "Are you okay?" he asked timidly. He didn't really want to know what the man did to Heather.

"I will be. Fortunately, he was killed before he…." Her voice trailed off.

Heather didn't want Bernie or anyone besides a psychiatrist to know what had happened to her that night.

"Thank God," they both said at the same time and Heather smiled at him again. "And thank you, Bernie, for coming to rescue me." She saw the scissors in his hand and held out her wrists for him to cut the thick tie. It was difficult for him but he finally cut completely through it and the bond fell off her hands. She rubbed them and swung her arms to get the feeling back into them. He then cut the tie around her ankles.

"Did Jeremy tell you where I was?"

"Yes, and sorry it took so long. He was trying to call me on your phone."

"My phone is somewhere along the road, along with my $300 purse, credit cards and money."

"No, I have it." And Bernie saw her face light up.

Bernie started to tell her the story of finding her purse and Jeremy losing track of her, but Heather stopped him.

"Please, tell me on the way if you don't mind. I need to get out of here. I keep thinking this guy is going to wake up any minute." Heather stood slowly and could hardly walk as she started for Bernie's car. She teetered and fell onto Bernie.

"I'm afraid I need help walking to the car, okay?"

Bernie turned his head so she wouldn't see his broad grin. "Okay!"

Once they were in the car, Bernie started with the threat on the morgue, stating that hopefully everyone got out. "We probably shouldn't go back there, but we can drive by and see if the police are there."

"So everybody came to the morgue as planned?" Heather was astounded. "How did Joe and Mary Beth know? I was supposed to call them this morning."

"I think Rachel called them last night to make sure they were going to be there."

"I obviously haven't had a chance to make the video I planned to do," said Heather. "I'm going to schedule it to go live on Youtube Tuesday morning and also be sent via Facebook, e-mail and a few other mediums unless I stop it. I will obviously stop it from being sent as long as I'm alive and well and able to stop it. But if not, it will be sent automatically. I have a feeling this video would go viral very quickly."

So that's what she had planned to do, thought Bernie. He told her everything he had done the night before and that morning, explaining that the group decided against his reading his speech in front of Mary Beth and Jon so that anyone watching them could see and hear it.

"Oh my goodness!" he said. "They must have still been able to hear us, because immediately afterwards Jeremy called and told us to get out of the building, that someone was coming to attack us. It's all my fault! If I hadn't read that speech, no one would have known what we were doing!" Bernie became quite distraught and Heather tried to comfort him.

"You don't know that, Bernie. This attack could have already been planned. If it's anybody's fault, it's mine. I'm the one who told Mary Beth and Jon. It could have been discovered last night that they were coming to the morgue to have their implants removed." Both of them were silent for a minute. "I sure hope everyone got out," she added softly.

Heather saw the McDonald's cup in Bernie's car cup holder. "Do you have any of that drink left? I really need to wash my mouth out."

"It's Coke, and it's probably watered down a little bit, but it's all yours."

Heather swished the Coke in her mouth and when Bernie stopped the car at a stop sign, she spit it out, then drank the rest of the cola. "Better," she said.

"I have Michael Michtenbaum's implants in a box in my trunk. I was going to meet a friend of mine and put it in the care of her Priest this morning, unless you have other plans for it."

"Wow, Bernie, I'm really amazed at what you've done. Thank you!" She gingerly leaned over from the passenger side of the car and gave Bernie a light kiss on the cheek. "I really hadn't decided where to put Michael's implants for safekeeping other than my safe deposit box. Do you trust this friend and her Priest?"

"I trust her and she really trusts her Priest, so yes."

Bernie could tell Heather wanted to ask more about how he could have made a friend in such a short time, but she didn't ask.

"Oh," Bernie added. "Dorgan's dead."

"What? What happened?"

"Don't really know, but Rachel thinks poison. Seems to be the weapon of choice with the agents, doesn't it?"

"Yes," she mumbled, then blurted out, "I have missed so much since last night!" She was thoughtful for a moment. "If Dorgan's dead, I wonder who ordered everyone killed at the morgue this morning."

Bernie hadn't thought about that.

They drove by the police station but decided to go on and drive past the morgue. From a mile away, they could see the smoke billowing into the sky. "Oh no!" cried Heather. "I hope they all got out!" she said once again.

The roadblock was being set up at Fair Avenue and Route 4 but they managed to turn towards the cemetery before the roadblock was complete. The road behind the morgue was being closed off as well, but Bernie and Heather managed to find a spot to park the car by the cemetery where they could see the morgue. It was now rubble.

Dorgan knew that faking his death could very likely lead to his real death. He knew that when the police found his body, they would call the coroner to the scene, who would insert the sharp thermometer into his liver to determine time of death, which would probably kill him. If it didn't, he would then be taken to the morgue and cut open for autopsy, which would definitely kill him. However, there was always the chance that the coroner would notice the blood from one of those wounds and realize he was still alive, or better yet, the coroner would be too busy with other dead bodies to do anything with his that evening. Whatever happened, he was prepared for either eventuality – life or death. He preferred life and was counting on Jeremy to have been watching him and listening to him as he explained why he needed to fake his death.

He knew for certain that he was a marked man. Someone higher up was after him and would not stop until they killed him. If his life was over anyway, he was going to end it on his own terms and not until he had finished his assignment, his way. If he faked his death, it might buy him a little time to complete what he had set out to do. If he died as a result of faking his death, then the provisions he had made to finalize the Freedom Project would go into effect.

His Saturday afternoon in the motel in Fairfield had been a busy one, primarily spent reading more of the highly classified file found in Jacob Barnes' folder. This file contained not only the details of every Freedom Project in existence, and there were more than he had known about, but also contained correspondence about eliminating certain individuals associated with the projects who were considered risks to its future existence and success. Assassin code names were included, some but not all with whom Dorgan was familiar. And even the most recent correspondence - correspondence from that very day - was in the electronic file.

The most recent Freedom Project went far beyond what even Dorgan could have imagined. This project was no longer experimental. It had been implemented on a national scale without the knowledge of the American people. Dorgan always believed in the small scale experiments so that when the time came, the overwhelming proof of the success of the implants would be made known to the public and they would embrace the technology as progress towards greatly improving their lives and their freedom.

It was amazing and miraculous, thought Dorgan, what the newest implants were doing. They were attaching to various parts of the brain and nervous system, continuously gathering and transmitting data to medical facilities for research. Not only could they gather and transmit information, they could receive information as well. Want to learn French in a day? No problem. The entire French vocabulary is downloaded into the implant located on one or both of the hippocampi near the cerebral cortex of the brain, becoming part of that person's permanent memory.

But even Dorgan knew there is no such thing as covert freedoms. You can't secretly insert foreign objects into human beings, grossly invade their personal privacy, and call it enhancing their freedom.

Since the 1940's, vaccinations for children against certain contagious and/or life-threatening diseases have been commonplace. Few, but some, children die from these vaccinations. Still, the higher good outweighs these tragedies in most people's minds. The American public has accepted the fact that they should have their children vaccinated. Now, thought Dorgan, these vaccinations include microscopic implants which attach to the eyes, ears, brain and various other organs so that the government is able to see and hear everything that child, eventually adult, sees and hears, and to gather medical research and other information. The project ensured that these implants were in the vaccinations given to the children entering the seventh grade. From what he had read, Dorgan knew that Freedom Project VIII had utilized the vaccinations, on a smaller scale, on infants, but there was a problem. One out of 200 infants was dying from the vaccination, so three years later they targeted older children, which produced a much better result. The American public was unaware of these additions to their children's vaccinations.

Dorgan was both thrilled and appalled at the newest Freedom Project. But he knew one thing for certain. It was wrong to do this without the public's knowledge. He intended one of his final acts to be to reveal the project. He copied the entire folder into his cloud storage and prepared a statement to be sent with the folder attached to go out one month from that day. If he was dead by then, the message would transmit automatically. If he was alive, he could decide whether to send the document or whether to cancel it and reveal the folder in a different way.

As part of his CIA field agent training, Dorgan kept several tools of the trade with him at all times. He wore a fake medical bracelet that contained all of these small items. The bracelet was permanently on his wrist and could only be removed with a special instrument. One item within the bracelet was a poison that would cause death within minutes...he wasn't yet ready to take that pill. Another was a drug that would slow his heartbeat and respirations to the point that he appeared to be dead. While similar to what was being used to chemically induce a coma, this drug was more specific and powerful, and could be timed to wear off in a few hours. This was the drug he had administered to himself late Saturday evening.

When Dorgan awoke and realized he wasn't dead, he also quickly realized he was sealed inside a metal tomb. It was pitch black and he could feel the cold metal all around him, within inches of his body above and beside him. He managed to move his arms and hands up beside his head to see if he could push open the heavy steel door behind him. He knocked as loudly as he could on the door – perhaps the coroner was still at the morgue. He figured it was sometime between 1:30 and 4:00 a.m. Sunday morning.

He was having a hard time breathing and knew the oxygen in the cold storage drawer was close to gone. He felt in the dark for his bracelet and removed the one other item it contained - a small putty substance and explosive. This was only the second time he had a need to use this explosive. He was uncomfortable with it being placed right next to his head, but there was no other way out. He would have to place it correctly on the door so that the force of the blast was outward...otherwise he would be blown up and the door would still be intact. Imagine the coroner's surprise if she opened the drawer and found a dead body blown into a thousand pieces. He smiled at the thought in spite of himself.

He had ten seconds after placing the putty on the door before it blew. He tried to scoot as far down and away from the blast as possible and placed his hands over his ears. The blast was designed to be somewhat quiet, but it would still be quite forceful next to his ears.

It was. The blast loosened the heavy steel door but didn't blow it off. He was able to push the door open and breathe the warm oxygen that now flowed into the drawer. His ears were buzzing loudly as he used his arms to reach out and pull himself out of the steel vault. He was otherwise perfectly fine. He looked down and noticed he was still fully clothed. He was even wearing his shoes.

He looked at the clock - 3 a.m. Before he left, he opened each of the other storage drawers to see if the other bodies were still there. There were three - his two agents that he himself had killed and the grave closer that Jones had killed. All had been autopsied and showed the telltale chest stitching.

Dorgan noticed that the blast had not damaged the door to his vault at all – it only forced the door open. He closed it and it looked normal to him. He smiled at the actual surprise the coroner would receive -- opening the door to find the dead body gone.

Dorgan left the morgue and hitchhiked to the spot in Fairfield where he had hidden his laptop and iPad. Back to work.

"Tell me again who threatened to attack you at the morgue this morning? And who are these people with you?" the Police Chief asked Rachel, who was seated across from him in his office. They both glanced out at the three other people sitting in the police station – Carol Moore and Joe and Mary Beth Singer. Carol was crying softly.

"I don't know who made the threat, only that a call came in and warned us to get out of the morgue right away; that we were going to be attacked. Based on everything that's happened in the past two days, I completely believed that we were in danger so we left right away and came here." Rachel didn't particularly want to answer the question about who the Moores and the Singers were, and why they were in the morgue at this early hour.

"And now tell me who those three are." Rachel and the Police Chief were more than colleagues. They were good friends and often attended the same social functions. But Rachel could tell the Chief was in no mood to be cordial or friendly at that moment. He wanted answers and he wanted them now. It was time to talk, she knew.

She took a deep breath to begin telling him the whole story when they were interrupted by an officer opening the Chief's office door without knocking. "Sorry to interrupt sir, but we've just gotten a call, several in fact, that the morgue was bombed! It's gone!"

Rachel gasped and thought of Bill and Jon. Did they get out?

The Chief was no longer surprised to hear such news. A helicopter had crashed into some trees near the river the night before and the pilot was still unconscious in the hospital. There were several eyewitnesses who swore they saw another large helicopter in the vicinity as well. They were still searching for Heather Barnes who was reported kidnapped. The Chief calmly told the officer to get several cruisers there right away.

"Let's go," the Chief said to Rachel. "Bring your friends as I'm sure this affects them as well, right?" He gave her a cold look.

"Right," she replied. "Carol's husband Jon might have still been in the morgue." She motioned towards the crying woman. "Bill too." Rachel's voice cracked when she mentioned Bill and the Chief softened.

"Tell me the story on the way," and the five of them headed for the Chief's car. They could smell the smoke as soon as they were outside the police station. Carol, Joe and Mary Beth had not yet been told what had happened but immediately associated the smell with their situation. "What's happened!" Carol cried in obvious anguish.

Rachel didn't want to tell her and looked at the Chief, who sighed and spoke. "We believe the morgue has been bombed. We're heading there now."

Mary Beth held Carol as they got closer to the morgue. Carol tried calling Jon's cell phone but when she heard it ringing, she remembered she was holding it for him in her purse while he was having surgery. As they approached and saw the black smoke billowing into the sky, she began to shake and Mary Beth held her tighter. "It will be okay," she whispered but she wasn't sure if she believed it herself.

The Chief crossed the roadblock already set up at Greenwood and Fair Avenues and pulled up behind where the morgue building used to be. He couldn't believe his eyes. The structure appeared to be completely gone but the buildings right next to it, only 30 feet away, were intact. It was hard to see what remained of the morgue, if anything, due to the heavy smoke. Several firetrucks encircled the structure and water was pouring onto it from all directions.

Carol was now inconsolable. She was out of the car and trying to run towards the smoking morgue. The Chief grabbed her and told Rachel, Mary Beth and Joe to keep her, and themselves, in the car while he assessed the situation. He couldn't spare an officer to watch them.

Rachel and Joe watched the Police Chief as he talked to the Fire Chief. Their faces were grim as the Fire Chief pointed at something. Both Joe and Rachel's eyes followed the pointing arm and saw the body bag lying nearby. It obviously had something, someone, in it. Rachel began to sob. Joe put his arm around his wife who was still holding Carol's hands in her lap and talking softly to her. Mary Beth turned at her husband's touch and saw the fear in his eyes.

A tap on the window caused the four of them to jump. It was Heather and Bernie. Rachel managed a smile and a hug for Heather after exiting the car on the front passenger side and coming around to the other side. Joe got out of the car as well, leaving Mary Beth to continue to console Carol in the back seat.

"There's a body bag over there," said Rachel quietly to Heather, nodding her head towards the bag. "I don't know who it is yet."

"I'm so sorry," said Heather. "This is all my fault. I should have just left it alone." She put her hands to her face, only for a second, then turned to Rachel. "Is there any way you can find out who is in the body bag? Perhaps it was a passerby and isn't Bill or Jon."

Rachel left to see if the Police Chief would let her look at the victim. She heard a phone ring behind her and saw Heather reach into her purse and answer it. The Chief was nowhere to be seen, so she headed for the body bag. She was the Coroner, after all.

"Rachel!" Heather shouted. As Rachel turned, Heather was hobbling towards her. "Someone is still alive in there! Look!" She held out her iPhone showing the red heat thermal image of a person lying down and moving, sent to her by Jeremy.

"Bill said he would put Jon in one of the storage slabs if he couldn't wake him. It must be Jon. The steel storage vault must have survived the blast!"

Rachel ran towards the firefighters and tried to get their attention. Heather followed her as quickly as her battered body would allow. The commotion caused Mary Beth and Carol to look as well and the two women got out of the car and joined Bernie and Joe.

As Joe looked around, he saw hundreds of people gathered at the edges of the quarantined area. A dozen or so cars were parked in front of the cemetery and dozens more were parking inside the cemetery and on the streets behind them. Joe counted six firetrucks, two ambulances, the Fire Chief's vehicle and seven police cruisers. There were probably more on the other side of Route 4 that he couldn't see. He saw that Rachel and Heather were now talking to the Police Chief and Fire Chief and Heather was showing them something on her phone. He also heard the Police Chief shout, "I thought you had been kidnapped!" and saw Heather giving an explanation to the Chief.

After talking with the Chiefs, Rachel once again started for the body bag but saw Carol watching her and decided against it. She walked back to the car instead. Heather followed.

"What's going on? Have you found out anything about Jon?" Carol asked in a pleading voice.

Rachel gave Heather a look and a nod which said she was deferring the answer to her.

"A friend of ours at Homeland Security," and Heather nodded towards Bernie indicating it was his friend as well, "has been watching via satellite as much activity here as he can over the past couple of days. He's the one that called and warned you to get out of the building, he's the one that found me in the woods and sent Bernie to get me, he's the one that gave the description of Rachel's attacker to the police on Thursday. He also has access to an infrared satellite that can detect the heat from a human body and he just called me and said someone is alive in there." Carol's hands flew to her mouth. Heather continued. "He is lying down flat and moving, so we believe it is probably Jon in one of the cold storage vaults. We've told the Fire Chief and they are going to check as soon as they can get close enough."

"Oh my God," cried Carol. "He's probably so scared…waking up in the dark in a tomb, not knowing where he is, or why. Oh, Jon!" She was crying again and Mary Beth was quietly telling her that he was alive and would soon be out. Carol nodded and tried to calm herself with deep breaths.

Heather noticed that Mary Beth was looking at her strangely. She realized that the only time she had been introduced to Mary Beth was when she was dressed as a man. Most likely, Mary Beth was trying to figure out why Heather looked familiar.

"Hi, you must be Mary Beth. I'm Heather Barnes. You probably remember me as Danny Wheatley." She didn't offer an explanation about her disguise, only a "sorry about that."

Rachel had to find out if it was Bill in the body bag and excused herself from the group. She asked two police officers if they would please discreetly move the bag to the other side of a firetruck where it would be out of view of spectators and especially out of view of Carol, who had not yet seemed to notice the black form on the ground.

She walked in the opposite direction of the two officers and came around to the other side of the firetruck after taking the long route around several police cars. She unzipped the bag. Rachel had seen death by almost every means – burns, car accident, gunshot wound, strangulation, poison, disease; but she had not yet seen death by explosion. Only portions of Bill's body were in the bag, including his head, which was intact enough that she knew it was him.

"I'm so sorry, Bill," she said to her friend and colleague. "Goodbye, my friend, and thank you."

Jeremy wondered if Jon Moore could feel the outside heat which had to be incredible from the blast. Was he roasting alive inside the metal vault? He was squirming, but that could be from waking and finding himself entombed. He sent the image to Heather to let the firefighters know to get the man out of there as soon as possible.

Jeremy now had three different satellites above the Butler County morgue scene. Audrey had been there throughout the dramatic event and he had quickly moved an infrared satellite to the scene to see if he could detect life after the missile hit and caused the explosion. At first, there was so much heat, he couldn't tell if any was human, but as the fire and heat subsided slightly, he was able to detect the human form within the former walls of the morgue. As Heather and Bernie left the woods and headed back towards the morgue, Jeremy brought Samuel to the scene as well. He used Samuel to see if the squirming form was indeed Jon. He called Heather again to let her know that Jon seemed well, just terrified. He watched his screen as Heather told the others standing around the Chief's car. Carol hugged Heather and then Mary Beth.

"Thanks again Jeremy," Heather told him and hung up. Jeremy realized he hadn't told her that Dragon was still alive, but then remembered he hadn't told her he was dead.

Jeremy was still wondering why Dragon wanted him to warn Rachel and the others at the morgue. Hadn't he been trying to kill them for the past two days? Why the change of heart? Jeremy wasn't sure of Dragon's motives, past or present, but he was certain that it was Dragon who had typed the message to him. He was certain Dragon was alive. Now he just had to find him again. Where would he be? It was almost 8:30 a.m. and Jeremy knew he needed to call the Secretary soon and give her an update. He wanted to find Dragon first before he called her. Now he was glad he hadn't told her Dragon was dead. That worked out quite nicely for me, he thought. Now I get to keep my job.

Ever since the blinds had been closed in Dragon's office and Jeremy knew he wasn't being watched by that camera, he had printed out copies of each of the assassin profiles that he had run through his MyBackdoor software and laid them out on his desk. As time permitted, he was researching each of them in even more detail. The one that intrigued him the most, which was the one he had lied about to Dragon, was Michael Michtenbaum's killer. He knew the name immediately when the photo had produced an identification and the Secretary had asked Jeremy not to reveal the name of the assassin to Dorgan.

The killer's name was legendary but his face was a mystery. The photo in the CIA database that Jeremy had hacked was fifteen years old and was only identified because of his eyes. Often assassins had plastic surgery to change their facial appearance, but usually didn't or couldn't change their eyes except for their color. This particular killer had somehow kept from being photographed over the years, so why would the man kill someone who was certain to be able to identify him through the video camera in his eye? It didn't make sense unless the killer didn't know who he was killing or why. It now seemed that lots of people knew about the Freedom Project, but three days ago that was not the case. Even though this agent was the assassin of choice utilized by the highest members of the U.S. government and its key agencies, Jeremy was sure he would not be privy to this top secret project. And although the man's talents were many, they did not include hacking into secret files, as far as Jeremy could tell.

It took hours of searching, but Jeremy found eighteen assassination missions that this particular agent had completed, all successfully, over the past twelve years. There were probably many more missions, but Jeremy had enough to complete a fairly accurate profile of the agent. Names were never listed as having hired the assassin, but the payment had to come from somewhere, and Jeremy had traced twelve of the eighteen missions so far. He also knew each target's name, most well known, and could form some conclusions based on the political or financial status of the victims. It appeared that at least two missions were assigned by the President of the United States himself. Homeland Security had paid for three. What chilled Jeremy's blood was that the most recent hire, the killing of Michael Ray Michtenbaum, was one of the three.

Jeremy had always had a healthy mistrust for authority, but now he truly didn't know who to trust or believe. What he believed to be true for the past two days, he now doubted. The person he thought to be the bad guy might actually be the good guy, or at least not as bad as he originally thought.

Jeremy believed he might find some answers in the file that he still had up on one of his monitors – the top-secret, 4000 page CIA file – the file Dragon was reading at the library - the same real-time file that someone accessed with the order to destroy the Butler County morgue and its inhabitants.

There was some activity at the morgue, and Jeremy watched as the firefighters brought out a traumatized but live Jonathon Moore from the smoking rubble. Carol ran to him and the two embraced for a full minute before the firefighters were able to get Jon seated and put an oxygen mask over his mouth and nose. Jeremy was glad that six of the seven people inside the morgue lived because of his phone call, which he made because of seeing the entry in the file, and because of John Dorgan.

Jeremy suddenly had a thought. The park. Maybe Dragon's at the park. Jeremy had watched Dragon the two times he had sat in the park and it seemed to be the place he enjoyed the most. It was worth a shot to move Samuel to that location and take a look. He had been watching Dragon's laptop carefully but nothing new had been entered since his last transmission, which still showed on the screen – *"Jeremy…call and warn them…now!"*

Keeping one eye on the morgue, he moved Samuel to the familiar location. Sure enough, there was Dragon sitting on the same park bench, his open laptop beside him. His eyes were closed but he would occasionally move slightly.

Jeremy was uncertain as to what to do. Should he contact Dragon? Was that what Dragon was sitting and waiting for? The ringing of his desk phone interrupted his thoughts and Jeremy looked at the caller ID – it was the Secretary, Rhonda Watterson. He hesitated for only a moment, contemplating whether to let it ring and go to voice-mail, then picked up the phone.

"Good morning Jeremy. Have you been there all night?" She sounded rested.

"Yes, but don't remind me or I'll feel tired."

The Secretary laughed briefly and then got down to business. "We haven't talked since yesterday when I stopped in and I was wondering if there's any news."

"Yes," said Jeremy. "John Dorgan is dead."

After skimming much of the CIA file, which apparently belonged to Heather's father, Jeremy made the decision to send Dragon the true identity of the man who killed Michtenbaum. It now seemed important that he know the truth. He utilized the software to "take over" another computer. Dragon was still sitting in the park. He typed two lines which would pop up on Dragon's laptop screen. "One casualty...six okay. Error on earlier ID – not Viktor Andronikov. Correct ID is Collin Reuth, code name Raptor."

Jeremy caused Dragon's computer to click to attract Dragon's attention. He watched from five feet above Dragon's head and saw that Dragon heard the click and looked at his computer screen. Instead of reaching for the laptop, Dorgan looked straight ahead and spoke softly aloud. "Jeremy. Can you hear me?"

Jeremy was taken aback but only for a moment. Dragon would guess that one of the satellites capable of receiving sound might be utilized. He typed "yes."

"Good man. I knew you would figure it out."

Jeremy typed again and watched Dragon read the message. "I'm not sure I've figured anything out other than I'm completely confused."

Dorgan smiled and spoke to the air. "That makes two of us. I *have* figured out that someone wants me dead. I'm just not sure if it's my current boss or my ex-boss giving the order."

As Jeremy typed his reply, he pulled Samuel up to 50 feet for a moment to make sure no one was in the park watching Dragon. He didn't see anyone and zoomed in close again. "Your current boss now thinks you're dead. So does everyone else in Hamilton as far as I know. That will change once the fire department goes through the morgue rubble."

"Yes, but it has bought me a little time. Will you keep my secret a day longer?"

"Okay," Jeremy typed.

"Thank you. And thank you for the identity of Michtenbaum's killer. At least I now know our own people killed him."

Jeremy thought about telling Dragon that his current boss was the one who had paid for the assassin, but decided against it, thinking he had bonded enough with the sly Dragon for one day.

"One more thing," Dorgan spoke again. "May I ask another favor?"

The pilot of the small helicopter that had crashed into the trees between the Great Miami River and Ohio Route 128 in Hamilton suffered a serious concussion and was unconscious for nine hours before awaking in Fort Hamilton Hospital. A police officer sat in his room and was the first face he saw when he awoke. The officer called his Chief before he notified the nurse that the patient was awake.

"Were you the pilot of the helicopter that crashed?" the officer asked the young man.

"Yes." The pilot still seemed dazed and the nurse told the police officer he might want to wait to question the man.

The officer ignored her. "Can you tell me what happened?"

The pilot thanked the nurse for the water she brought to him and turned his head slowly towards the policeman. "Is Mr. Barnes all right?"

"Mr. Barnes? Who's Mr. Barnes?" asked the officer.

The young man was slightly alarmed. "He was my passenger. Didn't you find him as well?"

"I'll check," stated the officer and again dialed a number on his cell phone. "I'll be right back." He walked into the hall to make the call to his Chief.

"There was another person in the helicopter?" The Chief was talking loudly as there was a great deal of noise at the morgue where he was still handing out assignments to officers to question any witnesses. He planned to personally question Rachel, the Singers and the Moores, and now Heather and Bernie, especially since they seemed to be the key to this whole mess, as soon as he could take them back to headquarters. But now he was considering taking a ride out 128 to see if another body was there. It was dark last night and although he hadn't gone there himself, he didn't believe the rescue team had searched the area other than right in and under the tree. He also had only moments ago found out that Heather Barnes was okay and her kidnapper was dead out off of 128 somewhere. Perhaps the helicopter crash was related and the dead body of the kidnapper was close by as well. He would take Rachel with him and have two of his officers take the others back to headquarters and keep them there.

"The man's name was Barnes," the officer told the Chief.

"What!" The Chief looked at Heather standing only a few feet from him. It seemed too great a coincidence that her last name was Barnes as well and that she had been in that same vicinity. Could it have been Heather's father or husband who shot and killed the kidnapper? Had they crashed right after making the shot? He decided it was best to not say anything to Heather yet until they found Mr. Barnes.

"Continue to question the pilot," the Chief instructed the officer at the hospital. "Find out where they were going, what they were doing, and why they crashed. And find out everything you can about the missing passenger."

Heather and Bernie managed to get a few minutes away from the Police Chief at the scene of the morgue bombing to discuss what to do with the one complete and intact package that held the electronic file of the Freedom Project, both of Michael Michtenbaum's implants and instructions on what to do with the package. Bernie wanted to give the package to Sheila's Priest.

Heather sighed. "You know the police are going to take us in again and this time I doubt they'll let us go anytime soon. We may not be able to give the package to anyone."

"I think I can sneak off and get back to my car," said Bernie. "No one seems to notice me much."

Heather smiled at him. "You'd make a great agent. In fact, you HAVE made a great agent." She looked around and realized it probably would be very easy for Bernie to just walk away unnoticed. "OK, why don't you get the package to Sheila's Priest."

"Great. I'll catch up with you later." Bernie walked through the throng of people watching the spectacle, towards the cemetery and his car.

Heather walked back to stand by Carol, Jon, Joe and Mary Beth. Rachel was nearby but in a private conversation with the Chief. Heather found herself watching the two couples as they stood there. Both men held their wives close to them and occasionally one would whisper to the other. Carol and Jon lightly kissed each other frequently as they stood there, still somewhat in shock. It was natural that they would be comforting each other since they had just been through the most traumatic few hours of their lives, but Heather sensed it was much more than that between both of these couples. What she had seen and heard from them so far told her that they were very much in love, even after 25 or 30 years of marriage.

Heather didn't know very many couples who had been married for years and still seemed to enjoy each other's company. While many of her friends were single, she had some married friends and knew many married couples through business or social events. They just didn't look at each other with love anymore and seemed to prefer conversation with someone other than their spouses. If marriage caused such a rift between two people, Heather wanted no part of it. She knew her feelings about marriage were a key reason she couldn't take the next step with Danny.

But in the past two days she had met three couples – the Singers, the Moores and the Michtenbaums – and all three couples were different than the couples she knew. Even in their grief, it was evident that Mitch and Celia Michtenbaum were deeply in love with each other. Perhaps it was possible to be married and still be happy.

"Heather!" She heard her name being called and looked up. Mary Beth had called her name as the two couples were being ushered into two separate police cruisers. "The officers are taking us back to the police station."

Heather was put in the cruiser with Joe and Mary Beth. She sat up front with the officer. Jon and Carol were in the back seat of another black and white car.

Rachel tapped on Heather's window and she rolled it down. "I'm going with the Chief to the site where you were kidnapped. Bernie needs to tell us or show us where it is." Rachel peered inside the car. "Where is he?"

"Did you check the other car?" Heather nodded towards the other cruiser that was backing up to pull out onto the road. The Police Chief had walked up to the car as well. "Yes, and he isn't in that car. Where is he, Miss Barnes?" His tone made it clear that he was in no mood for games.

Heather had planned on stating she didn't know where he was, which was somewhat true since she didn't know where he planned to meet his friend or where the Catholic Church was that they planned to visit. She still didn't want to mention the Catholic Church, but otherwise decided to tell the truth. "He's taking a copy of the file about the implant experiment to a friend to hold for us. It's obviously not safe with us. I'm sure he'll come to the police station after that."

His rage showed on the Chief's face, but he remained calm when he spoke. "Do you know the location of where you were taken last night?"

Heather thought a moment, then repeated the directions that Bernie told her he received from Jeremy. "There's a graveled clearing beneath the trees." Her voice trembled as she remembered where she spent the night.

"How did Bernie know where you were?"

Heather looked straight into the Chief's eyes. "We're from Homeland Security. We have eyes and ears on us almost every moment. These eyes and ears are the only thing that's kept the rest of us alive so far."

The Chief tapped on the roof of the car and the police officer left the morgue parking lot to take Heather and the Singers to police headquarters.

Rachel, the Police Chief and one additional officer tasked with taking photos had no trouble finding the tire tracks that led to the gruesome scene that caused all of them to stand in silent shock for several minutes, their eyes taking in the barbaric devices laid out on the ground. The officer then began snapping photos of the man slumped over a cage of rats, the discarded blanket several feet away, the harness and pulleys attached to two trees, the car left in the gravel drive as well as the tarp full of sadistic torture devices.

The Chief called in his crime scene experts as well as the bus which would soon take the body to the basement of Fort Hamilton Hospital, where it had been hastily decided the temporary morgue would be located.

Rachel wanted to move the body as it appeared the caged rats were eating what they could reach of the man laying slumped on top of them. "Do you really think it is Heather's father that was in the helicopter that crashed?" Rachel asked the Chief. He had filled her in on the phone call he had received earlier, especially since there could be yet another dead body. "If he wasn't in it, then he has to be on the ground somewhere nearby. Hopefully he's still alive."

"We'll go look once we leave here. I've already sent a team of people to look for him. In another hour or so, a crew will be there to remove the helicopter from the tree. I'd like to find Barnes before that if possible."

"How did they get the pilot out of the helicopter?" Rachel asked. "It was in the trees, right?"

"Yes. We sent for the Search and Rescue Air Team to locate the helicopter and to rescue the pilot from it. It was actually easier for them to raise the pilot into the helicopter and transport him to the hospital rather than lower him to the ground for ambulance transport. But paramedics were on the ground. I would think they would have seen Barnes if he had been lying on the ground." The Chief paused. "But it was awfully dark last night and even darker under those trees. If he wasn't right in their headlights or spotlight, he would be easy to miss."

The forensic team was there within a few minutes and Rachel waited patiently for them to do their thing. They then laid the body of the dead man on his back for Rachel to examine. He looked ghastly. The rats had eaten all of the flesh off of his nose and lips as well as part of his right cheek. Two fingers that lay next to the side of the cage had also been eaten in to the first joint. The police photographer took more photos before Rachel examined the body and stated the obvious – the man appeared to have died from a gunshot wound to the chest.

The entrance to the area where the helicopter had crashed was now well marked although there was no road to the site. A sheriff's vehicle was parked alongside 128 at the small clearing in the trees where the ambulance had entered and made its way through trees, bushes and weeds approximately 20 yards in from the road. The sun was now fully up and it was much easier to get to the site.

The Chief turned his car onto the path of flattened brush made by the ambulance and the vehicles of the search crew, who had just begun a grid search but stopped when the Chief arrived.

"We found these, sir," said one officer who handed a laptop and a cell phone to the Chief. The laptop was in two pieces as the monitor had broken off. The Chief took a few minutes to look at the recent calls and contact list in the cell phone. One recent call was to "Heather" so the Chief presumed the phone belonged to Barnes and that the two were indeed related, most likely father and daughter. He called the officer that was questioning the pilot at the hospital to see what else the man had said.

"Barnes had a weapon with him, ladies and gentlemen," the Chief told the search team, "so look for that as well. Also, let's not assume he's a friendly, so be careful." The pilot at the hospital had stated that another helicopter had caused them to crash, which was consistent with the eyewitness calls they received. The pilot also confirmed that Barnes had a pistol on him although he had not used it. The Chief wasn't convinced of that fact. If Barnes was indeed Heather's father, he could have been the one who shot the man who kidnapped his daughter. The man would have to be an expert shot. He sent the team on their search and then called his research expert and told him to find out everything he could about one Jacob Barnes.

Bernie had a little time before he was to meet Sheila at St. Julie Billiart Church. The metal box that he would give to her Priest was still well hidden in the trunk of his car.

He decided to run by the hotel to shower and brush his teeth before heading for the church. According to Sheila's directions, the church was only a block away from the Marriott.

Bernie didn't notice the car that had followed him from the time he walked away from Heather at the morgue, to his car parked in the cemetery, to the Marriott Hotel. The driver of the car stayed in the parking lot and waited for Bernie to return.

Bernie quickly showered and changed clothes. He was supposed to check out of the hotel today, so he gathered his few items and put them into his small suitcase. The phone in his room rang and startled him. He wasn't sure whether or not to answer it, but decided to do so.

"Hello?" he said tentatively.

"Bernie, it's Jeremy. You really need to get a cell phone, man."

"I've never needed one before, but I could sure use one this weekend."

"You're being followed and I wanted to let you know to be careful. It's a black sedan. I'd like you to keep this between us, but it's Dorgan following you. He's alive after all."

"You're kidding! Oh my gosh, he might try to kill me!" Bernie sounded shaken.

"Maybe, but I don't think so. He's actually the one who told me to warn you that the morgue was about to be attacked. I really don't know what his motives are any more, but he may have switched sides, so to speak. Still, I'd be careful if I were you. Where are you headed?"

"St. Julie Billiart Church. I'm going to give the Freedom Project file and both of Michael Michtenbaum's implants to a Priest there for safe keeping."

"Well, you might want to try and lose him. Do you think you can do that?"

"Uh, maybe." He didn't sound too certain at all. "I'll try."

"Good luck," Jeremy said, ending the call.

Bernie emerged from the hotel front door twenty minutes later in clean clothes and with his suitcase in hand, which he placed in the trunk of his car.

Now that he was paying attention, he noticed the black sedan pull out of the Marriott parking lot shortly after he did and turn in the same direction.

What would James Bond do? thought Bernie nervously. Well, for one, he wouldn't keep staring into the rearview mirror, Bernie chastised himself.

The church was only one block away, but Bernie decided to go in a different direction to try and lose Dorgan.

The light at the corner of Front and High had turned yellow and Bernie slowed in preparation to stop, but at the last second decided to run the light. He pressed hard on the gas pedal and his little Ford Focus lept forward across High Street. It had exactly the effect he wanted. High Street was fairly busy at the moment and Dorgan was unable to run the red light and follow him. Bernie knew as soon as he was able, Dorgan would run the light and be behind him again so, knowing Dorgan could see his car, he turned right onto Court Street and then immediately turned into a church parking lot and hid for few minutes. He slowly edged his car up to Front Street again from the parking lot. Dorgan was nowhere in sight, so Bernie turned left and headed back towards the hotel. He turned right onto Dayton Street and drove the block to St. Julie Billiart Church. He waited in the car to see if he saw the black sedan again, but it appeared that he had successfully eluded the tailing car.

Sheila was standing on the steps in front of the church watching for Bernie. She smiled and waved when she saw him approaching with a small suitcase. They walked into the church. Another figure entered the parish shortly afterwards. Seeing Bernie and Sheila seated about midway up the line of pews, he seated himself in the back.

Bernie didn't realize that Sheila intended for them to sit through mass first before talking with the Priest, but he rather enjoyed sitting beside her and spending a few quiet and calm moments in what had been an extremely chaotic and nerve-wracking twenty-four hours. At the end of the service, the Priest invited everyone to walk to the front of the church to partake in Holy Communion. Bernie looked at Sheila with a bit of panic in his eyes and she assured him it was okay if he didn't want to go up. He could just stay in the pew. He was relieved as he didn't want to leave his suitcase unattended; and, he hadn't taken communion since he was a young man attending church with his parents and would feel uncomfortable doing so now.

Sheila had already informed the Priest that she wished to meet with him immediately following the service, so he was waiting for them when they made their way to the front of the church. "How do you do?" the Priest began. "I'm Father Benjamin." He waited for Bernie to introduce himself and then asked how he could help them.

"Would it be possible to go somewhere more private to talk?" Bernie looked at several parishioners who were still milling about, talking.

"Certainly. This way." Father Benjamin led them through a

doorway and down a short hall. A well-furnished office was on the left and he ushered them inside, closing the door behind him.

Bernie opened his suitcase and removed a silver metal box, which he placed on the desk in front of the Priest. "I have a very unusual request. It may also be a very dangerous request, so I want to let you know that up front." Bernie waited a moment to see if that statement caused any reaction from the Priest, but it did not, so he continued.

"I'm not sure where to begin. I guess I'll start with the actual request. I need someone very trustworthy to keep this box in a safe place, perhaps for a day or perhaps indefinitely. It is very important that no one ever look inside the box or tell anyone else where it is. That's why Sheila suggested you, because you can be trusted to keep the secret and to not look at the contents."

The Priest nodded and raised a finger indicating that he wished to speak. "Thank you for your confidence in me," and he smiled at Sheila, "but I must ask a question before you continue. Is there anything illegal, immoral or hazardous in this box?"

Bernie looked bewildered at the question and the Priest clarified. "For example, is there a gun, or explosives, illegal drugs, or perhaps immoral photos in the box? Is there anything that the church would be embarrassed or worse, in trouble, for holding for you."

"Oh, no, no!" Bernie exclaimed loudly. "Nothing like that!" He took a deep breath. "It contains a computer file, on a USB drive, and some evidence of a very secret government experiment that has gone wrong. The contents themselves are not illegal or immoral, but many people would say that the experiment was, so if you look at it that way…." his voice trailed off.

"Sheila has already told me that the attempts on the coroner's life, which led to the deaths of two police officers, is because of this information. I understand there have been other tragedies as well, all related to this so-called experiment." The Priest was trying to make it easier for Bernie to tell the rest of his story.

"Yes. This morning another man died. The morgue was blown up and all of us got out but one." Bernie hung his head.

Both the Priest and Sheila were shocked at this news. Neither had heard about the morgue bombing yet. "Who was it?" Sheila asked.

"The assistant coroner, Bill. I don't remember his last name." Bernie replied.

"Bill Simmons! Oh dear," the Priest shook his head sadly. "He's a member here."

"He was a hero," Bernie said reverently. "He made everyone else leave and he saved another man who was unable to walk by putting him in one of the steel storage vaults where the dead bodies go. The blast destroyed everything except that steel vault. As I said, anyone involved in this could be in grave danger," Bernie continued. "Someone wants this information to stay secret and is willing to kill those that know about it. That's why I don't want to tell you any more about it and why it is important not to look at the information in the box. But I'll understand if you don't want to keep it. It could still put you and perhaps others in danger."

"What is the purpose of my keeping the box?" the Priest asked.

"There are seven of us that know about the experiment. We are all possible targets. We want this box to be an insurance policy to keep us alive. It's all explained here," and Bernie handed him a note. Bernie waited for the Priest's decision.

"I will keep it for you, for Bill's sake."

They discussed a few more details, then Sheila and Bernie left the Priest's office, leaving the silver package in his capable custody. "Are you staying in town a little longer?" Sheila asked Bernie as they walked through the church towards the door.

"I'm not sure how long, but probably not much longer. I'm supposed to be back at work tomorrow. Overtime for a holiday," he added with a small smile. The two walked slowly out the door, not quite ready to say what might be a permanent goodbye to a new friend that had brought each some excitement and joy into their lives. "Could you ever come to visit me in D.C.?" asked Bernie.

Sheila grinned at him. "Maybe I could! I've always wanted to see Washington D.C."

They exchanged phone numbers and as Bernie started to leave, Sheila hugged him and gave him a kiss on the cheek. She wasn't Heather, but the thrill he felt at her touch was more than he could have imagined.

The Police Chief dropped Rachel off at Fort Hamilton Hospital, where a makeshift morgue was already being set up in preparation for the body that had arrived. He assigned two officers to guard Rachel and the entrance to the morgue. Hospital security was also informed of the potential danger and were on high alert. The hospital scheduled extra security personnel on every shift to continue until further notice. While they didn't carry firearms, they were assigned to monitor all video cameras around the clock and make more frequent rounds of the facility and parking lot. They were to call in more police at the hint of anything suspicious.

While his detectives were currently questioning the five "guests" of the police department, the Chief planned to thoroughly question Heather himself. He had let her go with only a few questions the last time they spoke and he didn't intend to do that again. She was the key to this mess, he felt sure. Now that a Mr. Barnes whom he presumed to be her father was also involved, he had even more questions.

He pulled into the police station, which was also fortified more than ever before. All officers and SWAT personnel were on overtime and the parking lot was almost full. Two officers were assigned to simply watch the perimeter of the building, the parking lot, streets and sky. Everyone was on high alert.

He brought in the broken laptop and the cell phone of Jacob Barnes and temporarily deposited them on his desk. He wanted his expert to go through each of the devices thoroughly. But first he needed a cup of coffee, then wanted to check in with the two detectives assigned to question the Singers, the Moores and Miss Barnes. He surmised that his detectives were currently with the two couples as he saw Heather sitting alone in another room. She was making a phone call on her cell.

Suddenly the cell phone belonging to Jacob Barnes began chiming. The Chief was starting out his office door and went back to look at the display. It was Heather calling. He looked at her and he saw the question in her eyes as she listened to the phone chime in time with the ringing of her own phone. Then the realization passed over her face as to what was happening. She jumped up and hurried to his office.

"Is that my father's phone!" she cried loudly and several officers in the other room looked towards the Chief's office. She started to pick up the phone off of his desk and the Chief stopped her.

"Please, have a seat. I really need a cup of coffee. Can I get you one as well? Then we'll talk."

"What's happened to my father? Is he here?" Heather was frantic. "No, I don't want coffee!"

"Do NOT touch the phone or laptop. It's evidence. Give me 30 seconds and I'll be right back and explain everything."

He was gone longer than 30 seconds as he met the detective who had been talking with Jon and Carol Moore. The detective was amazed at the story he was hearing and told the Chief much of the same information he had already heard. So far, all of their stories were consistent.

"Please, tell me what's happened to my father," Heather pleaded as the Chief returned and shut the door to his office.

"We don't know where your father is at the moment," said the Chief. "I don't want to alarm you but there was a helicopter crash and he was apparently in the helicopter according to the pilot, but we haven't found him yet."

"So the pilot is okay?" questioned Heather.

"Yes, hurt but he'll be fine."

The Chief noticed that Heather relaxed somewhat as she asked the next questions. "What happened? How did the helicopter crash?"

"The pilot stated they nearly collided with another helicopter in the vicinity, which caused him to lose control of his small aircraft and crash into some trees. The helicopter was actually suspended in the trees. We found your father's broken laptop and his cell phone on the ground below the helicopter crash site this morning. The crash happened about 1:30 last night - this morning I should say - about the same time your kidnapper was shot." The Chief looked at Heather to wait for her comment to his last statement.

"Yes, I felt a breeze right as the bullet hit the man," Heather recollected, her voice low, meditative. "I didn't hear the helicopter though. Perhaps I was just too afraid. But a few minutes later, I thought I heard something else - a swooshing sound that could have been helicopter blades hitting something. Maybe it was dad's helicopter crashing into the trees that I heard. Was it close to where I was?"

"Yes, fairly close. Do you think it was your dad that shot the man who kidnapped you?" It was a logical question.

Heather's brows furrowed as she thought. "I don't know." Each word was spoken slowly, deliberately, as if Heather was still trying to make sense of what was happening. "It's possible, I guess."

It was obvious to the Chief that Heather was stunned by this news and had no idea that her father was in town or where he was now. "I have a team searching the area near the crash, just in case." He didn't have to say just in case what – he knew that Heather knew his meaning.

"Thank you" she replied.

"So, are you alright?" The Chief spoke softly and with genuine concern. He had just come from the crime scene and witnessed the variety of torture tools on the ground next to the dead kidnapper. And he could see the scrapes and bruises on Heather's arms and forehead.

Heather looked down at her lap. "I'll be okay. But I should go to the hospital to be checked out." She looked up and met his eyes.

"He hurt you."

"Yes," was all Heather said.

"Damn. I'm sorry." The Chief knew he should get her to the hospital immediately, but he wanted to question her now. "I'll take you to the hospital myself in just a few minutes, if that's okay."

"Of course."

The Chief took another gulp of coffee and asked Heather to tell him about the kidnapping. He had recognized the dead man as the man posing as her attorney and he felt a twinge of guilt at having released her to the stranger's custody. He couldn't really tell from the man's face, as it had been half eaten by the rats, but he recognized the man's hair and his expensive suit.

Heather told the story for the second time that morning, leaving out the details of her torture and rape. She ended by explaining how Bernie was able to find her, his news to her that the morgue was going to be attacked and their drive to the morgue immediately after the bombing.

"Who do you think is responsible for the bombing?" the Chief asked her.

Heather was thoughtful. "Two hours ago I would have said John Dorgan, but Bernie told me that you found him dead last night."

"That's right, but couldn't he have set it up yesterday? The bombing, and your kidnapping?"

"He could have." She didn't sound convinced. "I really don't know who else is involved in this cover-up, but it could go fairly high. There could be lots of resources behind keeping us quiet." They were both quiet and thoughtful for a long moment as the weight of that statement sunk in. Was this only the beginning? How many more people were going to die to keep this secret?

"I think I understand what you all were doing at the morgue this morning – well, not you of course – Rachel told me, but could you explain it to me as well?" Rachel had already told the Chief about the plan to remove the ear implants. Heather filled in some details that Rachel hadn't mentioned or didn't know.

Heather's phone was on vibrate and she heard it move in her purse. She was getting a call, but couldn't answer while the Chief was questioning her.

"That's where Bernie went this morning," Heather confessed, "to give a copy of the Freedom Project file to a trusted friend. I expect him to come here once he is finished."

The Chief started to ask about the file and the identity of the trusted friend, but commotion in the outer room drew his attention there. Officers were drawing their weapons and one detective was ushering his wards, the Moores, out a back door.

Nearly a dozen operatives dressed in black, including black cloth masks over their faces, burst into the large room and began shooting. The Chief's first thought was that he was thankful he had ordered everyone to wear a Kevlar vest. That might save some of them. He then realized as he heard the sound of a missile hitting the unprotected leg of one of his officers that the ninja-like intruders were using rubber bullets, not designed to kill but to temporarily immobilize. At close range, however, these bullets could still be deadly.

He motioned for Heather to crawl under his desk as he pulled a shotgun from a lower cabinet behind him.

These operatives were well trained, but his officers were putting up an excellent fight. The few seconds warning that they had received from one of the officers outside, plus the extra personnel, and the Kevlar, gave the Hamilton police a fighting chance against the professional team that now invaded them. And the police were using real bullets. Three of the operatives were down and three others were retreating into the stairwell at the barrage of bullets. However, two of the black ops had pulled Mary Beth and Joe from one of the side rooms and were using them as shields as they pulled them outside. Two others were now running across the room towards the Chief's office as their teammates were riddling the room with rubber missiles.

The Chief blew off the head of the first intruder that crashed through his door into his office. His teammate retaliated with several rubber bullets across the Chief's arms, chest and neck. As he fell to the floor, he saw Heather being dragged from beneath his desk.

Dragon's request for a favor was viewed by Jeremy as an order. After all, Dragon was still his boss. Deep down, both men knew that was no longer the case and that Jeremy could have refused to help him. Depending on the favor, he might have.

The favor was rather huge. Jeremy grinned as he thought about it. It was a hacker's dream. It was something he'd always wanted to do. It was the reason he would still use the excuse "my boss ordered me to" if and when he was discovered, fired then prosecuted. Depending on what he found, his punishment might be more permanent than firing and prosecution, he knew.

Dragon wanted Jeremy to hack into the secure files of three individuals – the Secretary of Homeland Security, The Director of the CIA, and the President of the United States. Dragon already had access to the current Freedom Project's Leader, Jacob Barnes', confidential files and didn't believe the man was working alone. He cautioned Jeremy to keep his search limited to the Freedom Projects and any related files, such as recent requests for resources.

Jeremy knew this job was a tall order, even for him. He knew he could hack into the internal classified files of the secretary rather easily, but the other two could take some time. He not only had to figure out how to break in, he had to figure out how to cover his tracks. Ass-covering took longer than an actual assignment.

Since the secretary would be the easiest, he started there. He began by listing every possible way his hacking could be discovered internally and by whom, then formulated separate plans for avoiding detection.

Keeping an eye on his monitors, Jeremy saw Dragon leave his park bench and begin walking. He was using Samuel to monitor Dragon and tried following him from a high enough distance to be able to continue to work on his hacking project as well. Dragon wasn't making it easy on him, however. Jeremy was beginning to think Dragon was trying to lose him. But Jeremy managed to follow him and work on his covert hacking plan at the same time. Forty-five minutes later, he was in Homeland Security's server that held the files of the leader of Homeland Security, Rhonda Watterson. During that time, Dragon had found an unlocked car, apparently with the keys in it and was now moving much faster. A few minutes later, he was in Greenwood Cemetery among all the other cars whose occupants were watching the disastrous scene at the morgue.

On another monitor, Jeremy saw Bernie walk away from the crowded morgue parking lot, cross the back street and head into the cemetery. Jeremy was pretty sure Bernie shouldn't be leaving the scene, but it didn't appear the police were going to stop him. Bernie left in his car. Jeremy wanted to follow him and positioned one of the old satellites over Bernie. He then noticed the black car that Dragon had stolen was following Bernie. He could follow both cars with just Samuel, but decided to keep both satellites on his targets in case they separated. He was glad when Bernie stopped at the hotel and went in, followed by Dragon, who remained in the car in the parking lot. While the two cars were stopped, Jeremy could finish hacking into the Secretary's secure folder and focus on reading some of her interesting files.

Only minutes later, Heather and the others were getting into police cruisers, and Jeremy stopped perusing files to watch the two cars as they made their way to police headquarters. A third car held the coroner and the Chief of police, but it drove on past the police station. Jeremy left the satellite positioned over the police station where Heather, Mary Beth, Joe, Jon and Carol were now going inside.

Jeremy found the Secretary's memo to file where she had assigned him, Jeremy, to follow and watch John Dorgan. She listed her justification as "…received a tip from colleague at CIA stating that John Dorgan may be involved in terrorist activity and acts of treason against the U.S." He also found her requisition for satellite Samuel that he had requested Friday evening. There were other notes regarding updates Jeremy had given her, but overall, the folder marked "Dorgan, John: Investigation" held little information.

Jeremy searched for anything in the Secretary's files regarding the Freedom Project but found nothing. He also looked for any evidence that she had hired the assassin Raptor, since he had seen the accounting that Homeland Security had paid for the killing of Michael Michtenbaum. The entry didn't say that – there was simply a dollar amount and the name Michtenbaum. He found nothing to indicate she personally had hired Raptor and could not find any requisition or evidence of payment to the man. Her financial records were meticulous, at least the ones that were in her secure file. It was possible that someone else within Homeland Security had hired the man and when murdering someone, you don't always ask permission and then document it. And there was always the possibility that an outside source, another agency, had planted the false expenditure.

Dragon was still in the black sedan in the parking lot of the hotel. Bernie was still inside. Jeremy wished Bernie carried a cell phone. Who didn't have a cell phone these days? Jeremy couldn't imagine that Dragon planned to do any harm to Bernie or the others, knowing that Jeremy was watching him, but he couldn't be sure just what Dragon was up to.

Jeremy called the Marriott and asked them to ring Bernie's room. There was no answer so Jeremy left a message for Bernie to call him. He waited ten minutes and tried again. This time Bernie answered and Jeremy told him about Dragon following him. He hadn't intended to tell anyone else that Dragon was alive, but he also hadn't expected Dragon to follow one of his friends. Yes, he thought to himself after hanging up the phone with Bernie, I now consider you a friend, you little gnome.

Jeremy watched as Bernie quickly lost Dragon at a traffic light. He was impressed that Bernie circled back around and lost Dragon permanently. Jeremy kept a close watch on Bernie and saw that he made it safely to St. Julie Billiart Church. Bernie spent several minutes with his head inside the trunk of his car before he finally emerged and walked towards the church with his suitcase. "Wait! What's this?" said Jeremy loudly to the computer monitor. Bernie was meeting a woman! "You didn't mention her, you sly dog," chuckled Jeremy. He then laughed heartily as he saw Bernie look up towards the sky and salute.

Tackling the job of hacking into the CIA Director's secure files was daunting. Jeremy had thought and dreamed of how he would do it should he ever have the professional need, or the personal death-wish, to do so. So most of the CYA work had already been done, but Jeremy began reviewing all of the possible scenarios in his mind. He couldn't afford to screw this up.

It was hard, however, to concentrate on his serious criminal computer activities while following and watching several people at the same time. He kept Samuel on Dragon, who was never able to find Bernie. Serves him right, thought Jeremy, who watched Dragon drive around the area for ten minutes before heading back to the Marriott. This time he went inside. Jeremy figured Dragon thought it was probably safe to go retrieve whatever was in his room now that the police thought he was dead, which is exactly what he did. "Please take a nap or something," said Jeremy. "I really want to hack into your old boss's files and I can't do that and watch you too!"

Jeremy's eye was then drawn to the screen showing the Hamilton Police station and surrounding area. Two black SUVs pulled into the police station parking lot and up to the front door. A police officer that had been standing near the front door ran inside the building before the vehicles stopped. Six black ops agents quickly exited each SUV and the dozen armed operatives went inside.

The last thing Heather remembered before falling into a deep slumber was being shoved into the back seat of a black SUV and seeing a man dressed in black with a gas mask over his face. That was long ago she somehow knew in the recesses of her mind. Now she was with Danny and they were sitting at a little outdoor café sipping wine and eating bread with oil and garlic. She was happy. Her father was approaching and had a file in his hand. He looked angry with her. As he reached her table, he slowed and glared at her but kept walking. Behind him, a man with a twisted, sadistic smile was looking at her and holding out his hands towards her, a large rat in each hand. She screamed and was no longer at the table but running in the woods, running away from the man with the rats. She fell and and realized she was tied up.

Heather awoke slowly and could hear in the distance an even roar of an engine. A few voices talked softly some distance away. She opened her eyes and tried to push the grogginess from her mind. She was sitting with a small pillow beneath her head and up against a window and quickly realized she was in a plane. She sat upright and looked around. In two seats across the aisle from her sat Joe and Mary Beth, both asleep. Two men were seated and talking quietly a row ahead of her, and two more men were behind her, one on each side of the aisle. These two appeared to be dozing.

She was in a small jet – there were only the seven passengers on the plane. She looked out the window at the bright sunlight and down at farmlands and fields below. She tried to think – it had been morning when she was abducted from the police station – it couldn't have been much past 10:30 a.m. How long had she been sleeping? She remembered the masked man putting a cloth over her mouth and nose – chloroform. That would have knocked her out for a while - apparently long enough for her captor to drive to an airport, secretly load three unconscious passengers onto a plane, and get into the air.

She remembered the conversation she was having with the Police Chief before she was taken. Her father was in Hamilton, Ohio. How did he know she was there? Did he figure out she had been in his files? She knew her father had called her last night, so that was probably it. He came home and was in the basement file room and realized she had gotten into that old forbidden file. He tried calling her, thinking she was in Fiji, and when he couldn't reach her, he called Danny.

Could it have been her father that shot and killed the psychopath that had kidnapped and raped her? She knew he was more than capable of making the shot and also capable of finding her if that was his goal, although she couldn't imagine how he possibly could know she was in a secluded wooded area almost completely out of view from above. How in the world did he find her?

She half stood in her seat and spoke to her captors. "Where are we going?" The two dozing men lept to their feet, with one beside her in an instant, placing his hand firmly on her shoulder and asking her to be seated.

"Where are you taking us!" Heather shouted at the man. One of the two men in the seats ahead of her stood and replied, "You'll find out soon enough. Just try and relax. If you're cooperative, you'll not be harmed. You have my word."

"Forgive me if *your word* doesn't mean much to me," Heather snapped, her voice dripping with contempt. She sat down and defiantly crossed her arms over her chest, as if that would help in some way.

"How much further?" Heather continued her demanding inquiry.

"Just try and relax," the man stated again and sat back down in his seat, continuing his conversation with his teammate.

The slight commotion had wakened Joe Singer who, in turn, woke his wife. Heather unlatched her seatbelt and turned to put her feet in the aisle and face Joe. She leaned in and spoke softly. "They won't tell me where we're going."

Heather wanted to say she was sorry, that she wished she had never gotten them into this mess, that it was all her fault. She felt all of those things, but as Bernie had told her earlier that morning, or perhaps it was yesterday now, it would do no good to dwell on those negative thoughts. If she lived through this, there would plenty of time later to wallow in guilt. But she still had to say the words again to these two people who had lived a happy, normal life until they met her. She whispered, "I'm sorry," and tried to keep the tears from flowing.

Heather leaned her head back on the seat, closing her eyes. She wanted Joe and Mary Beth to be able to spend these moments together in private. None of them knew if these moments might be their last. She finally peeked across the aisle and was again amazed at the bond between these two. Even in their fear, they smiled at each other with a look of absolute love. They truly found comfort and peace from the other's presence. Heather thought of Danny, wishing he was next to her at this moment and that she could pull comfort from his embrace.

Her thoughts were temporarily interrupted by an overwhelming urge to pee and she stood and asked if she could use the restroom.

"Of course," the man answered. He then nodded to one of the men behind the hostages indicating that he should stay close to her. Heather looked at herself in the small mirror in the airplane lavatory. She was a mess. She had spent last night in the woods in the company of the psychopath and desperately needed to bathe, change clothes and brush her teeth. Her arms were scratched and bruised. Her right shoulder was displaying a nasty bruise from where it had slammed into the tree several times. The top of her head felt tender and when she touched it, she realized there was a large knot there. She ached all over from the trauma her body had undergone. Her mascara had run from crying and her eyes had the subsequent black smudging under them.

She washed her face and brushed her teeth with her finger as best she could and ran her fingers through her very short black hair.

When Heather returned to her seat, one of the men produced a cooler with a variety of sandwiches, snacks and cold drinks, which were offered to the three captives as well as the captors. Heather, Joe and Mary Beth all gratefully accepted the food and drink, the first they had had that day.

Feeling slightly cleaner, and with food now filling her stomach, Heather felt better. Joe and Mary Beth seemed stronger as well. The three began talking about various things, starting with Joe and Mary Beth's daughter, Lauren. Joe passed his cell phone housing numerous photos across to Heather. "Wow, she's beautiful," said Heather truthfully. The young woman was obviously photogenic, each photo capturing a large, warm smile and round, laughing blue eyes. Her straight blond hair was at different lengths in the various photos that spanned a two or three year period of the young woman's life.

"She just graduated from Miami University and leaves for Europe next week," Mary Beth told Heather. She stopped only momentarily and the three knew they were all thinking the same thing – please let us be alive and home next week. She continued with pride in her voice. "She has a 3.9 average."

Heather thought of her own 3.9 GPA upon graduation from Cornell and her 4.0 from John Hopkins. "She sounds like a wonderful daughter. I know you must be very proud of her."

"We are," Joe answered. "How about you? Is there anyone special in your life?"

"Yes, there is." She told them how she was supposed to be in Fiji with Danny. "I've always felt love for Danny, but lately I've been pushing him away, more than usual. I guess I believe that the love will eventually go away if we get married and be replaced by indifference, or simply tolerance of each other, or even hatred. I've seen it happen too many times to others. But, seeing you two, and Jon and Carol, and even Mitch and Celia – you all seem very much in love after years of marriage." Heather laughed slightly. "I meet three couples this weekend and all three just happen to be poster couples for a happy marriage. Hopefully that isn't just because you're all scared out of your minds."

The three laughed out loud, which drew the attention of the men in the plane with them, but only momentarily.

"Well, you're right that we have a very happy marriage," stated Mary Beth. "Would you like to know why? There is a secret to living a happy married life."

"I'd like to know that myself," Joe chuckled. "I've obviously been doing it, though." He paused a moment and the expression on his face changed. "We're starting to descend."

Dorgan bought a cup of coffee and a bagel from the hotel restaurant and took them up to his room. He approached cautiously even though he believed the police would no longer be watching this room since he was now believed to be dead. He had his room key and hoped it still worked.

The room had been searched by the police and his personal

items were gone. He sat down to wait for the two phone calls he was expecting. He turned on the Cincinnati local news with the headlines being several stories from Hamilton, Ohio, the top one being the bombing of the Butler County morgue, resulting in one death. A local news crew was on the scene showing the still smoldering remains of the morgue in the background. The story was now focusing on the miraculous event of a man found alive in one of the steel body storage vaults.

The next story was about a helicopter crash in which the helicopter was lodged in trees near the Great Miami River. The Civil Air Rescue team had retrieved the pilot from the suspended helicopter and flown him to the local hospital where he was listed in good condition. Dorgan hadn't heard about the helicopter accident and watched the news coverage carefully as he was certain it had something to do with him. "A passenger in the helicopter, identified by the pilot as Jacob Barnes of Fairfax, Virginia, is currently missing," stated a reporter who was on the scene, surrounded by trees and police vehicles. A recent photo of Jacob was briefly shown on the screen.

"Barnes!" Dorgan hissed, rising from his chair. "So you're here as well!"

Dorgan knew if Barnes was missing, it was because he wanted to be. He was out there somewhere.

There was a brief news story about his own death. "The man wanted for questioning by police in several area murders was found dead in a Fairfield motel." It showed a picture of the motel where he had stayed.

His cell phone rang. He answered without saying a word, and hung up without anyone but himself hearing "three passengers en route to compound."

Hmmm, three, thought Dorgan. He wondered which three. If they included Mary Beth Singer and Jon Moore, then perfect, three was all that was needed. However, if either Jon or Mary Beth had not been taken, then his work was not yet complete. He continued to watch the news as he was certain the story of the invasion on the Hamilton City Police Station would soon be another top story.

Dorgan smiled slightly at the recent memory of tailing Bernie, whom he was certain had the implants of Michael Michtenbaum. He was smiling partly because he was impressed that the man lost him so easily, but primarily because he had another person following Bernie and that person had not lost him. The hired man had followed Bernie to St. Julie Billiard Church on Dayton Street. Now Dorgan would be able to get the Michtenbaum implants.

Dorgan could never be certain if Jeremy was watching or listening so during the night, after escaping from the vault in the morgue, he contacted two operatives via text so that he could not be heard. Dorgan no longer cared about protecting certain individuals in high places involved in the Freedom Project since he was pretty sure they were the ones who were planning to kill him, but he was still determined to finalize FP-I until it was both officially and unofficially over. For him, that meant the retrieval of all implants from the three individuals involved in the original experiment.

As Bernie approached the police station, he saw a body bag being loaded into an ambulance. Another ambulance sat close by and by the time Bernie had parked his car and started walking towards the station, a second body bag was brought out of the building and placed in this vehicle. No sirens or lights were needed as the two emergency vehicles left the street, heading in the direction of the hospital morgue.

Bernie was frantic, not knowing whose bodies were in those bags. Could one of them be Heather? Was one of them Joe, or Jon, or one of their wives? A SWAT van was parked close by and the special weapons team was standing guard outside.

He was stopped by one of the SWAT members, gun pointed in his general direction although not directly at him. "What happened?" Bernie asked the man.

"What's your business here," the policeman asked, eyeing him a little suspiciously.

"I was with the people at the morgue right before it blew up. I believe they were all here at the police station and I was supposed to join them. Are they all alright?" Bernie had walked closer to the doorway, ready to go inside.

"I don't know, but you can't go in. You can wait here and I'll try to find out." Bernie stayed put and the police officer opened the front door and called to another man inside the building.

A few minutes later, a detective came out the front door. It was the same man who had talked with Bernie after the foiled bombing incident the day before. "Bernie, come with me." This time the SWAT officer nodded at Bernie as he walked inside.

The detective was also the one who had been interviewing Jon and Carol Moore less than 90 minutes before when an officer had run in and warned the building occupants of the attack that would happen within seconds. He had hastily hustled Jon and Carol out of the station, out a back door and into his car, to safety. Not knowing where to take them, he had deposited them at his own home and stayed with them a while before returning to the station to find out the other three people being interviewed in regards to the morgue bombing had all been taken by the intruders. Several Hamilton police officers, including the Chief himself, had been wounded, but fortunately, none was killed. The news of the attackers using rubber bullets had spread throughout the police force. Three of the invading shooters had been killed and one was badly wounded and under police guard at the hospital.

"We were attacked and three of your friends were taken, alive," the detective added the last word when he saw the anxiety on Bernie's face. "Do you have any idea who took them?"

"Who was taken and where are the others?" Bernie cried.

The detective was patient with Bernie. "The Singers and Miss Barnes were taken. The Moores are safe for now."

"What about Rachel, the coroner?" Bernie asked.

"She wasn't here. So I assume she's safe as well. Now my question again - do you know who may have done this?"

"The same people that blew up the morgue I assume!" Bernie was exasperated that the police hadn't figured out that the power and resources of the federal government were most probably behind this. "And that kidnapped and almost killed Heather!"

"Do you have a name, I mean," stated the detective. "You gave us a name before, remember?"

"Yes, I remember." And now Bernie wondered if Dorgan was behind this as well. He was still alive, after all, and had followed him earlier that morning. "I know that John Dorgan is still alive. He might have done it, but I don't know for sure."

The detective was genuinely surprised. "Dorgan? He's the one that was dead in the motel last night, right?"

"Right."

"How do you know he's still alive? And how could that be possible? He was pronounced dead yesterday and taken to the morgue."

"Well, he was following me this morning, so I know he's still alive. I really don't know how it's possible that he was pronounced dead yesterday unless it was a different person perhaps?"

"Where were you this morning?"

Bernie hesitated as he didn't want to reveal where he had taken the package that held the implants from Michael Michtenbaum, which the police would still consider as evidence in that unsolved murder.

"I took a copy of a confidential Homeland Security file to a person for safekeeping."

"Does that file have to do with all of these attacks?"

"Yes, I believe so. We – all of us that were at the morgue this morning – plus Heather, thought whoever is trying to kill us would stop if we threatened to reveal the experiment to the media." Bernie hung his head. "But it doesn't seem to have worked."

"Perhaps it is time you let the police see that file. It might hold other clues as to who else is involved in these kidnappings and deaths." The detective took a deep breath. "And besides, it is personal now. They've killed two of our officers and wounded five more today, two quite seriously."

"Yes, you're right," said Bernie. "I have the file in my car." The two walked to Bernie's car and retrieved the small memory stick from his glove box. They returned inside the building and the detective asked Bernie more questions concerning Dorgan and where Bernie had taken the package. Bernie finally told him about Father Benjamin at the church and what had transpired that morning. "Your fellow officers should be bringing in the man who stole the box soon."

The detective wasn't sure what to do with Bernie now. He couldn't stay there. The police station looked like a war zone and with seven officers dead or wounded and two on constant duty at the hospital morgue, they were short staffed. "What are you going to do now, Bernie? I can take you to stay with the Moores."

Bernie wasn't sure what to do. He knew he should drive back to D.C. as he was supposed to be at work the next day even though it was a holiday. But he didn't want to leave until he found out where Heather was and if she was alright. He needed to talk to Jeremy and hoped he was tracking her.

"Ok, I would like to see the Moores. But I need to take my car. I should be heading home soon, if that's okay."

"Of course. You can follow me. Just give me a few minutes and we'll go." The detective left Bernie sitting there as he went to give the evidence on the flash drive to the acting Chief.

Bernie looked around. Heather's purse was sitting on the floor about twenty feet away. On an impulse, he walked over and picked it up, going unnoticed in the chaotic aftermath of the recent attack on the station. He took the purse to his car and waited outside the door for the detective. He took advantage of the time to call Jeremy. He now had a cell phone – Heather's.

"I'm tracking them," Jeremy explained. "They left in two black SUVs and went to a small airport in Hamilton, where they left in a Learjet 45. I called both the Hamilton and the Fairfield police as I was tracking them, but they didn't get to the airport in time to stop them. I've just checked with the airport to see if the pilot filed a flight plan, but he didn't, so I don't know where they're headed. I'll call and let you know as soon as I know anything more. Keep Heather's phone on you, okay?"

"I will. Unless I hear from you that the plane has landed somewhere close, I'll probably head back to D.C. soon."

"That's about all you can do, man. If they do land somewhere fairly close, I'll let you know. Otherwise, see you tomorrow."

The detective found Bernie outside. "Oh, here you are. Ready?"

Bernie hung up and got in his car to follow the detective. Ten minutes later they pulled up to a modest ranch-style home. It had white aluminum siding and black window shutters, no garage but a carport on the side of the house and a white fenced back yard. Bernie saw a golden retriever in the back yard, who seemed excited to see them.

"Who lives here?" asked Bernie as he walked from the street where he parked his car towards the detective who was now near the front door.

"I do. I didn't have anywhere else to take them for now." Bernie noticed the officer glance both up and down his street for any cars coming their way. There were none. The two entered the front door. Jon and Carol Moore had been watching from a window, so greeted them when they saw it was the detective and Bernie.

"Are the others okay?" Carol asked breathlessly as soon as the two men entered. They had been watching television for any news of the incident, but so far nothing had appeared.

"Everyone is alive, as far as we know," explained the detective, "but Miss Barnes and Mr. and Mrs. Singer were taken by the intruders."

Carol and Jon both gasped and held on to each other.

Bernie felt he should tell what further information he knew. "They just took off in a plane about fifteen or twenty minutes ago."

The detective stared at him. "How do you know that?"

"My friend back at Homeland Security is tracking as many of us as he can via satellite. He watched them leave in two black SUVs and go to a small airport in Hamilton where a Learjet was waiting. He doesn't know where they're heading though."

The detective was irritated that Bernie hadn't told him this information before and was calling the station. Bernie assured him that Jeremy had already called the Hamilton police and had already checked with the airport, but the detective still called.

Carol, Jon and Bernie went and sat at the kitchen table, where Carol had made coffee earlier. She poured a cup for each of them and asked Bernie where he had gone when he disappeared from the morgue earlier. Bernie explained about taking the package to a trustee, but didn't reveal who the trustee was or where he was located. It was best if they didn't know.

"Well, it's good one of the packages is in safe-keeping," said Jon. "I guess the other file copies and my other implant were blown up at the morgue. "

"Oh wait!" exclaimed Carol, reaching into her pant pocket. She placed the small ear implant on the table. "The coroner gave it to me when she took it out of your ear. I forgot I had it."

It hit all three of them at the exact same time and they each looked from one to the other, not saying a word. *Was someone listening to them?* Jon was still wearing his eye patch so that no one could see where they were.

"I'm heading back for the station." The detective had finished his call and walked into the kitchen. "Bernie, I need the name and number of your contact at Homeland Security before I go."

"Sure," said Bernie, and got up to walk outside with the officer.

When Bernie returned, Carol and Jon were wrapping a towel around the ear implant and putting it inside several layers of paper and plastic bags, then inside a cardboard box. "Ok, think Jon," said Carol breathlessly. "Did we say anything that could lead them to us now? I don't even remember the detective's name, so I don't think we said we were at his house, did we?"

"I don't think so, but I'm not sure. We've been talking a lot since we've been here."

"Perhaps we should leave here and go somewhere else," suggested Bernie. "I have my car."

"Yes, that's a good idea," agreed Jon.

Father Benjamin kept several small gifts given to him by his parishioners, young and old. These treasures were displayed on shelves, walls and the top of his desk in his office. Most were homemade – a lace doily, hand-made and given to him by the elderly Mrs. Gilbert, who passed away almost a decade earlier; a crayon drawing of Jesus and angels made by a sick little girl who had died a week later.

Father looked at one of his most prized possessions – a small doll made from a piece of burlap, stuffed with cotton, and tied about the neck and the waist with red ribbons. The doll had not been given to him by a member of the church but had belonged to his mother. It was the only remembrance of her that he owned. One of the button eyes was missing from when a visiting family's child played with the doll and pulled the button off, losing it in the process. He now reached for the doll sitting on the corner of his desk and carefully unstitched the back of the burlap, gently removing a portion of the stuffing. He reached into his pocket and pulled out a small glass vial holding a small flash drive and two tiny silver discs wrapped in aluminum foil. He gently placed the vial within the doll and re-stitched the burlap.

Father Benjamin locked the small silver case that Bernie had given him in the wall safe located in his office, behind a large painting of the Mother Mary.

The man who had followed Bernie to the church waited through mass and communion in the back row until the service was over. He watched as Bernie and the woman walked with the Priest down a hallway at the front of the church before following them further. He saw the door close to the room they entered and hid himself in a closet across the hall, leaving the door slightly ajar. When he heard the three leave the room, he slid silently across the hall to search for the package. The man who hired him was specific in his instructions. He was not to harm anyone in his retrieval of the package although he could threaten to harm, a skill at which he was quite adept. He was to keep property damage to a minimum, if possible, but if not possible, so be it. But he was not to return without the package. If he wanted to get paid, he must complete his assignment, which he fully intended to do.

Since nothing resembling the items for which he was searching was lying in plain view, the man assumed the package had already been hidden within the office. He found the safe right away behind the painting and quickly applied an explosive beneath some putty.

"What are you doing?" boomed a voice behind him. The man quickly turned to see the Priest standing in the doorway.

The man lit the fuse, smiling slightly at the Priest as he did so. "Surely you were told others would be looking for these items."

"Stop! I'll open the safe. Please don't destroy it!" the Priest cried, walking towards the man.

The man pulled the fuse and moved slightly to allow the Priest to open the safe. The silver box had been set in the back of the safe and the Priest reached in to retrieve it.

"Here. Now go!" the Priest said sternly as he handed the box to the man, "unless you'd like to confess your sins first," he added sarcastically.

"That's okay padre," and he motioned for the Priest to sit. "This is the least of my many sins." He leaned down and faced the Priest. "Give me five minutes before you call the police or I will come back and torch your lovely church."

The Priest gulped and nodded.

The man exited the church and ran towards his car, tossing the silver box onto the passenger seat as he climbed into the driver side. As he started the car, two police cruisers merged on him, blocking his way in both directions. Within seconds, four guns were aimed at him and he didn't need to think too long about it – he chose surrender over death.

"Put both hands outside the window!" one of the officers yelled and the man did so. He looked beyond the police and saw the short, stocky man he had followed to the church, with the woman, standing there. He's not as stupid as he looks, thought the man.

Jacob awoke to the sound of motored vehicles heading his way. His head hurt like hell and the rest of his body didn't feel so great either.

He had fallen from the tree, he recalled, although he didn't remember hitting the ground. It was now broad daylight so that had to have been seven or more hours ago. He had been unconscious or asleep that entire time.

He stood gingerly, keeping one hand on a tree trunk to steady himself. He needed to see if any bones were broken. His left leg was quite sore but did not appear to be broken. His left arm and shoulder hurt as well but were otherwise intact.

Two police cars and a van arrived, stopping only 20 or so yards from where he was standing and he immediately went to his hands and knees behind some brush. He could see several people but from the sound of the voices as they emerged from the vehicles, there were a dozen or more.

"The Chief will be here soon, but we are to start the search now," boomed one voice as the others became silent. "We will do a grid search – ten wide – from this point to the river. We're looking for the passenger in the helicopter, but call if you find anything else as well, such as a piece of the helicopter."

Jacob cursed silently. If they had not already found his phone and laptop, they would now. He felt his right leg – his small handgun was still there, and his wallet was still in his back pant pocket.

As the team began their search, Jacob began moving slowly and silently in the opposite direction towards the road. He was grateful that he hadn't broken any bones – that would have slowed him down considerably. It took him five minutes to make his way through the heavy brush to the road. As he approached the road, he saw another police car turn into the brush, heading towards the crash site. A man and a woman were in the car.

Jacob was glad when a sheriff's cruiser parked by the road left the scene. Still, he didn't want to risk walking in clear view for fear of being seen by newly arriving, or leaving, police vehicles. He also wasn't optimistic about his chances of being picked up by a passing car if he hitchhiked. He was dirty, bloody and had torn clothing.

A car was approaching and from his vantage point behind a tree near the road, Jacob could see that the car appeared to contain only a driver, no passengers. He made a quick decision and pulled the gun from its holster under his right pant leg. He walked deliberately into the road, stopped, and aimed the gun straight at the approaching driver.

Jacob was ninety percent certain the driver would slam on the brakes, especially since he could now see that the driver was a woman. There was always that ten percent chance she would run him down. The favorable statistic prevailed and the woman screeched her car to a halt, screaming as she did so. "Get out please," Jacob told her in a firm voice, still aiming the gun at her. He checked the road both ways – still no oncoming traffic. "Open the trunk," he ordered.

The woman was in her late fifties or early sixties and somewhat overweight. Jacob felt badly about having to put the woman in the trunk but it couldn't be helped. He had no intention of hurting her or keeping her any longer than absolutely necessary, but at the moment he needed to get away from this location quickly.

The woman became hysterical as he ordered her into the open trunk. He could see a car coming in the distance and he slammed the trunk lid shut quickly. He slipped into the driver's seat and proceeded down the road, trying to formulate a plan for what to do now that he was without his phone, laptop, pilot, helicopter and familiar surroundings.

At the stoplight at a bridge, Jacob rummaged through the woman's purse, looking for a cell phone. She had a simple flip phone with no internet access. He crossed the bridge, heading for what was apparently downtown Hamilton based on the buildings he could see in the distance, and he dialed 411 for information.

"I need the phone number of the closest AT&T wireless store," Jacob started when the operator answered the phone, and he told her where he was located. She gave him the number of the store in Bridgewater Falls, about two miles from town.

Susan was awakened by a noise, or at least she believed she was. Did she only dream that she heard a noise? Jacob had left abruptly last evening, telling her to make herself at home and he would be back as soon as he could. She missed having him beside her in bed, a condition that she had only recently gotten used to, but she felt very comfortable in the big house and had stayed up until well after 1 a.m. waiting for a call from him. Eventually, she gave in to her nodding head and drooping eyelids and climbed into Jacob's bed alone. Could he be downstairs now, home and treading quietly so as not to wake her? She smiled at the thought. She couldn't believe that she had met the man of her dreams at this stage of her life. Fireworks had gone off in her nervous system the moment she first laid eyes on him. When he turned and noticed her as well, holding her gaze with a breathless look on his face and then smiling shyly, she knew she would fall head over heels in love with this man. Now she was going to get to live the rest of her life with him.

She yawned, stretched and turned to her right side, closing her eyes to go back to sleep when another sound caused her to sit upright in fear, her eyes wide open and trained on the closed door to the bedroom, the cream color merely a slightly lighter version of the darkness that enveloped the room. The clicks were unmistakable –

she knew her guns - the sound was that of a Glock semi-automatic being primed to fire.

Without a second's hesitation, Susan was out of bed and running to where she remembered the door to the safe room to be, which was still partially open from the earlier tour of the house Jacob had given her. As she pushed the heavy door a little wider open to allow herself to slip in, the shooting began. She heard the slugs hitting the bed, each a soft dull thud hitting in rapid succession. She pulled hard to close the safe room door and heard a voice curse softly as its owner realized what had just happened.

As the impenetrable door solidly closed and locked, the automatic lighting system came on. She was panicked but fought to control her breathing as she tried to listen to any noise outside the safe room. I won't be able to hear anything through these walls, she thought. She knew there was an intercom system, but she did not want to talk to the intruder. A loud sob escaped her lips and she allowed herself a few moments to be afraid, sliding down the wall, sitting on the floor and trying not to panic.

A few moments was all she needed. She knew she must stay in control and keep her wits about her. She stood and began examining more closely the few important items in the room. There was a small refrigerator, fully stocked, several cabinets housing everything from first aid and medical supplies, to non-perishable food items, to books and dishes. There was a water cooler with an extra 30-gallon bottle of water, a small couch, and a toilet partially hidden behind a partition – everything one would need to be somewhat comfortable if sequestered for more than a day. On the wall were several weapons including a Glock 22 pistol like the one the intruder had used and an M24 rifle. Most importantly, however, there was a phone. She lifted the receiver and got a dial tone. She remembered Jacob explaining how the wiring for this phone was 20 feet underground, encased in a virtually indestructible material - just in case an intruder decided to cut the outside wires on the house.

She dialed 911.

"What is your emergency?" came the woman's voice. Susan explained the situation as calmly as she could and gave Jacob's address to the 911 operator. "I don't know how the intruders got in, so the downstairs doors may still be locked. Have the police break in if need be. I'm in the upstairs master bedroom, in the safe room. I'll turn on the intercom so that I can hear when they arrive and they can let me know when it's safe to come out."

The operator told Susan that help should arrive within five to seven minutes and that she should stay on the line until they arrived.

Susan looked at the intercom on the wall. There was a mute button that would allow her to hear anything going on in the bedroom but would not allow sound from the safe room to be heard. She turned on the intercom and immediately pressed the mute button. All was quiet. Was the intruder still out there, waiting? Or would he assume that whoever ran to the safe room would be able to call for help and therefore he had fled.

Susan speculated as to the reason for the attack. She greatly doubted that it was merely coincidence that Jacob had received disturbing news earlier in the evening, and soon after bullets are being blasted into his bed. Didn't the would-be killer know that Jacob had left? Susan shuddered as it occurred to her that perhaps the killer was targeting *her*, not Jacob. Jacob's daughter was in trouble – could someone be going after the people Jacob loves? Suddenly, she desperately needed to talk to Jacob – to make certain he was okay, and to let him know what was happening at his house.

"Operator, I need to call someone. I'm going to hang up and wait for the police to arrive, okay?" Susan hung up the phone after the 911 operator told her to call back if she needed to and she dialed Jacob's cell phone number. It went to voice-mail and she quickly explained what had just happened, but that she was safe and the police would be arriving at any moment. "If you get this message soon and can call in to the phone in your bedroom safe room, please call me. I need to hear your voice!" Susan finished the voice-mail and hung up, feeling very alone.

The master bedroom was still silent. No police yet. How long had it been? Susan was getting very nervous, but realized it had only been three minutes or so since the operator had called the police. Give them time, she told herself, taking deep breaths to control her rising panic. She got a cup from one of the cupboards and filled it with water, drinking it quickly. She sat on the edge of the couch, ready to jump to the intercom and unmute it when she heard the police arrive.

Susan knew Jacob was CIA. She knew nothing specific about what he did other than that he was in an office job – nothing dangerous, he had said – and that he was retiring in three months. She felt certain this home invasion had to do with his job, although she hoped and prayed that the intruder was a psychopath targeting homes randomly. Please don't be after Jacob, or his family, she cried to herself. For that would mean even if the intruder were caught, another one would be ready in an instant to finish the job.

Ten minutes passed and no police. "Where can they be!" Susan was getting a horrible feeling that they were not coming. Did the intruders kill them? Could the intruders have intercepted the 911 call and it was not the police that she spoke with at all?

The minutes dragged on.

"Susan, can you hear me?"

Susan went pale at the sound of her name by the soft, low voice. She hadn't heard police barging in, announcing themselves. She hadn't heard any sirens in the distance or shoes running up the hardwood stairs. She didn't hear any other voices or anyone moving about in the bedroom. The police weren't there. The voice was that of the intruder, a stealthy, professional killer. A psychopath perhaps, but definitely not a random one.

"Susan, I know you can hear me," the voice said softly but firmly. "Turn on the two-way intercom and let's talk."

Even though Susan felt certain the man could not possibly get into the safe room, she lifted the M24 off the rack and checked the magazine. She sat on the edge of the couch again with the gun aimed towards the door. Okay, she reasoned to herself, it would be easy enough for them to know who she was and that she was alone in the house, but how did they intercept the 911 call as well? How could they possibly do that when the phone wires aren't even visible or nearby? Did they hear her call to Jacob as well? As she feared, the police were not coming. As the impact of her new situation began to seep into her brain, Susan set the shotgun on her lap and put her head into her hands as she tried to think straight and consider what her next step should be.

"I can wait. I'll just lie here on the bed until you feel like talking," the intruder said.

She knew she had water and food for at least five days.

Surely the killer would know that she could wait until Jacob returned with help. Then it hit her: they might have gotten to Jacob already. He may never get her voice-mail. The thought that something might have already happened to Jacob physically sickened her and she began vomiting on the concrete floor of the room.

George Davies, the Hamilton Chief of Police, was recuperating at Fort Hamilton Hospital from painful and temporarily disabling, but not life-threatening, injuries. As soon as he awoke and was able, he set up a makeshift office in his bed and began making phone calls to get up to speed on the events of the past few hours. He had learned that Heather and both of the Singers had been kidnapped and their whereabouts was unknown other than they were taken on a small private jet. The Moores were safe and temporarily staying at an officer's home. Since the assailants had used rubber bullets, there were no fatalities on their side, but several officers were injured, all released except for himself. The assailants weren't so lucky – three had been killed and one was seriously wounded – he was still in surgery. The police station was still a crime scene with lots of broken glass but they were doing their best to continue working out of that facility.

"And oh," said the officer who was updating the Chief, "the Fire Chief wants you to call him." The Chief left word for his second in command, who had been acting as the interim Chief in his absence, to call or come see him right away.

The Fire Chief had finally left the scene of the morning's bombing and had returned to his home. When the Police Chief called, he was informed that after a thorough search of the rubble, they determined that one corpse was missing. Rachel had told them to look for four dead bodies that were housed in the storage coolers and they found only three.

"What!" exclaimed the Police Chief. "Which body was it?"

"Uh, the most recent one," the Fire Chief said slowly as it was obvious he was searching for the name on his list, "John Dorgan."

The Chief groaned and mumbled to himself, "It would have to be him." To the Fire Chief he asked, "How is that possible? Could he have been incinerated by the bomb?" The Fire Chief explained that all of the bodies were in the cold storage vault according to Rachel and that the entire steel vault survived the bombing.

Since the storage vaults holding the dead bodies, and the live body of Jonathon Moore, were basically undamaged, Dorgan's body should have been intact. The Chief hung up and sent word to Rachel, who was working in the morgue in the hospital basement, that he would like to talk with her at her earliest convenience. He also called to talk to the detective who hid Jon and Carol Moore at his home and asked him to find Bernie and bring him to the hospital for a talk as well. He wished he could talk with Heather Barnes, but that wasn't possible right now and perhaps never would be. He felt a twinge of guilt that he had not taken her to the hospital immediately once he knew she had been raped. As it now stood, they didn't have a clue where she and the Singers were taken or even if they were still alive. All they knew was that a private jet had taken them away within fifteen minutes of the abduction. But he needed answers as to what happened to John Dorgan, the perpetrator who was responsible for the deaths of two of his police officers and several other people.

The Chief closed his eyes and rubbed his temples. The past 48 hours had been a non-stop nightmare. The one good thing about getting shot was that he had gotten a couple of hours of much needed sleep, even if they were because he was unconscious.

A tap came on his open hospital room door and he looked up to see Rachel standing there. He smiled weakly, "Thanks for coming."

"How are you feeling?" asked Rachel.

"I'm fine," replied the Chief gruffly. "Just bruised and tired."

Rachel nodded, indicating her understanding and empathy. "I've been wondering why the assailants used rubber bullets. The MO the past few days has been to kill. Why do you think they changed tactics?"

"I've been trying to figure that out as well," replied the Chief. "Perhaps it's a different group of people after Heather and the others. Or perhaps it's the same group, but they don't want to kill the Moores and the Singers and therefore couldn't risk sending in troops with real bullets that could possibly hit one of them."

Rachel just nodded, but was deep in thought.

The Chief continued. "Speaking of the same group, have you

heard that our key suspect, John Dorgan's, body is missing from the morgue?" He waited for her reaction.

She lifted her eyes to his, the fatigue showing, and shook her head slowly. "That's impossible," she said in a low voice. "I put his body in the cooler myself." She was still shaking her head. "There must be a mistake."

"I don't think so." The Chief waited to see if Rachel had any other explanation to give. While he didn't really believe she could have anything to do with his disappearance, he knew it was possible and wanted to give her the opportunity to explain. He watched her closely, and waited. "Did you check his liver temp last night?"

It was obvious that Rachel was exhausted. Her movements, and speech, were slow. "No. I didn't do anything with the body but put him on a slab, still fully clothed. I was so tired and angry with him, actually, that I left him for Monday or Tuesday morning."

"Is it possible that someone broke in the morgue during the night and stole his body?" the Chief offered.

"I guess it's possible," Rachel replied. "But why, I wonder?"

"Maybe he thought he'd be blown to bits assuming he's the one who set up this morning's bombing of the morgue. He knew he might be killed and wanted to have his dead body sent back to his family in one piece so pre-arranged it."

"I guess." Several seconds of silence passed. "Or..." Rachel's voice now sounded more interested, more like herself, "or, maybe he wasn't even dead. He had someone rescue him during the night. He has used two rather sophisticated poisons to kill two people so far. Perhaps he used a drug on himself to mimic his own death."

The Chief could see that she was thinking more about that possibility. "But why would he risk it? Even though he probably knew I was backed up with autopsies, I still might have cut him open, or stuck the thermometer in his liver, or just decided to decimate his corpse because I'm so pissed at him!" They both laughed briefly as she added the last portion of her statement. "Really though, why would he risk actually dying and what would he have to gain by faking his death? No, you're right, the stealing the body in the night scenario makes more sense, even though it still doesn't make a lot of sense to me."

"None of this has made much sense to me, even though now

that I know about the implants, I can see why certain people would not want that information and evidence to become public knowledge," the Chief added.

An aid brought in a tray of food for the patient. He had been unconscious when lunch was served and when he awoke, famished, he had requested some food. "I haven't eaten since yesterday," the Chief mumbled as he began shoving meatloaf and mashed potatoes into his mouth. Rachel smiled as she watched him finish his meal in under two minutes.

The Chief's phone rang and he answered it. It was the detective who was keeping Jon and Carol at his house. "Hold on a moment," the Chief said to the detective. "You're welcome to stay if you like," he directed the comment towards Rachel, "but I don't have anything else for you right now."

He was glad that Rachel took his comment as her cue to leave, and she touched his arm and told him to get well soon, then left.

"Did you find Bernie?" the Chief asked the detective.

He scowled at the answer he heard. "No, Bernie is gone and apparently Jon and Carol Moore went with him. I can't find any of them, but I've put out an APB on Bernie's car since you still want to talk to him. We had told him he was free to go and we can't hold the Moores other than for their own safety."

"Shit!" growled the Chief. "I just heard that our prime suspect John Dorgan, who died last night, damn him, is missing from the morgue rubble. I thought this Bernie guy might have an idea as to what happened to him."

"Oh, that." The detective sounded a little embarrassed.

"What do you mean, oh, that!" shouted the Chief.

The detective cleared his throat. "Bernie said Dorgan is alive, and that he, Dorgan that is, was following him this morning."

"And when was someone going to tell me this!" The Chief was close to losing his temper. Even though he'd only been awake 40 minutes or so, that was plenty of time for someone to have updated him on such an important matter as John Dorgan being alive, he fumed.

"Murdoch knows," said the detective quietly. Murdoch was the officer in charge while the Chief was unconscious. "Everyone that can be spared is out looking for the guy."

"Okay. Not your fault. Murdoch hasn't been available yet."
The Chief shifted position in the hospital bed, groaning at the pain it
caused him.

The intruder at Jacob Barnes' house knew it would be futile to
try and lure Susan out of the safe room and made the assumption
that she would call her boyfriend Jacob. Barnes was his primary
target and he knew that eventually Barnes would return home. He
need only be patient and wait. So he left the bedroom for the second
time, closing the door behind him.

Unlike many operatives in his line of work, he did not work
alone, at least not for this assignment. His team consisted of one
woman and two other men, all well-trained assassins. As usual, he
did not know exactly which high level government official, or even
which branch of the government, ordered this hit. He only knew his
assignment and targets.

Since he had also made the assumption, and accurately so,
that there was a phone in the safe room and that Susan would call
the police, the team was ready when the police arrived only minutes
after Susan locked herself inside the safe room.

The woman on his team, now dressed in pajamas, came
running down the stairs just as the police knocked down the front
door.

"It's okay! It's okay!" she shouted towards them. "It's a false
alarm! I'm upset but fine. Thank you for coming; I was so scared!"

She continued to quickly walk towards them and extended
her hand. "I'm Susan Combs. It was a false alarm. I'm so sorry to
have made you come, and (she glanced at the broken front door and
made a face) to have caused damage to Jacob's house, but hopefully
he'll forgive me."

"So there was no intruder?" one of the officers asked.

"Oh, yes, there was, but it was just a friend of Jacob's.
Apparently Jacob lets him stay here on occasion when he's in town.
I, of course, didn't know this and the friend, likewise, didn't know
that I was here."

"Why would this friend come into the house in the middle of
the night?" one of the officers asked.

"Exactly!" the woman exclaimed loudly, raising her hands for emphasis. "I asked him the exact same question!" The police waited for her continued explanation.

"Apparently he parties with clients until the wee hours of the morning, then crashes here. Jacob gave him a key so he let himself in."

"Is the friend still here?"

"Yes, he went in the bathroom, I think; oh, there he is."

The leader of the group had quickly left Jacob's bedroom after Susan had locked herself in the safe room and changed from his Kevlar and black jacket and hood to a long sleeved polo shirt, anticipating the quick arrival of the police. His imitation of a somewhat drunken house guest was convincing as he walked down the steps. "Oh shit, you called the cops!" and he stopped in his tracks. "She told you guys I'm a friend, right?" When no one spoke, he continued. "Jake *never* has a woman here. I had *no* idea. I'm *so* sorry." He addressed the last comment to the fake Susan.

"No harm done," she said quietly, "well, except to the door."

The leader looked at the front door lying on the entryway floor. "Oh, man. Tell Jake I'll pay to have that fixed."

"I do think under the circumstances I will stay at a hotel the rest of the night," the fake Susan continued. She went on to explain to the police that right after she called 911, she called her boyfriend Jacob and he told her to turn on the intercom and ask who was there. She explained that Jacob stayed on the line and heard the voice of his friend, so she came out just a few minutes ago as they, the police, arrived.

The two assassins were very convincing. Their goal was to convince the police that all was well so that they wouldn't ask to see the safe room or ask to call Jacob to verify their stories. Either of these requests could lead to the agents having to kill the police officers, which would spoil the entire mission. Other police would swarm the house looking for the original two squad cars and four officers. The woman had just noticed that there were two squad cars outside, but only two officers inside. She surmised that the other two were checking the perimeter of the house. Would they be able to tell that the security system had been disabled, she wondered.

"Do one of you officers mind dropping me off at the nearest

hotel? I just need to change quickly." It would be an inconvenience to have to make her way back to this house in the dark, but it couldn't be helped.

"Are you sure?" said the man posing as Jacob's friend. "You can stay here and I can go to a hotel."

The woman held out her arm and hand towards the broken front door indicating she wouldn't stay in a house with no front door.

"Oh, yeah." He shrugged. "I'll just lock myself in the safe room!" he laughed.

The two officers seemed satisfied that all was well and told the woman they would wait while she changed. Two other police stepped in the doorway and relayed that there did not seem to be any signs of forced entry anywhere around the house.

They took the name and contact information of Jacob's friend, which he readily supplied, then the police left with Jacob's "girlfriend" in the back seat of their cruiser.

The AT&T store at Bridgewater Falls would not open for another hour. Jacob needed clean clothes and something to eat. He parked his stolen car with its occupied trunk in an empty restaurant parking lot and walked across several parking lots to a Panera Bread restaurant. He visited the men's room first to wash his face and hands and try to look more presentable in his torn and dirty clothes. He then ordered coffee and an egg and bacon bagel sandwich.

He wanted to call Susan, and Heather, but hesitated at using the woman's cell phone. He didn't want their numbers traced from her phone. Not that it really mattered. He was certain his identity was either already known or would be very soon as being a passenger in the wrecked helicopter. And soon, they would figure out that it was he who kidnapped this woman and stole her car, so why would it matter that he called his daughter and his girlfriend. He decided to do so, and just keep her phone, which might delay the call tracing for a short while.

He dialed Susan's cell number. She should be out of bed by now. It went to voice-mail, which he somewhat expected since she wouldn't recognize the calling number.

"Hi, hon, it's Jacob. I really miss you. I'm so sorry I had to leave you alone on the very first day of our week together. I promise I'll make it up to you. I'm not sure how long I'll be, but hopefully not long. Oh, I'm using someone else's phone right now. I should have mine back by noon or shortly thereafter. If you get this message right away, you can call me back on this number. I love you. Bye."

He started to call Heather and realized he didn't even know the last four digits of her number. It was programmed into his phone and he always just tapped her name or spoke to his phone..."call Heather." He only knew Susan's because it was new to him and he had memorized it the day she had given it to him.

Jacob felt guilty for not looking for his daughter in the woods instead of hijacking the car. He knew she couldn't be far from where his helicopter crashed. But he also knew he might be searching for hours without the exact coordinates which were in his laptop and phone, neither of which was currently available to him. He also knew that her captor was dead and that she was most likely okay. As soon as he got his phone, he would find her.

Jacob drank his coffee and ate his sandwich and thought about the recent events involving his daughter. For some reason still unknown to him, Heather was now involved in the initial Freedom Project, a project that the CIA officially terminated years ago but that its former project leader, John Dorgan, was still unofficially assigned to monitor. The murder of one of the three test subjects triggered not only Dorgan's involvement, which would be expected, but also Heather's involvement, which was totally unexpected and a mystery to him. As he knew would happen to anyone who learned of any of the nine Freedom Projects, and made that knowledge known, her life was now in danger. She had been arrested earlier for taking evidence, the implants from the murdered subject, then was abducted by a killer that Jacob recognized as a well known psychopath. Thank God the psychopath was killed before he had a chance to hurt Heather. Jacob truly hoped the man had not had a chance to hurt Heather. He did not know that for certain but could not bear to think about that possibility.

While Jacob did not know of everyone who hired this particular psychopath to torture then kill their targets, he knew of several people who did. Which one of them was not content to just kill his daughter but wanted her tortured? Wanted HIM tortured knowing that his daughter had been tortured? Surely the selection of this particular killer was about him - Jacob - and not about Heather.

Jacob realized he was squeezing his coffee cup tightly as the anger seethed up in him and he took a deep breath to calm himself.

He hardly knew Dorgan. Surely it's not him who has it in for me, is it? Jacob thought. While he was the most likely person to want to eliminate Heather if she was snooping around his project, he would just have her shot or poisoned.

He considered his boss, the Director of the CIA, as a close friend. The two played golf and poker together regularly and had lunch or dinner at least once a month. There was absolutely no way it was him.

He thought carefully about each Freedom Project committee member, both past and present. There were two he did not particularly care for and they most likely felt the same way about him, but he still could not remember any disagreement between them that would cause them to go to this extent.

To his knowledge, this current Homeland Security Secretary had never stooped so low as to use this madman killer.

As he took the last bite of his sandwich, it occurred to him that perhaps Heather's capture by this crazed killer had nothing to do with the Freedom Project at all but was due to another vendetta against him. That would broaden the suspect pool considerably.

Jacob checked his watch and ordered another sandwich and two bottles of water to go. He took a round about way to the parked car. Since the trunk was facing away from the stores and other parking lots, Jacob and his captive could not be seen when he opened the trunk.

"Here, I've brought you some water and a sandwich."

"Please let me go! You can have my car!" she pleaded. The woman's face was streaked with mascara from crying.

"What's your name," Jacob asked kindly.

"Barb," she sniffed.

"Barb, I need another hour or two and then I will let you go, you and your car. I promise. I do not intend to hurt you. I just can't have you calling the police before I finish what I need to do. Just stay quiet and try to relax and you'll be home soon." He spoke calmly and soothingly and noticed that the woman started to protest, but then just nodded her head.

Jacob shut the trunk once again, and headed for the JC Penney store to buy some new clothes.

Once Jacob's data downloaded onto his new phone, he saw that he had two voice-mails. Both were from the same number, which he recognized as his own safe room phone number. He listened to the voice-mails as soon as he left the store. He heard Susan's voice.

"If you get this message soon, and can call in to the phone in your bedroom safe room, please call me. I need to hear your voice! Someone broke in and shot at me! He tried to kill me!" Jacob could hear Susan's sobs. "Please call me as soon as you get this!"

This first message broke Jacob's heart. The second message froze it.

"Jacob, I know it's the middle of the night, but please, please wake up and call me. The police never came. I called them over an hour ago and they never came. I'm so scared. The man talked to me…he knew my name. He's after me, or you, or both of us. I hope you're okay…I hope they didn't get you." Jacob couldn't stand to listen anymore as she cried into the phone and he hung up and dialed his safe room number.

Susan answered immediately. "Jacob! Jacob, is it you?"

"Yes, honey, oh my God, I'm so sorry! Are you all right?" He tried to stay strong but his voice was shaking.

"I'm not hurt, but I'm scared to death. Where are you? I'm so glad you're okay."

"I'm still in Ohio looking for Heather but I'll come there right away. As long as you stay in the safe room, you'll be fine - no one can get in that room, I promise you." His voice softened. "I'm so sorry, Susan, I'm so sorry." He paused. "Is he still there?"

"I don't know. It's been quiet for a long time. A few hours ago I could hear some noise from downstairs through the intercom, but I haven't heard anything for several hours. Oh Jacob, he knew my name! He tried to get me to turn on the intercom to talk to him but I wouldn't. I didn't want to talk to him!" She was crying audibly and Jacob so badly wanted to be there and comfort her - and kill the bastard in his house.

"I'm on my way honey. Just sit tight. I'll call you again when I'm in the air, okay?"

"Hurry, please!" she pleaded. "And Jacob, I think there's more than one of them."

Bernie, Jon and Carol stopped at a gas station off Highway 129 before getting onto Interstate 75 to start their long drive to Washington, D.C. Jon was not at all certain that it was a good idea to travel to the very city where those wishing to kill them were located.

"We can't go home," Carol reminded him. "Not yet at least. And it wouldn't be wise to stay with relatives and put them in danger."

The gas station sold fresh donuts and they bought a half dozen, two coffees and a chocolate milk. Jon and Carol sat in the back seat and Bernie kept Heather's purse on the front seat beside him. Her phone was out in case Jeremy called or Bernie needed to call him. He had never used a cell phone while driving so planned to stop the car or give the phone to one of his passengers to answer if it rang. He decided to call Jeremy before leaving the gas station to let him know Jon and Carol were with him and that they were headed for D.C. Jeremy would be able to track them through the GPS on Heather's phone, he told them. Jeremy also had some news regarding the whereabouts of Heather, Mary Beth and Joe. Their plane appeared to be heading for Boston.

Jon, Carol and Bernie talked as they ate their donuts and drank their coffees and milk. It was a relief for them to know that Jon's ear implant was safely wrapped and encased and in the trunk of the car, and they could speak freely. Physically, Jon now felt great with the horrible screeching and buzzing noises gone from his head, but emotionally he, like the others, was a wreck and he couldn't enjoy his restored health. His mind was reeling. Who will run my business while I'm gone? What should we tell our children? Will we live to the end of the day?

By the time they reached I-71, which would take them north towards Columbus, Ohio, where they would turn east towards Pennsylvania, they all fell silent. Jon and Carol had stayed awake most of the night before, so both were tired and closed their eyes to try and rest. Bernie was surprisingly alert from his four hours sleep in his car and he began thinking about that morning's events. Sheila looked great in her church clothes and he lightly touched his cheek where she had kissed him.

Maybe she would be his girlfriend. She could move to D.C. and get a job at the café where he ate dinner every day and they could smile at each other. They wouldn't have to talk much during the forty-five minutes while he ate his dinner because he would get to talk to her later, for hours, after she got off work.

But what about Heather? Heather was his true love. He wasn't sure he wanted anyone else but her, even if she would probably never be his girlfriend. Still, he would call Sheila in a couple of days and thank her again for her help.

Bernie's thoughts changed from Sheila to the great idea that had come to him the night before when he was copying the Freedom Project file onto the flash drives. He knew it was a spy-worthy idea at the time and it had already paid off. He made up a decoy package with a blank flash drive and two silver watch batteries that closely resembled the implants and put those items into the silver case, which was the case Father Benjamin put into his safe and the case that the man who followed him to the church stole that morning.

Bernie had tried to think like a spy and prepare for every eventuality. He thought it was quite possible that someone could follow him or Heather to whichever trustee they decided upon, so planned accordingly. If Jeremy can watch their every move, so can others.

Fortunately, the man was caught and the fake file and evidence was in the custody of the Hamilton Police. Bernie knew Father Benjamin would find a very safe and secure place for the real evidence, also ensuring that should something happen to him that the evidence would be entrusted to someone else.

He knew Heather would be proud of him, wherever she was.

Jacob knew that he would not be able to access Heather's implant video from his phone. He wanted to make sure she was alright before he left Hamilton. He tried calling her but it went to voice-mail. "Honey, it's dad. Please call me right away."

He could, however, now access the longitude and latitude coordinates of Heather's last known position and he decided to make a quick trip back to the wooded area off 128. Perhaps she was still there.

He called in another favor to one of his CIA colleagues – a small jet and pilot to meet him in forty five minutes at the coordinates he gave, which was a field not far from where he was heading. He called the local hospital to check on the status of his first pilot and was informed that he was in good condition.

Jacob easily found the spot where his daughter had been. She was no longer there, but crime scene investigators were, so he immediately turned the car around and left. He hated to leave Hamilton without knowing where Heather was as he was certain that she was still in danger. He hoped he would be able to find her before he left.

It would be over a half hour before his "ride" would arrive. He began thinking of the people that Heather mentioned when he saw her being arrested. "Call Rachel and Jeremy," she had told the man in the room with her, whose identity was also a mystery to Jacob. He was fairly certain that Rachel was Rachel Curry, the local Butler County Coroner, and he called information to get her number. It was not listed.

He called his CIA friend again. "Bob, are you able to check the Homeland Security employee list at the Nebraska Avenue complex?" Bob informed Jacob that he could. "See how many Jeremys are listed."

Ten seconds later Bob replied, "Eighteen."

"Do any of them work in the same department or general area as my daughter?" Bob was well aware of Heather's position and status at DHS. "No, not that I can see."

Jacob thought for a moment. "What about working with John Dorgan in Intelligence and Analysis?"

"We have a winner," said Bob only seconds later. "Jeremy James, Surveillance Technician."

"Do you have a cell number for him?"

Bob gave Jacob the number. Jacob pulled the car off the road to a shady spot under a tree where he hoped poor Barb would be cooler in the trunk. He got out of the car, putting the keys under the floor mat, and walked to the rear of the vehicle.

"Barb?" No answer. "Can you hear me?"

"Yes," she said quietly.

"I just wanted to let you know I'm leaving now. I will call the police in about ten or fifteen minutes and let them know where you are and they will come and let you out. I'm really sorry to have put you through this, really I am."

She didn't reply.

"Barb, are you okay? Do you have enough water?"

"Yes, I'm okay. I just want out of here."

"As I said, the police will be here soon. You will be fine."

Jacob then walked along the road the short distance to where his plane would be arriving. As he walked, he dialed Jeremy James' cell phone number.

"Hello." The greeting was quick and curt.

"Is this the Jeremy James who works with John Dorgan at Homeland Security?" Jacob's voice was low and even, his words succinct and deliberate, his tone professional, not conversational.

"Yeah, who's this?" Still curt but now with caution.

"My name is Jacob Barnes. Do you know my daughter Heather?"

There was a brief silence. "Yes, I know her."

"Do you know where she is right now? I can't reach her on her cell and I think she may be in danger."

Slight pause. "Last I heard she was going on vacation with her boyfriend."

Jacob's monotone continued with a slightly more menacing tone. "She didn't go. She went to the same city where your boss is. Are you sure you don't know where she is."

"I'm sure." Dial tone.

"Little lying prick," Jacob said aloud. He then saw the plane approaching and called the Hamilton police from Barb's phone, sprinting the rest of the way to his ride home.

The 500 mile trip to Fairfax, Virginia took 75 minutes in the expensive small jet designed for speed and comfort. On the way,

Jacob formulated his plan to rid his home of the pests that currently plagued it and he called for needed resources. So far, none of the resources he requested yesterday or today was sanctioned or approved by the CIA. Once these were lined up, he called Susan to let her know he would be there in 30 minutes or so. She still hadn't heard any noise whatsoever and wasn't sure they were still in the house.

Ten minutes out, Jacob received a text with a video attached. It was a thermal image of the inside of his home. There were no warm bodies in his house other than Susan.

Jacob texted back asking for images of both neighboring houses. A few minutes later the next video came. It was of the large two-story home to the right of Jacob's property and Jacob knew that the owners were currently in Italy. The home should be vacant. The video, however, showed that two people were in the house, positioned in opposite corners of the home.

The video that came next was of Jacob's other neighbors, a sweet elderly couple. Three warm bodies were in this house, two of which appeared to be close together and not moving. Oh my God, thought Jacob. Did he hurt them? There was then a slight movement between the two and Jacob relaxed a little. He was sure the two were his neighbors, most likely bound and gagged by the intruder, but alive.

Further surveillance found another person in Jacob's pool house at the rear of his property.

"There are four of them," Jacob said to the pilot and he nodded. "I need to know which one is the leader."

The pilot landed at a nearby airstrip where he traded the jet for a fighter helicopter that was waiting for them. They were only a few minutes from their destination but Jacob wanted to watch more video to determine which of the two single operatives, the one in his pool house or the one with his neighbors, was the squad leader. He ruled out the two in the other neighboring house and felt fairly confident the leader was the one holding his two elderly neighbors hostage.

The helicopter landed and the pilot was waiting for Jacob's instructions. Jacob watched for a few minutes more the thermal image of the man he thought to be the leader - the one he believed had shot at and terrified Susan. He saw the man pull something from his side and tap on it. He was most likely sending a text message to the others. Jacob's contact confirmed that the other three appeared to look at their devices shortly afterwards.

Though not proof positive, Jacob was going with this man as being the leader. Too bad for him.

"You take the south house and the pool house," Jacob told the pilot and showed him the buildings on the map in relation to his house. The pilot had viewed the map before and was confident of the location of the buildings and the three individuals inside, none of whom had moved significantly from their original locations.

"Then stop on the rear lawn of the north house." Jacob jumped out of the chopper.

As the pilot lifted off again, Jacob took off on foot, watching the now streaming feed of the satellite image of the leader, watching his every move within the house. While the other three invaders were stationary, at least within one room, his target moved among three rooms - the kitchen, dining room and great room. Jacob was outside his neighbor's home within five minutes just as a quiet but deadly missile hit the first corner of his other neighbor's home. The missiles were new technology. They would easily penetrate the brick and other layers of building materials, leaving only a one inch circular hole, and explode a deadly gas once inside the building. The gas would kill any occupants within 50 feet in any direction, but would then dissipate quickly, leaving no trace.

The helicopter was on the other side of the house in seconds delivering the second missile. The pilot completed his duty by sending a third missile into Jacob's boat house. He received confirmation from Jacob's satellite contact that all three targets were down.

Jacob slipped in through a window in the lower master bedroom of the house and made his way down the hall. The intruder was in the kitchen and not in his view so he waited for the man to return through the dining room to the great room. The man stood looking out the window, for only a few seconds, but that was all the time Jacob needed.

Many men were stronger than Jacob, and younger and more powerful, but few were better trained. Jacob disarmed and immobilized the man quickly. The helicopter was now landing on the back lawn.

Jacob made sure the man could not move then quickly cut the ties from the wrists and feet of his neighbors, removing the hoods that had been placed over their heads. "Are you two alright?"

"Oh Jacob!" the woman cried when she saw him, with both fear and relief in her eyes. When they saw the man on the floor, tightly bound, the elderly man responded. "Yes, Jacob, we're okay. What's going on? How did you know we were in trouble?"

"I can't explain right now. I have to remove this trash," and he looked with contempt at the man on the floor, "but I'll be back to check on you later, okay?"

"Yes, yes, thank you!"

Jacob pulled the man to his feet and dragged him out the back door to the helicopter. He sat him on the ground by the vehicle.

"You have 60 seconds to tell me who sent you and why."

The man just sneered at Jacob and didn't say a word.

"It's your choice whether you die quickly and painlessly," he paused, "or *not*." He waited a few more seconds. "30 seconds."

If Susan was not terrified and waiting for him to rescue her, and if Heather was not God-knows-where in grave danger, he would interrogate and torture this man until he told him what he wanted to know. But alas, there was no time for interrogation.

"Pick Susan and me up at the other spot in fifteen minutes," Jacob told the pilot as he tied a bungee cord to the ankles of the man on the ground.

As Jacob ran towards his own house, to the front door which was conspicuously missing, the helicopter lifted off with a screaming man dangling upside down underneath.

Jeremy was very tired and now he was very scared as well. He had accessed and perused a top secret CIA file belonging to Jacob Barnes, the same file that Dorgan had been reading. The document was over 4000 pages long so he had read very little of it, but he had scanned through much of the document. Based on what he had seen so far, he knew that the information contained in the document would get anyone knowledgeable of its contents killed. There was no way Barnes or anyone else named in this document would risk letting the public know about these projects.

Even though Jeremy hadn't hacked into the file himself, but had used the username and password that Dorgan had used the day before, he knew his access to the document could now be traced by Barnes. It scared Jeremy to death and he wished he had never seen the incriminating file.

The document listed the names of every subject of every Freedom Project with the exception of the two most recent projects where the subjects were too numerous to document. In those cases, it listed the names of the children who had died from the vaccinations and documented all batch numbers of the vaccines as well as the pharmaceutical companies involved. Every Freedom Project committee member, every high level government official, every pharmaceutical and American Medical Association executive, everyone involved or associated with one of more of the projects was named. Several were now deceased and the report documented who had died of natural causes and who had been assassinated and by whom.

Most terrifying, however, was the most recent entry. At 7 a.m. that morning the names of Jon and Carol Moore, Joe and Mary Beth Singer, Rachel Curry and Bernie Kossack were documented as targets to be eliminated. There also was the recent order to blow up the morgue. Heather wasn't on the list, but then, she *was* his daughter. Why was she kidnapped last night if she wasn't on the list? Jeremy wondered. The initial attempt on her life, the car bomb, was by one of Dorgan's men, who also made the first two attempts on Rachel's life. This morning's bombing of the morgue, however, was not Dorgan. This document proved to Jeremy that it was Barnes. Perhaps the kidnapping was instigated by him to keep Heather away from the morgue and to scare her into going home and forgetting about this Freedom Project. He hired the worst psycho he could find to truly scare her into giving up this quest, knowing he would stop the killer before the man had a chance to harm her. But would Barnes take that chance? What if the man *had* hurt her or killed her? Or what if Jeremy had found her sooner and she had made it back to the morgue before the bombing?

Maybe Dorgan had pre-arranged last night's kidnapping.

Then, after reading this document, he changed his mind and had someone stop the killer.

Jeremy wasn't convinced of either of those scenarios. He did believe, however, that Dorgan's change of attitude was due to the CIA file. Anyone who read it would be appalled and sickened by its contents. It was after he had read parts of it and saw that Dorgan was being set up as the fall guy that he had decided to help Dorgan.

Another question bothering Jeremy was, if Heather's name wasn't on the list, why was she kidnapped again today with the Singers? Was Barnes or Dorgan trying to take her to safety? The fact that the attackers and kidnappers at the Hamilton police station used rubber bullets made Jeremy think it might be Dorgan running that operation. However, he had not seen or heard him give any such orders.

Perhaps Barnes *does* plan to have his own daughter killed, Jeremy thought, but chose not to document it.

He remembered a few hours earlier when his cell phone rang. Jeremy had been reading a few pages of Barnes' secret file when his phone chimed. It was as though the man could read his mind. It was Barnes on the other end of the line, or at least someone claiming to be Barnes. Jeremy wasn't about to tell this person, father or not, where Heather Barnes was.

Jeremy glanced at the monitor that showed Satellite Samuel following Dorgan. Samuel was capable of automatically tracking and following moving objects such as a commercial plane or ship as long as the satellite was remotely linked to the object while it was stationary. This tracking was so much easier since it was on auto pilot. Not so with automobiles; therefore, he had not been able to track the car of last night's kidnapper. A couple of hours ago, Dorgan had driven to the Cincinnati airport and Jeremy moved the satellite to follow the plane he boarded. The plane was headed for Boston and would arrive shortly.

Jeremy jumped when his cell phone rang again. He looked at the display. It wasn't Barnes again but one of his gaming buddies, the one he had let down by not participating in last night's tournament. His friends never called him at work, but it was Sunday. Owen most likely assumed Jeremy was home by now.

"Hey man," Jeremy answered.

"Hey, you home?"

"Nope. Still at work. How'd the tourney go? You guys win?" He chuckled, pretty certain they hadn't won without him.

"Really, Jeremy," Owen said sarcastically, but good-naturedly. "We were out after the first hour."

"Again, I'm really sorry." Jeremy paused, waiting for Owen to end the conversation as he was busy .

"But that's not why I called," Owen said cheerfully. "I'm sending you a link to a crazy YouTube video. It was posted about 30 minutes ago by some guy in a small plane and it's had over a million views already. It's really crazy. You need to see it. Sending to you right now."

"OK, thanks Owen, I'll check it out."

Jeremy could see that Dorgan was texting from his phone, but he couldn't read the phone's display.

Jeremy's phone pinged indicating he had a text and he opened the attached video. A man was hanging upside down from a helicopter, his body flying in different directions depending on which way the helicopter turned. The pilot flew over some trees and while the helicopter cleared the trees, the man did not. He smacked into them and was dragged through the treetops, exiting on the other side with the man still dangling.

Soon afterwards, the pilot maneuvered around a building, and the swinging man hit the corner of the building.

It was unclear whether this video was of a stunt man or of a pilot who was unaware someone was hanging from his helicopter. The other possibility, thought Jeremy, was that the pilot knew exactly what he was doing. The man was definitely alive when he was being dragged through the trees. Although the video was somewhat hard to follow as it was being taken by another moving object, a few fairly close shots of the man showed that he was screaming and moving his arms, which appeared to be tied together at the wrists. After hitting several buildings, the man was most likely no longer alive. The small plane taking the video had backed off and was recording from a greater distance.

The final few seconds of the video showed the man falling from the helicopter to the ground. He looked like a rag doll as he fell. Most likely most of his bones were broken before he hit the ground.

"Geez, that was bizarre," Jeremy said out loud.

"What was bizarre?" a voice said, causing Jeremy to nearly jump out of his skin. No one else was around today, at least not in his office.

Jeremy looked up at the tall figure standing in front of him. He knew the terror he felt showed on his face but he tried to maintain his composure. He knew the man from his picture in the CIA file.

It was Jacob Barnes.

There was no reason for John Dorgan to stay in Hamilton any longer. Mary Beth Singer, one of the project subjects, was on her way to Boston. Ideally, Jon Moore would have been on that plane as well, but the police had been somewhat prepared for the invasion and had managed to get Jon and his wife out. Dorgan knew where they were at the moment and would track Jon down later. It would no longer do any good to access Jon's implant video as he was keeping an eye patch over his right eye and his defective ear implant had been removed. He would have to get Jon's implants later – some other way.

The other man he sent to follow Bernie had been arrested after stealing Michtenbaum's implants. The man was a local thief and car-jacker and Dorgan had managed to find and hire him to follow Bernie and retrieve the package. The thief had texted Dorgan as soon as he arrived at St. Julie Billiart Church where his target had gone and Dorgan had walked the short distance from the hotel to the church to watch. He saw the police arrest his hired man, while Bernie and some woman stood by. So he was still without the Michtenbaum implants. They were most likely at the police station and he would have to retrieve those another time. He needed to get out of Hamilton and get to Boston. At least he would be able to get Mary Beth's implants after her surgery.

Dorgan had accessed Heather's government issued cell phone not only to track the GPS but to record and transmit any conversations from the phone, another nifty little trick now possible on smart phones. Thirty minutes earlier, Bernie had used the phone to call Jeremy. "...going to see Jon and Carol Moore," Bernie had told him. Dorgan was watching Heather's phone as it moved away from the residence where Jon and Carol were staying.

Dorgan drove towards the interstate to head for the Cincinnati airport. As he drove through downtown Cincinnati, another recorded call from Heather's phone came through to his iPad. It was Bernie calling Jeremy again. Bernie's voice saying "...Jon and Carol are with me...heading for D.C. to my sister's house" and Jeremy telling Bernie "...plane appears to be heading for Boston."

Dorgan still did not understand why Bernie, the file clerk, and Heather, the assistant to the top DHS leader, were in Hamilton and involved in a decades-old secret government experiment or why his employee Jeremy James was watching and helping them. He didn't think the three of them even knew each other. Well, he thought, if we all manage to live a few days longer, I will have to ask them.

Heather had flown to Boston many times and recognized Logan Airport when the plane carrying her, Mary Beth and Joe touched down. A limousine was waiting by the plane when it taxied to a stop and they were quickly moved from the plane to the car. Heather thought about screaming as soon as she exited the plane in order to attract the attention of airport workers or passengers staring out the windows, but she thought better of it and remained silent.

Joe held Mary Beth's hand for the limo ride, which lasted only ten minutes. The three looked at each other with puzzled expressions when they arrived at a large medical center in the middle of town, bustling with activity – not exactly a place you would pick to hide three kidnapped adults.

The three were escorted by two of their captors into the facility and onto an elevator. One of the men used a key to select their floor. The elevator opened into a well lighted hallway and the three of them were deposited into an attractive apartment.

"You'll be staying here for a little while so make yourselves comfortable," said the man.

After the men left, Joe tried the door. "Locked," he said, stating the obvious. The three walked around to examine their temporary home.

"There's a bedroom in here," Mary Beth called as she opened a door and went inside.

"And the bathroom is here," Joe had opened the other door on the same wall.

Heather found fresh clothes in a closet. She excused herself to take a shower. She was still a dirty mess from spending the night lying on the ground, but mostly she felt dirty inside, which no amount of hot water and scrubbing could cleanse. For the most part, she had remained strong and in control the past few hours but now, alone in the shower, she allowed herself to cry over the horrible violation done to her. Would she be okay, or had her body been damaged beyond repair? Not only was she cut and sore inside, her head, shoulders and arms were bruised from the battering against the tree, and her back was scraped and cut. She cried more as she remembered all she had endured last night.

The hot water felt good and Heather's muscles and mind began to relax. She was able to think beyond the previous two days, which had been the most harrowing and terrifying of her life. Why were they in Boston and what was going to happen to them? It certainly seemed that they were not going to be killed, at least not soon. Why fly them to another city, provide them with a limousine, apartment, new clothes and food if the end game is going to be death?

Heather let the water flow over her for 30 minutes before she finally dried off, dressed in fresh clothes and brushed her teeth. She felt much better. She looked around the apartment more carefully. There were no windows. She tried the door once more but it was locked from the outside. She looked through the cabinets and refrigerator in the small kitchen. It was fully stocked with a variety of food and drinks. "I'm going to make coffee," she called to Mary Beth and Joe.

The three sat and sipped their coffee for the next half hour, holding their collective breath each time they heard footsteps in the hallway. They jumped at the sound of a man's voice, seemingly coming from inside the room. "Mr. and Mrs. Singer and Miss Barnes, please prepare for a visit in ten minutes." The message was repeated a second time.

There was no use speculating as to what the visit was about, who would be coming for them or what they would want. So the three of them sat nervously, quietly, until they heard a quick knock on the door, a courtesy only. The door opened.

Two men entered the room, both in white coats. Both were smiling and friendly, shaking their hands and asking how they were. Heather, Mary Beth and Joe relaxed a little.

When the older man, whom Heather guessed to be around 80, introduced himself as Dr. William Banks, Heather gasped. That name was fresh in her memory. He looked at her curiously and then knowingly and she noticed that his eyes were warm and kind and his smile genuine. Despite what he had done, she found herself liking the man.

The other doctor introduced himself as well and the two explained that they were going to surgically remove the implants from Mary Beth. They explained exactly what the procedure would entail and how long it would take. They answered all of Mary Beth's and Joe's questions about the surgery.

Dr. Banks added, "As Heather knows and perhaps the two of you have also concluded, I am the doctor who put these devices in you, Mary Beth, on the night you were born. I'm sorry for that. I want you to know that I had no choice." He bowed his head. "I had a young wife and daughter at the time."

Mary Beth nodded her understanding, unable to speak, tears in her eyes. Heather wasn't sure what to say, so stayed silent. Joe spoke up first. "Do you know who brought us here? And what is going to happen to us once the surgery is over?"

"I received a call early this morning from the Secretary of Homeland Security," Banks explained.

"What?" Heather was shocked at this news.

"Yes, although I do not know her personally. I understand you work for her."

"Yes." Heather was confused. How could her boss be involved in this? Did Jeremy tell her? "Are you sure it was her? Perhaps it was a woman claiming to be Rhonda Watterson."

"We talked via FaceTime. I could see her as well as hear her. It was definitely her. I've seen her on TV many times." Banks was patient as he knew they needed answers and reassurance. "She said she was sending someone today to bring you back to Washington safely, after your surgery of course," and he looked at Mary Beth. "I assume they will send you and your husband home after that. She didn't give me any details," Banks concluded.

After a few moments of silence, the younger doctor interjected, "Mary Beth, if you're ready, you can come with me and we'll prep you for your surgery."

Joe went with his wife and the younger doctor, leaving Dr. Banks and Heather alone in the room. She offered him coffee, which he accepted.

As he reached for the cup, he said to her, "Heather, I want to talk to you about something else as well, something I'm sure you don't know and are not going to like."

Heather cried uncontrollably for twenty minutes after Dr. Banks left. Implants! Inside her! Smaller ones, better ones, ones with GPS tracking! Oh my God!

Heather's only question to Dr. Banks had been "did my father know about this?" Dr. Banks had shook his head and said he didn't know, but a brief flicker of his eyes gave him away. Her father knew. She couldn't stop crying at that thought.

Dr. Banks asked her if she wanted him to remove the implants today. He had not known she was coming and had not planned the surgery so would have to make arrangements quickly, he told her. Could she be ready in 30 minutes or so. "Yes!" she shouted.

He told her he remembered that day, over 29 years ago, when he performed surgery on the beautiful baby daughter of Jacob Barnes, whose mother had died shortly after the baby's birth. "You were my last implant surgery. I never did another one after you. I hoped that was because they stopped doing the experiments and not because newer technology eliminated the need to perform individual surgeries."

Thirty minutes later, a nurse came to get Heather to prepare her for surgery.

Barnes did not have another laptop computer at home. His

laptop was currently in the custody of the Hamilton, Ohio, Police Department, most likely broken. Even if intact, there was no way they could get into any files or programs on the laptop - he wasn't worried about that - but it meant he no longer had access to the program that would allow him to find his daughter.

He had rescued his new girlfriend, the love of his life, Susan, and had taken her to a safe house in D.C., where he assigned two agents to watch and protect her around the clock. He wished he could have stayed with her for a longer period of time, to comfort her, and to try and restore a sense of calm and balance to himself, so important to him now that he was planning a new life. The past sixteen hours were of his past life, his secret life, the one he was ready to leave. But he couldn't leave until he found his daughter.

He couldn't go to his office to access Heather's implant file as there was always the possibility of internal monitoring of computer activity. He never accessed the Freedom Project files from his office, especially not Heather's file. She was not even known to be a test subject by those who were privy to the identity of all test subjects. There were only three living people who knew Heather Barnes had four government implants inside her. He wanted to keep it that way if possible.

He knew Jeremy James of Homeland Security had lied to him on the phone that morning. After checking Heather's phone for all incoming and outgoing calls, he had seen several to and from the same number, which turned out to be James. I need to go pay him a visit, decided Jacob, and thirty minutes later, he was granted access to the Homeland Security building on Nebraska Avenue and was standing in front of a twenty-something year old computer tech watching a video on his phone.

Jeremy got over his shock of seeing Jacob Barnes standing in front of him long enough to push his "panic button" to simultaneously shut down his eight computer screens. He stared at Barnes, having scooted on his computer chair as far to the other end of his workstation as he could, waiting for Barnes to make the first move. He noticed that Barnes crinkled his nose and looked at the makeshift chamber pot situated behind Jeremy. Yes, it probably does stink a bit in here, thought Jeremy.

Nervous, Jeremy finally broke the silence. "You're Heather's father." It was more a statement than a question.

"Yes. And you're Jeremy James, I assume."

Jeremy nodded.

"I'm still trying to find my daughter, as I told you on the phone earlier; and I believe you know where she is." He paused to give Jeremy time to think about his answer.

"How do I know you're really her father?" What Jeremy wanted to say was how do I know you're not planning to kill her when you find her, you murdering bastard, but that didn't seem the appropriate thing to say to a father, or to a murdering bastard who was currently standing in front of you.

"You seemed to recognize me just now, so I assume you know what I look like. However, feel free to run my face through your software if you wish. You'll get confirmation quickly."

Mainly to buy some time to think, Jeremy said he'd like to do just that and he snapped a quick photo of Jacob on his phone. He fed it into his facial recognition software. A fairly recent CIA photo of Jacob Barnes came back within seconds. Not enough time to think.

Jeremy nodded slowly. "I don't know who to trust," he said meekly.

"Neither do I," Barnes replied. He took a deep breath and let it out slowly. "Listen, I think you already know my daughter is in grave danger. I know someone tried to kill her last night - not only kill her, but torture her." He choked a little on the last two words. "Thank God the man was killed and she got away. I now know she was kidnapped this morning from the Hamilton, Ohio, police station."

Jeremy started to ask how he knew these things, but he realized it would be easy for almost anyone to find out that information, and *very* easy for someone like Jacob Barnes to find out that information. So instead, he asked, "Have you talked to Heather in the past two days?" Surely, if the two of them were close, Heather would have called her dad for help.

Jacob nodded slightly, indicating he knew what Jeremy was asking. "I last talked to Heather early Thursday evening. She told me she was leaving on vacation Friday but wanted to talk to me about something. She said it could wait until she got back. I didn't think anything more of it. Saturday evening when I got home I discovered that Heather had been at the house and had looked at an old CIA file I had, a highly confidential, top secret government project file. I then wondered if that was what she wanted to talk to me about."

Jeremy was keeping a careful eye on Jacob as he spoke and noticed that Jacob was watching him closely as well. He had mentioned the top secret file. Was he trying to ascertain what Jeremy knew?

"My first thought was, why in the world would she have looked at that file? Do you know the one I mean?"

Jeremy had to make a decision, fast. He could admit he knew about the Freedom Project, only the initial one, the one involving Michael Michtenbaum and the other two subjects. Or he could feign ignorance of the project, which he was sure Barnes would be able to see right through.

"Yes, Dorgan assigned me to watch three people when I started working here, just via satellite, but when one of them, Michael Michtenbaum, was murdered, I found out about the Freedom Project."

Barnes continued. "I figured something must have happened with the experiment that brought attention to it, even though I still can't figure out why Heather would hear about it or what she would have to do with it. When I couldn't get hold of her Saturday evening, I called her boyfriend. He said she went to a funeral in Ohio."

Jeremy knew the answer but figured Barnes would expect him to ask the question; "Why would you have had a file on this experiment?" then he also added because he wanted to know, "and why would Heather even know you had it?"

"May I sit?" Barnes sighed.

Jeremy said he could use a high stool so that they could stay on their respective sides of the computers and still see each other.

"You know I'm CIA?" asked Barnes, and Jeremy nodded.

"For a brief time, I was the project leader for this particular experiment; then it was turned over to your boss, John Dorgan, whom I assume you also know used to be with the CIA." Again Jeremy acknowledged that he knew this. "I had the original file from the 1960s. I wasn't with the agency then, of course, but I inherited the file when I took over the project." Barnes got a pained look on his face. "Heather actually saw the file once when she was fourteen years old. I'll never forget that day as long as I live..."

After telling Jeremy an abbreviated version of the story of that day fifteen years ago, he continued by telling him why John Dorgan was still in charge of this project, even though he was no longer CIA and the experiment was no longer considered active. "Once a project of this security level, the highest security level, is terminated, the project leader is still responsible for its monitoring, albeit infrequent or sporatic as it may be without funding, but more importantly, for its continual secrecy and the protection of any persons involved, until either the Project Leader dies or everyone involved is dead."

Jeremy had not known any of this information. That certainly explained why Dragon left immediately for Ohio once learning of Michtenbaum's death.

"I know your boss, John Dorgan, mainly by reputation, and I know he will do whatever he must do to keep the project a secret." Barnes emphasized *whatever*. "When I heard about the police killings and about the attempts on the coroner's life, and then knew that Heather had gone to Ohio as well, I knew that I must go and get her. I knew she would be in danger and I was right. He tried to have her killed last night. And now she's been kidnapped. There have been several other murders in Hamilton, the morgue was blown up, all of which are related to this project and to John Dorgan. He tried to kill me and my girlfriend last night as well."

Jeremy could not reveal to Barnes why he was so afraid of him and why he did not trust him. He knew Barnes hadn't mentioned that while Dorgan took over as leader of Freedom Project I, Barnes was still the leader of the other eight Freedom Projects, numbers II through IX. He could not tell him that he had seen the 4000 page file, Barnes' file, which told of the many Freedom Project atrocities, the many murders committed because of these projects, the notes explaining how Dorgan would be set up to be killed, the order to have the morgue bombed, and the most chilling notes of all - the names of everyone, except Heather, who knew about the project and were to be terminated. At that moment, he realized that his own name had not been on the list but would surely be added now.

Jeremy was sure that Barnes saw the look of fear that crossed his face.

"So how did you get involved in this? Are you and Heather friends?" Barnes asked.

"Not exactly," Jeremy replied cautiously. "I know her from work, that's all."

When Jeremy didn't offer anything further, Jacob began to lose patience. "Jeremy, I need to know where my daughter is so I can get her to a safe place until Dorgan is captured. I know you know where she is or how to track her and I truly don't understand why you won't help me when you know she's in danger."

Jeremy tried to sound innocent and convincing. "Mr. Barnes, I really don't know where she is. I lost her after the kidnapping. They put her on a plane, I know that much, but then I lost her."

"Then why has she called you three times today already," Jacob snapped.

Jeremy was taken aback for a moment but knew the truth would help him in this case since it wasn't Heather, but Bernie, who had called him from Heather's phone. The truth, however, could hurt Bernie, Jon and Carol. But he had to tell Barnes something. "Heather doesn't have her phone. It was in her purse, which was left behind at the police station when she was kidnapped." He didn't offer who had Heather's phone. Jeremy also realized that Barnes must not be able to track the GPS in the phone or he would know it was at this moment traveling east on Interstate 70 in Ohio, heading for Pennsylvania.

"I've tried to call her several times and no one has answered. Obviously, you are communicating with someone on her phone, and I greatly doubt it is the police as I know they would *love* to talk to me and wouldn't ignore my calls." He raised his voice to a more ominous tone. "Who has Heather's phone, Jeremy. And where is Heather? Tell me now!"

"If you're going to kill me, just get it over with!" shouted Jeremy, jumping up from his chair. "Stop torturing me!"

Jacob opened his mouth, seemingly dumbfounded. "What! Why would I want to kill you?" Then Jacob's tone changed and he eyed Jeremy suspiciously. "Unless you're working with Dorgan. Are you helping Dorgan?" he almost shouted.

"No!" Jeremy screamed, assuming he meant helping Dorgan kill people. Then he realized he was sort of helping Dorgan, or at least he wasn't hindering him in any way. "No," he said more calmly. "I'm just following him. Secretary's orders."

"How long have you been following him?" asked Barnes, again sounding surprised.

"Since Friday morning." Jeremy sat down again and waved an arm at his blank and unresponsive semi-circle of flat screen monitors and added rather dejectedly, "but I've most probably lost him now. He was in a plane and I had eyes on him when you walked in, but he will be gone by now."

Jeremy was not about to tell Barnes that Dorgan was in Boston, where Heather and the Singers also were. While he still didn't completely trust Dorgan and wanted to watch him, he trusted Barnes even less and decided it was best to pretend to have lost both Heather and Dorgan.

"Then, by all means, get back to work and find him!"

Dorgan's flight arrived in Boston and he took a taxi to the large medical center where his three kidnappees were taken. He had flown under his false name of Marcus Stone. He didn't know if Jeremy, or someone else, was still following him via satellite, but he would proceed as if they were. Not that it would change what he planned to do.

He had kept an eye on the Hamilton, Ohio, on-line news throughout the day and there had not been any public announcement of a missing body from the morgue. He was certain the police had to know by now that his body was not in one of the cold storage units that had survived the morning's blast. Would they realize he was not dead or would they think his body had been stolen? He hoped he was still considered dead, although he wasn't worried about the police finding him. Others, yes.

The patient that Dorgan had come to retrieve was still in surgery. He had called in a favor last night to Rhonda Watterson before taking the chemical to slow his heart to ensure that the best doctor in the country was in Boston and ready to remove Mary Beth

Singer's implants.

Dorgan was met at the door by his contact and escorted to a viewing room where he could watch the remaining portion of the surgery. It was almost over and he was told the eye implant, the most difficult part of the surgery, was complete and went well. There was a man in the viewing room whom Dorgan recognized as Mary Beth's husband, Joe. Heather was not there.

Dorgan nodded at Joe but then asked his contact if they could speak in the hall. "Do you know where the other woman is - Heather Barnes? I expected her to be here as well."

"She's in surgery with Dr. Banks," the man replied. "They just started an hour ago, so that one may take a while longer."

"What do you mean, she's IN surgery? Is she watching another surgery?"

"No," the man replied. "I mean she's being operated on."

"Oh, no!" Dorgan said loudly, then caught himself as a nurse down the hall stopped to look at him. He spoke more quietly, but with irritation in his voice. "There's been a mistake - she's not the other test subject. And Dr. Banks! Why is he here? Banks shouldn't be performing any more surgeries - the man is almost a hundred years old, for crissake!"

The man did not seem shaken by Dorgan's comments.

"First of all, I assure you that Dr. Banks is still very capable of performing the most delicate operations. His eyes are perfect, his hands are steady and his mind is sharper than anyone I know. You don't have to worry about him. And there is no way he would perform a surgery on someone who didn't need it. Perhaps it is for another reason."

"Let's go find out," barked Dorgan.

The other operating room in which Dr. Banks was performing his surgery did not have a viewing room beside it and the two men could not see inside, nor were they permitted to go in. There was no one at the door to keep them out and briefly Dorgan considered just walking in and talking to Banks from the doorway but decided against it. He asked a nearby nurse if it would be possible to get a note to Dr. Banks. "It's very urgent I speak with him right away," he said.

The nurse seemed to know Dr. Banks and to be familiar with

what he would or would not permit. She said she could call him over the intercom in the room. "Please tell him I'm with Homeland Security and I must speak with him right away."

"May I give him your name?" the nurse asked.

"Tell him I'm here with the authority of Rhonda Watterson, Head of Homeland Security."

Several minutes went by and Banks had not yet come out of the operating room. If he was holding an eyeball in his hand, thought Dorgan, it might be difficult for him to get away right that moment.

Dorgan was a little surprised that this fairly young woman knew Dr. Banks. "Is Dr. Banks here often?" he asked her. "I thought he was retired," he quickly added.

"Dr. Banks is retired and no longer officially affiliated with the hospital, but occasionally he will request the use of our facilities. He's a genius, you know, and sometimes, like today I guess, someone has requested only him."

"Do you know what operation he is performing?" Dorgan thought he would find out what else she knew.

The other man, his contact, shot Dorgan a frown, meaning stop talking to this woman about this subject.

"I have no idea," she replied. He basically just rents our surgery rooms and equipment, but he brings his own staff. The hospital isn't involved from a medical standpoint."

Dorgan knew once Banks came out, he would have to talk to him out of earshot of this nurse. There were doors to the outside of the hospital about 30 feet down the hallway with a vestibule. It was as good a place as any.

It was half an hour before Banks emerged from the operating room, pulling off his mask and gloves and throwing them in a hazardous waste receptacle. He did the same with his coat, which had blood on it.

Dorgan nodded at Banks without saying a word, indicating that he should follow him down the hall. Once they were in private, he introduced himself.

"I'm only a third of the way through this surgery. I need to get back to it right away. May I ask what this is about?" Dr. Banks said calmly.

Dorgan got to the point. "I'm very familiar with your part in the past experiments with the implants. I knew your colleague would be operating today on Mary Beth Singer to remove her implants, but this woman, Heather Barnes, was not one of the test subjects. You shouldn't be operating on her."

The doctor looked at Dorgan and smiled. "Heather is Jacob Barnes' daughter, right?"

Dorgan nodded, "Yes."

"You should ask him why I am operating on his daughter." He turned to walk away and Dorgan grabbed him by the arm.

"I'm asking you," he said firmly.

Dr. Banks sighed. "You know there have been more subjects than just the original three?" It was a question.

"Yes, many more," confirmed Dorgan. The truth then hit Dorgan before the doctor could make the next statement.

"Heather was one of the subjects of a later experiment, so I'm fixing one of my past mistakes today."

Dorgan was stunned. He had read every name of every project test subject in the top-secret file of Barnes that he had hacked into. Heather's name was not on it. Did Barnes even know that Heather had these implants?

Dr. Banks had already turned again to head back to the operating room.

"How much longer on this surgery?" Dorgan called to him.

"About three hours," Banks called back.

Dorgan decided against waiting with Joe Singer in the recovery room after Mary Beth's surgery and chose instead to spend the next few hours in a nearby visitors lounge with a vending machine turkey sandwich, a cup of coffee, his laptop and cell phone. Once Heather was awake after her surgery, he would meet with all three of them to explain that he was taking them back to D.C. per orders of the DHS Secretary. He knew he would have a tough time convincing Heather since she most likely believed he tried to kill her. Technically, he did try to kill her, but that was yesterday. Today was Plan B - he wanted to save her. And he needed to retrieve the implants - two sets of them now.

He was stunned at the news that Heather was part of one of the later Freedom Projects - one that implanted devices in both of the eyes and both ears, each equipped with tracking capability. Jacob Barnes would be able to know exactly where his daughter was at all times, as well as what she was doing. Surely he would know she was here, in Boston, the current home city of Dr. Thomas Wilhelm and his protégé Dr. William Banks, and that she was with Mary Beth and Joe Singer; that is, if he knew about Heather's implants. Why hadn't he interceded and tried to stop them from coming here? Why was he letting these operations take place? If Barnes, indeed, was the man behind the bombing of the morgue, thought Dorgan, then he doesn't want anyone alive that knows about any of the Freedom Projects. And his own daughter now knows of at least two of them. Dorgan thought that there were some answers in Barnes' CIA file.

It would take days, if not weeks, to thoroughly read the 4000 page document that he now had backed up on his cloud then deleted off his hard drive. He no longer cared that such a breach of security, if found, would cost him his job and probably his life, but he couldn't risk continued hacking into Barnes' CIA files. He had password protected the file on a separate cloud service and put a failsafe program in place to erase the document should the wrong password be entered three times.

He sat in a comfortable leather chair in a corner of the room and continued reading where he had left off that morning.

An hour passed, then two, with Dorgan completely engrossed in reading the document on his laptop. Suddenly a pop-up box appeared on his screen, interrupting his task. "President assigned Dr. Randall Thyssen to take over FP effective in 3 months." There was an "acknowledge" button within the box and Dorgan clicked it. The box and message disappeared.

"Hmmm," murmured Dorgan. "Jeremy must have succeeded in hacking into the President's documents." He was impressed at the talents, and the balls, this young man possessed. He rather regretted not being friendlier to him the past four years. But no time for regrets now.

"Thyssen." He was remembering their brief meeting Thursday morning and how he took an instant dislike to the young Director of Clandestine Services. So that's how he knew about

Freedom Project I. And that's why the President or director sent him to tell me about Michtenbaum, Dorgan thought. Dorgan knew Jeremy had accessed Rhonda Watterson's files and had not found anything incriminating, but he had not received any word about whether Jeremy had been successful in hacking into the CIA Director's secure files.

"So which of them is out to get me?" Dorgan said aloud. Barnes? Thyssen? The Director of the CIA? The President? Perhaps all of them? His money was still on Barnes although he knew that most likely someone above him ordered it. He had already decided that Rhonda was not the one who wanted him dead. They had a long telephone conversation on Saturday evening and his gut told him it wasn't her.

Dorgan closed down the document he was reading and switched his thoughts to the political ramifications of change of leadership of the Freedom Projects.

It had been a long time since he had used his serious hacking skills but the situation called for it. He hoped he was at least half as good as Jeremy James at maneuvering satellites and other spying paraphernalia.

Heather opened her eyes to see Dr. Banks standing over her. He smiled at his patient who had come through the surgery with flying colors. Since she had confided in him about her recent rape, he made certain she was thoroughly examined and her injuries treated by an attending gynecologist while she was still under the anesthesia. She would need to spend a couple of hours in the recovery room. The implant removals, though very delicate and invasive, did not require a lengthy recovery at all. Heather might have a little discomfort, but could see, hear and otherwise go about her normal life as soon as the anesthetic had completely worn off and her vitals were stable. Her injuries from the rape, however, might prove more problematic.

"How are you feeling?" he asked her.

"Groggy, but otherwise good," she replied, trying to sit up.

"No, no, stay lying down for a little while. A nurse will be here shortly to check your blood pressure and respirations." He went on to tell her that the operation went well and she would be better than new. He winked at the last comment.

"Where are the implants?" Heather asked in a slow, sleepy voice. "May I have them?"

"Of course. I'll get them for you." Dr. Banks looked at Heather, his smile gone. "I believe there might be tracking devices in each of them which are still operational. Keep that in mind. Also, a man claiming to be from Homeland Security is here. He said he is to take you and the Singers back to Washington, D.C., as soon as you feel well enough to travel."

The hair on Heather's neck and arms rose and she became instantly alert. "What does he look like?"

"I thought you might want to know, so I asked the nurse to take a picture of him on her cell phone." He held up the nurse's phone and Heather saw the photo of a man she thought was dead - John Dorgan.

Barnes walked around from the front of Jeremy's partitioned cubicle to the side. "I need to go in Dorgan's office," he told Jeremy. "I need to use his computer."

Jeremy knew he was asking him to open the office. "I don't have access to his office but I know he took his laptop, so it isn't in there."

Jeremy had only begun to look for Dorgan again, or at least pretend he was looking for Dorgan again. He had no intention of finding Dorgan, Heather, or anyone for Barnes.

"Do any of your computers here," and Barnes nodded towards the row of monitors at Jeremy's workstation, "have Ebicon II software? I need to access a site and need that software to do so." Jeremy was quite familiar with the software - it was required to access the Freedom Project implant video recordings.

Jeremy thought quickly about the ramifications of letting Barnes use one of his computers, several of which had the software on it that Barnes needed. Jeremy knew that Barnes would not be able to find Jon since his ear implant had been surgically removed and he wore a patch over his right eye. And, he had been watching and listening to Mary Beth's site and something was going on with hers as well. He was able to hear voices for a while, but not any longer. And her screen was completely black. So if Barnes wanted to find Heather or Dorgan or any of the others by tracking one of those two, he would get nowhere. And neither of them had any GPS devices on them, so he wouldn't be able to track them that way either. And, he reasoned, if he let Barnes use his computer, he could track his keystrokes afterwards and know what he had accessed, which could prove very beneficial. He decided to let him use one of the laptops.

"I have Ebicon II on this one. It's needed for my facial recognition and a few other secure websites." He thought it best not to come right out and offer the use of his laptop to Barnes, since so far he had been quite uncooperative. But he knew the admission that he had the software was enough of an invitation for Barnes to come into his workspace and ask to use the computer.

"Wow, it kind of stinks back here. Do you mind emptying that pot while I use your computer?"

Jeremy would have liked to have watched him, but knew Barnes couldn't access any of his other computers. He had them all on shut-down and only he knew how to turn them back on, which he proceeded to do with the one laptop, also activating the keystroke software while he was at it.

"Sure," was all he said, knowing Barnes wanted him out of there. He could really use a break anyway and he badly wanted to be away from Barnes. He grabbed his cell phone and the makeshift toilet.

As soon as he was down the hall and around a corner, Jeremy accessed his keystroke software program from his phone. He wanted to know immediately what Barnes was doing. For a few seconds, nothing was being entered, so Jeremy continued down the hall towards the men's room, phone in one hand in front of his face, chamber pot in the other hand, as far from his face as he could get it. He watched as letters began to appear on the screen of his phone. "Oh God!" he cried out loud and dropped the pot in the middle of the hall, spilling its smelly contents. Jeremy just wanted to get out of the building and away from Barnes. He turned the pot upside down over the mess in the hall and ran towards the stairs and out of the building as fast as he could. He ran across the street and behind the shelter of a doorway of a building where he could stop and think, and see the entrance to the Homeland Security building.

Barnes had entered the username barnesheatherm17225. Heather! Could it be? thought Jeremy. Did Barnes have implants placed in his own daughter that he was now accessing? Barnes was even more of a monster than Jeremy had thought. He leaned forward to catch his breath and try to decide what to do. Should he call the Secretary and let her know that he was in way over his head now? He would need to tell her he had lied to her. Well, not so much lied as withheld certain truths. He hadn't told her Dorgan was still alive and that he had given Dorgan the identity of Michael Michtenbaum's killer, which she had specifically told him not to do. He hadn't told her that Heather, her key right hand person, was involved in this mess from day one and was in grave danger. He hadn't told her another Homeland Security employee, Bernie, was just as involved. He hadn't told her he had been somewhat involved in the Freedom Project every day since he was hired, but his boss Dorgan had told him not to tell *anyone*. But now he needed to tell her the true culprit was Heather's father, who was currently sitting in the Homeland Security building, accessing Freedom Project information from Jeremy's own computer.

Jeremy couldn't actually view from his phone what Barnes was seeing on his computer monitor. He was only able to see Barnes' keystrokes. He would have to wait until he got back to his office to check the recorded video to see what Barnes was viewing and try to tell if Barnes was able to figure out that Heather was at a prestigious medical center in Boston.

More keystrokes showed that Barnes was now accessing some of Heather's recorded video. He entered that day's date, two p.m. Jeremy thought quickly to remember where Heather would have been at that time. She was kidnapped from the police station at precisely 11:10 a.m., and the plane that took her to Boston landed at approximately 1:45 p.m. At 2 p.m., she would have been en route to the medical center.

Within minutes Barnes changed the time to 2:30. By that time, Jeremy thought, Heather and the Singers were inside the medical center. Jeremy was keeping an eye on the door to the Homeland Security offices - the door that Barnes would most likely use to leave the building, which Jeremy hoped would be soon.

Almost an hour passed without any new keystrokes being entered and Jeremy began to wonder if Barnes was still on his computer. He had barely finished that thought when Jeremy's phone pinged and he watched the screen as Barnes logged out. Within five minutes, Barnes exited the building, hailed a cab and headed southeast on Massachusetts Avenue.

As soon as the cab was out of sight, Jeremy went back to his office. He stopped first to clean up the mess in the hallway, then went to the men's room. He washed up, throwing water on his face and combing it through his hair with his fingers. He rubbed a little soap on his armpits in lieu of deodorant. When had he last taken a shower, he wondered as he looked at his tired reflection in the mirror. When had he had a decent meal that didn't consist of all junk food? He made one more stop at the break room and grabbed a couple of sandwiches and a cup of coffee.

Jeremy entered the username and password used by Barnes to access Heather's implant video and audio and first watched a minute of live coverage, which revealed nothing. The screen was completely black and although he could hear some sounds, they were very distant. Jeremy had learned enough about the original implants of Jon, Mary Beth and Michael to know that a completely black screen wasn't good. Even when one's eyes were closed, there was usually some light that could be seen. Of course, Heather had newer technology and the implants most likely were different.

He then entered the same time that Barnes had entered - 2:30 p.m. - and began watching the recording from that afternoon. The implants had worked fine at 2:30. Heather was in a bathroom brushing her teeth.

Jeremy felt strange watching the video. He feared that the live coverage of her dark screen and distant sounds meant she was dead and he wasn't sure he wanted to watch the video for the next hour as Heather's father had done. Was he going to watch Heather being killed? Is that what Jacob saw as well, and if so, was he enraged and grieving at his daughter's death, or simply accepting of the fact that the necessary task was over.

He watched as Heather prepared to shower. Feeling guilty, he fast-forwarded through the next half hour and up until the time the two doctors came into the room to talk to the Singers. He watched as Dr. Banks broke the news to Heather about her implants. "Heather, I want to talk to you about something else as well, something I'm sure you don't know and are not going to like."

Jeremy continued to watch and listen to Heather's implant video up until Dr. Banks began to remove one of her eyeballs and decided he didn't want to watch anymore. He could watch zombies tear apart humans and aliens annihilate a whole city of people, but he couldn't watch a real-life surgery being performed, especially from the viewpoint of the person on the table.

Jeremy assumed that Heather was okay - that the black screen meant her implants had been removed and not that she had died on the table. It then occurred to him that Barnes was most likely on his way to Boston. What would he do now that Heather knew about her own implants? She now knew there had been subsequent Freedom Projects, that she had been part of one, and that her father most likely sanctioned it. She was probably pretty pissed off about it.

Jeremy knew he should call the Secretary and bring her up to speed on the day's events. There were two reasons, however, why he wouldn't. One, he had to find Dorgan again. It had been two hours since he had last tracked him, prior to the unwanted visit of Jacob Barnes. Most likely Dorgan was at the same medical center where Heather was, and he now positioned the huge satellite Samuel to go into the facility and look for both Dorgan and Heather.

The second reason was that he could not think of any way to tell the Secretary that Barnes was a threat without telling her how he came by this knowledge. He didn't want to reveal that he knew about all of the Freedom Projects conducted over the past fifty years. He didn't want to reveal that to anyone. That knowledge petrified him.

Jon and Carol awoke from a short nap in the back seat of Bernie's car when he stopped for gas. They had crossed the state border into Pennsylvania and still had a long drive ahead of them. Jon offered to drive and let Bernie rest, so Carol moved to the front passenger seat and Bernie to the back. He didn't feel like sleeping though. He wanted to talk.

"I still can't believe this is happening," Bernie started. "I've worked for the government all my life and nothing like this has ever happened that I know of. I mean, you see stuff in movies, but..." he paused so Jon interrupted.

"I believe it," he said with anger in his voice. "I can't believe it happened to ME, but I definitely believe the government spies on people all the time and in ways we never know about. Never in a million years would I have thought this, though."

"And it's one thing to perform such an experiment," added Carol. "But it's another thing entirely to then murder people who know about it. Will we ever be safe?" Her voice was full of anguish and Jon reached over to squeeze her hand. He had to turn his head to see her since he had no peripheral vision in his right eye due to the patch he was wearing.

"How well do you know this Dorgan guy, Bernie?" Jon was looking in the rearview mirror and could see Bernie's face.

"Not at all, really. I've met him a couple of times to give him a file or something, but never talked to him much." Bernie thought about Friday when he gave the USB drive to Dorgan – the one that had the Freedom Project file on it. Dorgan hardly even looked at him and threw the small device into his desk drawer. He was definitely a jerk, but that didn't make him a killer. Still, he was behind several of the killings in Hamilton, Ohio, of the past two days. Bernie was certain of that.

"Jeremy, the guy at Homeland Security that's been helping us, says that Dorgan is the one who warned us about the bombing of the morgue, so he seems to have switched sides."

"Hmmm, why do you think that is?" Jon contemplated.

"I don't know. Maybe he hadn't meant for the guys he hired to actually kill anyone, or maybe only the coroner. I'm sure the killing of the two policemen was not planned. Maybe they were only supposed to get the implants from the dead guy, Michtenbaum. Each of his hired guys killed people they weren't supposed to kill - the other one killed the man at the gravesite - and then Dorgan killed them, so they must have really screwed up."

"Yeah, maybe." Jon didn't sound convinced. "Of course that means if it isn't Dorgan, then someone else is trying to kill us, or worse, lots of someone elses."

They were quiet for a moment as that thought hit each of

them. Bernie shuddered at the thought that someone else at Homeland Security might be involved in trying to kill them. What were the chances that Dorgan was the only one involved in this. The thought of his boss, Mr. McElroy, or the head of Homeland Security being behind this didn't seem possible, he decided. He just wouldn't let himself believe that. However, he was seriously considering calling in sick tomorrow.

"Mary Beth Singer - the other woman with the implants - you know," Carol started, and both Jon and Bernie nodded that yes, they knew who she was talking about although they had all met only briefly that morning at the morgue. "She was telling me that she knew this other guy with the implants that was killed. They grew up together."

"Well now that's really odd isn't it?" Jon said.

"Not really," Bernie decided to explain. "I believe all three of you were born on the same night in the same hospital, so it would make sense you might have grown up together. You were born in Hamilton weren't you, Jon?"

"Yes, I was, but we lived in Trenton all my life, so I went to school there. So you're saying the experiment was conducted on three of us babies born that night at Mercy Hospital."

"Yeah, I guess it was easier for the doctor to do it all at once in the same place, although I have no idea why that hospital in that city was chosen."

"Lucky me," Jon said sarcastically.

"Another thing Mary Beth said," Carol continued, "and you said the same thing, Jon. The nurse that was on duty that night with the newborns disappeared and was never seen again. I now believe that disappearance was because of the surgeries that were conducted on the three of you that night."

"I'm sure it was." Jon said quietly. "I wonder how many innocent people have died because of this experiment."

After a while, they changed the subject and talked about their families. Carol and Jon were proud of their children and grandchildren and spent an hour bragging on them all.

"I'm getting hungry and could use a break," Carol finally said. They all agreed they wanted to get back on the road as soon as possible so decided to stop at a fast food restaurant.

As they left the Wendy's Restaurant after eating, Bernie noticed a black sedan parked a few spaces from his car. It hadn't been there when they arrived and the only reason he noticed it was because of the government plates and tinted windows. He couldn't tell if anyone was inside but since no one else had entered the restaurant while they were inside, he assumed whomever was driving the car was still in it.

As soon as they got in Bernie's car, he told Jon his suspicion that the black car might be following them. The brief period of relaxation they had felt while talking about family and getting some food was gone.

"Don't turn around to look at them," Jon instructed both Carol and Bernie. So far the black car *was* following them, though quite a distance behind. "I'll keep an eye on them in the mirror and Carol, maybe you can see them through the mirror on your visor."

The car kept its distance behind them and after a while they began to wonder if they were just being paranoid. Still, Jon tried to stay as near other vehicles on the road as he could, especially large trucks. He didn't want to give the black car a chance to pull up beside them.

After several minutes of silence, Bernie commented, "I'm wondering if they're tracking us through Heather's cell phone, or whether they're watching my car by satellite or some other way."

"Good point," said Jon. "Maybe we should get rid of the phone. Of course, they now know where we are and which way we're headed, so could pretty easily find us even without the phone."

"I sort of hate to give up Heather's phone," Bernie interjected. He felt a responsibility to Heather to get it back to her safe and sound. He knew, though, she'd rather have the three of them safe and sound instead of her phone.

As if it could hear Bernie's thoughts, Heather's phone chimed. It was Jeremy and Bernie answered it. Earlier, Heather's father had called, twice actually, but Bernie had decided not to answer and let it go to voice-mail.

"Hi Jeremy," he answered. "I think we're being followed."

"Which car?" asked Jeremy. "I've managed to keep eyes on you so far."

The black car was five cars behind them and Bernie thought

that Jeremy would be able to see it. Jon sped up a little but the black car remained about the same distance behind them.

"Slow down and see what happens," suggested Jeremy.

Jon slowed to 55 miles per hour and soon the nearby cars, including the black car with the tinted windows, passed them.

The three let out a collective sigh of relief. The black car sped on around a semi truck. Carol grinned. "We have every right to be paranoid, you know."

Bernie giggled. "I, for one, am glad we were wrong. So Jeremy, did you call to let us know about Heather?"

"Me too," started Jon. "Oh shit!"

Bernie and Carol tried to look at Jon but were jerked sideways as Jon swerved violently into the middle lane.

"Oh shit!" Jon screamed again. "Get down!"

The windshield cracked, followed by the shattering of the left back window next to Bernie.

Carol screamed. Jon swerved the car again, back into the slow lane, pulling up alongside a tractor trailer, keeping it between them and the black car that had fired upon them.

Jon scanned the terrain on both sides of the highway. On his right, it was too steep and wooded to attempt to escape that way. The median of ground between the east and west bound traffic was steep as well, but it was a hill instead of a gully. He wouldn't be able to cross it and reverse their direction in an effort to get away from the attacking vehicle, which would surely be upon them again in a few seconds.

The black car was in front of them again. The barrel of a rifle was visible out of a hole in the rear window of the car. Jon slammed on the brakes. Another shot hit the windshield and lodged in the upper portion of the back seat, missing Bernie by inches as he attempted to lay down as best he could with a shoulder belt on.

As Jon started to maneuver back into the middle lane behind the truck, the huge truck surprised him by jerking quickly to the right, slamming into the black car, shoving it off the road, through a guardrail and into the deep wooded ravine.

Jon could see the car go to the bottom of the steep hill, much too steep for the car to climb out, and he couldn't believe that once again they had been spared from death. He was now shaking and wanted to stop, but first sped up alongside the truck, which had returned to the middle lane. He wanted to motion to the tractor driver, who might want them all to stop and call the police.

The driver of the tractor trailer simply nodded knowingly at them but did not slow down or motion for them to stop. Jon, Carol and Bernie all waved to him and mouthed the words "thank you."

"Wow," was all Bernie could say and was thankful there were people who would do what they felt was right to help someone, even if it was normally wrong. He picked up Heather's phone from the floor where it had fallen. "Jeremy, are you still there?"

"Yes, I saw the whole thing. You guys all okay?" Bernie confirmed that they were.

"Get rid of your phones. Now. Stop some place safe and get a disposable phone and if possible, a different car. Maybe you should get off I-70 – hold on while I check a map – not too far ahead you could get off on Route 43 and take it south to 68 east. Stay away from cameras if you can. And disguise yourselves in some way – they're looking for two men and a woman together, one with an eye patch. Have Jon stay in the back seat – he's too conspicuous – and you or Carol wear a ball cap or put down the sun visor – anything to keep cameras from recognizing you."

"Ok. We will. Oh, have you heard from Heather yet?" Bernie asked.

"She and the Singers were taken to Boston. They're safe for the time being," Jeremy replied, followed by a long, tired sigh. "Bernie, maybe I should call Watterson and get help. This situation is way out of hand. We need help. You and the others are in grave danger."

"I've been wondering why we haven't done that before, unless you think she's in on it."

"I don't think so," said Jeremy a bit hesitantly. "I'll call her. In the meantime, I'll keep watching you via satellite, but in case I lose you, call and let me know your new number once you get it. Now toss your phones."

Both Carol and Bernie threw their iPhones out the window. They rode in silence until they exited off of I-70 and stopped at a town called Brownsville. Jon parked Bernie's car in a small, dark lot across the street from a Walmart store.

Bernie took Heather's purse with him and the three walked across the street to Walmart, entering separately and from the sides of the building to be less conspicuous to the parking lot cameras. "What should we do?" Carol asked when they met inside, the anguish visible on her face.

"I don't think we can rent a car without a credit card and it isn't wise for us to use our card in case they're checking," Jon replied.

"Who are THEY anyway!" Carol had raised her voice and attracted the attention of some nearby shoppers. "I'm so sick of THEM! How dare THEY do this!" She was crying now, and Jon reached out to hold her.

"Wait," Carol sniffed. "I have my boss' credit card with me."

Jon and Bernie looked at each other. "It might work," Jon said. Bernie shrugged as he didn't own a credit card and had never rented a car in his life so didn't know the protocol.

"If there's a car rental place nearby," added Jon. "Why don't you two go ask about that while I buy a cheap phone and card." Jon headed down an aisle. "I'll meet you back here in five minutes."

Carol and Bernie found out that there was an Enterprise car rental store just a half mile up the road.

When Jon returned with the phone, he gave it to Bernie. "Just follow the instructions here to add these minutes to the phone, then call your friend and let him know where we are and our new phone number. You stay here. Carol and I will walk to the car rental place and come back and get you."

Bernie sat down at a table in the small café area of Walmart. He read the instructions carefully and managed to get the phone working and loaded with one hundred minutes of talk time. He programmed Jeremy's phone number into the phone.

Bernie then went outside to a side corner of the store to wait for Jon and Carol. He felt a little silly standing there with a purse. As he waited, he noticed a for sale sign in an older car parked on the edge of the lot. It was an old Ford Taurus, at least twenty years old, and in bad need of a paint job.

Bernie checked Heather's wallet. There were three one hundred dollar bills, as well as several smaller bills. He called the phone number on the sign.

"Dr. Banks, that is the man who has been trying to kill us, and has already killed several people. There's no way the Secretary of Homeland Security sent him here to get us. She's been having him surveilled for possible crimes. Mary Beth and Joe and I need to get out of here. Can you help us?" Heather had only been in the recovery room a few minutes but again started to sit up and look for her clothes.

Under normal circumstances, Dr. Banks would have objected to a patient trying to leave before spending sufficient time in recovery, but he understood Heather's dilemma. "Come with me."

He took her to an unused office where no one would come looking for her and had her sit quietly while he went to get Mary Beth and Joe. "You're still groggy from the anesthetic, so don't move until I get back." Then he looked both ways along the hall before leaving the office.

Twenty minutes later Heather, Mary Beth and Joe were being ushered out a back door to a car. "Here's some cash so you can't be tracked by your credit cards. And here's a cell phone in case you need it. Get rid of any traceable phones you may have." Dr. Banks then handed the car key to Joe and told them to be careful. "The man who is here to get you still thinks you're in surgery, Heather. I instructed the nurse to tell him that - so I can delay him perhaps another hour at best."

Mary Beth found herself hugging the doctor, the man who had placed the implants in her when she was born, and then the three of them climbed in the small car. Heather rolled down the window and asked, "Whose car is this by the way? If all goes well, we will get this money and car back to you eventually."

"The car belongs to a patient who died. I know he has no family, so I'm sure he won't care if you have it." Dr. Banks smiled at them. "And don't worry about the money. I feel I owe it to you. I'll keep your implants safe for the both of you in case you ever decide to use them as evidence."

As Joe pulled out of the hospital parking lot, Heather counted the cash. Twenty $100 bills. That should be enough for a few days should they need to hide. She gave $700 each to Joe and Mary Beth so that all of the money would not be with one person should they get separated, or worse.

"Where to?" Joe asked as he continued to drive as fast as possible away from the hospital.

"Um, let's head towards D.C. for now. We can always change our minds and go somewhere else." Heather grinned at Joe. "And it looks like you're going to have to navigate the old fashioned way. Either stop and ask for directions or get a map."

"D.C. seems the last place we'd want to go," commented Mary Beth. "And I don't know about you, but I'm totally confused. Who brought us here? If this Dorgan guy wants to kill us, why in the world would he bring us here to remove my implants?   And why wasn't he keeping a close eye on us every second at the hospital?"

"I know. It doesn't make sense," Heather agreed thoughtfully.

Mary Beth's voice took on a slightly different tone, one of slight suspicion, Heather noticed. "I was in the recovery room for an hour and then back in the apartment they gave us for at least another hour before Dr. Banks came and got us. Dorgan never came to either place.   And you weren't in the apartment, Heather, or the waiting room or recovery room, so we were worried about you." She waited a moment. "We asked Dr. Banks where you had been and he said you'd explain it to us when you were ready."

Heather didn't speak for a moment. "Yes, I will, but I can't bring myself to talk about it right now.   Let's just leave it that I underwent surgery as well, just like you." She said each of the last three words slowly.

"Oh my God!" and Mary Beth's hand flew to her mouth. "Oh Heather, I had no idea!"

"Me either," Heather mumbled with her head down, then looked towards the front seat. "Is it okay if we don't talk about it now. It's too upsetting."

"Of course," said both Joe and Mary Beth at the same time, and they both gave her a sympathetic look.

Joe had managed to find his way to I-95 heading south without the aid of a map or without emasculating himself by asking for directions. Once on the expressway, Heather said that she would make a few phone calls and try to find out any new information that she could. She started with Jeremy, the only person besides Bernie and her newfound friends that she felt she could truly trust. Even her father was no longer in that circle of trust.

Heather felt sure her new little phone couldn't be traced and was confident that Jeremy knew how to keep his cell phone from being traced or tapped as well. She wasn't sure if he would answer, not knowing the number that was calling. Most likely his caller ID would show "private" or "unknown" or perhaps say "Boston, MA."

He answered on the third ring, sounding rather tentative. "Hello?"

"Jeremy, it's Heather."

"Oh, Heather, good to hear from you. You guys all alright?"

"Yes, we're all okay. Have you heard from Bernie?"

"Yes, the other couple, the Moores, are with him. They're on their way back to D.C." He paused. "So you've left the hospital already?"

Heather smiled. Of course he would know where they'd been. Did he know about her surgery as well? "Yes, we're driving now but not sure what to do. Have you figured out who took us from the police precinct and what they plan to do with us? We're a little afraid to head to D.C."

"I don't blame you there," he said. "I'm not positive who had you taken but I have two theories, one of which you're not going to like at all." He waited for Heather's reply.

"I don't like any of this, so go ahead and tell me."

"Well, it might have been Dorgan. He…"

Heather interrupted Jeremy. "Oh, Dorgan is at the hospital! I thought he was dead! He told the doctor he has authority from Rhonda to bring us back to D.C. Fat chance! So we snuck out, with the help of Dr. Banks."

"Yes, I tracked him to the hospital as well as you guys. That's one of the reasons I think it's him. The other is, as you know, or maybe you don't know, the intruders at the police station that took you used rubber bullets so as not to kill anyone. Dorgan has found out some information that has changed his game plan. I still don't trust him but I don't think he's out to kill any of you anymore and didn't want any other collateral damage either."

"What information? Why would he try to kill me one day and then help me the next?" Heather found it very hard to believe that

Dorgan was now on her side.

"Well," Jeremy said slowly, "you now know, personally, that there was at least one more Freedom Project in addition to the original one." Even though Heather was probably the only person in the world he would consider telling about her father's secret file, he was extremely uncomfortable talking about it. He waited for her response.

So he did know that she had implants. "Yes."

"Dorgan found out a lot of information that he hadn't known before which I believe changed his mind as to how he was going to clean up the Michtenbaum implant situation."

"Why would he say he was under the authority of the Secretary to pick us up from the hospital? Surely that's not true! How much does she know about all this?" Heather needed answers and hoped Jeremy had them.

"That I don't know. I haven't told the Secretary anything at all in the past 24 hours and I certainly don't think she knows any of these details, so it doesn't seem logical that she sent Dorgan to get you guys. In fact, she's going to be pretty pissed off at me when I tell her about you and Bernie being involved. I've kept a lot from her." Jeremy took a deep breath. "Maybe Dorgan just told the doctor that story to get access to you, or to hopefully gain your trust."

"Well, that's not going to happen anytime soon. Do you think it was Dorgan who had me kidnapped last night by the crazy madman?"

"Again, I don't know for sure, but I don't think so. He's the one who warned me that the morgue was going to be bombed. And I don't think he'd use a guy like that." Jeremy didn't want to say any more about the reputation of the psychopathic killer.

"Who else could it have been? Who else is after us?"

Joe and Mary Beth were listening intently to Heather's side of the conversation. Although the phone was on speaker, they could not hear most of what Jeremy said.

"Now for the part you're really not going to like." Jeremy added quickly but not convincingly, "but I don't think this guy is after you, Heather, not you. So it still doesn't answer the question of last night."

"So who?" Heather was getting impatient.

Again the deep breath. "Your dad."

Heather looked at Mary Beth to see if she heard. She did. What a silly emotion to be having at this moment - one of embarrassment and disgrace that someone else might learn that her father was involved. That emotion was mixed with many other emotions - disbelief, betrayal, but mostly shock - the same shock she felt a few hours ago when she learned she, too, had implants since birth and that her father knew about it.

"Why... how do you know... why do you think this?" Heather stumbled over her words. She could feel the conflict that Jeremy was having with himself as to what to tell her. "Just tell me," she said quietly.

"Dorgan had hacked into a file belonging to your father. It was about the Freedom Project." Jeremy didn't go into the contents of the file except for the few recent entries. "An entry was made a few days ago about having Michael Michtenbaum killed and thus setting in motion a way to frame or kill Dorgan, as well as permanently end this project. That's the entry Dorgan saw yesterday that I think made him change his course of action."

"Do you think he could have called the Secretary after that and told her? She was investigating him based on a reliable tip she received. He didn't know that, I presume. So he might have called her when he saw this information."

"Maybe," agreed Jeremy. "She searched his office yesterday in front of a camera he was watching, so I kind of figured he might not trust her, so it didn't occur to me that he might have filled her in, but it's possible."

"But there's more, Heather, much more." He went on to tell her about the entry made that morning to "terminate" all of those associated with the Freedom Project. He told her it listed everyone's name except hers and his own. Heather was relieved that Joe and Mary Beth couldn't hear everything Jeremy was saying. He then went on to tell her about the phone call and visit he received from her father that day. "He truly didn't seem to know where you were, but my theory is that you weren't supposed to be kidnapped, only the others. It didn't go as planned, and Jon and Carol got away, and you were taken."

"I don't know what to say," Heather finally said. "I'm more

confused than ever. I know dad has probably had to do some horrible things over the years, but this doesn't even seem in the realm of possibility. I just can't believe he would have innocent people killed." But she wasn't entirely convinced. He knew she had implants - he probably agreed to it when she was born - did she really know him at all?

Then a thought hit her. "What time did you say that entry was made this morning?"

She could hear Jeremy clicking a keyboard to check. "7:30. Why? What are you thinking?"

"Well, sometime last night dad was in a helicopter crash in Hamilton. The police had his cell phone and laptop when I was at the station around 10:30 this morning which would mean those must have fallen out of the helicopter. If he had made that file entry from either of those two devices, he would have them with him, right?"

"Could he have had an iPad or perhaps went somewhere and used another device?"

"Yes, I suppose. They couldn't find him at the scene this morning, so he may have gone somewhere and used another computer."

They were both quiet as they tried to think of other explanations.

"What do you think we should do, Jeremy? Should we come to D.C. and if so, go where and do what? Two people that I completely trusted this morning, my dad and my boss, I'm not so sure about now. I would have felt safe in my dad's house, but I can't go there now."

"Bernie and the Moores are headed to his sister's house. You could go there as well, or come here to the office. I'll give you the sister's address in case you decide to go there."

"Jeremy, you just mentioned that dad made an entry a couple of days ago about having Ray Michtenbaum killed? Have you been able to confirm that it was really him that ordered that hit? Maybe it's possible someone else is framing dad?" She didn't really believe this herself but badly wanted to. The father she had known all her life, with the exception of ten minutes when she was fourteen years old, was not capable of doing any of these things he was now being accused of.

"Interesting you should mention that. On the surface, it showed payment to the hired killer as coming from Homeland Security, but when I checked further, it came from the CIA. I couldn't trace it to a particular person or terminal though." He added that last sentence to let her know there was the possibility that it wasn't her father.

Heather started to say something more but Jeremy interrupted. "Hey, you just called Michtenbaum by his middle name - Ray. Why?"

"That's what Mary Beth and his parents call him." Mary Beth looked quizzically at Heather when she heard her name. "Your friend Ray went by his middle name right?"

"Well," said Mary Beth, "only his parents called him Ray. I occasionally do when I'm with them. Other personal and business acquaintances called him Michael."

"Let me do some more digging. I'll call you later," said Jeremy and he hung up before Heather could respond.

Dorgan looked at his watch and figured Heather was out of surgery and had most likely been in recovery for an hour. He had been engrossed in reading other details of Barnes' Freedom Project file and the hours had flown by. He knew he had to approach Heather which might be a difficult meeting. She might know that it was his hired man that tried to blow up her car yesterday and she definitely knew a bug had been planted in her purse, so he assumed she would be less than willing to accept his protection to take her back to the Homeland Security office. Worse, he must try and convince her that it was not him, but her father, who had blown up the morgue in an attempt to kill all those with knowledge of the Freedom Project. He was trying to protect her from her own father.

Dorgan had searched the 4000 page file looking for Heather's name as a subject in one of the '80s projects, but he could not find her name anywhere. He would have thought that Dr. Banks was just having a "senior moment" and got her mixed up with someone else except for the fact that he operated on Heather for hours. If the man's memory had been faulty and Heather did not actually have any implants, he would have discovered that fact early on in the operation. Dorgan was convinced that Barnes was the one who had Michtenbaum murdered, was now trying to murder the other test subjects as well as those who had knowledge of this project and who was setting him up to take the fall. If all had gone according to his original plan, no one would have died and Michael Michtenbaum's implants would have been recovered, with no one the wiser. He approved the killing of Rachel Curry if absolutely necessary, but then Heather and Bernie showed up, the police got involved, and everything got out of hand. So he knew he was not blameless in this situation and was willing to take his lumps for his part in this fiasco, but he did not intend to take the blame for Barnes' actions.

So far, his satellite surveillance had revealed nothing of value. He had managed to take over one of DHS's newest satellites, the "twin" of Samuel affectionately called Delilah. But it was time to go and he would have to continue that surveillance later, once he landed in D.C. with Heather, Joe and Mary Beth in tow.

He turned off his computer and packed it into its case and left the waiting room to find Dr. Banks to take him to Heather and the Singers. As he neared a corner in the hall, he could hear voices, one of which was Dr. Banks and the other of which was asking about Heather.

Dorgan stopped to listen and stayed behind the wall so he wouldn't be seen.

"How did she react when you told her about the implants?" the voice said quietly. Dorgan didn't know Barnes well, but he knew that it was his voice.

"She was shocked of course, and upset," answered Dr. Banks. "And, she asked me if you knew about them. I think the fact that you knew about the implants upset her more than anything else."

Dorgan could hear Barnes sigh before he said, "Yes, I've really messed up with her and she may never forgive me."

Dr. Banks seemed to like Barnes, Dorgan thought. However, he had a gentle and kind way about him with everyone. "Oh, don't be so sure. Your daughter loves you and I know you love her. It may take a little time, but don't underestimate that love."

Dorgan knew he needed to get to Heather and the Singers before Barnes did. But the only way to get to them was across the nurse's station area where the two men were standing.

"If you've come to get Heather," continued Dr. Banks to Barnes, "I'm afraid you're too late. She has already left."

"What!" exclaimed Barnes, and Dorgan was thinking the same thing. "What! Left! When and how?"

"She was anxious to leave. I believe she was afraid that someone was after her and she left shortly after her surgery."

"How long ago did she leave and did she say where she was going?"

"It's been a half hour ago and no, she didn't say where she was going. But the man she was afraid of is still in the hospital I believe. She said his name was Dorgan from Homeland Security."

Dorgan heard the clip of Barnes' gun being inserted and he moved quickly back down the hallway, retreating into an open doorway.

Dorgan readied his own weapon should he need to use it. The minutes ticked by. After twenty minutes of Barnes not appearing, Dorgan crept out of the waiting room, watching carefully around each corner, and finally made his way to the exit and to an awaiting cab.

Heather stayed quiet in the back seat while Joe and Mary Beth talked softly as they drove along I-95 towards D.C. Heather was trying to digest the information about her father. Could he really be the monster behind the Freedom Project? Could he be the one who bombed the morgue? Could he have ordered the hits on the Singers, Moores and others as Jeremy had said? Could he and Dorgan be working together?

Even if all of this were true, she refused to believe he could have been the one who had her kidnapped by that awful sadist.

It made Heather physically sick to think about her father at that moment. Even if he was not involved, he DID know about her implants and she wasn't sure she could ever forgive him for that.

She switched her thoughts to how to ensure the safety of Mary Beth, Joe and herself. If someone was after them, or at least after Joe and Mary Beth, why hadn't they been killed already? Why take them to Boston and have Mary Beth's implants removed? No, whoever did that was helping them.

At least now, with their implants gone, they couldn't be tracked that way. Heather had made the decision not to keep her implants as evidence. So the threesome in the car had no devices with GPS tracking. The automobile they were driving could not be traced unless Dr. Banks were to talk and Heather felt sure the doctor would die before revealing any information.

The trio's biggest issue would be staying on the expressway. In addition to surveillance cameras, her dad, Dorgan, or whoever was after them might expect them to be heading south on I-95 and use the highway cameras or other means to look for them.

They had been driving almost an hour before Heather spoke again. "I think I should call my boss and see if she really did send Dorgan. What do you think?"

"How much do you trust your boss?" Joe asked.

"Well, Friday morning I would have said about 98%, but that percentage is much lower now; not because I truly think she's involved, but because I trust almost no one now."

"Will she be able to find us if you call her? I mean, track us?" he continued.

"I don't think so. Not if the call is brief. I just need to know if she sent Dorgan and, if so, why."

Joe took a deep breath. "And will you be able to tell if she's lying? If she says no, she didn't send him, then Banks was either lying or was duped. I personally don't think he was lying and he struck me as too wise to be duped. And if she admits that she did send him, then chances are the explanation is going to take longer than the time we will want to have her on the phone. I vote to not call her."

"Me too," said Mary Beth softly. "I'm sure everyone in the government isn't out to get us, but right now, it sure feels like it. I don't trust any of them."

"Okay, you're right," Heather conceded. She paused a moment. "I was thinking you two might be safest at a hotel instead of going to D.C. You have enough cash to last several days."

"What about you?" Mary Beth turned around to look at Heather. "You make it sound like you're only talking about us."

"I am. I'm going to D.C. to end this one way or another. But I don't want you to come. It's too dangerous."

"No way," interrupted Joe. "We're not letting you go alone."

"Yes, it's the best plan." Heather's tone was calm and firm. "They're looking for three of us together, so we'll split up." Her voice was mixed with both anger and sadness as she continued. "And if it is my father behind this, then he'd better kill me anyway, because I won't be able to go on living with that knowledge."

Joe had pulled off the side of the road in order to be able to turn and look at Heather as she spoke. "You two need to be somewhere safe to figure out what to do next, and hopefully to hear from me that this nightmare is over."

Joe and Mary Beth exchanged a knowing look that they were both ready for this horrible day to be over.

It was dark when they said their goodbyes at a Hampton Inn off of I-95.

Jacob Barnes conducted a quick search of the hospital floor for Dorgan, but when he couldn't find him after ten minutes, he changed his focus to finding Heather. He questioned Dr. Banks about Heather's quick exit and knew the good doctor was holding something back when he mentioned giving her cash but said he did not know where they were going or how they were getting there.

Barnes didn't push the doctor further. "Thank you for removing the chips from my daughter," Jacob said as he left Dr. Banks. "I've always felt guilty about that decision and even though our relationship may never be the same, I'm glad it's out in the open."

Barnes' preferred method of transportation was helicopter, but when he needed to move fast, he used a Learjet built for speed. He was heading back to D.C. to once again visit the uncooperative Jeremy James and find out where Heather was. As he tried to relax while his pilot flew, he dialed Susan's number. He wanted to hear the voice of at least one person he loved.

Once again Barnes was able to enter Homeland Security's offices unattended, a privilege of his rank at the CIA. The building was mostly deserted and quiet at this hour and he quickly made his way to the Office of Intelligence and Analysis and to Jeremy James.

He did not believe he would be able to persuade the young man to talk to him. That tactic had not worked the previous two times they had talked. He therefore was prepared to use more drastic measures to find out what he wanted. He released the canister of clear, odorless gas beneath the closed door leading into Jeremy's office and waited ten minutes before picking the lock.

The Hamilton Police Chief checked himself out of Fort Hamilton Hospital early Sunday evening and was back on the job, as much as he would have enjoyed a few days rest in the hospital.

His city was a mess. The county morgue was gone, blown to pieces, and television crews as well as the curious public had made the fire department's job of combing through the rubble even more difficult.

He counted ten deaths attributable to this whole Freedom Project implant business, eleven counting Michael Michtenbaum – his two officers; the Greenwood Cemetery employee; Bill Simmons, the assistant coroner; three of the soldiers that invaded his precinct to kidnap Heather and the Singers; Heather's other kidnapper, the fake attorney; and the two men found dead at the Marriott Hotel, both apparently hired agents to steal Michael Michtenbaum's implants and each responsible for the deaths of at least three of the four innocent people who died.

To make matters worse, he had spoken with Jeremy James of Homeland Security earlier and learned that Coroner Rachel Curry was probably still in danger and should have protection at all times.

They had arrested a man for stealing a metal box from a church and threatening a Priest. They had rescued a woman from the trunk of her car who had been kidnapped by a man who came out of the trees along Route 128, the man now determined to be Jacob Barnes. He had a federal warrant out for his arrest.

Apparently this Dorgan monster was still alive and on the loose.

The only good news was now that all of these persons associated with the Freedom Project had left town, the dead body count stopped. There hadn't been a new entry to the morgue since the three precinct assailants and Heather's kidnapper that morning.

The police had not released the story about the eyeball found at the cemetery and so far had been able to keep the family of Michael Michtenbaum unaware of that piece of unpleasant news. However, the story of the grave closer killed and placed in a new grave was all over the news.

Citizens had been calling in all day regarding helicopters, smoke and suspicious-looking characters. Yes, his city was a mess.

Before he left the hospital, the Chief visited Rachel in the basement morgue and told her she could still be a target. "How about staying here at the hospital until further notice. I'm sure they can find you a bed."

With hospital security doubled and on high alert and with a police officer with the coroner 24/7, the Chief explained that she would be safer there than at home.

"Sure, Chief. I might go climb into one of those beds now."

"Bernie!"

Bernie heard Carol call his name and he headed in the direction of her voice. Jon and Carol were standing outside the front door of Walmart with no rental car in sight.

"They wouldn't rent us a car," complained Jon. "The credit card name has to be the same as the driver's license name," he grumbled.

"It's okay," said Bernie. "I just bought us a car."

"What?" laughed Carol.

"Come on. I don't like us being out in front of security cameras." Bernie started to walk to the furthest end of the parking lot.

"You bought a car?" Jon was truly surprised.

"Yes. Heather had $300 cash in her purse so I offered the guy that much for his car and he took it. He signed the title but I'll have to get it legal later. This is better. Unless we're being watched right now and let's pray we're not, we can't be traced to this car at all."

They had reached the car. Jon climbed in the back and Bernie pulled on a ball cap he'd just purchased. Carol pulled down her sun visor and the three continued their journey to Washington, D.C.

The hours passed slowly as Heather drove through the night. Her thoughts shifted constantly from her father to Bernie and the Moores, back to her father and then to Danny. It seemed weeks, not days, since she'd spoken to him, and a lifetime since he'd held her and told her he loved her. At that moment, in the wee hours of a Monday Memorial Day morning, not certain if she would live another day, not certain if she had a father anymore, the realization hit her. She loved Danny and she wanted to marry him.

"I love Danny!" she said out loud in the car, laughing. "And not because I've had the worse weekend of my life," she kept shouting. Well, maybe because of it, she thought. This weekend has made me appreciate the good things I have. It's made me realize married couples can stay in love forever. And it's made me a stronger, more capable person. Again she shouted out loud. "I plan to live through this and ask Danny to marry me!"

"Oh!" She was startled by the phone ringing. She had programmed only two numbers into the phone when she stopped to let the Singers out – Jeremy's and her own cell number, although Bernie hadn't answered it when she tried calling around midnight. She wanted to make sure he'd arrived safely at his sister's house.

The display showed that Jeremy was calling. "Hi!" Heather said cheerfully, still excited about thinking of Danny.

"Heather, honey, I'm so glad you're okay."

Heather froze. For the second time in her life, the sound of her father's voice frightened her.

"Heather, where are you? I've been calling you since last night."

"I'm okay," Heather managed to say. Her voice had lost its cheery tone. "I haven't had my phone since yesterday evening, Saturday evening, so I didn't get your calls." She knew that wasn't exactly the truth. She'd had her phone briefly Sunday morning and had seen calls from him.

Barnes' voice became solemn as well. "Honey, I know we have a lot to talk about and I know you're very upset with me right now. I don't blame you, but please, it's important that we focus on your safety. I'm sure Dorgan is trying to find you as we speak."

"Where's Jeremy?" Heather just realized her father was with Jeremy. "Is he okay?"

"He's fine. He's sleeping and I borrowed his phone."

"Sleeping? Right." Heather wondered what he really meant by *sleeping*. "Let me talk to him," she demanded.

"Heather, Jeremy is fine, I promise you. I think he's been at this for days and was simply exhausted and fell asleep." Jacob paused. "I came here to get him to tell me where you are and saw his phone so thought I'd check it for a number for you. Now please, where are you? I can pick you up and get you somewhere safe."

"Wake Jeremy up and let me talk to him and then we'll see." Heather's gut told her that her dad had done something to Jeremy.

"I'm in a different part of the building right now."

"I'll wait," said Heather defiantly. Then it occurred to her that he might be able to trace her whereabouts if she was on the line any longer.

"On second thought, gotta go," and Heather hung up on her father, or whoever this man was that she had always loved but now feared.

The joy she had felt only minutes ago was dispelled with this call. She still wasn't ready to believe her father was a murderer – that he would order the deaths of innocent people. There had to be another explanation.

"I was thinking," started Bernie, talking loudly enough so Jon, who was lying down in the back seat, could hear him. "If whoever is trying to kill us was tracking us through our cell phones before, they may have heard that we're going to my sister's. Maybe we shouldn't go there."

Jon propped himself up on an elbow. "I've been skeptical about going to any family members anyway. Way too easy for them to find us there. We should go someplace else."

Carol had been resting her eyes, but became alert at the conversation. "We won't be able to call and let your sister know we aren't coming. Her phone may be tapped. Do you have a place in mind to go?"

"I was thinking of going to my work – to Homeland Security.

We at least know Jeremy is there and that he's on our side."

"But there's probably a million cameras there. We'd be spotted both outside and inside, wouldn't we?" Jon asked.

"Yeah, you're right."

"Why don't we just find an all-night restaurant or even just a safe place to park and hang out until daylight at least," Jon continued. "I'm not too fond of walking into the frying pan, so to speak."

"I agree," said Carol.

"There's a 24-hour Waffle House nearby." Bernie smiled as he made this suggestion, thinking of Sheila and his recent Waffle House experience. Chocolate milk and waffles sounded wonderful right now.

Dorgan listened to the last call made between Jeremy James and Bernie on Heather's phone.

"Hi Jeremy, I think we're being followed."

"Which car? I've managed to keep Audrey on you so far."

Dorgan listened to the entire conversation, including the minutes during which there was no real conversation but obviously a lot was happening as the car in which Bernie and the Moores were riding was under attack. Dorgan still felt strongly that Barnes was the key person assigned to frame him and kill those involved, so it had to be him who sent someone to kill these three. But what about Thyssen – was he involved at all, or was he just next in line to have to perform such unsavory deeds at the behest of the higher ups. He had been watching Thyssen for several hours now, but so far the man was spending his Sunday at home.

Although Dorgan still wondered about Heather's and Bernie's involvement with these Freedom Project subjects, he no longer suspected they were agents sent to spy on him. For one thing, when he decided to confront his boss, Rhonda Watterson, the evening before, he could tell she was truly surprised when he asked her if she sent her assistant to Hamilton, Ohio. "You're wrong, John. It can't be Heather. She is in Fiji!" Rhonda exclaimed.

After talking with her for half an hour, Dorgan was convinced Rhonda did not know anything about this particular

Freedom Project prior to their conversation. He filled her in on the experiment and explained the reason for his continued involvement. He finally told her he wanted to have the implants removed from both Jon and Mary Beth, to end this project once and for all, and asked for her support to forcibly take them to Boston for surgery, and then to D.C. for a briefing. After numerous questions from Rhonda as to why they needed to be flown to Boston without their consent, she finally agreed. Since his boss had mentioned Heather's father, Dorgan also told her his suspicions about Jacob Barnes. "I'm 90% sure he's behind all this."

"Other than the fact that Heather may have been familiar with the project because of her father, I have no idea why she would be involved. And I'm quite worried about her," Rhonda added.

Dorgan continued to listen to the call between Bernie and Jeremy.

"She and the Singers were taken to Boston. They're safe for the time being." It was Jeremy's voice. "Bernie, maybe I should call Watterson and get help. This situation is way out of hand. We need help. You and the others are in grave danger."

"I've been wondering why we haven't done that before, unless you think she's in on it."

"I don't think so," said Jeremy a bit hesitantly. "I'll call her. In the meantime, I'll keep watching you via satellite, but in case I lose you, call and let me know your new number once you get it. Now toss your phone."

The call ended. "So Jeremy is calling Rhonda as well," Dorgan thought. "At least he will be confirming with her some of the information I've given her." Dorgan was frustrated that he couldn't listen to any other conversations of Jeremy or of Heather; however, he felt certain Jeremy would tell Heather where the others would be. It was a pretty good bet that she would head for Bernie's sister's house. So that's where he would be too.

He thought about calling Jeremy. He was starting to respect that kid. But he had no real reason to call him and felt confident that Jeremy was watching and listening to him anyway. It was surely Jeremy who kept him alive after he faked his death. Not only had the coroner not conducted an autopsy, she hadn't checked his liver temp for time of death. So Jeremy must have heard his instructions from Saturday night before he took the drug. "Jeremy, if you can hear me, listen carefully. You can save my life by not letting the Hamilton police or coroner touch my body. Tell them it must be held until someone from DHS or the CIA arrives. I'd consider it one last favor."

And Jeremy had sent him the information from the President's files about Randall Thyssen being next in line to lead the Freedom Projects after Barnes' retirement. Jeremy seemed to be on his side, but one could never be sure.

Dorgan was struggling with his mixed emotions. As of now, he no longer cared about retrieving the sets of implants from the three Freedom Project subjects. He still cared about it this morning, although only slightly, but no more. Never, not once in his working life, could he say that he had not given a hundred and ten percent towards successfully achieving his mission, no matter what it was, and his success rate was nearly one hundred percent. He never deliberately changed course and purposely failed to complete his task. But he was now. Even though he had failed to retrieve Michael Michtenbaum's implants and failed to bring Jon Moore to Boston to have his implants removed, those tasks were still achievable. He now simply chose not to achieve them. He didn't even attempt to get Mary Beth's implants, which was a primary purpose of his trip to Boston. He no longer cared about his original mission. He now had a new mission - reveal and destroy all Freedom Projects and those behind them.

Dorgan continued to watch Thyssen on his laptop screen. The man had finally left his house and just met up with someone in downtown D.C. Dorgan immediately recognized the *someone's* face.

It was midnight and The Man would be up most of the remainder of the night. He had learned that many of those associated with Freedom Project-I would soon be meeting at a house in a Baltimore subdivision. Heather, for one, another Homeland Security employee who was now privy to the project secrets, and one of the original experimental project subjects and his wife. What would the outcome of this meeting be? The Man wondered if it would support his original plan or if he would need to create a diversionary story to take focus away from his ultimate goals.

MONDAY

Calls came from Jeremy's phone twice more over the next hour as Heather arrived in the Baltimore area on her way to Bernie's sister's house. She did not answer the calls. It was most likely her father, still in possession of Jeremy's cell phone.

Without her Garmin or iPhone to use for GPS, Heather had to rely on her knowledge of the Baltimore area, as well as the brief directions Jeremy had given her. Bernie's sister and her family lived in a modest three-bedroom house in a 1950s subdivision. Heather drove by the sister's house. The porch light was on but the house appeared dark inside. Her gut told her to keep driving and she turned the corner at the next block, making one additional turn before parking three blocks down that street.

Something didn't feel right and her senses were on high alert. Why weren't the lights on in the house if Bernie and the Moores had arrived safely and were waiting for her? She had tried numerous times over the past couple of hours to reach Bernie who had her phone but there was no answer.

She decided to call Jeremy. Perhaps her father had returned his phone to him. There was no answer. She wasn't sure of his extension on his office phone, but called the main number and entered his name at the voice prompt to get an extension number. He did not answer his desk phone either. Surely something had happened to him.

She began walking the five blocks to Bernie's sister's house. She wanted to be able to approach the house from the back to prevent being seen going to the front door. Therefore, when she reached the street she should have turned onto, she kept going to the next block in order to cut through a yard and reach the back of the house.

Before she reached the next street, Heather heard a noise. It was coming from a row of shrubbery that bordered the lawn of the house she was walking past. The hairs on the back of Heather's neck began to rise. She kept walking but a muffled click sound caused her to stop and whirl around. She saw no one but knew someone was there, watching her, perhaps following her.

The night was dark but she could see well enough to know

there was no one within her line of sight and she was afraid to go into the shrubbery. No other sounds came for the next several seconds so she continued to walk, more rapidly now.

As Heather approached what she thought would be a yard that would lead her to the back of Bernie's sister's house, her heart sank and she almost screamed. The back of the house that had before appeared dark inside was now glowing. The glow was moving and growing as the flames inside began to engulf the house.

Heather ran as fast as she could to the far end of the block and continued running towards the street where she had parked the car given to her by Dr. Banks. Something hit her hand sharply and her cell phone fell to the ground. She kept running.

A noise woke Jeremy with a start. He looked around. Something wasn't right and yet everything in his office looked the same. He must have dozed off sometime after his last conversation with Heather and he tried to focus his groggy brain. When was that?

"Damn idiot!" he admonished himself. He had been awake since five a.m. Saturday morning and it was now two a.m. Monday morning. It would be understandable if he had fallen asleep, but his gut told him that was not what had happened. Never once had he fallen asleep on the job and he had spent many such vigils as this one when tracking terrorists. But he had no other explanation for his unacceptable and totally uncharacteristic behavior. No one had been in his office to drug him or knock him out.

He needed to find Heather and Bernie again, right away, which might prove to be difficult since he had not followed them for the past three hours. He began moving Satellite Samuel to the coordinates of Bernie's sister's house as that was the only location where he knew to look. At the same time, he started a fresh pot of coffee to try to rid his head of the fog that seemed to be enveloping it.

He remembered part of the conversation he had had with Heather before he fell asleep. She had asked if it was possible if someone besides her father could have made the Sunday morning entry into his file – the one ordering the hits on Bernie, Rachel and the others – and the entry of a week ago about arranging to have Michael Michtenbaum killed. That's right, he now remembered, he had begun investigating and had determined that it could not have personally been Jacob Barnes that made those entries. Both entries had been made from Barnes' office computer and Barnes was definitely not in D.C. either time.

But Barnes was not off the hook yet. A colleague or co-conspirator may have made the entry from Barnes' computer at his instruction. And it was obvious to Jeremy that Barnes was involved in every one of the nine separate Freedom Projects he'd read about in this top secret document.

But the fact that Barnes didn't personally make the entry on a file that appeared to be Barnes personal notes made Jeremy wonder if perhaps Barnes, like Dorgan, was being set up. Was this file left vulnerable for Dorgan and others to find by someone out to get both Barnes and Dorgan? And Barnes did say someone had attacked his home. Of course, that's assuming he's telling the truth, Jeremy mused.

Jeremy noticed that the light on his office phone was on, indicating he had a voice-mail. That must have been the ringing noise that woke me, Jeremy surmised. He saw that the call was from Heather's new cell phone number. "Jeremy, I hope you're okay. My dad called me from your cell phone and said you were asleep. I'm near Bernie's sister's house and the house is dark. Something feels wrong. Please call me if you get this message."

Barnes! Jeremy grabbed his cell phone and sure enough, three calls had been placed to Heather's number, with only the first one recording any time. How did Barnes manage to drug him without coming in the room? What else had he been able to do from Jeremy's computers?

He dialed Heather's number. There was no answer. At least he now had Samuel focused above Bernie's sister's house and the surrounding area, hoping to find not only Heather, but Bernie and the others as well.

Jeremy saw movement and zoomed in to see Heather walking towards Bernie's sister's house, still two blocks away. He also found the car she was using parked under a streetlight.

As he started to dial Heather's phone again, Jeremy saw a man behind some bushes only yards away from Heather. He saw her stop and turn. She must have heard the man.

And now another man was visible another street away, lurking in the dark behind the house that Jeremy soon realized was Bernie's sister's. The man ran away as a glow began to appear inside the house. Oh no! thought Jeremy. He frantically searched for the phone number of Bernie's sister. He had it earlier to give to Heather. He dialed but no one answered. No one emerged from the house either. He dialed Bernie.

"Still awake?" said Bernie.

"You're not at your sister's?" Jeremy didn't bother with niceties.

"No, we decided it might put her in danger, so we're hanging out somewhere else."

"Good. And you're right. I don't want to worry you, but someone just set her house on fire. I've tried calling her but no answer. Does she have a cell phone you can call?"

"Oh, my gosh!" Bernie cried. "I'll call you back!"

It was time to call the big boss before anyone else got hurt or killed. Jeremy knew he could, probably would, lose his job over this, but he could no longer justify keeping Secretary Watterson in the dark and the stakes were way too high now. He had no authority to call in help for his friends, but she certainly did. No matter that it was the middle of the night - he dialed her cell phone number. It went to voice-mail, as he expected it would, and he left a message for her to call him as soon as possible.

Jeremy was glad Bernie hadn't mentioned where he and the Moores were at the moment. It occurred to him that Barnes may have planted a listening device in Jeremy's office while he was unconscious. He quickly checked his cell phone to see if a device had been planted in it. He found nothing.

Heather continued to walk towards Bernie's sister's house. Jeremy tried calling her once again but didn't hear her phone ring, nor did she indicate she felt it vibrate. Since both men were hiding nearby, Jeremy called 911. As he relayed the emergency information to the 911 operator, he simultaneously used that time to search his office for any transmitters Barnes might have planted. His sweeping device did not detect any bugs, nor could he find any visibly during his brief search. "Please hurry!" he told the operator. He gulped down a cup of coffee. His head was starting to clear.

Keeping one eye on Heather, who now had seen the fire and began running, Jeremy looked for evidence that Barnes had searched his computers. He started with the same computer Barnes had used previously. Jeremy still had the keystroke program activated and sure enough, Barnes had used this computer.

She was now certain that she was being followed. It was a terrifying revelation and she tried to quell the panic that was rising in her by focusing her mind on what she needed to do. I need a weapon! she screamed to herself, but all she had was the car key in her hand, which she readied by sticking the shaft out of her fist.

Her car was still three blocks away. There was no moon. The night was dark. She no longer had her cell phone They made sure of that. She was in a residential neighborhood and wanted to go to a door and ask for help. But she knew no one could help her. If those after her wanted her dead, she would be dead and so would anyone who tried to help her. Her only hope was that they wanted her followed, not killed. Or, if she were attacked, that she could strike a well-placed blow of the key into the eye or ear and subsequently into the brain of the assassin. Slim chance.

She thought of Danny and how she wished she had told him she loved him. She thought now she would probably never see him again. She wished her father knew where she was, for if she died tonight, chances are no one would ever find her body or know what happened to her.

Focus! Two more blocks. She knew she could probably outrun her stalker if only she knew where to run. It was 3 a.m., pitch black, and she had never been in this neighborhood in her life. So running would be futile. If the person following her was unarmed, she would have a fighting chance. She was strong and agile.

Would they at least have the decency to tell her father she was dead? He knew these people; hell, he trained these people. But no, they probably wouldn't tell him and he would agonize the rest of his life, wondering what happened to her. So would Danny. Maybe not the rest of his life, since he was only 33 and would hopefully find someone else to love, but it would hurt him deeply not knowing where she was or why she had left without saying goodbye.

I should have gone on vacation with Danny. I should have kept my nose out of this. I have only made things worse, not only for me, but for others. What was I thinking? I was trying to help someone, that's what I was thinking. I was trying to help a lot of someones, that's what I was thinking. I'm trying to do the right thing, and it's probably going to be the last thing I ever do.

One block to my car. Then she was struck with another thought and stopped running. What if they have tampered with my car? Is that how they plan to kill me? But I have to use my car to get out of here. I can't keep walking aimlessly. I don't know this area at all. I have to risk using my car. And, if I die in the car, at least Danny and dad will know what happened to me. She continued her brisk walking and could now see her car up the street.

An occasional streetlight cast a circular glow around its base, and fortunately her car was underneath one such light. Unfortunately, so was the man who was after her.

"Heather!" The shout that broke the extreme silence of the night came from behind and Heather swirled around to see - could it be! - her father! She momentarily forgot her fear of him and started to smile when she saw the gun in his hand and his arm raising towards her. As she screamed, he fired.

"So that's how he found her." Jeremy saw that Barnes had requisitioned a small surveillance drone to follow his daughter. After drugging him, Barnes would have been able to see all eight of Jeremy's computer monitors. He would have seen Heather's car traveling south on I-95 and determined her exact location. The drone would then follow her and feed Barnes information on her whereabouts after he left Jeremy's office.

He returned his focus to Heather. She was now running and the man from the bushes was following her, cutting a different path across residential lawns in order to get ahead of her. The man stopped briefly. Was he aiming a gun at Heather? She looked down but did not stop running and the man continued to run as well. As Heather stopped on the street where her car was parked, Jeremy now saw the whole picture. She was surrounded as three other men emerged out of the shadows. Even from a hundred feet, he thought he recognized the men. He zoomed in. One was Barnes. Another was Dorgan. He heard sirens in the distance and as he zoomed out, he could see the pulsing and rotating lights of three police vehicles on their way.

Instinctively, Heather fell to the ground. She lay there for several seconds, her mind shut down from fear and panic. Another shot rang out, then another. She heard someone moan. As the seconds ticked by, her face buried in one of her arms, she tried to assess whether she was dying. Did she feel pain from the shot? It didn't seem so. Was she bleeding? She tried to peek beneath herself without moving too much. It didn't appear that she was bleeding. She could hear her father's voice. He was shouting at someone.

"On the ground! Face down! Arms above your head!" He repeated it.

She raised her head to look. Her father had a man on the ground, his arms now behind his back as Jacob Barnes placed handcuffs on him. He also tied the man's feet and left him laying on the ground.

Heather sat up and looked around. Two other men lay on the ground, one of them only two yards behind her.

It was dark but the man's face was clearly visible to her. It was John Dorgan. The other was lying near her car under the street light.

Both men appeared to be dead. Lights had come on in a few of the neighboring houses. Two men were standing on a porch across the street, watching, but holding the door open, ready to hurry inside if necessary.

Heather could hear her father calling in the shooting.

"...near Anntana and Gerland Avenues...will need two buses." As he continued to fill in the person on the other end of the line, he turned towards Heather and their eyes met. He immediately said into the phone and towards Heather, "I'll call you back in a minute. I have to go hug my daughter."

He helped her up from the ground and hugged her for a full

minute. She found herself returning the hug and sobbing on his shoulder. She finally backed up to look at him. "Dad, what's going on!"

"They were here to stop you and your friends. You may have seen what they did to your friend's house?" Heather nodded and choked the question. "Are they okay, do you know?"

"I don't believe anyone was in the house so as far as I know, they're all okay."

"But Bernie's sister and her family?"

"I moved them out an hour ago. The Bernie guy wasn't there."

Heather just nodded, relieved, but her mind was still reeling. She stayed quiet and let her dad hold her for a few moments more. An ambulance arrived.

"Honey, I know we have a lot to talk about..." he broke off, looking at the paramedic who didn't know which of the two dead bodies to approach first.

"Go, dad, and take care of this. I'll be okay. We can talk later." She sat down on a large rock on the lawn of the house littered with bodies. Her father and the two paramedics were checking to see if either of the two men who had been shot was still alive. Neither was, so they talked quietly with the local police, waiting for the FBI and CIA to arrive.

Jeremy heard footsteps in the hallway. He quickly shut down his computers and fled to a co-worker's cubicle, all empty at 5 a.m. on a holiday morning. A few would be arriving soon, however, and perhaps the footsteps were of those wanting to get an early start to their day.

He heard someone try to open the door from the hall to his main office area. He had started keeping the door locked after the first visit by Barnes.

A knock followed the attempt to open the door, timidly at first and then louder. "Jeremy?" a muffled voice called.

Jeremy recognized the voice and sprung from his hiding place to run open the door for Bernie and the Moores. "I thought you'd call me back," Jeremy said as he let them in and re-locked the door.

"Sorry," Jon Moore said. "That was my fault. Carol and I were using the phone to talk to our kids." He extended his hand to Jeremy. "Jon Moore. This is my wife Carol. You must be Jeremy."

Jeremy nodded. "Nice to meet you."

"My sister and her family are fine," said Bernie. "They're at a friend's house for now. Heather called me right after that and said for us to meet her here. I think her dad got my new number from my sister. She and her dad and the FBI are on their way right now."

Jeremy nodded, then suggested everyone sit at the other end of the room, away from the glass doorway. He grabbed his cell phone and joined them.

Within minutes, more footsteps and voices were heard in the hallway and Jeremy opened the door for Heather, Jacob Barnes and two FBI agents assigned to protect those in the room. Jacob gave instructions to the two agents as to where each of them should be positioned – one inside the room and one outside the door. Two other agents were stationed downstairs, one at the main entry and one near the elevator and stairs.

Before Jeremy could speak, Heather grabbed and hugged him for a full ten seconds, followed by a kiss on the cheek and a whispered "thank you." While he was recovering, she did the same to Bernie. She gave a quick hug to Carol and Jon. "I'm so glad you're all okay!"

Jeremy wished he could just talk to Heather, or at least just look at her, but Jacob Barnes ruined any chance of that. He still didn't trust Barnes at all and didn't like being in the same room, or even the same building, as he. He needed to keep one eye on that man at all times.

As if reading Jeremy's thoughts, Barnes stated, "Well, I have some phone calls to make and need to get a bite to eat. I'll be right down the hall if you need me."

"Where is Mary Beth and her husband?" Carol asked.

Heather quickly explained that they were safe in a hotel. "I'll tell you all about our ordeal in a minute."

The group made their way back to the far cubicles of the room in order to talk without being overheard by the FBI agent stationed near the door.

"Why here?" Jeremy asked, meaning why was the Homeland Security building chosen to house and protect them.

"It was my idea," said Heather. "Overall, I feel safer here than anywhere else. And you're here. And the three of us (she looked at Bernie and Jeremy) know our way around here. Dad made arrangements for the FBI to stay here and protect us until we can figure out who is trying to kill us. Hopefully, we've ruled out my dad?" She looked hopefully at Jeremy.

"Well, all I know for sure is that he is not the one that documented the hits on all of you."

"What! There are actual hits out on us?" Carol gasped. Jon put his arm around her, his face grim. "This just keeps getting better and better."

"I'm afraid so," continued Jeremy. "So, we know Barnes didn't document it, but that doesn't mean he isn't involved." He tried to be as tactful as he could and not hurt Heather, but he knew there was no way for this talk to not hurt her. Everyone looked towards Heather.

"I know," she said. Jeremy could tell she had so many mixed emotions – love for her father, fear of him and embarrassment at being his daughter right now. "But keep in mind he could have killed all of us – me included – on the way over here. And he didn't have to have FBI agents assigned to protect us. I know he isn't completely innocent in all this mess, but I truly don't think he has anything to do with wanting to kill any of us."

"So that leaves who?" questioned Jeremy. "Dorgan possibly, but now he is dead so if your dad thought it was him, which I think he does, why does he feel we still need protection?"

"Dorgan's dead?" Bernie had a slight grin on his face, "are you sure this time?"

"*I'm* sure," said Heather. "I was there when he was shot. The paramedics said he was dead."

"Oh my goodness!" exclaimed Carol. "What happened!"

Heather quietly told her story. "Let me start from when we were taken from the police station." She told an abbreviated story of the abduction, plane ride, Mary Beth's surgery and how the doctor had helped them escape. She left out the part about her own implants and surgery and she saw Jeremy give her a sympathetic look.

　　She went on to tell about arriving at Bernie's sister's house, the fire, and the man that was following her. She finished with telling about the shoot-out. "Dad admitted afterwards that Dorgan was not aiming his gun at me although he was standing behind me. Dad thought he was going to shoot me, so he shot Dorgan. But it was Dorgan who shot and killed the man who was following me. So I think dad now thinks someone else besides Dorgan is involved." Everyone was quiet for a moment as they digested this information. "And there was another man," she looked at Jeremy as she knew he had watched the entire shoot-out. "The FBI have him in custody right now. He is most likely the key to who is really behind all this. He's alive and well and hopefully talking."

　　"Yeah, I got a snapshot of his face, sort of. It's running through my facial recognition software right now."

　　"That reminds me, Jeremy," Heather looked at him. "Ray Michtenbaum was murdered, and maybe his murder was associated with the fact that he was a test subject of the initial Freedom Project. Have you thought to check his implant video to see if you can tell who murdered him?"

　　The others looked expectantly at Jeremy. "Yes, I have." If it had been anyone other than Heather or one of the other three people sitting in front of him who had asked that question, he would have had a sarcastic and scathing reply for them. Of *course* he would have done that.

　　"It was a hired killer, so yes, I'm sure Michenbaum was murdered because of...hey, you said Ray again." Before Heather could comment, Jeremy was out of his chair and sprinting over to his desk and computers. "I think that's it!" he called out. The agent by the door watched him but did not interfere.

　　At his desk, Jeremy opened the 4000 page document of Jacob Barnes that he had stored on a flash drive. He had not come close to reading the entire document yet but he had skimmed all of it and read hundreds of pages. He began skimming again. In the early portions of the document and a few times throughout, Michael Ray Michtenbaum was referred to as Michael, Michael R. or Michael Ray and his last name. Only in the last few entries – and specifically the one ordering Michtenbaum's murder – is he listed as Ray

Michtenbaum. Jeremy did a quick electronic search for Ray and while there were other Rays listed in the document, the only times the name Ray was associated with Michtenbaum was in the last few entries, all made within the past week. Jeremy removed and securely stored the flash drive, quickly checked his facial recognition software, which was still searching, and then checked his e-mail. He opened one from the Secretary of Homeland Security. "Meet me in my office at 7:30 a.m." He quickly acknowledged to her that he would be there.

"Who else would know that Michtenbaum went by the name Ray to his family?" queried Jeremy to Heather, Bernie, Jon and Carol as he sat back down with them. "If we find that out, we find out who is behind this and who is trying to kill us." Jeremy included himself in the "us" even though he hoped his name was still not on the list.

"Mary Beth knows that, but I'm pretty sure it isn't her." They all smiled at Heather's statement.

"I think we can rule out his actual family and close friends,." Jeremy said. "It most likely would have to be someone who had access to viewing and hearing the implant videos, which goes back to both Dorgan and Bar – your dad – but I'm sure others have that access as well."

"Did you?" Bernie asked Jeremy, and quickly added, "I know it wasn't you, but didn't you have access to the videos too?"

"Good question, but no, not until a couple of days ago. Yes, I was tasked with surveilling the three of you," – he looked at Jon – "but only from a satellite that viewed outdoors only, and no sound, so I was to check for a minute once or twice a day and make sure each subject was okay – going to work each day, going home, etc. I think I was mainly checking in case someone died, like Michtenbaum. I had no idea why I was watching you guys, or that you had implants and were part of this Freedom Project."

"So what were you just looking at that makes you think the person or persons behind this knows Ray's nickname, so to speak." It was Carol asking.

"Without going into a lot of detail," Jeremy would never go into detail with anyone about the secret document, "whoever made the final entries on a document about the Freedom Project - the entries that ordered the murder of Michtenbaum and," he stopped.

He didn't want to mention again about the order to kill them as well. But he could see on their faces that they knew. "Whoever made these entries called Michtenbaum by his middle name Ray. All entries made before this past week referred to him as Michael or Michael Ray, but never just Ray. "

"That's not a lot to go on is it?" said Jon.

"Maybe not, but it tells me loud and clear that someone else added these comments at the end."

"I'm still not following you." Both Jon and Carol agreed with Heather's comment. "Do you know who made the original entries? "

"I'm not sure." Jeremy had already revealed too much, and certainly didn't want to reveal that the original entries were made by Jacob Barnes, even though he had already told Heather. If Heather mentioned to her father anything about the conversation they just had, he would be able to figure out that Jeremy had access to his top-secret Freedom Project file. But Jeremy now knew that Barnes was being set up by someone else, as was Dorgan. He would get Heather aside later and tell her at least that much.

"I know this information doesn't help us much, but it will if I can find out who else has had access to the Freedom Project implant video files and calls Michtenbaum by his middle name. I'll start working on that right after my meeting with the Secretary at 7:30."

"In the meantime, what do we do?" implored Carol. "We are still targets!"

"Well, while it doesn't ensure our safety," Heather said, "I plan to schedule the Freedom Project file, including photos, to be sent via e-mail, cloud and on Youtube to numerous officials and reporters next week unless I cancel it before then. I had planned to do that Saturday night," she looked at Bernie and he nodded knowingly," but I was interrupted and haven't had a minute, or internet access, since then. If anything happens to any of us before then, lots of people will know about it."

"I've already done the same thing," Jeremy said quietly. "With a different document."

They were all silent for a moment, then Jon spoke. "Hopefully the man they have in custody will talk and this will all be over soon."

With a little anger in her voice, Carol added, "And when it is, I think we should sue the government! I know, fat chance of winning, but I think we should make a stink! They've violated our – which amendment is it?"

Bernie had been pretty quiet throughout the conversation, but jumped in when he knew the answer. He loved American history and had memorized much of the constitution, the bill of rights, and other important documents. "The fourth amendment is *'The right of the people to be secure in their persons, houses, papers, and effects, against unreasonable searches and seizures...'*

"Exactly!" cried Carol. "Well, we haven't been secure in our persons or in our house, and we've been unreasonably searched!" She was looking at her husband.

"Everyone agrees with you, honey. I just doubt we'd get very far trying to sue the federal government."

"I'm not so sure. " It was Jeremy speaking. "The Privacy Act offers some remedy for individuals when it comes to their records, and these video recordings are records maintained by a government agency. You have the right to sue the federal government if it violates the law and I'm pretty sure we can find a few violations. For one thing, I know it says there can be no personal record-keeping system whose very existence is secret. One major violation already!

"I know first hand that none of us are ever alone, at least potentially," Jeremy continued. "With security cameras, cell phone cameras, satellites, drones, traffic cameras, it is possible to watch our every move if someone so desires. There is nothing on our laptops or iPads or cell phones that is private. It's possible that our every telephone conversation is being recorded." Then he added, "And, of course, there are those with unknown implants. "

Noise was heard at the door and Jeremy got up to look. One of his co-workers had arrived and the FBI was detaining him. Jacob Barnes arrived at that time and motioned for Jeremy and the others.

"I understand you're meeting with Rhonda shortly," Barnes said to Jeremy. "I'll take the others to a secure office and we'll wait for you. I've spoken with her on the phone and we think it best to get you all to a safe house at least for today." He directed this statement to the whole group. "You can clean up and get some rest while we try and find out who is after you – and me." He turned back to Jeremy. Meet us here when you're finished," and he showed Jeremy an office number written on a piece of paper.

"I need to go clean up a little before I go to her office," said Jeremy. He kept a change of clothes in his desk and retrieved them, bidding goodbye to the rest of the group.

"Make the call." The lead FBI agent holding the man captured at the scene of that morning's fire and shooting in a Baltimore neighborhood had already made a deal with him. The perpetrator would receive probation instead of jail time if he made a call to the man who hired him. The FBI hoped the fabricated story would implicate the person on the other end of the line who had ordered the deaths of several people.

The phone rang three times and was then picked up. "Yes?" Two of the FBI agents wore headphones and were able to hear the conversation.

"Last night's job is done. Six dead – four of them our targets."

"How?"

"Immobilized them with gas, then set the house on fire. You should hear about it on the news soon."

The man had already heard – he just wanted confirmation. "Describe them."

His hired agent gave accurate descriptions of Bernie, Jon and Carol, Bernie's sister and brother-in-law, and Heather, adding "damn shame to have to kill such a gorgeous woman."

It was obvious to the listening FBI that the man on the other end of the line would have preferred to say very little. He was being careful and he didn't want his voice recognized. However, he apparently had much to say to this former CIA agent, now freelance killer.

"You were supposed to call me by 3 a.m. It's almost 8. What the hell have you been doing for the past five hours?"

"Hiding. Dino and I barely made it a block or so from the house fire before several other people showed up, including two of your old friends. I think you know who I mean." The speaker's words were dripping with accusation. "Anyway, the place was soon crawling with police, FBI and CIA. I had to hide in the bushes for hours while they talked and investigated. Dino was out in the open and was killed. Anyway, I couldn't leave or they'd see me and I couldn't call you or they would hear me. I just left there twenty minutes ago and wanted to get some distance between me and that neighborhood before I stopped."

The lead FBI agent nodded to the man they had arrested. He was doing fine.

There was a brief silence on the other end of the line. "I didn't send them, by the way. They have been tracking our targets as well and it's coincidence that they arrived at the same time."

"I told you Dorgan was a threat to national security." CIA Director of National Clandestine Services Dr. Randall Thyssen stood in front of Homeland Security Secretary Rhonda Watterson in her office at 7:20 a.m. Memorial Day morning. She had just arrived to find him waiting outside her office door. All hell had broken loose when they heard of the chaos and deaths set in motion by John Dorgan since Friday.

"I wish John was here to tell his side of the story," Secretary Watterson interjected. "But he's dead and it's going to take some time to unravel this mess."

"You wanted to see me, ma'am." Jeremy James poked his head into the Secretary's partially open door.

"He ordered the death of Ray Michtenbaum, which is what started the whole mess," Thyssen continued as if Jeremy wasn't there.

"Wait outside!" the Secretary snapped at Jeremy. "And close the door!" She clearly was not happy with her top surveillance tech. "What about Jacob Barnes. He is the one who shot and killed Dorgan. What role does he play in all of this?" The Secretary had known Dorgan for over 20 years, way before he had begun working for her, and she could not believe he was solely responsible for all that had happened. He could be ruthless, yes, but he never killed without orders or very just cause. Neither seemed to be the case here. And she believed Dorgan when he called her Saturday night. He said someone, most likely Jacob Barnes of the CIA, was after him.

"I've never trusted that guy, and he's very clearly involved, and more than just trying to rescue his daughter. He may very well have set Dorgan up to take the fall, instigating the hit on Michtenbaum himself. That's my theory anyway."

"Well, the FBI investigative task force is being assembled as we speak. Mark Jamison is leading it – he's good – so the investigation will be done right."

Rhonda looked at the probable future CIA Director sitting in front of her desk, impeccably dressed, immaculately groomed, and felt slightly disgusted. He was the most ambitious man she had ever met, and she had met many. Three months ago he had tried to seduce her – not because he was attracted to a woman twenty years his senior – but because he wanted to be "in bed" with anyone who could further his career. She had put him in his place immediately, and he had simply smiled at her and continued their previous business conversation.

Now once again she wanted to dismiss him. She had nothing further to discuss with him. She hadn't invited him and she needed to talk to her employee Jeremy James. Jeremy had disappointed her greatly by not keeping her informed about all of Dorgan's activities, and she was going to put him on a leave of absence while she investigated his involvement in this mess. She didn't believe he was involved in any criminal activity, but he acted recklessly by not informing her of the involvement of other DHS employees, and of additional murders and attempted murders that were being committed during the course of his surveillance.

"Randall, thanks for stopping by – please keep me apprised of any new developments." She walked to her door and opened it, clearly indicating to Thyssen that she wanted him gone.

She looked into her outer office. Jeremy James was also gone.

Jeremy sprinted to the second floor and pounded on the locked office door. "It's me, Jeremy!"

Barnes opened the door and Jeremy practically fell inside. "It's the CIA guy! Bernie, the guy that came to see your boss and Dorgan on Thursday!" Jeremy was hoping Bernie knew the man's name. "He's our guy! I think he's the one that's after us! And he's here in the building!"

"Dr. Thyssen," Bernie informed them.

"Oh, that's Thyssen?" Jeremy knew the name as the one the President was assigning as the new Freedom Project Leader, but he hadn't been introduced to the CIA man who visited his boss on Thursday morning so hadn't put the face and name together.

Jeremy could see on Barnes' face that the mention of Thyssen's name hit a nerve. "How do you know he's the guy?" Barnes asked Jeremy.

"Because he called Michael Michtenbaum by his middle name, Ray. I just heard him. According to reliable sources, only his parents and one or two close friends called him Ray. I'm guessing Thyssen knew this because he's been spying on him recently - because he ordered the hit on him in order to frame Dorgan." Jeremy spoke calmly, even though he knew he was now in dangerous territory. He didn't mention the document and hoped no one else in the room would mention it either. He also didn't mention that by ordering the hit in writing in a secret file maintained by Jacob Barnes that Thyssen was also implicating Barnes should anyone ever see that document.

Everyone remained quiet. Barnes nodded at Jeremy. "Where is he now?"

"He was in Watterson's office five minutes ago."

"You stay here and keep the door locked." Jacob directed the order to the group. "I'll be back soon." As he started to leave, he turned back and pulled a small revolver from beneath his pant leg. "Do any of you know how to use this?"

"I do," said Jon. Jacob gave it to him and left.

Although he didn't doubt that Randall Thyssen was the man behind Michael Michtenbaum's, and several other, murders, Jacob was glad to get confirmation from the FBI as he headed upstairs to Rhonda's office. They confirmed that their captive was cooperating and had just contacted Thyssen, claiming he had killed four of the intended targets.

"Do you have the present coordinates of Thyssen's phone?" Jacob asked. "I plan to arrest him right now."

"GPS signal coming to your phone in a few seconds," said the FBI agent in charge.

Jacob asked two of the four agents standing guard to meet him on the fourth floor and the other two to have the building secured, letting no one in or out. As Jacob opened the door from the stairwell to the fourth floor, Randall Thyssen was walking towards him, heading for the elevator. Their eyes met, and Jacob knew that Randall knew why he was there.

Jacob raised his gun so there was no misunderstanding. "Put your hands on your head," Jacob said quietly.

A woman walked out of a doorway behind Thyssen and Jacob yelled at her to go back inside. She obeyed.

The stairwell door opened again and an FBI agent joined Barnes, following his lead by raising his weapon. The second agent appeared at the other end of the hall.

"Gentlemen, that won't be necessary," stated Thyssen. "I'll come peacefully."

"Shut up and put your hands on your head." Barnes asked the FBI agent to arrest and Mirandize the prisoner.

The foursome took the stairs to the first floor. Thyssen's hands were now bound behind his back and the weapon he had carried in had been removed. Barnes watched him closely as they walked down the steps. Thyssen held a smug smile on his face as if to say, "I'm not worried."

Barnes wondered if Thyssen was behind everything – the attempt on Susan's life, Heather's kidnapping, the bombing of the morgue. He had to suppress the urge to smash the smile off the man's face.

They reached the lobby and waited inside. Dozens of confused Homeland Security employees stood outside waiting to get into the locked-down building.

"A car will be here shortly," said one of the FBI agents. "Five minutes at most." Barnes decided that he was going to ride with the FBI and prisoner. If this man was behind the personal attacks on his family, he wasn't letting him out of his sight.

The door to the stairwell burst open and Heather came running into the lobby, slightly out of breath. She headed straight for Thyssen and sucker punched him in the face. "You bastard!" she screamed at him.

"Heather!" Her father pulled her away from the man as Thyssen was pulled backwards by the two FBI agents flanking his sides.

Blood seeped out of Thyssen's nose and dripped onto his expensive shirt and tie. He grinned at her, then returned his facial expression to its previous smug, knowing smile. It was as though he knew he would be acquitted of any crimes he had committed.

"He ordered my torture and murder! He's the one who had me viciously raped!" She pulled from her father's grasp and handed him a cell phone, touching the screen to begin playing a video.

Barnes had not known about the rape. He stood, shocked. Guilt enveloped him and he wasn't focusing on the video. He was thinking of how he had left Hamilton without finding her; had stolen a car instead of looking for his daughter being held captive by a madman in the woods. He stared with hatred at Thyssen. What exactly was that look on Thyssen's face when Heather mentioned her rape? Was it confusion?

"Dad, watch the video! Jeremy just received this on his phone from Dorgan who obviously programmed it to send before he died." She started the video again.

The video clearly showed Thyssen meeting with another man. Barnes was one of only a few people in the world who knew this other man by sight. He was known as Raptor. The two men walked on a busy city street, surrounded by people and by noise. Whoever captured this video – Dorgan apparently – did a superb job of filtering out the background noise and capturing the two men's faces and voices.

Thyssen spoke first. "You're the only one of the many I've hired that successfully completed his mission, so I need you to finish everyone else's assignments. You'd have thought I'd hired fucking amateurs," hissed Thyssen. He regained his composure on the tiny screen. "Ten targets, as soon as possible. Four or more of them are meeting tonight at this address – memorize it." The man studied the address for only a few seconds and Thyssen lit the small piece of paper with a lighter.

The live version of Thyssen, standing ten feet away from Barnes and Heather, showed no emotion as he heard his own voice talking to the top assassin in the world – an assassin who was now dead – killed only hours earlier by John Dorgan. But no matter, he thought, the smug grin still on his face. He would soon be released and would keep trying until he completed his mission to rid his new Freedom Project organization, and the soon to come FP-X, of any and all who might want to reveal or stop the project. He was greatly annoyed, though, that someone had managed to capture and record his meeting with Raptor. It was almost impossible to have a private conversation anymore, he mused.

Barnes continued to watch the video. "I know nine of the targets," said Raptor. "Who's the tenth?" The two men then stepped inside a building doorway and, although the satellite soon followed, it did not pick up Thyssen's reply to the question. Thyssen then left and the video ended.

Barnes glared at Thyssen. Never before had he wanted to kill someone so badly.

"They're here," said one of the agents with Thyssen. More FBI arrived in two cars, one car to be used to transport the prisoner. DHS security, with the approval of the FBI, unlocked the front doors to let the employees in first before the group of men left.

Heather watched her father leave the building with Thyssen and the two FBI agents, then turned to head back upstairs to return Jeremy's phone to him. She was shaking with rage.

Outside, Barnes whispered to Thyssen. "I *will* get you for this."

"We'll see who gets who." That smug smile again. Then he added, "But your daughter is wrong. I didn't have her kidnapped or raped."

Barnes heard a faint ping and a slight thud. He watched Thyssen crumple to the sidewalk, a bullet hole between his eyes.

An hour passed before Barnes returned to the office where Heather, Jeremy, Bernie, Jon and Carol waited.

"Thyssen is dead. Not by me," he added when Heather looked at him with surprise.

"Good." she said.

"The President has asked for a meeting with all of you, the

Singers and me for tomorrow at 2."

"The President!" Bernie exclaimed. "Of the United States?"

"Yes. He is appalled and concerned over what has happened. I can still take all of you to the safehouse for the night if you wish, or a hotel. I do think you're safe now with Thyssen dead. Those of you who live locally may want to go home. But we need to meet tomorrow and go to the White House together."

"I should probably go tell my boss where I am first," said Bernie. "I'm definitely late for work. I'd love to stay in a hotel tonight," he grinned.

"A hotel sounds good to me," said Carol.

"I still have to get chewed out by Rhonda, and if I still have a job tomorrow, I'll probably be right here, but tonight I'm going home."

"I'm on vacation," Heather said with a resolute firmness, "and I'm heading for Fiji on the next plane. Give the President my regards."

"Heather," Barnes said in a fatherly tone. "Perhaps not a wise decision. Can't Fiji wait one more day?"

"Actually I think it's one of my wisest decisions, and no, it can't."

Linda Jayne

TUESDAY

"You know that Thyssen was going to take your place as Project Leader for the Freedom Projects. With him gone, I need you to continue leading the projects." Jacob Barnes jumped quickly out of his chair at these words from the President of the United States. They were now alone in the President's office after the twenty minute meeting at two p.m. when the President spoke with the Moores, the Singers, Bernie and Jacob. He apologized to the group for the horrific behavior of John Dorgan and Randall Thyssen and assured the group that they were no longer in danger. He promised some compensation to the Moores and the Singers and ensured Jon that his eye implant would be removed promptly.

"Now Jacob, calm down. It's only for a short time – six months, maybe a year. We have to find a suitable replacement for you. And one who doesn't want total control by killing all the other players," the President said sarcastically, referring to Thyssen.

"Respectfully, Mr. President, no. I'm retiring on August 31 - two months from now. I'll oversee it until then, but no longer. I'm getting married in September and plan to start a new life, leave my former life behind me forever."

"You can still get married in September. You can still go home every night to the little woman. I'm not asking you to go to war, for godsake. I'm not even asking you to stay in your current job. I'm just asking you to lead the Freedom Project a little longer. It doesn't even need to be full time on your part. I think you'll agree with me that none of the current FP committee members are able or willing to lead the program. We need to find and quickly acclimate your replacement." The President spoke with his usual forceful tone, indicating that his word was final.

"What about Symmes? He's young and ambitious and has been on the committee for two years. While he may not be perfect for the job, he's trainable."

"No, I have other plans for him. He won't be on the committee much longer." The President rose from his chair and walked towards the door. "It will be fine, Jacob, you'll see."

Barnes also walked towards the door. "No sir, it won't. I am staying until the end of August and not a day longer. I will do everything in my power to find a suitable new committee member before I leave that can take my place eventually, but I'm not staying to mentor him, or her."

The President glared at Jacob Barnes as he left the oval office. He closed his door and sat back down at his desk, grateful for a few moments of solitude. He had underestimated Jacob Barnes. The man was obstinate and ungrateful, as was his daughter who didn't bother to come today. But every man has his price and the President planned to find out what Barnes' price was and either pay it or remove the need to do so, as he had had to do with Randall Thyssen.

Linda Jayne

FOUR WEEKS LATER

"I can pick you up at the airport. And you can stay at my place. I'll either sleep on the couch or I can stay at my sister's. She just moved into that great new house. Anyway, with your cousin's Skymiles for a free flight, the trip won't cost you too much." Bernie was excited that Sheila had agreed to come visit him if she could afford the trip. They talked on the phone at least three times a week and he now considered her his girlfriend. Jon Moore had let Bernie keep the cell phone he had bought at Walmart, so he could now call her from anywhere.

Bernie had talked to Jon and Carol Moore the day before. Jon was doing fine now that his surgery to remove his eye implant was over. They talked to the Singers and neither of them had received any compensation yet as the President had promised.

"Most of the places we'll visit won't cost anything and I can usually get a discount or free tickets to the ones that do cost something."

Since Sheila often worked nights, her best time to talk on the phone was mornings. Bernie no longer cared about his exemplary record of never making personal calls during working hours. Never is a bit long, he concluded, and it was time he changed his standard to no more than three personal calls per week of three minutes or less in duration if on company time, or as many personal calls as he wanted if it was during his break or lunch times.

Today he talked with Sheila during his morning break. He rarely went to the break room anymore as Heather had taken a personal leave of absence from work and he was trying to give up chocolate milk to lose weight.

"So whatever happened to the guy that stole the fake package we gave the Priest?" Bernie had recruited Sheila as his information liaison on updates in Hamilton related to that horrific (albeit incredibly exciting now that he looked back on it) weekend. Recent updates from Sheila included the county's plans to build a new morgue, with a proposal to name it the William L. Simmons Memorial Morgue, and a plaque that would be placed on the outside of the new building, donated by Coroner Rachel Curry, with the names of the two slain police officers.

"Well, the paper mentioned him but didn't say what his punishment was, so I had to get my cousin who, as you know, is the dispatcher at the Sheriff's Office, to find out for me. She knows some of the guys at the city police who said he got two years 'cause he wouldn't tell who put him up to it. I think, 'cause the police think, he didn't even know who put him up to it, but the police already knew who it was anyway. What a dumb-ass." Sheila laughed her musical laugh that Bernie had come to love.

"Father Benjamin says hello and said to tell you your real things will stay safe and sound, even though I told him what you said – that your friend had the information on the computer so that it would send to a bunch of people if any of you were threatened, but that you thought the threat was over and you all were safe."

"So," Sheila continued, hardly stopping to take a breath, "what if I decide I really, really like Washington?"

Noon is a nice time to wake up, thought Jeremy as he climbed out of bed at 12:15 p.m. on a bright Wednesday afternoon. It was day 26 of his 30-day unpaid leave from his job, punishment by Rhonda Watterson, he concluded, for his unprofessional handling of Dorgan's surveillance. She was actually conducting an investigation to see whether or not he should lose his job over his failure to keep her properly informed of events in his most recent assignment, but she had informed him yesterday that he could return to work on Monday.

Did he want to? He was still pissed off at Watterson and he would now have a new boss with Dorgan gone. He never liked Dorgan, but he might like his new boss even less.

The NSA had been courting him for three years and he finally interviewed with them. "Whatever you're making now, we'll double it," the high level recruiter at the agency told him. Higher pay, more sophisticated surveillance equipment and opportunities to spy on just about everyone in the entire world. Very tempting. He would have to let them know his answer soon.

Jeremy fired up his computer at his oversized wooden desk, which took up most of the space in the living room of his three room apartment. He was greatly enjoying his unexpected vacation time.

He had participated in an international gaming competition for Battlefield and came in third in the world. He spent his prize money on a trip to Hawaii, surfing off Maui with his buddy Owen. Best of all, he'd had several meetings with Heather as the two of them began drafting a class-action lawsuit against the federal government on behalf of the Singers, the Moores and Michael Michtenbaum's estate. They also had drafted proposed amendments to The Privacy Act and would be making their unprecedented presentation in exactly five hours.

"Let's see what else we can find," said Jeremy to his computer as he opened another personal file of his former boss, John Dorgan. He wasn't sure what he was looking for, but he wanted answers to several unanswered questions about the events of Memorial Day weekend. For one, who saved Heather from the creep who kidnapped her? For another, why would Thyssen want Dorgan out of the way so badly that he would expose the initial Freedom Project and kill or attempt to kill numerous people? Jeremy hoped he could find answers to these and other questions in Dorgan's private files, those not on the server of Homeland Security.

Jeremy had documented every keystroke that Dorgan had made on his laptop before he died. He was still able to see any keystroke made on the laptop, which was now in the possession of the FBI. They had combed everything in the first few weeks after Dorgan's death, but not at all in the past week. Jeremy had accounted for every entry except one. He felt certain that the two sets of twelve-digits entered were either a username and password, or two passwords, but had not yet figured out to what program or file. It was entered by Dorgan about six hours before he died.

"OK, here's something." Jeremy found another cloud account of Dorgan's and tried the first twelve digit password. It opened. "Excellent!" There was only one file listed in the account and when he clicked on it, it prompted him to enter a password. He entered the second twelve digits. "Well, that turned out to be easier than I thought."

As he suspected, it was the secret file of Jacob Barnes, the same 4000-page file that he himself had hidden away on a flash drive as well as attached to a mass e-mail that would automatically send should he be unable to stop it each month. It was a dangerous game to play. What if he forgot to stop the document from sending that month by failing to push the send date out once again? Still, it was the only way to know that he could reveal the project should anything happen to him, or to the others who knew about the Freedom Project.

Apparently Dorgan had the same idea. The top-secret file, which revealed everything about nine separate Freedom Projects, every name, every death, was scheduled to send to every major news media organization in the world - in exactly forty-eight hours. "Oh, my God!" Jeremy jumped to his feet, not knowing what to do. A failsafe was in place and only Dorgan could stop it.

As happened every day and almost every night, Heather's thoughts returned to one or more of the nightmare events that happened to her only a few short weeks ago. Today she focused once again on the psycho who had kidnapped her from the Hamilton Police Headquarters, raped her, and planned to torture and kill her. She was saved by a sniper's bullet that killed her would-be assassin. So far, she did not know who the good Samaritan was who saved her. She wasn't even a hundred percent certain that it was Thyssen that had arranged for her kidnap and death. Her father, her boss, Jeremy – none of them knew the answer to those questions nor had they been able to find out. This haunted her. It was an unresolved piece of the puzzle, and she knew she would never get over that terrible event until she learned why it happened and why it was stopped.

She tried to remember every word that was said that night when she was in the car with that madman, and afterwards. He had not asked about Michael Michtenbaum's implants. He had never asked about the implants. Wasn't that what he was after? Perhaps not – perhaps Thyssen just wanted her dead, along with all the others who knew about the Freedom Project. But Jeremy had told her that her name was not on the list that he had seen, the list they now knew had been written by Thyssen in one of her father's files. Did he only want her frightened and raped, but not killed? Did he order the hit, but then stop it before she was killed? Was it even Thyssen at all?

Not knowing was torturing her. And now she had a new torture. The week before, the Hamilton, Ohio, Police Chief had called her and told her about a tiny video camera that had been collected from the scene of her rape. Along with all of the other evidence, this camera was logged and held. The Chief called to let her know they had found this camera but did not know how to access any video that it might have recorded, nor did they want to violate her privacy by doing so. Her rapist was dead. They did not need the evidence. He asked if she wanted the tiny camera and suggested that perhaps the FBI or her friend Jeremy could access the video if she wanted that done.

She had received the device in a secure package today. Would this video give her any indication of who had ordered her torture and murder? Would it tell who had stopped it? She doubted it. She didn't want to see the video and definitely didn't want anyone else to see the video. Just having the tiny device in her home made her anxious and nervous. She wanted to destroy it. But she decided she would keep it for the time being and put it in her safe deposit box, out of her home.

She changed her thoughts to her father.

Heather did not know how long it would take for her and her father to return to the same relationship they had before that weekend in May that had changed her life forever, for better and for worse. Probably never. She had forgiven him for allowing implants to be placed in her as a newborn – at least she told him that she forgave him. Would she ever really forgive him? She wasn't sure. He assured her that no one had ever accessed and watched her – ever – except for himself the one time she was seven years old and then when he was looking for her that Sunday. She didn't know if she believed him.

And even though she now felt certain that he was not the one who orchestrated any of the events of that weekend, she knew he was not innocent. Jeremy had uncovered a lot more information about her father than he was willing to reveal, even to her, but it was evident that Jeremy feared her dad.

She learned about the woman he had kidnapped briefly in Hamilton. Somehow he made that charge disappear, or paid the woman to not press charges. She also wondered about the man who was murdered by being dangled from a helicopter. That event happened the day her father's home was invaded – the same 24-hour period he had arrived in Hamilton by helicopter - and she could tell from the Youtube video that some of the scenery was near her father's home. She hadn't asked him if he did it, however – she wasn't sure she wanted to know if his answer was yes, and she wasn't sure she would believe him if his answer was no.

But she would be a good daughter and be maid of honor for Susan at their wedding. She really did like Susan, and she was truly happy that her father had found such a great person to share the rest of his life with. She did not reciprocate and ask Susan to be maid of honor at her own wedding, though, nor did she ask her father to walk her down the aisle. Was it because she wanted to hurt her father a little bit that she asked Danny to marry her right then and there in Fiji? No wedding – no family in attendance – no money paid out by the father of the bride that would obligate a daughter to be grateful.

Mainly, she remembered, she just wanted to be with Danny, right then and forever. They were living in her condo and he had sublet his apartment for the remainder of the lease. After returning from Fiji, she had returned to work for one day only, specifically to ask her boss for an indefinite leave of absence for personal reasons. Rhonda Watterson interpreted those personal reasons as being stress-related and the leave of absence was granted. Heather's reasons, however, were only partially due to continued stress, but mostly due to continued and growing outrage over the Freedom Projects. She needed time to conduct research. She needed time to draft documents. She needed time to make sure she didn't fail at stopping any current and future Freedom Projects.

For now, she would have to be content with presenting proposed amendments to the Privacy Act that included a new system of third party oversight and audit of records. She and her new friend, Jeremy James, had been granted a private meeting with the President of the United States to present their proposal, all the more remarkable since both she and Jeremy had declined his invitation of a month ago to meet with him. She was also requesting that any and all video recordings of the Singers, the Moores and Michael Michtenbaum be destroyed. Jeremy had strongly suggested she not mention her own implants which would alert the President to the fact that she knew there was more than one Freedom Project. "Trust me on this. For us to remain safe, we can only talk about the initial Freedom Project."

Heather was not a fan of this President. She had met him for the first time a year earlier at a dinner to which her father was invited and brought her as his guest. The dinner conversation among the men had turned somewhat lewd, very inappropriate for the collective group and the austere location, and she, unlike the other timid or political women at the table, boldly excused herself and did not return. She found a ladies room nearby and hid out there for a while. When she exited an hour later, the President was walking down the hall towards her. He apologized in words, but his tone and facial expression denoted anger towards her. He then proceeded to make a pass at her and she shoved him to the floor. She had been fortunate there wasn't a secret service person nearby.

But she would be cordial to him today and then spring the lawsuit in a few weeks.

The Man sat with his head in hands, massaging his temples as the start of a headache spread across his forehead. Not everything had gone according to his plan but Dorgan was dead and that was a good start. Thyssen's death was unfortunate but necessary. Thyssen's ambition and hunger for power had caused him to cross the line. Only he, The Man, had the right to do that.

He thought about Heather and what he should do. He had punished her, although she could never know that it was he who had done it. Even if she or others found the small video camera that was left at the scene of her rape, which they most likely did, there was no video to access. It only fed the live scene to him that Saturday night in May, never to be accessed again.

He thought back to last year. How dare she mock him publicly and scorn him in private.

The door to his office opened and his assistant stepped inside.

"Mr. President. Miss Barnes and Mr. James are here to see you."

Linda Jayne spent her 35-year career in "Corporate America" managing quality, human resources, marketing and other functions for three multi-location companies, as well as owning and operating her own consulting firm. She now devotes much of her time to her first love, writing. The Privacy Act is her first novel, with her second novel, The Freedom Project, coming soon.

Made in the USA
Middletown, DE
06 June 2015